DEDICATION

The story of *Lion of Macedon* was born on a Greek island, in the shadow of a ruined acropolis, beneath the walls of a fortress built by Crusader knights. The first ideas surfaced in a bay that was said to have sheltered Saint Paul on his voyage to Rome. Lindos, on the island of Rhodes, is a place of quiet beauty and great charm, and her people echo her qualities.

This novel is dedicated with great affection to those people who have made my journeys to Lindos full of enchantment: to Vasilis and Tsambika of Flora's Bar, to "Crispy" and "Jax," and Kate and Alex.

And to Brian Gorton and his lovely wife, Kath, for the gift of the "Eyes."

THE BLIND SEERESS

"Why was I chosen to be a seeress?" Derae asked. "And at such a terrible cost."

Tamis replied, "Because you love Parmenion. The Dark God is coming, Derae, and all the world will fall to him. He must be stopped."

"And Parmenion can destroy him?" Derae asked.

"When first I saw the shadow of the God, I prayed for a way to defeat him. I saw Parmenion then and heard his name echo across the vaults of Heaven."

"Show me Parmenion," Derae said. "Then I will give you my answer."

"Take my hand, child, and close your eyes."

The world lurched, and Derae felt she was falling. All around her were stars, huge and bright. Then she found herself floating above a night-shrouded city. Derae looked. She saw Parmenion, and saw, too, the woman who lay with him.

"Take me back," Derae whispered to Tamis. "You may have my gift; you may take my eyes."

Legend
The King Beyond the Gate
Waylander
Wolf in Shadow
Ghost King
Last Sword of Power
Knights of Dark Renown
The Last Guardian
Quest for Lost Heroes

LION OF MACEDON

DAVID GEMMEL

A DEL REY BOOK

BALLANTINE BOOKS · NEW YORK

Copyright © 1990 by David A. Gemmell

All rights reserved under
International and Pan-American Copyright Conventions.
Published in the United States by Ballantine Books,
a division of Random House, Inc., New York.

Originally published
in Great Britain by Random Century Group
in 1990.

LIBRARY OF CONGRESS CATALOG CARD NUMBER:
92-72773

ISBN: 0-345-37911-X

Cover painting by Tom Stimpson

MANUFACTURED IN THE UNITED STATES OF AMERICA
First American Edition: September 1992
10 9 8 7 6 5 4 3 2 1

ACKNOWLEDGMENTS

My thanks to my editor Liza Reeves, copy editor Jean Maund, and test readers Val Gemmell, Edith Graham, Tom Taylor, and "young Jim of the Penguin," who forced me to rewrite from scratch. And special thanks to my researcher Stella Graham, who plowed through scores of heavy tomes seeking inspiration, and to Paul Henderson, who checked the manuscript for historical accuracy.

Contents

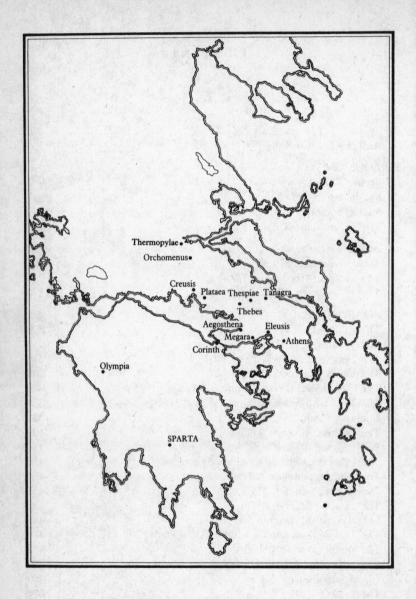

Thermopylae•

Orchomenus•

Creusis
•

Plataea Thespiae Tanagra
•   •   •

Thebes
•

Aegosthena   Eleusis
•   •

Megara•   •Athens

Corinth•

Olympia
•

SPARTA
•

Author's Foreword

The world of the ancient Greeks was one of turmoil and war, intrigue and treachery. There was no Greek nation; the divided land was ruled by scores of city-states that fought continually for domination.

For centuries the great cities of Athens and Sparta battled across land and sea for the right to become the leaders of Greece. Thebes, Corinth, Orchomenus, Plataea—all changed sides time and again, and Victory flew between the warring factions, always the harlot, moving on, sweet with a promise she would not keep.

The Greek wars were financed by Persia, fearful that a united Greece would seek to dominate the world. The Persians grew rich, and their empire flourished across Asia and Egypt, their power felt in every city of the civilized world. But still their wary eyes watched events in Greece, for twice the Persians had invaded the Greek mainland and twice had suffered terrible defeats.

The Athenians and their allies crushed the army of Darius on the field of Marathon. Darius' son, Xerxes, then led a massive army, numbering more than a quarter of a million men, to subdue Greece once and for all.

A small Spartan force blocked their way at the pass of Thermopylae and held them for days. The Persians won through at last, sacking the city of Athens and ravaging the countryside, until finally they were decisively beaten in two battles. On land five thousand Spartans, led by the general Pausanius, inflicted a humiliating defeat on the Persian horde, while at sea the Athenian admiral Themistocles destroyed the Persian fleet at Salamis.

— Persia would never again invade, seeking instead to rule by intrigue.

The events detailed in *Lion of Macedon* (i.e., the taking of the Cadmea and the battles at Thermopylae, Leuctra, and Heraclea Lyncestis) are all historically based. The main characters (Parmenion, Xenophon, Epaminondas, and Philip of Macedon) all walked those ancient mountains and plains, following their own paths of honor, loyalty, and duty.

But the story of the *Lion of Macedon* is my own. History has all but forgotten Parmenion. No one can know whether he was the king of the Pelagonians, a Macedonian adventurer, or a Thessalian mercenary.

Yet whatever the truth, I hope his shade will smile in the Hall of Heroes when this tale reaches him.

David A. Gemmell
Hastings, 1990

BOOK ONE

A wonderful people are the Athenians. They elect ten new generals every year. In all my life I have known only one—and that is Parmenion.

PHILIP II OF MACEDON

SPRING, 389 B.C.

IT had begun with a morbid fascination to know the day of her death. She had tracked the limitless paths of the future, tracing the myriad lines of possible tomorrows. In some futures she had died of illness or plague, in others of seizures or murder. In one she had even fallen from a horse, though riding was distasteful to her and she could not imagine ever being persuaded to mount such a beast.

But as she idly traced the possibilities, she became aware of a dark shadow at the edge of her last tomorrow. No matter when she died, the shadow was constant. It began to gnaw at her. With all the thousands of futures, how could this shadow remain? Tentatively she moved beyond the days of her death and saw the futures expand and grow. The shadow was stronger now, its evil palpable. And in a moment that touched her beyond terror she realized that even as she knew of the shadow, so it was becoming aware of her.

Yet Tamis was not without courage. Steeling herself, she chose a path and flew to the heart of the shadow, feeling the power of the Dark God eating into her soul like acid. She could not hold her presence here for long and fled back to the transient security of a solid present.

The knowledge she had gained became a terrible weight that burdened the old priestess. She could share it with no one and knew that at the most critical moment, when the evil needed to be challenged, she would be dead.

She prayed then, harder than she ever had, her thoughts spinning out into the cosmos. A darkness grew inside her mind, then a single light shone and she saw a face, lined but strong, hawklike with piercing blue eyes beneath a helm of iron. The face blurred and faded, to be replaced by that of a boy. Yet still the eyes were piercing blue, the mouth set in a determined line. A name came to her. But was it that of a savior or a destroyer? She could not know; she could only hope. But the name echoed in her mind like distant thunder.

Parmenion!

Tʜᴇʏ came at him silently from the shadows, faces hooded and masked, wooden clubs raised.

Parmenion darted to the left, but two more attackers ran into his path and a club slashed past his head, grazing his shoulder. His fist hammered into the masked face, then he cut to the right and sprinted toward Leaving Street. The cold, marble eyes of the statue of Athena gazed down on the boy as he ran, drawing him on toward her. Parmenion leapt to the base of the statue, clambering up to stand against the stone legs.

"Come down! Come down!" chanted his tormentors. "We have something for you, mix-blood!"

"Then come up and give it to me," he told them. The five attackers ran forward. Parmenion's foot lashed into the face of the first, hurling him back, but a club cracked against his leg to knock him from his feet. He rolled, kicking out and sending an assailant sprawling, then he was up again and leaping high over them to land heavily on the street. A hurled club took him between the shoulder blades, and he staggered. Instantly they were upon him, pinning his arms.

"Now we have you," said a voice, muffled by the woolen scarf masking the mouth.

"You don't need the mask, Gryllus," hissed Parmenion. "I'd know you by the smell."

"You will not contest the final tomorrow," said another voice. "You understand? You should never have been allowed to take part. The general's games are for Spartans, not half-breeds."

Parmenion relaxed, his manner becoming subdued, his head dropping. The hold on his arms eased . . . suddenly he wrenched free, his fist thundering into Gryllus' face. They swarmed in on him then, punching and kicking, driving him to his knees. Gryllus hauled him up by his hair as the others pinned his arms once more.

"You asked for this," said Gryllus, drawing back his fist. Pain exploded in Parmenion's jaw, and he sagged against his captors. The blows continued, short, powerful hooks to the belly and face.

Parmenion did not cry out. *There is no pain,* he told himself. *There is no . . . pain.*

"What's going on there?"

"It's the night watch!" whispered one of his captors. Loosing their hold on Parmenion, the youths sprinted off into an alleyway. Parmenion fell to the street and rolled. Above him loomed the silent statue of Athena of the Road. As he groaned and lurched to his feet, two soldiers ran to him.

"What happened to you?" asked the first, gripping Parmenion's shoulder.

"I fell." Parmenion shook loose the helping hand and spit blood.

"And your friends were assisting you to rise, I suppose," grunted the man. "Why don't you walk with us for a while?"

"I need no escort," Parmenion told them.

The soldier looked into the youth's pale blue eyes. "They are still in the alley," he said, keeping his voice low.

"I did not doubt it," answered Parmenion, "but they'll not take me unawares again." As the soldiers moved away, Parmenion sucked in a deep breath and began to run, ducking into alleys and cutting left and right toward the marketplace. For a while he heard his pursuers, but then there was only the silence of the city night.

They would expect him to make either for the barracks or for the home of his mother. He would do neither. Instead he ran through the deserted marketplace and on to the sanctuary hill above the city.

Back at the statue of Athena an old woman stepped out into the moonlight, leaning on a long staff. She sighed and sat down on a marble seat, her body weary, her mind touched with sorrow.

"I am sorry, Parmenion," she said. "Strong though you are, I must make you iron. You are a man of destiny." She thought then of the other boys in the barracks. How easy it was to make them hate the half-breed, such a simple enchantment. To heal a boil took more psychic energy than to encourage hatred. It was a disturbing thought, and Tamis shivered.

Glancing up at the statue, she saw the blind marble eyes staring down at her. "Do not be so haughty," she whispered. "I know your true name, woman of stone. I know your weaknesses and your desires, and I have more power than you."

Tamis pushed herself to her feet.

A face came to her mind, and she smiled. Despite the enchantment Parmenion had one friend, a boy impervious to the fuel of hatred. Although it went against her plans, yet still she found the thought comforting.

"Sweet Hermias," she said. "If all men were like you, then my work would not be necessary."

Parmenion sat on a rock waiting for the dawn, his belly hungry but his jaw too bruised to chew on the stale bread he had saved from the previous day's breakfast. The sun rose slowly over the red hills of the Parnon range, and the water of the Eurotas River sparkled into life. The sun's warmth touched

Parmenion's wiry body, causing him to shiver involuntarily. Spartan training taught a man to ignore pain, to close his mind to cold or heat. To a great degree he had mastered this, but the new warmth served only to remind him how cold he had been on this long night, hidden upon the sanctuary hill above the city.

The statue of Zeus, Father of Heaven—twelve feet tall, majestic and bearded—stared out over the lands to the west of the city, seeming to study the towering Mount Ilias. Parmenion shivered once more and took a tentative bite from the dark bread, stifling a groan as pain flamed from his jaw. The punch from Gryllus had been powerful, and held as he was, Parmenion could not roll with the blow. He lifted a finger to his mouth. A tooth was loose. Tearing the bread, he pushed a small piece to the right of his jaw, chewing gently. Having finished his meager breakfast, he stood. His left side was tender. Lifting the *chiton* tunic, he examined the area; it was an angry purple, and there was blood above the hip.

He stretched, then froze as he heard movement on the climbing path. Swiftly he ran behind the marble sanctuary to the Muses, crouching to wait for the newcomers, his heart pounding. He picked up a sharp shard of broken marble; it had an edge like an ax blade. If they came at him again, someone would die!

A slender boy in a blue tunic walked into view. He had dark curly hair and thick brows. Parmenion recognized his friend Hermias, and relief washed over him. Dropping the stone, he pushed himself wearily to his feet. Hermias saw him and ran forward, gripping him by the shoulders. "Oh, Savra, my friend, how much more must you suffer?"

Parmenion forced a smile. "Today will see the end of it. Maybe."

"Only if you lose, Savra. And you *must* lose. They could kill you. I fear they will!" Hermias looked into his friend's pale blue eyes and saw no compromise there. "You are not going to lose, though, are you?" he said sadly.

Parmenion shrugged. "Perhaps—if Leonidas is more skillful, if the judges favor him."

"Of course they will favor him. Gryllus says that Agisaleus is coming to watch—you think the judges will allow a nephew of the king to be humiliated?"

Parmenion laid a hand on Hermias' shoulder. "Since that is the case, why are you worried? I will lose. So be it. But I will not *play* to lose."

Hermias sat down at the foot of the statue of Zeus and took two apples from his hip pouch. He passed one to Parmenion, who bit carefully into it. "Why are you so stubborn?" Hermias asked. "Is it your Macedonian blood?"

"Why not the Spartan blood, Hermias? Neither people is renowned for giving ground."

"It was not meant as an insult, Savra. You know that."

"Not from you, no," said the taller youth, taking his friend's hand. "But think on it, you all call me Savra—*lizard*—and you think of me as a half-breed barbarian."

Hermias pulled away, his expression showing his hurt. "You are my friend," he protested.

"That is not at issue, Hermias, nor is it an answer. You cannot help what you are—you are a Spartan, pure-blooded, with a line of heroes that goes back far beyond Thermopylae. Your own father marched with Lysander and never knew defeat. Probably you have friends among the helots and the other slave classes. But you still see them as slaves."

"You also had a Spartan father who came back on his shield, with all his wounds in front," insisted Hermias. "You are Spartan, too."

"And I have a Macedonian mother." Parmenion removed his tunic, wincing as his arms stretched over his head. His lean body was marked by bruises and cuts, and his right knee was swollen. His angular face was also bruised, the right eye almost closed. "These are the marks I bear for my blood. When they took me from my mother's house, I was seven years old.

From that day to this I have never known the sun to shine on a body that did not carry wounds."

"I, too, have suffered bruises," said Hermias. "All Spartan boys must suffer—else there would be no Spartan men, and we would no longer be preeminent. But I hear what you say, Sav . . . Parmenion. It seems Leonidas hates you, and he is a powerful enemy. Yet you could go to him and ask to serve him. Then it would stop."

"Never! He would laugh at me and throw me out into the street."

"Yes, he might. But even so, the beatings would end."

"Would you do that if you were me?"

"No."

"Then why should I?" hissed Parmenion, his pale eyes locking to his friend's face.

Hermias sighed. "You are hard on me, Parmenion. But you are right. I love you as a brother, and yet I do not see you as Spartan. I do inside my head—but my heart . . ."

"Then why should the others—who are not my friends—accept me?"

"Give us time—give us all time. But know this: Whatever you choose, I will stand beside you," said Hermias softly.

"That is something I never doubted. Now call me Savra—from you it has a good sound."

"I shall be at your side for the contest, and I will pray to Athena of the Road for your victory," said Hermias, smiling. "Now, would you like me to stay with you?"

"No, but thank you. I will remain here awhile with Father Zeus, and I will think, and I will pray. I will see you at Xenophon's house three hours after noon for the contest."

Hermias nodded and wandered away. Parmenion watched him go, then swung his attention to the awakening city.

Sparta. The home of heroes, birthplace of the finest warriors ever to walk the green earth. From here, less than a century before, the legendary sword king had set off for the pass of Thermopylae with three hundred warriors and seven hundred helots. There the tiny force had faced an army of

Persians numbering more than a quarter of a million.

And yet the Spartans had held, hurling back the foe until at last the Persian King Xerxes sent in his Immortals. Ten thousand of the finest warriors Persia could muster from her great empire, highly trained, the elite corps. And the Spartans humbled them. Parmenion felt his heart swell as he pictured those grim-eyed men in their full-faced helms of bronze, their blood-red cloaks, and their shining swords. The might of Persia—the might of the world!—broken upon the swords of three hundred Spartans. He turned to the southeast. There, out of sight now, was the monument to the king who died there. Betrayed by a Greek, the Spartans had been surrounded and massacred. They had known of the betrayal, and the king had been urged by his allies to flee the field. His words were engraved on the hearts of all Spartans: "A Spartan leaves the battle carrying his shield—or upon it. There will be no retreat." It seemed ironic to Parmenion that his greatest hero and his worst enemy should share the same name and bloodline—Leonidas. And at times he wondered if the king of legend had been as cruel as his namesake. He hoped not.

Parmenion climbed to the highest point of the acropolis, gazing down at the city that circled the hill. Fewer than thirty thousand people dwelt here, yet they were held in awe from Arcadia to Asia Minor, from Athens to Illyria. No Spartan army had ever been beaten in a pitched battle by a foe of equal numbers. The Spartan foot soldier—the *hoplite*—was worth three Athenians, five Thebans, ten Corinthians, and twenty Persians. These scales were drummed into Sparta's children and remembered with pride.

Macedonians did not rate a mention in Spartan scales. Scarcely considered to be Greek, they were barbaric and undisciplined, hill tribes of little culture save that which they stole from their betters. "I am a Spartan," said Parmenion. "I am not a Macedonian."

The statue of Zeus continued to gaze at the distant Mount Ilias, and Parmenion's words seemed hollow. The boy sighed, remembering the conversation minutes before with Hermias.

*"You are hard on me, Parmenion. But you are correct. I love
you as a brother, and yet I do not see you as Spartan. I do
inside my head—but my heart . . ."*

*"Then why should the others—who are not my friends—
accept me?"*

As a young child Parmenion had experienced few problems
with other youngsters. But at seven, when all Spartan boys
were taken from their parents and moved to barracks for
training as warriors, he had first suffered the torment of his
tainted blood. It was there that Leonidas—named for the king
of glory—had taunted him, demanding that he kneel to him as
befitted a man from a race of slaves. Smaller and younger,
Parmenion had flown at him, fists lashing at the older boy's
face. Leonidas had thrashed him then—and many times since.
Worse, Leonidas was of a noble Spartiate family, and many of
the other boys in the barracks of Lycurgus had sought his
favors. Parmenion became an outcast, hunted, hated by all
save Hermias—even Leonidas could not turn on *him*, for he
was the son of Parnas, the king's friend.

For eight years Parmenion had borne the blows and the
insults, convinced that one day he would see their eyes look
upon him as a brother Spartan. Today should have seen the
hour of triumph. He had succeeded beyond his dreams in the
general's games, battling his way to the final. But who should
be his opponent among all the youths in Sparta? None other
than Leonidas.

As Hermias had warned, victory would bring only more
pain, yet he could not—would not—consider playing to lose.
Every year the general's games were the high point of the
calendar for the apprentice warriors in Sparta's many barracks. The winner would wear the laurel crown and hold the
victory rod. He was the *strategos*—the master!

The game pitched two armies against one another, the com-
petitors acting as generals, issuing orders, choosing formations. The soldiers were carved from wood: there was no
blood, no death. Losses were decided by two judges who
threw numbered knucklebones.

Picking up a stick, Parmenion traced a rectangle in the dust, picturing the Spartan phalanx, more than a thousand warriors with shields locked, spears steady. This was the main force in the game, the cavalry coming second. To the right he sketched a second block: the Sciritai, Spartan vassals who always fought alongside their masters. Doughty men, hard and ungiving, yet never were they allowed into the front rank of the battle. For they were not Spartan and were therefore almost subhuman.

This was his army, three thousand men, Spartan foot, horse, and the Sciritai reserve. Leonidas would command an identical force.

Closing his eyes, he recalled the previous year's final, which had been played in Menelaus barracks. The battle had taken two hours. Long before the conclusion, Parmenion had grown bored and had wandered away into the marketplace. It had been a battle of attrition, both phalanxes locked together, the judges throwing knucklebones and removing the dead until at last the white army overwhelmed the red.

A pointless exercise, Parmenion had decided. What good was such a victory? The winner had fewer than a hundred men at the close. In real life he would have been overwhelmed by any second enemy force.

A battle should not be fought in such a way.

Today would be different, he decided. Win or lose, they would remember it. Slowly he began to sketch formations, to think and to plan. But his mind wandered, and he saw again the great race three weeks ago. He had planned for it, trained for it, dreamed of the laurel wreath of victory upon his brow.

Twenty miles under the grueling summer sun, out over the foothills, up the scree-covered slopes of the Parnon mountains, legs aching, lungs heaving. All the young men of Sparta in one great race, the ultimate test of juvenile strength and courage.

He had outdistanced them all: Leonidas, Nestus, Hermias, Learchus, and the best of the other barracks. They ate his dust and struggled behind him. Leonidas had lasted better than the rest, hanging grimly to his shadow, but twelve miles from home even he had been broken by Parmenion's final burst.

And then Parmenion had run for home, saving the last of his energy for the sprint to the *agora*, where the king waited with the laurel of victory.

With the city in sight, white and beckoning, he had seen the old man pulling his handcart along Soldiers' Walk at the foot of the olive grove, had watched in dismay as the right wheel came loose, tipping the cart's contents to the dust. Parmenion slowed in his run. The old man was struggling to loosen a looped thong from the stump at the end of his right arm. He was crippled. Tearing his eyes from the scene, Parmenion ran on.

"Help me, boy!" called the man. Parmenion slowed and turned. Leonidas was far behind him and out of sight . . . he tried to gauge how much time he had. With a curse he ran down the slope and knelt by the wheel. It was cracked through, yet still the Spartan boy tried to lift it into place, forcing it back over the axle. It held for a moment only, then broke into several shards. The old man slumped to the ground beside the ruined cart. Parmenion glanced down into his eyes; there was pain there, defeat and dejection. The man's tunic was threadbare, the colors long since washed away by the winter rains, bleached by the summer sun. His sandals were as thin as parchment.

"Where are you going?" Parmenion asked.

"My son lives in a settlement an hour from here," replied the old man, pointing south. Parmenion glanced at the wrinkled skin of his arm; it showed the cuts of many sword blades, old wounds.

"You are Spartan?" inquired the boy.

"Sciritai," the man answered. Parmenion stood and stared down at the cart. It was loaded with pots and jugs, several old blankets, and a breastplate and helm of a style the boy had only seen painted on vases and murals.

"I will help you home," said Parmenion at last.

"Was a time, boy, I would have needed no help."

"I know. Come. I will support the axle if you can steer and pull."

Hearing the sound of running feet, Parmenion glanced up. Leonidas sped by along the crest of the hill; he did not look down. Swallowing his disappointment, Parmenion took hold of the axle, heaving the cart upright. The old man took his place at the handles, and the two made their way slowly south.

It was dusk when Parmenion finally trotted through the gates. There to greet him were many of the youths from his barracks.

"What happened, mix-blood? Did you get lost?" they jeered.

"More likely lay down for a rest," sneered another. "There's no stamina in half-breeds."

"Last! Last! Last!" they chanted as he ran on to the marketplace, where his barrack tutor, Lepidus, was waiting to count his charges home.

"What in the name of Hades happened to you?" asked the soldier. "Lycurgus barracks should have won the day. We finished sixth, thanks to you."

Parmenion had said nothing. What was there to say?

But that was in the past—and the past was dead. Parmenion grew hungry and wandered down into the marketplace and on along Leaving Street to the barracks. In the mess hall he got in line with the other boys of Lycurgus and sat alone with his bowl of dark soup and chunk of black bread. No one spoke to him. Leonidas was on the other side of the hall, sitting with Gryllus and a dozen others; they affected not to notice him. Parmenion ate his meal, enjoying the feeling of a full stomach, then left and walked through the streets to the small home of his mother. He found her in the courtyard, sitting in the sunshine. She glanced up at him and smiled. She was painfully thin, her eyes sunken. He touched her shoulder and kissed her gently, his lips touching bone beneath the dry, taut skin.

"Are you eating well?" he asked her.

"I have no appetite," she whispered. "But the sun is good for me, it makes me feel alive." He fetched her a goblet of water and sat beside her on the stone bench. "Do you contest the final today?" she asked.

"Yes."

She nodded, and a strand of dark hair fell across her brow. Parmenion stroked it back into place. "You are hot. You should come inside."

"Later. Your face is bruised?"

"I fell during a race. Clumsy. How are you feeling?"

"Tired, my son. Very tired. Will the king be at Xenophon's house to see you win?"

"It is said that he will—but I might not win."

"No. A mother's pride spoke. But you will do your best, and that is enough. Are you still popular with the other boys?"

"Yes."

"That would have pleased your father. He, too, was popular. But he never reached the final of the general's games. He would have been so proud."

"Is there anything I can do for you? Can I get you some food?" Parmenion took her hand, holding to it tightly, willing his own strength to flow into her frail limbs.

"I need nothing. You know, I have been thinking these last few days about Macedonia and the forests and the plains. I keep dreaming of a white horse on a hillside. I am sitting in a field, and the horse is coming toward me. I so long to ride that horse, to feel the wind on my face, whispering through my hair. It is a tall horse with a fine neck. But always I wake before he reaches me."

"Horses are good omens," said Parmenion. "Let me help you inside. I will fetch Rhea—she will cook for you. You must eat, Mother, or you will never regain your strength."

"No, no. I want to sit here for a while. I will doze. Come to me when you have played the game. Tell me all."

For a while he sat with her, but she rested her head against a threadbare pillow and slept. Moving back into the house, he washed the dust from his body and combed his dark hair. Then he pulled on a clean *chiton* tunic and his second pair of sandals. The *chiton* was not embroidered and was too small for him, barely reaching midway to his thighs. He felt like a helot—a slave. Parmenion walked to the next house and rapped his knuckles on the door frame. A short red-haired woman came out; she smiled as she saw him.

"I will go in to her," she said before he spoke.

"I do not think she is eating," said Parmenion. "She is becoming thinner every day."

"That is to be expected," answered Rhea softly, sadness in her voice.

"No!" Parmenion snapped. "Now the summer is here, she will improve. I know it."

Without waiting for her to speak, he ran back beyond the barracks and on to Leaving Street and the house of Xenophon.

On the day of the game Xenophon awoke early. The sun was just clearing the eastern peaks, long thin shafts of light spearing through the warped shutters of his bedroom window. He rolled to his side and groaned. He always enjoyed dining with the king, but as life so often proved, all pleasures had to be paid for. His head was pounding, his stomach queasy. He took a deep breath and sat up, pushing back the thin sheet that covered him and gazing down at his torso. The muscles of his belly were ridged and tight, belying his forty-seven years, the skin of his face and body burnished gold from frequent naked exercise in the early-morning sunshine.

The general rose and stretched before his bronze mirror. His eyesight no longer had the keenness of youth, and he was forced to peer closely at his reflection, noting with distaste the slight sagging of skin beneath the blue eyes and the silver streaks appearing in the gold of his hair. He hated the process of aging and dreaded the day when lovers would come to him out of duty or for money rather than desire.

The youth last night had been charmed by him, but more than anything he had wished to be seen with Xenophon, hero of the march to the sea, the rebel Athenian acknowledged as one of the greatest generals of the age. At this morale-boosting thought Xenophon chuckled and moved back from the mirror. He opened the shutters, felt the sun on his skin, then sat once more on the firm bed.

The march to the sea: the year of glory. Was it the Fates, the will of Athena, or blind luck? he wondered. How could a man ever know? Outside the sun was shining, the sky cloudless, just like that day at Cunaxa when all his dreams and beliefs were put to the test, when Cyrus had fought for his birthright. Xenophon's eyes lost their focus as the events of the day swarmed up from the dark corridors of memory. Cyrus, as handsome as Apollo and as brave as Heracles, had led his troops into Persia to fight for the crown that was rightfully his. Xenophon had known they could not lose, for the gods would always favor the brave and doubly favor the just. And the enemy, though superior in numbers, had neither the strategic skill nor the valor at arms to defeat the Greek mercenaries who loved Cyrus. When it came, the battle was a foregone conclusion.

The two forces had met near the village of Cunaxa. Xenophon had been a junior officer under Proxenus then, and he remembered the sudden rush of fear as he first saw the enemy, stretched out in a vast battle line. He had ordered his men into close formation and waited for orders. The Persians set up a great roar, clashing spear hafts to shields, while the Greeks stood silently. Cyrus galloped his charger along the front line, shouting, "For the gods and glory!" Outnumbered, the Greek phalanx charged into the Persian horde, which broke and ran. Cyrus, looking like a god on his white stallion, then led a ferocious assault on the enemy center, sending his treacherous brother—Artaxerxes the king—fleeing from the field. The glory of victory, the fulfillment of destiny!

Xenophon shivered and walked to the window, staring out over the rooftops, but he did not see them. What he saw was sunlight on lance points, what he heard was the screams of the dying and the cacophonous clash of sword on shield at Cunaxa as the Greeks, in four-deep formation, routed the barbarians.

Victory was theirs. Justice had prevailed, as all men of good heart knew that it would. And then?

Xenophon sighed. And then a common Persian soldier—a peasant by all accounts, unable to afford armor or sword—had thrown a rock that struck Cyrus on the temple, toppling him from the saddle. The enemy, in the process of flight, saw him fall. They regrouped and charged, coming upon the valiant Cyrus as he struggled to rise. He was stabbed a score of times, then his head and right hand were cut from his body.

Victory, like a fickle wife, flew from the Greeks.

The gods died that day in Xenophon's heart, though his intellect battled on to sustain a tenuous belief. Without gods the world was nothing, a place of torment and disillusion lacking order and reason. Yet after Cunaxa, he had rarely known peace of mind.

The general took a deep breath and struggled to suppress the bitter memories. A discreet knock came at his door. "Enter," he said, and his senior servant, Tinus, came in, bringing him a goblet of heavily watered wine. Xenophon smiled and thanked him.

Two other male servants fetched spring water for his bath, then toweled him dry. His armor had been polished until the bronze gleamed gold and his iron helm shone like purest silver. One servant helped him into his white linen tunic, while the second lifted the breastplate over his head, fastening the straps at Xenophon's side. A bronze-reinforced leather kilt was slung around his waist and tied at the hip. Bronze greaves were fastened to his shins. Xenophon waved the servants away and took up his sword belt. The leather was pitted, the bronze scabbard showing many dents, but the sword within was iron and keen-edged. He drew it, enjoying the exquisite balance of its short blade and leather-bound grip. Sighing, he slammed the blade home in the scabbard before buckling the sword belt at his waist. He lifted his helm and brushed the white horsehair crest.

Holding the helm under his arm, he turned toward the

door. Tinus opened it, and Xenophon walked out into the
courtyard. Three female servants bowed as he passed; he
acknowledged them with a smile and lifted his face to the
sunlight. It was a fine day.

Three helots were preparing the sand pit to the judges'
instructions, shaping hills, valleys, and streams. Xenophon
stopped to examine their work. "Make that hill higher and
more steep," he told one of the men, "and widen the valley
floor. That is where the battle will be fought, and there must
be room to swing the line."

He walked on through the open courtyard gates and out
toward the hillside and the shrine to Athena of the Eyes. It
was not a large shrine, three pillars supporting a low roof, but
within was the sacred altar. Xenophon entered the building,
removing his sword and standing it in the doorway. Then he
knelt beneath the altar, upon which stood the silver statue of
a woman, tall and slender, wearing a Doric helm pushed back
upon her head and carrying a sharp sword.

"Praise be to thee, Athena, goddess of wisdom and war,"
said Xenophon. "A soldier greets thee." He closed his eyes in
prayer, repeating the familiar words he had first used five
years before when leaving the lands of the Persians.

"I am a soldier, Athena. Do not let this be an end to my
glories. I have achieved so little. Let me live long enough to
carry your statue into the heartlands of the barbarian."

He glanced up at the statue, hoping for a response yet
knowing that only silence would follow. Xenophon rose and
backed from the shrine. He saw movement on the acropolis
and watched two boys embracing. Narrowing his eyes, he
recognized one of them as Hermias. The other, then, must be
the half-breed, the one they called Savra: a strange boy often
seen running across rooftops and high walls. Xenophon had
only seen him twice at close quarters. With his curved, hawklike nose he was neither handsome like Leonidas nor beautiful
like Hermias, yet there was something about him. His blue
eyes had a piercing look, both guarded and challenging, and
he bore himself with a pride his poverty did not warrant. Once

Xenophon had seen him running along Leaving Street, pursued by four other boys. On the second occasion Savra had been sitting with Hermias by the temple to Aphrodite. He had smiled then at some light comment from Hermias, and his face was transformed, the brooding glare disappearing. The change had shocked Xenophon, and he had stopped to stare at the boy. Savra had looked up then, seeing that he was observed. Swiftly his expression changed, like a mask falling into place, and the Athenian felt a sudden chill as those pale eyes focused on him.

Xenophon's thoughts turned to the brilliant Leonidas. Now *there* was a true Spartan, tall and beautifully proportioned, proud of stance, with hair like spun gold. There was a greatness in Leonidas, Xenophon believed, a true gift from the heavens. It was not often that the Athenian looked forward to the general's games, but today he was relishing the battle of wills to come.

The general approached the training ground known as the planes. Here, usually at dusk, the younger boys would fight mock battles, using sticks instead of swords. But every sixth morning the Spartan army would engage in maneuvers. Today was special, Xenophon knew, as he crossed the low bridge to the south of the planes; today saw the manhood parade. His admiration for the Spartan military system was undiminished, despite causing his banishment from Athens. The Spartans had evolved the perfect army, using principles so simple that it was a source of wonder to Xenophon that no other city-state had copied them. Men were ranked according to their years from manhood at twenty. Children who had grown together, learned together, and forged friendships in infancy would stand together, in the phalanx. And as the years passed they would stay together, fighting alongside one another until they reached the perfection of twenty years from manhood, when they would be eligible to retire.

That was what made the Spartan army invincible. The phalanx formation was multilayered, the first line made up of men of thirty, ten years from manhood—tough, seasoned, yet still young and strong, men used to iron discipline, who had fought in and won many battles. Behind them were the warriors twenty years from manhood, proud, battle-scarred, and mighty. One row back were the new recruits, seeing at first hand how Spartan warriors fought. And behind them the manhood lines from two to nineteen. Was it any wonder that no Spartan army had ever been defeated in the field by a foe of equal numbers?

"Why will you never understand?" Xenophon wondered aloud, picturing his native city of Athens. "You wanted to be supreme. You should have been supreme. But no, you would not learn from your enemies." Athens and Sparta had fought a long and costly war across the Peleponnese. It saw the worst period in Xenophon's life, when the Spartan army had besieged Athens twenty years before. The city of Athena, blessed by the gods, had surrendered. Xenophon would never forget the shame of that day.

Yet as a soldier studying the art of war, how could he hate the Spartans? They had lifted the art to heights undreamed of.

"As always you come equipped for battle," said Agisaleus, and Xenophon blinked. His mind had been far away, and he grinned almost sheepishly. The Spartan king was sitting on a narrow bench seat of stone under the shade of a cypress tree.

"My apologies, my lord," said Xenophon, bowing, "I was lost in thought."

Agisaleus shook his head and stood; only then did his twisted left foot become apparent. A handsome, dark-bearded man with piercing blue eyes, Agisaleus was the first Spartan king in history to suffer a deformity, and it would have cost him the crown had not the General Lysander argued his case before gods and men.

"You think too much, Athenian," said the king, taking Xenophon's arm. "What was it this morning? Athens? Persia? The lack of campaigns? Or are you longing to return to your estates at Olympia and deny us the pleasure of your company?"

"Athens," Xenophon admitted. Agisaleus nodded, his shrewd eyes locking to the other's face.

"It is not a simple matter to be called a traitor by your own people, to be banished from your homeland. But perspectives change, my friend. Had you held a senior position in Athens, perhaps the war would not have been so terrible—perhaps there would have been no war. Then you would have been a hero. I, for one, am delighted you did not command an army against us. Our losses would have been much higher."

"But you would not have lost?" queried Xenophon.

"Perhaps the odd skirmish," Agisaleus conceded, chuckling. "For a battle is not just about the skill of generals but also the quality of the warriors."

The two men walked to the crest of a low hill and sat on the first row of stone seats overlooking the planes.

The manhood line, numbering two hundred and forty men, was being incorporated into the eight formation, and Xenophon watched with interest as the new recruits practiced—alongside three thousand regulars—the charge and the wheel, the surge and the flanking hook.

There was a marked difference in their enthusiasm as the sweating men saw the king on the hill above them. But Agisaleus was not watching them; he turned to Xenophon.

"We have been too insular," said the king, removing his own red-plumed helm and setting it on the seat beside him.

"Insular?" responded Xenophon. "Is that not Sparta's greatest strength?"

"Strength and weakness, my friend, often seem as close as husband and wife. We are strong because we are proud. We are weak because our pride never allowed us to grow." He flung out his arm, encompassing the land. "Where are we? Deep in the south, far from the trade routes, a small city-state. Our pride does not allow for intermarriage, though it is not against any law, and the number of true Spartans is therefore held down. On that field are three thousand men, one-third of all our armies—which is why we can win battles but never build an empire. You feel the pain of Athens? She will survive and prosper long after we Spartans are dust. She has the sea; she is the center, the heart of Greece. We will beat her in a thousand battles yet lose the war."

Agisaleus shook his head and shivered. "The ice beast walked across my soul," he said. "Forgive my gloom."

Xenophon swung his eyes back to the fighting men on the planes. There was a great truth in the king's sorrowful words. For all her military might, Sparta was a small city-state with a population diminished by the terrible wars that had raged through the Peleponnese. He glanced at his friend and changed the subject.

"Will you present the prize at the general's games?"

Agisaleus smiled, and the melancholy passed from him. "I have a special gift today for the winner—one of the seven swords of Leonidas the king."

Xenophon's eyes widened. "A princely gift, my lord," he whispered.

Agisaleus shrugged. "My nephew is of the bloodline and carries the king's name; it is fitting he should have the blade. I would have given it to him anyway on his birthday in three weeks' time. But it will make a nice occasion and will give the boy a fine memory of the day he won the games. I won them myself thirty years ago."

"It will be a fine gesture, my lord, but . . . what if he does not win?"

"Be serious, Xenophon. He is pitted against a half-breed Macedonian, one step from being a helot. How can he not win? He is a Spartan, of the blood royal. And anyway, since you are the chief judge, I am sure we can rely on a just result."

"Just?" countered Xenophon, turning away to mask his anger. "Let us at least be honest."

"Oh, do not be stiff with me," said Agisaleus, throwing his arm around his friend's shoulder. "It is only a child's game. Where is the harm?"

"Where indeed?" replied Xenophon.

* * *

Parmenion slowed in his run as he approached the white-walled home of Xenophon. Already the visitors were gathering, and he could see Hermias at the edge of the crowd, talking to Gryllus. Anger flared as he remembered the short, powerful hooked punches, and he felt the desire to stalk across the crowded street, take Gryllus by the hair, and ram his foul head into the wall until the stones were stained with blood.

Calm yourself! He knew Gryllus would be present—as Xenophon's son, this was his home; secondly, he would carry the black cloak for Leonidas. But it galled Parmenion that Gryllus was accepted—even liked—by other youths in the barracks. How is it, he wondered, that an Athenian can win them over but I can't? He has no Spartan blood, yet my father was a hero. Pushing the thought from his mind, Parmenion eased himself through the crowds, closing in on the two youngsters. Gryllus saw him first, and his smile froze into place, his eyes darkening.

"Welcome to the day of your humiliation," said the Athenian.

"Get back from me, Gryllus," warned Parmenion, his voice shaking. "The sight of you makes me want to vomit. And know this: If you come at me again, I will kill you. No blows. No bruises. Just worms and death!"

Xenophon's son staggered back as if struck, dropping the black cloak he carried. Swiftly he gathered it and vanished into the doorway of the house.

Turning to Hermias, Parmenion tried to smile, but the muscles of his face were tight and drawn. Instead, he reached out to embrace his friend, but Hermias drew back. "Be careful," said Hermias. "It is a bad omen to touch the cloak!"

Parmenion gazed down at the dark wool draped across Hermias' arm. "It is only a cloak," he whispered, stroking his fingers across it. The loser of the game would be led from the battlefield, cloaked and hooded to hide his shame. No Spartan could be expected to look upon such a humiliation with anything but loathing. But Parmenion did not care. If Leonidas won, that would be shame enough. Wearing the cloak would worry him not at all.

"Come," said Hermias, taking Parmenion's arm. "Let us walk awhile—we do not want to be early. How is your mother?"

"Getting stronger," answered Parmenion, aware of the lie yet needing it to be true. As they walked away, he heard a cheer and glanced back to see the arrival of the golden-haired Leonidas. He watched with envy as men gathered around to wish him luck.

The two youths walked up the stony path to the sanctuary of Ammon, a small, circular building of white stone fronted by marble *hoplites*. From here Parmenion could see the sacred lake and, beyond the city, the tree-shrouded temple of Aphrodite, goddess of love.

"Are you nervous?" asked Hermias as they sat beneath the marble statues.

"My stomach is knotted, but my mind is calm," Parmenion told him.

"What formation will you use?"

"A new one." Swiftly Parmenion outlined his plan.

Hermias listened in silence, then shook his head. "You must not do this, Savra! Please listen to me! It is unthinkable!"

Surprised by his friend's reaction, Parmenion chuckled. "It is just a mock battle, Hermias. Wooden soldiers and knuckle-bones. Is not the object to win?"

"Yes, yes, but . . . they will never allow it. Gods, Savra, can you not see it?"

"No," answered Parmenion. "Anyway, what does it matter? No one will have to sit through a two-hour ordeal. Win or lose, it will be over in minutes."

"I do not think so," whispered Hermias. "Let us go back."

Xenophon's courtyard was crowded, the guests climbing to the banked seats against the western wall, where they could sit in the shade. Parmenion was uncomfortably aware of the poverty he showed in his ill-fitting *chiton*, but then, his mother had only the one small landholding, and from that meager income she had to find enough money for food and clothing and to pay for Parmenion's training. All Spartan youths were charged for their food and lodging, and inability to pay meant loss of status. When poverty struck a family, they lost not only the right to vote but the right to call themselves Spartan. It was the greatest shame a man could suffer. Ejected from his barracks, he would have to take employment and become little better than a helot.

Parmenion shook himself clear of such somber thoughts and stared at the ten-foot-square killing ground shaped in sand. The carved wooden soldiers stood in ranks beside it. Gold on the left, blood on the right. Unpainted and unadorned, yet still they were handsome. Reaching down, he picked up the first gold *hoplite* line; it had been carved in white wood, but the years had stained it yellow. There were only ten figures pinned to the small support plank, but these represented a hundred heavily armored warriors bearing round shields, spears, and short swords. They had been carved with care, even down to the leather kilts and bronze greaves. Only the helms were now outdated; full-faced and plumed, they had been discontinued thirty years before. But these carvings were old and almost sacred. The great Leonidas of legend had used them when he won the eleventh games.

Parmenion replaced the Spartan file and moved to the Sciri-tai. These were less well carved and not as old. The men here carried no spears and wore round leather caps.

A shadow fell across Parmenion, and he glanced up to see a tall man wearing a yellow tunic edged with gold. He had rarely seen a more fine-looking warrior: his hair was golden, streaked with silver, his eyes the blue of a summer sky.

The man smiled at him. "You would be Parmenion. Welcome to my house, young general."

"Thank you, sir. It is an honor to be here."

"Yes, it is," Xenophon agreed, "but you have earned that honor. Walk with me."

Parmenion followed Xenophon into a shaded alcove decorated with a magnificent display of purple flowers that draped the wall like the cloak of a king.

"The straws have been drawn, and you will make the first move. Now, tell me the first three orders you will give," said Xenophon. Parmenion took a deep breath. For the first time his nerves seemed to fail him, and he found himself staring back at the crowd in the courtyard. In a real battle, once the fighting started, it was almost impossible to change the strategy swiftly, not when thousands of men were struggling together with swords and shields clashing. That was why, in the game, the first three orders were given to the judges so that no competitor could suddenly change his mind if faced by a superior move from his opponent.

"I am waiting, young man," whispered Xenophon. Parmenion turned his pale blue eyes on the handsome Athenian. Then he told him, watching the older man's reaction.

Xenophon listened without expression, then he sighed and shook his head. "It is not for the senior judge to offer advice; therefore, I will say only that if Leonidas chooses any of four—perhaps five—options, you will be routed catastrophically. You have considered this, of course?"

"I have, sir."

"Have you also considered the question of tradition and of Spartan pride?"

"I merely wish to win the battle."

Xenophon hesitated. Already he had exceeded his duties. Finally he nodded and returned to the ritual. "May the gods favor you, Sparta," he said, bowing. Parmenion returned the bow and watched the Athenian stride across to where Leonidas waited. He swallowed hard. If the general was a friend to Leonidas and should impart even a clue as to Parmenion's battle plan . . .

Do not even think it! Xenophon is a great general, Parmenion chided himself, and would never stoop to anything so base. This was the man who, after the defeat at Cunaxa, had seen his friends brutally assassinated and had taken command of a demoralized Greek army and fought his way across Persia's vast empire to the sea. Xenophon would not betray him.

But he is also the father of Gryllus, thought Parmenion, and a friend to the family of Leonidas.

The crowd rose, and Parmenion watched as Agisaleus entered, flanked by his generals and two of his lovers. The king bowed as the crowd applauded him, then limped to his seat at the center of the first row, directly beside the sand pit. Parmenion's mouth was dry as he walked to where Hermias stood, averting his eyes from the cloak.

Xenophon called the other two judges to him. For some minutes he spoke to them, then took his seat beside the king. The first of the judges—an elderly man with short-cropped white hair and a closely trimmed beard—approached Parmenion.

"I am Clearchus," he said. "I will place the army as you have commanded, General. You may ask my advice on matters of time delay, but nothing else." He opened a pouch at his hip and removed from it three knucklebones. In the six indentations on each bone were painted numbers, from three to eight. "To decide losses, I will roll these bones. The highest figure and the lowest figure will be removed, and the remaining number will be regarded as the fallen. You understand?"

"Of course," Parmenion replied.

"A simple yes is required," Clearchus stated.

"Yes," said Parmenion. Clearchus moved to stand alongside the yellow wood army as the second judge positioned himself on the other side of the pit by the red wood soldiers.

For the first time Parmenion locked his gaze to Leonidas. The other youth grinned at him, his eyes mocking. Leonidas was considered beautiful, but despite the yellow-gold hair and the handsome mouth, Parmenion saw only the ugliness of cruelty.

As was the custom, the two combatants walked around the pit to face one another.

"Will you give ground to the Spartan gold?" asked Parmenion, following the ritual.

"The Spartan red never gives ground," replied Leonidas. "Prepare to die."

The crowd applauded, and the king rose, raising his hands for silence. "My friends, today I offer a special gift to the victor: one of the seven swords of Leonidas the king!" He held the iron blade aloft, where the sunlight caught it, turning it to silver. A great roar went up.

Leonidas leaned in close to Parmenion. "I will humble you, mix-blood."

"Your breath smells worse than a cow's ass!" replied Parmenion, enjoying the flush of color that leapt to Leonidas' cheeks. Both youths returned to their places.

"Begin!" ordered Xenophon.

Clearchus stepped forward. "The general Parmenion has ordered the troops into Lysander's fifth formation, with the Sciritai on the left, sixteen deep, the Spartans at the center, sixteen deep, and mercenary javelin throwers behind the cavalry on the right. The general positions himself *behind* the center." Parmenion saw several warriors in the crowd shaking their heads in disapproval and could guess their thoughts. No general could expect his men to fight for him if he did not have the courage to stand with them in the front lines.

Three helots moved forward, lifting the ranks of wooden soldiers into place on the sand.

The second judge addressed the crowd. "The general Leonidas has ordered the third Agisalean formation, the Spartans on the right, ten deep, the cavalry in the center, Sciritai and javeliners on the left. He positions himself in the second line of the center." Applause went up, and Leonidas bowed. As a Spartan general should, he had chosen to place himself close to the front rank.

The crowd leaned forward, staring intently at the formations. It was obvious that Parmenion was planning a defensive battle, ready to repel a frontal assault. Leonidas had stretched his line and was planning the traditional angled attack from the left while moving to encircle the enemy. Much would now depend on the rolling of the knucklebones to decide casualties.

Clearchus cleared his throat, and all in the crowd knew the words that would follow—the formations made it obvious. No move. The Spartan gold would wait until Leonidas attacked, relying on the knucklebones to decide the outcome. But conversation ceased as Clearchus spoke.

"The general Parmenion orders the cavalry forward at the charge, veering toward enemy center." All eyes swung to the judge by Leonidas. The first three moves could not be changed, and much would depend on Leonidas' use of cavalry. It was unusual—though not unheard of—for a cavalry charge to be signaled at the onset.

"The general Leonidas orders the javeliners and Sciritai to advance on the right."

Now the whispers began, for Leonidas had not anticipated a cavalry attack and had issued no orders to his own horsemen.

A helot with a measuring rod moved the yellow wood horsemen forward. The judges conferred, and Xenophon addressed the crowd.

"It is agreed unanimously that the speed of the charge has routed the opposing cavalry, forcing them back into the *hoplite* ranks. Casualties are sixty suffered by Leonidas and nine by Parmenion."

The voice of Clearchus then rose among the clamor. "The general Parmenion instructs the Spartans and Sciritai to merge lines and advance at a run, thirty-two deep, at the enemy's right."

Parmenion stood stock-still, eyes locked to Leonidas, who was staring horror-struck at the massed advance. Parmenion could understand how he was feeling; he was facing not one improbable plan of action but two. No Spartan force would ever consider merging with the Sciritai, and no Greek army would ever attack the enemy's right—its strongest point. To do so meant exposing a vulnerable flank, for the shield was borne on the left arm, and therefore the advancing phalanx would be open to javelins, rocks, arrows, and stones.

But not here, thought Parmenion. Not today. For Leonidas'

center had been wrecked by his own cavalry, and there were no peltasts or archers close enough to wreak havoc on his advancing line with missiles. He looked up, wanting to see, to remember, every change of expression on the face of his enemy, longing to see and memorize the moment when defeat first registered.

"The general Leonidas orders the rear six lines to move out and encircle the enemy."

Parmenion was exultant, but he hid his feelings, making a mask of his features, only the flaring nostrils and the quickening of his breathing betraying his excitement. Leonidas was beaten. A massed charge was bearing on his right, and he had thinned his line to only four ranks.

The helots lifted the wedges and carried them forward. There was no need for the judges to confer; every soldier in the crowd knew what must happen when a phalanx thirty-two deep struck a line of four ranks. The strength and courage of the few could not stop the weight of the charge. Leonidas was not merely beaten—he was crushed. The golden-haired Spartan stared at the soldiers, then stepped back and spoke swiftly to his judge. The man's words stunned Parmenion.

"The general Leonidas is asking the judges to countermand the second order of the general Parmenion on the grounds that it has no credibility. If such an order were given in battle, the Spartans would no doubt refuse to obey it."

Parmenion reddened and looked to the king. Agisaleus sat back and began a conversation with the young man on his right. Xenophon called the judges to him, away from the crowd, but all could see that the argument that followed was heated.

Parmenion's heart sank as he stared down at the tiny battlefield and the wooden soldiers locked in frozen battle. Could they disqualify him? Of course they could. He gazed up at the rows of spectators. Who are you, Parmenion? he asked himself. You are a poverty-stricken half-breed. What do they care for you? This is a day for Leonidas, and you have spoiled it for them.

Xenophon walked back to the sand pit. The crowd waited for the verdict, and even the king sat forward, his eyes on the Athenian.

"The challenge is an interesting one, which has split the judges. It is true that the merging of lines with the Sciritai would not be considered honorable, nor even likely." He paused, and Parmenion saw heads nod in agreement, felt the eyes of Leonidas on him. His opponent allowed himself a smile. Parmenion swallowed hard. "However," Xenophon continued, "it seems to me that the question is not one of honor but of tactics and discipline. The general Parmenion, knowing the strength of his enemy and that his enemy had used this formation in his last five battles, chose an unusual course of action. I am an Athenian, but I speak with the authority of one who admires beyond all men the qualities of the Spartan army. And the question here is of discipline. The challenge stands or falls on one point: Would the Spartans refuse to obey such an order? The answer is a simple one. When, in all of their glorious history, have Spartan soldiers *ever* failed to obey an order?" Xenophon paused once more, his eyes sweeping the ranks of the spectators and resting at last on the king. "The move stands," said Xenophon. "The general Leonidas is defeated and, since he placed himself at the second line, is also slain. The Spartan gold have the day. The general Parmenion is the supreme *strategos.*"

There was no applause, but Parmenion did not care. He swung to Hermias, who threw aside the dark cloak and rushed forward to hug his friend.

The crowd was stunned. King Agisaleus fixed Xenophon with an angry look, but the Athenian merely shrugged and turned away. Then the whispers began as old soldiers discussed the strategy. Leonidas rose and stumbled back. Gryllus moved forward behind him, offering the cloak of shame, but Leonidas waved it away and strode from the courtyard.

An elderly helot moved from the shadows, touching Parmenion's shoulder. "Sir, there is a woman at the gates. She says you must come quickly."

"A woman? What woman?" asked Parmenion.

"It is something to do with your mother, sir."

All sense of triumph and joy fled from Parmenion. He staggered as if struck . . . then ran from the courtyard.

The crowd fell silent as the young Spartan sped from the gates. Agisaleus pushed himself to his feet and moved toward Xenophon, his dark eyes angry.

"This was not supposed to happen!" hissed the king.

Xenophon nodded. "I know, sire," he replied, keeping his voice low, "but then, none of us expected Leonidas to perform so badly. He showed no strategic skill and treated his enemy with contempt. But you are the king, sire. You are the foremost judge in Sparta. It is your right—should you desire it—to set aside my judgment."

Agisaleus turned to look at the wooden soldiers lying forgotten in the sand pit. "No," he said at last, "you were correct, Xenophon. But I'll be damned if I'll present the sword to the half-breed. Here! You give it to him."

Xenophon took the weapon and bowed. The king shook his head and walked away, the crowd dispersing after him. As the Athenian moved into the shade of the *andron* porch and sat quietly, his thoughts turning to Parmenion, his son Gryllus approached him.

"That was disgraceful, Father," said the boy.

"Indeed it was," agreed the general. "Leonidas did not wear the cloak of shame. It was not seemly."

"That is not what I meant, and you know it. The Spartan army would never allow mongrels like the Sciritai to merge lines. No one could have expected it. The game should have been restarted."

"Go away, boy," said Xenophon, "and try not to speak of matters of which you have little understanding."

Gryllus stood his ground, his face reddening. "Why do you hate me, Father?" he asked.

The words shook the Athenian. "I do not hate you, Gryllus. I am sorry that you believe it." Xenophon stood and approached the boy with arms spread, ready to embrace him.

"No, don't touch me!" cried Gryllus, backing away. "I want nothing from you." Turning, he ran across the courtyard and out onto the main street. Xenophon sighed. He had tried so hard with the child, painstakingly teaching him, trying to fill Gryllus with thoughts of honor, loyalty, duty, and courage. But to no avail. And Xenophon had watched him grow, had seen the birth of arrogance and cruelty, vanity and deceit. "I do not hate you," he whispered, "but I cannot love you."

He was about to enter the house when he saw an old man standing by the sand pit, staring down at the soldiers. As the host, Xenophon was compelled by good manners to speak to him, and he strolled across the courtyard.

"May I offer you refreshment?" he inquired.

The old man looked up into the general's face. "You do not remember me?" he asked, lifting the stump of his right arm.

"Pasian? Sweet Hera! I thought you dead!"

"I should be—sometimes I wish I was. They cut my right hand away, General, leaving me to bleed to death. But I made it home. Sixteen years it took me." Pasian smiled, showing broken, rotted teeth. "Home," he said again, his voice wistful. "We fought our way clear of the Persians and forted up in a circle of boulders. We could see Agisaleus and the main force and thought they would come to our aid. But they did not. We were only Sciritai, after all. One by one we died. I killed eleven men that day. The Persians were not best pleased with me, Xenophon; they took my hand. I managed to stop the bleeding, and I found a farmer who covered the wound with boiling pitch."

"Come inside, my friend. Let me fetch you wine, food."

"No, though I thank you. I came only to see the boy, to watch him win."

"Leonidas?"

"No. The other boy, Savra. He's no Spartan, Xenophon, and may the gods be praised for that!"

"How do you know him? He was not born when you marched into Persia."

"I met him on the road, General . . . when I was almost home. You know, I had not realized how old I had become until I saw the hills of my childhood. All these years I have struggled to come home, and there I was, a decrepit cripple with a broken cart. I called out to him for help, and he came. He took me to my son's house. And not once did he tell me I had lost him the great race. Can you imagine that?"

"He finished last, I believe," said Xenophon.

"He was first—in sight of the city. And I have nothing to give him. No possessions. No coin. But I will pay my debt, Xenophon, by claiming another. Twice I saved your life. Will you honor my debt?"

"You know I will, as I hope you know that, had I been in Persia with Agisaleus, I would have come for you."

Pasian nodded. "I do not doubt it, General. I understand the boy is a mix-blood, with little money and less influence. Help him, Xenophon."

"I shall, I promise you."

Pasian smiled and walked away, stopping for one last look at the sand pit. "I enjoyed the battle," he said over his shoulder. "Nice to see the Spartans humbled."

Parmenion raced out through the gates and into the noon-deserted streets. He did not feel the intensity of the sun on his skin or the pain of his bruises. He did not see the houses as he passed them, or hear the yapping dogs that snapped at his heels.

His head was full of the roaring of anguish, and all he could see was his mother's face floating before his mind's eye—soft and smiling, calm and understanding.

She was dying.

Dying . . .

The word hammered at him over and over, and his vision blurred, yet still he ran. He knew then that he had always known. When the weight fell away from her once beautiful face, when her limbs had become skeletal and her eyes had grown dull. And all the other signs of blood and pain. Yet he could not face what he knew and had turned his eyes and his mind away.

He came to Leaving Street and cut off through the poorer quarter, cannoning into a fat trader and knocking him from his feet. The man's curses followed him.

The doorway of his house was blocked by neighbors standing silently. He pushed his way through them and found Rhea sitting by the bedside. The doctor, Astion, was standing in the small courtyard with his back to the room. Parmenion stood in the doorway, his heart pounding as Rhea turned to him.

"She has gone," said the woman, rising and moving to Parmenion, her plump arms circling him. "There is no more pain."

Tears flowed to Parmenion's cheeks as he stared at the slender body on the bed. "She did not wait for me," he whispered.

Rhea hugged him for a moment and then moved to the door, gently pushing back the neighbors and friends, closing the door on them. Then she returned to the bed and sat, taking Artema's small hand in hers. "Come," she told Parmenion. "Sit by her on the other side. Say farewell." Parmenion stumbled forward and took his mother's right hand, and together they sat in silence for a while. Astion entered, but they did not see him and he left quietly.

"She talked of you at the end," said Rhea. "She spoke of her pride. She wanted to wait, to see you, to know how you fared."

"I won, Mother," said Parmenion, gripping the lifeless fingers. "I won before them all." He gazed down at Artema's face. The eyes were closed, the features still.

"She looks peaceful," Rhea whispered.

Parmenion shook his head. He could not see the *peace*, only the terrible finality of death, the total stillness, the separation. Yet her hand was warm and the fingers supple. How many times had she stroked away his pains or patted his face with these hands? He felt a terrible knotting in his stomach and a swelling in his throat. Tears fell more freely, coursing down his face and splashing against his mother's hand.

"She talked of a white horse," said Rhea. "She could see it on a hillside. It was coming for her, and she said she was going to ride it all the way back to Macedonia. I do not know if that is a comfort. She also said she could see your father, waiting for her."

Parmenion could not speak, but reaching out, he touched the skin of his mother's face.

"Say good-bye," whispered Rhea. "Tell her good-bye."

"I can't," sobbed Parmenion. "Not yet. Leave me for a while. Please, Rhea!"

"I need to prepare the . . . I'll come back in a while." She walked to the door and stopped. "I loved her; she was a fine woman and a good friend. I will miss her, Parmenion. There was not an evil thought in her; she deserved better."

When he heard the door close, Parmenion felt the floodgates of his grief give way, and he sobbed uncontrollably, his mind awash with images. He could remember his father only dimly as an enormous dark giant moving about the house, but his mother had been with him always. When, as was the Spartan custom, he had been taken at seven to live in a barracks with other boys, she had wept and held him to her as if his life were in danger. He had sneaked out often, climbing over walls and rooftops to see her.

Now he would see her no more.

"If you loved me, you'd come back," he said. "You would never have left me." He knew the senselessness of the words, but they were torn from him.

He sat with the corpse until the light began to fade. Hearing a door open, he expected Rhea's hand upon his shoulder.

"I bring your trophy, General," said Xenophon softly. "Cover her face and we will talk in the courtyard."

"I can't cover her face!" protested Parmenion.

Xenophon moved to the other side of the bed. "She is not here, boy; she is gone. What you see is the cloak that she wore. It is no terrible thing to cover her." His voice was gentle, and Parmenion blinked away his tears and stared up at the Athenian.

Tenderly Parmenion lifted the white sheet over the still face.

"Let us talk for a while," said Xenophon, leading the boy into the courtyard and sitting on the stone seat. The Athenian now wore a long cloak of blue-dyed wool over a white linen tunic and calf-length sandals of the finest leather. Yet still he looked every inch the soldier. He was carrying the sword of Leonidas, which he placed in Parmenion's hands.

The youth put it to one side without even looking at it. Xenophon nodded.

"It will mean more to you in days to come. But let it pass. You are young, Parmenion, and life holds many griefs in store. Yet none will ever touch you like this one. But you are a sensible lad, and you know that all people die. I have spoken to your neighbor about your mother; she was in great pain."

"I know of her pains. I know of her struggles. I wanted . . . I wanted to build something for her. A house . . . I don't know. But I wanted to make her happy, to give her things she desired. There was a cloth in the market she wanted, edged with gold, a shining cloth to make a dress for a queen, she said. But we could not buy that cloth. I stole it. But she took it back. She had nothing."

Xenophon shook his head. "You see too little. She had a husband she loved and a son she adored. You think she wanted more? Well, yes, she may have. But this is a cruel world, Parmenion. All any man—or woman—can expect is a little happiness. According to your neighbor, your mother was happy. She knew nothing of your . . . troubles . . . with the other youths. She sang, she laughed; she danced at festivals. And yes, she is dead—she will sing no more. But then, neither will she feel pain. Nor did she grow old and withered and outlive her son."

"Why did you come here?" asked the boy. "You could have sent the sword."

Xenophon smiled. "Indeed I could. Come home with me, Parmenion. We will dine, and you will tell me of your mother. It is important that we speak of her and send our praises after her. Then the gods will know what a fine woman she was and will greet her with fine wine and a dress of shining cloth, edged with gold."

"I don't want to leave her," said Parmenion.

"It is too late; she has already gone. Now they must prepare her for burial, and it is not fitting that a man see a woman's mysteries. Come."

Parmenion followed the general out of the house, and they walked in silence along Leaving Street and on beyond the market to the larger houses of the nobility.

Xenophon's house looked different without the crowds and with the sand pit removed. The scent from the purple flowers on the walls was everywhere, and a servant brought several lamps to light the courtyard. The night was warm, the air heavy, and Xenophon listened as Parmenion told the story of his mother's life.

Servants brought watered wine and sweetmeats, and the two men sat together long into the night. At last Xenophon led Parmenion to a small room at the rear of the house.

"Sleep well, my friend," said the general. "Tomorrow we will see to your affairs." Xenophon paused in the doorway. "Tell me, young man," he asked suddenly, "why did you finish last in the great race?"

"I made a mistake," answered Parmenion.

"Is it one you regret?"

Parmenion saw again the old man's face, the despair in his eyes. "No," he said. "Some things are more important than winning."

"Try to remember that," the Athenian told him.

Tamis sat by the dying fire, watching the fading shadows dance on the white, rough-hewn walls of the small room. The night was silent save for the dry rustling of leaves as the night wind whispered through the trees.

The old woman waited, listening.

I was not wrong, she told herself defiantly. A branch clattered against her window as the breeze grew stronger, the fire flickering into a brief blaze, then dying down. She added dry sticks to the flames and pulled her thin shawl around her shoulders.

Her eyelids drooped, fatigue washing over her, yet still she sat, her breathing shallow, her heartbeat ragged.

As the night deepened, she heard the sounds of a walking horse, the slow, rhythmic thudding of hooves on hard-baked earth. With a sigh Tamis pushed herself to her feet, gathering up her staff and moving to the open doorway, where she stood watching the shadow-haunted trees.

The sound was closer now, yet no horse was in sight. Closing the eyes of her body, she opened the eyes of her spirit and saw the tall white stallion cross the clearing to stand before her. It was a huge beast of almost eighteen hands, with eyes the color of opals.

Tamis sighed and put aside her shawl, taking up instead a cloak of gray wool, which she fastened to her shoulders with a brooch of turquoise. Leaving the door open, she walked out into the night toward the city, the ghostly horse following behind.

Her thoughts were somber as she made her slow way through the nearly deserted market square, her staff tapping against the flagstones. Parmenion's mother had been a good woman, kind and thoughtful. *And you killed her*, whispered a voice in her mind.

"No, I did not," she said, aloud.

You let her die. Is that not the same?

"Many people die. Am I responsible for all deaths?"

You wanted her dead. You wanted the child to suffer alone.

"To make him strong. He is the hope of the world. He is the one destined to defy the Dark God. He must be a man of power."

The voice was stilled, but Tamis knew she was unconvinced. You are getting old, she told herself. There is no *voice*.

You are talking to yourself, and such debates are meaningless. "I speak with the voice of reason," said Tamis. "She speaks with the voice of the heart."

Is there no place now within you for such a voice?

"Leave me be! I do what must be done!"

A group of men were sitting close by in the moonlight, dicing with knucklebones. Several of them looked up as she passed, one surreptitiously making the sign of the circle to ward off evil. Tamis smiled at that, then put the men from her mind.

Arriving at the house of Parmenion, she closed her eyes, her spirit moving inside, hovering within the death room where Artema lay swathed in burial linen. But what Tamis sought was not here, and the sorceress returned to her body. Wearily she walked along the moonlit streets, the stallion following, until she stood before the gates to Xenophon's home. Once more her spirit soared, moving through the house and up the stairs to a small room, in which Parmenion lay, lost in dreams.

There by the bed stood a pale figure, white and ethereal, like sculptured mist, featureless and glowing. Tamis felt the overpowering emotions within the room, love and loss and harrowing heartbreak. Parmenion's dreams made him groan aloud, and the figure shimmered. Now Tamis sensed confusion and pain. A pale arm reached toward the boy but could not touch him. "It is time," whispered Tamis.

"No." The single word hung in the air, not a denial but an entreaty.

"He could not see you, even were he awake. Come away. I shall lead you."

"Where?"

"To a place of rest."

The figure turned back to the bed. "My son."

"He will be a great man. He will save the world from darkness."

"My son," said the wraith, as if she had not heard.

"You are no longer of his world," said Tamis. "Say your farewells swiftly, for soon it will be the dawn."

"He seems so lost," whispered the wraith. "I must stay to comfort him." The mist hardened, the features of Artema shining through. She turned to Tamis. "I know you. You are the seeress."

"I am."

"Why do you want to take me from my son?"

"You are no longer of his world," repeated Tamis. "You . . . died."

"Died? Oh, yes, I remember." Tamis steeled herself against the grief born of knowledge that emanated from the ghost. "And now I will never hold him again. I cannot bear it!" Tamis swung away from the anguish in Artema's eyes.

"Follow me," she commanded, and returned to her body. For a while she stood in silence beyond the gates until at last the ghostly figure moved out into the courtyard.

"You say he will be a great man," said Artema. "But will he be happy?"

"Yes," lied Tamis.

"Then I must be content. Will I be reunited with his father?"

"I cannot say. For where you will ride I cannot go. But I pray it will be as you desire it. Mount the horse, for he alone knows the paths of the dead, and he will carry you safely."

The figure of mist flowed to the stallion's back. "Will you look after my son?" asked Artema. "Will you be his friend?"

"I will look after him," promised Tamis. "I will see that he has all he needs to meet his destiny. Now go!"

The stallion lifted its head and began to walk toward the burial hill. Tamis watched until it was out of sight, then sank back to sit on a marble bench.

But will he be happy?

The question gnawed at her, changing her mood from sorrow to anger.

"The strong do not need happiness. He will have glory and fame, and his name will be whispered in awe by men of all nations. Generations will know happiness because of him. Surely that is enough?"

She glanced up at the window of Parmenion's room. "It will have to be enough, *strategos*, because it is all I can give you."

Parmenion awoke in the night, his mind hazy and uncertain. He sat up, unsure of where he was. Moonlight was streaming through the open window. He looked up at the moon and saw again his mother's face, cold in death. Reality struck him worse than any blow he had received from Gryllus or the others, hammering home into his heart. He rolled from the bed and moved to the window that opened out onto the courtyard. He stared down at the empty square and saw that the sand pit had been removed, the scene of his triumph once more merely cobbled stone. He thought of his victory, but it was as nothing against the enormity of his loss. A child's game—how could it have meant so much? He glanced back at the bed, wondering what had awoken him. Then he remembered.

He had been dreaming of a white horse galloping over green hills.

He looked up at the moon and the stars. So far away. Unreachable, untouchable.

Like his mother . . .

The sense of separation was unbearable. He sat down on a high-backed chair and felt the cool night breeze bathing his skin. What did it matter now that he was despised? The one person who loved him was gone.

What will you do, Parmenion? Where will you go? he asked himself.

He sat by the window until the dawn, watching the sun rise over the peaks of the Parnon mountains.

The door opened behind him, and he turned to see the man Clearchus, his judge from the games. Parmenion stood and bowed.

"No need to accord me your respect," said the man. "I am little more than a servant here. The master of the house invites you to break your fast with him."

Parmenion nodded, and the man made as if to leave, then turned. His hard face softened. "It probably means nothing, boy, but I am sorry about your mother. Mine died when I was eleven; it is not a loss that you forget.",

"Thank you," said Parmenion. Tears welled, but he forced his face to remain set and followed Clearchus to the courtyard, where Xenophon sat waiting. The general rose and smiled. "I trust you slept well, young *strategos*."

"Yes, sir. Thank you."

"Be seated and take some food. There is bread and honey. I found the benefits of it when campaigning in Persia; it makes a good start to the day."

Parmenion cut several slices from the fresh loaf and smeared them with honey.

"I have sent a message to the barracks," said Xenophon. "You do not have to attend muster today. So I thought we would ride out toward Ilias."

"I am not a good rider, sir," Parmenion admitted. "We cannot afford a horse."

"Then how can you know if you are a good rider or not? Enjoy your meal and then we will see how good you are."

They finished their breakfast and moved back through the house to the long stables at the rear, where there were six stalls and five horses.

"Choose," said Xenophon. "Examine them all and select a mount."

Parmenion entered each stall, making a show of examining the horses. Not knowing what to look for, he stroked each mount, running his hand over their broad backs. There was a gray with a fine curved neck and strong back, but he looked at Parmenion with a jaundiced eye that seemed to promise pain. Finally the youngster chose a chestnut mare of fifteen hands.

"Explain the choice," said Xenophon, slipping a bridle over the mare's head and leading her out into the yard.

"When I stroked her, she nuzzled me. The others merely stood, except for the gray. I think he wanted to bite off my hand."

"He would have," Xenophon admitted, "but you made a

fine choice. The mare is sweet-natured and swift to obey. Nothing shakes her." The general laid a goatskin shabraque on the mare's back. "It will not slip," he told Parmenion, "but remember to grip her with your thighs, not your calves." On the back of the gray he placed a magnificent leopardskin shabraque. "In Persia," he said, "many of the barbarians use hardened leather seats strapped to the horse's back. But that is for barbarians, Parmenion. A gentleman uses only a blanket, or at best an animal skin."

The air was fresh, the early-morning sun lacking the strength-sapping power it would show within a few hours. They walked the horses across the planes and out to the rolling hills north of the city. Here Xenophon cupped his hands and helped Parmenion mount; then the general took hold of the gray's mane and vaulted to the gelding's back. The move was smooth, sure, and graceful, and Parmenion found himself envying the older man's style.

"We will start by walking the horses," said Xenophon, "allowing them to adjust to the weight." He leaned forward, patting his mount's long neck.

"You care for them," said Parmenion. "You treat them like friends."

"They *are* friends. There are so many fools abroad who believe that a whip will subdue a horse and make it obey. They *will* subdue it—no doubt of that. But a horse without spirit is a worthless beast. Answer me this, *strategos*—who would you rather depend on in battle, a man who loves you or one you have tormented and beaten?"

"The answer is obvious, sir. I would rather have a friend beside me."

"Exactly. Why is it different with a horse or a hound?"

They rode across the hills until they came to a level plain covered with dry grass. "Let them have their heads," said Xenophon, slapping the rump of the gelding. The beast took off at a run, the mare following. Parmenion gripped the mare's belly with his knees and leaned forward. The thunder of hoofbeats filled his ears, and the exhilaration of the rider swept over him. He felt alive, truly, wondrously alive.

After several minutes Xenophon swung his horse to the right, heading for a cypress grove to the east. There he slowed the gelding to a walk, and Parmenion cantered alongside. The Athenian leapt to the ground and smiled up at Parmenion. "You handled her well."

The youngster dismounted. "She is fine. Very fine," he said.

"Then pat her and tell her."

"Can she understand me?"

"Of course not, but she can hear your tone and know from your touch that you are pleased with her."

"Does she have a name?" Parmenion asked, running his fingers through the dark mane.

"She is Bella, Thracian stock with the heart of a lion."

They tethered the horses and sat beneath the cypress trees. Parmenion suddenly felt uncomfortable. Why was he here? What interest did this legendary Athenian have in him? He did not want to be seduced by Xenophon, nor did he wish to be put in the position of having to reject such a powerful suitor.

"What are you thinking?" asked the general suddenly.

"I was thinking of the horses," lied Parmenion.

Xenophon nodded. "Do not fear me, youngster. I am your friend—no more than that."

"Are you a god to know my thoughts?"

"No, I am a general, and your thoughts are easy to read, for you are young and naïve. In your battle against Leonidas you fought to keep the elation of triumph from your face. That was a mistake, for you made of your features a mask and yet your eyes gleamed with the purest malice. If you wish to disguise your feelings, you must first fool yourself and when you look upon a hated enemy, pretend in your mind that he is your friend. Then your face will soften and you will smile more naturally. Do not try to be expressionless, for that only tells your enemy you are hiding something. And where you can, try to use a little honesty; it is the greatest disguise of all. But these are thoughts for another day. You wonder why Xenophon has taken an interest in you? The answer is not complex. I watched you play Leonidas, and your breadth of vision touched me. War is an art, not a science, and that is something you understand instinctively. You studied Leonidas, and you learned his weakness. You took a risk, and it paid off handsomely. Also, you used your cavalry well—and that is rare in a Spartan."

"It did not impress the audience," said Parmenion.

"There is a lesson there, *strategos*. You won, but you allowed a greater share of the glory to go to the Sciritai. That was not sensible. If the slave races ever believed they were the equal of the Spartans, there would be another revolt. And then city-states like Athens or Thebes would once more combine their forces to invade Spartan lands. It is a question of balance—that is what the warriors in the crowd understood."

"Then I was wrong?" Parmenion asked.

"In a game? No. In life? Yes."

"Why, then, did you give me the victory?" asked the youth.

"You won the battle," answered Xenophon. "It matters nothing—in a game—that you would have gone on to lose the war." The general stood and walked to his mount, and Parmenion followed him.

"Will you teach me?" asked the younger man before he could stop the words.

"Perhaps," said Xenophon. "Now let us ride."

Leonidas took three running steps and hurled the javelin high into the air, watching its curving arc as the sunlight caught the iron tip. The weapon dropped gracefully to thud home in the sun-baked earth a dozen paces farther than the longest throw of his peers. Leonidas swung and raised his arms, and a score of youths applauded.

At this stage their barrack officer, Lepidus, would normally complete a throw, and Leonidas turned his eyes on the man.

Lepidus shook his head and took up his javelin. He strode back seven paces, tested the weapon for weight, then ran forward and, with a grunt of effort, launched it. Even as it left the officer's hand Leonidas allowed himself a smile of triumph.

Lepidus saw the javelin fall less than three paces short of Leonidas' mark. He swung and bowed to the younger man. "You have a good arm," he said, smiling warmly, "but you are not dipping your body back far enough on the launch. There is at least another eight paces in you. Work on it."

"I will, sir," promised Leonidas.

"Now I'd like to see you Spartan gentlemen run," Lepidus told them. "Twenty laps of the racecourse, if it please you."

"And if it does not?" shouted a boy at the back.

"Twenty-five laps," said Lepidus. A groan went up, but the youngsters ran off to the start. Lepidus wandered to a wooden bench seat in the shade and watched the young men. Gryllus took the lead, followed by Learchus. But Leonidas had eased himself into fourth place behind Hermias. Lepidus rubbed at his shoulder, where a Persian lance point was still buried under the bone. The joint ached murderously in winter, and even in summer any effort, such as throwing a javelin, caused a dull ache.

Lepidus looked up as the sweating youngsters passed him. He envied them their youth and their energy, remembering his days in the barracks, his longing to march with the phalanx into battle.

He saw a boy at the back of the pack. "More effort, young Pausias!" he yelled, and the boy sprinted into the group, trying to hide from his critical eye.

Lepidus' mind wandered, and he saw again his own youth. Sparta was different then, he told himself, more true to the principles laid down by the divine Lycurgus. The boys in the barracks were allowed two tunics, one for summer and one for winter. There were no minstrels performing in the Theater of Marble, no plays, no parties at the homes of the rich. One bowl of black soup a day for the youngsters, and iron discipline maintained by the birch. A race bred for battles. He looked at the runners. Good boys, strong and proud, but Leonidas had many tunics and a warm cloak against the winter wind. And

Hermias spent most of his evenings at home with his parents, eating good food and drinking watered wine. Young Learchus had a gold-embossed dagger made by a craftsman in Thebes, while lazy Pausias filled his belly with honey cakes and ran with all the speed of a sick pig. These boys did not survive on a bowl of soup a day.

Transferring his gaze to Leonidas, he saw that the youth had moved up into second place and was loping along behind Gryllus. The Athenian was a fine runner, but Lepidus knew that Leonidas would accelerate into the last bend and leave him gasping. Only the boy Parmenion could live with the pace Leonidas could set, but never over twenty-five laps, when Leonidas' greater strength would count.

Using Sciritai alongside real men! Lepidus shook his head. That morning he had been summoned to the senior over the move.

"It was none of my doing, sir," he said to the grim-eyed old man.

"Then it should have been," snapped the aging general. "The king was displeased, and one of our finest young men was shamed. Are you saying the boy had never attempted such a move in practice?"

"Never, sir," answered Lepidus, his unease growing. This man had been his commanding officer in seven campaigns, and although both were now past forty years from manhood, the general still inspired awe in Lepidus.

"Put him right, Lepidus. Where will we be if we allow Spartan men to develop such appalling methods?"

"He is a half-blood, sir. He will never be Spartiate."

"His father was a fine warrior," answered the general, "and the mother bore herself well. But I hear what you say. Blood will out. Send the boy to me."

"He is with Xenophon, sir. His mother's burial is today, and the Athenian has him as a houseguest."

The general's fist slammed down on the table. "I don't want one of my boys as that man's catamite!"

"I will see he is back tomorrow."

"Do so," grunted the old man. "And Lepidus, there will be no presentation of the victory rod."

"Sir?"

"No presentation this year."

Lepidus looked into the old man's eyes and swallowed hard. "I do not much like the boy, sir, but he won. How can we refuse him the rod?"

"An example must be set. Do you know that my helots are talking of his win, that it is common knowledge among the Sciritai?"

Lepidus had said no more. Now he sat, grateful for the shade from the tall cypress tree, and watched the boys run. He had little time for Parmenion, whom he saw as a sly, cunning youth, but he had earned the rod, and it was unfair to deprive him. He wondered how the other boys would take the decision. Parmenion was not popular, but the award night was usually a riotous affair and much looked forward to.

The race was entering its final stages: Lepidus stood and walked to the center of the field.

Gryllus still held the lead, but Hermias was now alongside Leonidas and vying for second place, blocking the taller youth's chances of an outside run at Gryllus. Leonidas cut to his right, barging Hermias aside. The slender youth staggered and lost ground, but Leonidas surged forward, catching Gryllus just before the line and breasting home ahead. Hermias came in fifth.

Lepidus waited while the youngsters regained their breath, then called them to him.

"A fine run—save for you, Pausias. Five more laps, if you please." The boys jeered at the fat youth as he set off on his lonely run. "Now, gentlemen, the notices. First, the Olympiad trials. Leonidas and Parmenion will represent this barracks in the middle and long races. Leonidas will also compete in the javelin with Nestus. Hermias and Asiron will represent us in the short race. I will speak to the athletes when you are dismissed. Second, four boys were late for muster yesterday. This is not showing a good example to the younger members of the barracks. We are Spartans, gentlemen, and that means we understand discipline. It will not happen again. Third, the presentation of the victory rod . . ." His eyes moved to Leonidas, and a fleeting smile touched the boy's face. *He knows, then,* thought Lepidus, and anger flared in him like a candle flame. "The presentation will not take place this year, and there will be no celebration." To Lepidus' amazement a great cheer went up, and his face darkened. "Gentlemen!" he yelled, raising his arms. Silence fell. "I do not understand the cause of this joy. Would someone explain it to me? You, sir," he said, pointing to Learchus.

"Savra cheated," Learchus answered, and Lepidus saw several heads nod in agreement.

"He did *not* cheat!" roared Lepidus. "He won! And that is what Spartans are supposed to do. And let me make something very clear to you all. Had Leonidas ordered his own cavalry forward, they would have intercepted the charge. Then, as Parmenion advanced, his right would have been exposed to javelins and arrows. Parmenion would have been annihilated. I do not excuse his use of the Sciritai, but when I see Spartans whining about defeat, I despair. You are dismissed!"

Spinning on his heels, he stalked from the training ground, leaving a stunned audience behind him.

"I didn't think he liked Savra," whispered Learchus.

"What he said was right," Leonidas said.

"No, Savra cheated," put in Gryllus.

Leonidas stood and turned to the others. "He was right! I took Savra lightly, and he humbled me. I should have worn the cloak of shame. There were a dozen ways I could have crushed him, had I guessed at his plan, and three that could have won me the battle even though I failed to read his intent. I did not use them. Now let that be an end to it."

Leonidas walked away, and Gryllus turned to Learchus, leaning in close. "The mix-blood is staying at my father's house today," he whispered. "But tonight he will go home for the burial night."

"So?"

"So he cannot run in the Olympiad trials if his legs are injured."

"I don't know."

"He humbled our friend!" hissed Gryllus.

"What if your father finds out?"

"It will be dark. And Savra will not name us."

"Tonight, then," Learchus agreed.

The body, wrapped in white linen, was lifted from the bed and laid on a length of stout canvas hung between two poles. Parmenion watched as the women carried his mother from the house of death toward the burial hill. There were four bearers dressed in white, and plump Rhea followed behind as the mother of mourning. Behind her came Parmenion, and beside him the Athenian general, Xenophon.

The burial ground was beyond the Theater of Marble in the east of the city, and the small procession made its way through the teeming marketplace and on past the monument to Pausanius and Leonidas.

They reached the cave mouth, where an old woman sat waiting, her white hair fluttering in the slight breeze.

"Who seeks to walk with the dead?" she asked.

Rhea stepped forward. "My friend Artema," she answered.

"Who carries the river price?"

"I, Parmenion." He dropped a silver tetradrachma into her outstretched palm. She cocked her head to one side, her pale eyes turned toward him. For a moment she sat as still as death, then her eyes swung to where Xenophon stood silently.

"The one who is and the one who is to be," whispered the old woman. "Invite me to your home, General."

The departure from ritual shocked Xenophon. He took a deep breath. "As you wish, old mother."

"Bring the dead to rest," she said. Rhea ordered the bearers forward, and the darkness of the cave mouth swallowed them. The two men stood at the entrance.

"I could not afford mourners," said Parmenion. "Will the gods look unkindly on her for that?"

"An interesting debating point," answered Xenophon. "Are the gods swayed because of faked tears and wailing? I would doubt it. Good men have died unmourned and unnoticed, while some of consummate evil have had thousands of mourners at their funerals. It is pleasant to believe that the gods are a little more discerning than men."

"Do you believe that?"

"I believe there are powers that govern our lives. We give them many names."

"She will live again, then, you think?"

"I like to believe so. Come, we will walk awhile. The day is not too hot."

Together they strolled back to the monument to Pausanius and Leonidas. It was a huge marble cube, topped with a statue of a Spartan *hoplite*, the base engraved with the story of the mighty battle at Plataea, where the invading Persian army had been crushed by the power of the Spartan phalanx. Xenophon removed his white cloak and sat in the shade. An elderly widow approached them, offering fresh pomegranates. Xenophon dropped a coin in her palm and bought three. He tossed one to Parmenion.

"What was the lesson of Plataea?" asked Xenophon, taking a dagger from his belt and quartering his fruit.

"The lesson?" queried Parmenion. He shrugged. "They advanced on the Persian center, which broke and ran. What should we learn?"

"Why did they run?"

Parmenion sat beside the general. Peeling the skin from his fruit, he ate swiftly, spitting the pips to the ground. "I don't know. They were frightened?"

"Of course they were frightened," snapped Xenophon. "Think!"

Parmenion felt embarrassed, his face reddening. "I do not know enough of the battle," he admitted. "I can't answer you."

Xenophon seemed to relax. He finished the pomegranate and leaned back against the cool marble. "Examine the evidence, Parmenion."

"I don't know what you want!"

"If you can answer me this question, then I will do what you asked of me—I will teach you. If not . . . there would be no point. Think about it and come to me this evening." Xenophon rose and walked away.

Parmenion sat for a long time, puzzling at the question, but the answer eluded him. He wandered down to the market-place, crept behind a stall, and stole two pies. He was spotted by the stallholder, but he ducked into an alley and sped along Leaving Street before the man could catch him. Spartan youths were encouraged to supplement their meager meals by theft. If caught, they were punished severely—not for the theft itself but for the crime of being caught.

In Leaving Street he saw two elderly men sitting close to the palace of Agisaleus. He walked over to them and bowed. One of the men looked up after a while, acknowledging his presence. "Well?" he asked.

"Sir," said Parmenion, "what was the lesson of Plataea?"

"Lesson?" answered the man. "What lesson? The only lesson handed out was to the Persians and the world. You don't take on a Spartan army and expect to win. What a foolish question to ask!"

"Thank you, sir," said Parmenion, bowing and moving away.

What kind of a riddle had Xenophon set him? Was the answer so obvious? If so, why did the Athenian put it in the first place? Parmenion ran to the acropolis, where he ate his pies and stared out over the Taygetus mountains.

"*Examine the evidence*," Xenophon had said. What evidence? Five thousand Spartan warriors had met with Xerxes' great army on the field of Plataea. The Persians were crushed, the war won. Pausanius had been the Spartan general.

What lesson?

Parmenion rose and loped down the hill to the monument.

There he read the description of the battle engraved on the marble, but it told him nothing he did not know. Where, then, was the evidence?

He began to get angry. The Athenian did not want to train him and had found this clever excuse. Set him a problem that had no answer, then turn him away. But even through his rage Parmenion dismissed the thought. Xenophon needed no excuses. A simple no would have been sufficient.

The monument to Pausanius and Leonidas . . .

It loomed above him, its secret hidden in stone. He stared up at the *hoplite* statue. The warrior's long spear was broken, yet still he looked mighty.

Was he Leonidas or Pausanius, Parmenion wondered, or just a soldier?

Leonidas? Why did the king slain at Thermopylae appear on the monument to Plataea? He was killed months before. The Greeks had asked the Spartans to spearhead their army against the coming Persian invasion, but the Spartans were celebrating a religious festival, and the priests refused to sanction such a move. However, the Spartan king, Leonidas, was allowed to take his personal bodyguard of three hundred men to the pass of Thermopylae. There they had fought the Persian horde to a standstill, and even when betrayed and surrounded, the Spartan line still held. The Persians, too frightened to attack, finished off the defenders with arrows and javelins.

Like the sun coming through cloud, the answer to Xenophon's question shone in Parmenion's mind. What was the lesson of Plataea? Even in defeat there is victory. The Persians, too frightened to tackle even the remnants of the three hundred, had finally come face to face with five thousand Spartan warriors. They had watched the line advance, spears leveled—and they had run. That was why the monument was shared. Plataea was also a victory for Leonidas the king, a victory won by courage and defiance and a hero's death.

He gazed up at the marble *hoplite*. "I salute you, Leonidas," he said.

* * *

Xenophon's servants moved back as the old woman entered the gates of his home. None dared to approach her. She could see their fear and smiled mirthlessly as she stood leaning on her staff, waiting for the lord of the house.

She felt the pressure of many eyes upon her. Once those eyes would have glowed with lust; once the mere sight of Tamis would have inflamed passions and had men willing to kill their brothers merely for the right to hold her hand. The old woman hawked and spit. Once upon a time . . . Who cared any longer about once upon a time? Her first husband had died in a war against Athens, her second in a battle in Thrace. The third had contracted a fever during a hot summer when the water went bad and had died in agony while Tamis was visiting Delphi. The last she could have saved—had she known of his illness. Could have? Might have? What did it matter now? The past was dead.

She heard a door open and the confident steps of the Athenian general approaching her. She watched him with the eyes of her body and her talent, seeing both the handsome general and the glow of his soul fire.

"Welcome to my home, lady," he said.

"Lead me to the shade and allow me a drink," she told him. His hand touched her arm, and she felt his power. It disconcerted her, reminding Tamis of days of youth. The strength of the sunlight faded as he led her to an alcove to the right. Here she could smell the perfume of many flowers and feel the cool stone of the wall. She sat and waited in silence until a servant brought her a goblet of cold water from the well.

"You have a message for me from the goddess?" inquired Xenophon.

Tamis sipped the water. It touched a raw nerve in a rotting tooth, and she placed the goblet on the stone table. "You will not find what you desire, Athenian. No more distant wars for you. No more glory on the battlefield." She felt his disappointment, sharp and raw. "No man achieves all his dreams," she said more softly. "Yet you will be remembered by men for a thousand years."

"How so, if my glories are ended?"

"I do not know, Xenophon. But you can trust my words. However, I did not come here to speak of you. I came to talk of the cub."

"Cub? What cub?"

"The boy who buried his mother. The one who is to be. He will know glory, and pain, and tragedy, and triumph. He is the important one."

"He is just a child. He is not a king, nor even a gentleman. What can he do?"

Tamis drained the water. She was comfortable here and yet unwelcome. It would have been pleasant to pass the day in the shade, thinking back to happier days in her long, long life. She sighed. "His destiny is of glory, but his name will not be remembered like yours, even though he will lead armies across the world. It is your duty to teach him, to give him that which you hold."

"I hold nothing!" snapped Xenophon. "I am not rich, nor do I have a command."

"You have everything he needs, Athenian, stored in your mind. You know the hearts of men and the ways of battle. Give him these gifts. And watch him grow."

"He will take Sparta to glory?"

"Sparta?" she laughed grimly. "Sparta's days are done, Xenophon. We have the crippled king. They did not listen to the oracle. Lysander thought he knew best—as men are wont to do. But there will be no new glory for Sparta. No, the boy will go elsewhere. You will send him when the time comes." Tamis stood.

"Is that all?" asked Xenophon, rising. "You feed me riddles. Why can you tell me no more?"

"Because that is all I know, Athenian. You think the gods allow their servants to share all their knowledge? I have done what I had to do. I know nothing more."

With that lie upon her lips, Tamis walked back into the sunlight and out into the street.

Tamis made her slow way through the streets of Sparta and on past the lake and the small temple to Aphrodite. She followed a narrow track to the door of her house, a low, mean dwelling, one-roomed with a central fire pit and an open roof to allow the smoke to drift clear.

There was a thin pallet bed in one corner but no other furniture. Tamis squatted down in front of the dead fire. Lifting her hand, she spoke three words and flames leapt from the cold ashes, burning brightly. For a while she stared into the dancing fire, until at last the weight of her loneliness bore her down. Her shoulders sagged.

"Where are you, Cassandra?" she whispered. "Come to me."

The flames licked higher, curling as if seeking to encircle an invisible sphere. Slowly a face formed within the flames, a regal face, fine-boned with a long, aquiline nose. Not a beauty, to be sure, but a handsome strong-featured face framed with tightly curled blond hair.

"Why do you call me from my sleep?" asked the fire woman.

"I am lonely."

"You use your powers too recklessly, Tamis. And unwisely."

"Why should I not call upon you?" the old woman asked. "I, too, have need of friends—of company."

"The world teems with the living," the fire woman told her. "That is where your friends should be. But if you must talk, then I must listen."

Tamis nodded and told Cassandra of the shadow in the future, of the coming of the Dark God.

"What has this to do with you?" Cassandra asked. "It is part of the perennial battle between the source and the chaos spirit."

"I can stop the birth, I know that I can."

"Stop the . . . what are you saying? You have seen what is to be. How can you change it?"

"How can you ask that question?" countered Tamis. "You know as well as I that there are a thousand thousand possible futures, all dependent on limitless decisions made by men and women and, aye, even children and beasts."

"That is precisely what I am saying, Tamis. You were not given your powers in order to manipulate events; that has never been the way of the source."

"Then perhaps it should have been," snapped Tamis. "I have studied hundreds of possible futures. In four, at least, the Dark God can be thwarted. All I needed to do was trace the lines back to the one element that can change the course of history. And I have done that!"

"You speak of the child Parmenion," said the fire woman sadly. "You are wrong, Tamis. You should cease your meddling. This matter is beyond you; it is greater than worlds; it is a part of the cosmic struggle between chaos and harmony. You have no conception of the harm you can do."

"Harm?" queried Tamis. "I know the harm that will be caused should the Dark God live to walk the lands in human form. The mountains will be bathed in blood, the rivers will spout smoke. The earth will be desolate."

"I see," said Cassandra. "And, of course, you alone have the power to stand against this evil?"

"Do not patronize me! You think I should live as you did, giving prophecies that no one believed? What use were they? What use were you? Begone!"

The fire died down, the face disappearing.

Tamis sighed. Right or wrong, the course was set, the lines laid down. Parmenion would be the warrior of the light, holding back the darkness.

Do not meddle! Who do they think destroyed the plans of the last coming more than twenty years ago, when the child was due to be fathered by the Persian king? Who was it that entered the concubine's mind on the night of conception and made her walk to the top of the tower to fling herself to the stones below?

"It was I!" hissed Tamis. "I!"

And you were wrong! said a small voice deep in her mind. *You are wrong now. Parmenion has his own life to live. It is not for you to alter his destiny.*

"I am not altering it," she said aloud. "I am helping him to fulfill it."

He must be allowed choices.

"I will give him choices. At the cusp moments of his life, I will go to him. I will offer him choices."

And what if you are wrong, Tamis?

"I am not wrong. The Dark God must be stopped. He will be stopped. Leave me be!"

In the silence that followed Tamis glared around the squalid room, heavy of heart. With her powers she could have ensured a palace of riches, a life of splendor. Instead she had chosen this.

"I have made my gifts to the source," she told the room, "and the light is with me in all that I do."

There was no one to argue, but Tamis was still unsure. She pointed to the blaze and called out a name. A man's face appeared.

"Play for me, Orpheus. Let the music ease my heart."

As the sweet notes of the lyre sounded in the room, Tamis moved to her bed, lying back and thinking of the futures she had seen. In three of them the Dark God had been born in Sparta, the ruling city of Greece.

Three possible fathers. Learchus, who could rise to greatness. Nestus, related to the royal family. And Cleombrotus, who would be king.

Tamis closed her eyes. "Now we will see your destiny, Parmenion," she whispered. "Now we will see."

Parmenion lay on a hillside to the east of the city, watching the young girls run and play. His interest in their activities surprised him, for this was not a pastime he would have consid-

ered before last summer. He recalled the day when a new
kind of joy entered his life. He had been running up and down
the hillside when a voice as sweet as the birth of morning
spoke to him.

"What are you doing?"

Parmenion turned to see a young girl, perhaps fourteen
years of age. She was wearing a simple white tunic through
which he could see not just the exquisite shape of her small
breasts but also the nipples, pressing against the linen. Her
legs were tanned and smooth, her waist narrow, her hips
rounded. He glanced up guiltily, aware that he was reddening, and found himself gazing into wide gray eyes set in a face
of surpassing beauty.

"I was . . . running," he answered.

"I saw that, she said, lifting a hand and pushing her fingers
through her red-gold hair. It seemed to Parmenion that sunlight became trapped in her curls, glinting like jewels. "But
tell me why," she went on. "You run up the hill. Then you run
down the hill. Then up again. There is no sense to it."

"Lepidus—my barrack master—says that it will strengthen
my legs. I am fast."

"And I am Derae," she told him.

"No, my name is not Fast."

"I know that. I was joking with you."

"I see. I . . . I must be going." He turned and fled up the
hill. Surprisingly, considering his previous exertions, he moved
at a pace he had not considered possible.

For almost a year since this meeting he had come to the hills
and the fields beyond the lake to watch the girls run. Lepidus
had told him that only in Sparta were women allowed to
develop their bodies. Other city-states considered such exercise indecent, claiming that it incited men to commit grave
crimes. Parmenion felt this could well be true as he lay on his
belly in acutely pleasurable discomfort, his eyes following
Derae.

He saw the girls line up for the short race. Derae was on the
outside. She won easily, her long legs stretching out, her feet

scarcely seeming to make contact with the grass.

Only twice in the year had he found the courage to speak to her as she approached the field. But always she greeted him with a cheerful smile and a wave, then was away and running before a conversation could develop. Parmenion did not mind. It was enough that he could gaze on her every week. Besides, there would be little point in getting to know her, since no Spartan man was allowed to marry before he reached manhood at twenty.

Four years. An eternity.

After an hour the girls finished their exercise and prepared to return to their homes. Parmenion rolled onto his back, closing his eyes against the harsh glare of the sun. He thought of many things as he rested there, his hands behind his neck. He thought of the battle with Leonidas and the endless torment of the barracks, and of Xenophon, and of Hermias, and of Derae. He tried not to think too much about his mother, for the wound was too fresh, and when her face floated before his mind, he felt himself unmanned, out of control.

A shadow fell across him.

"Why do you watch me?" asked Derae. Parmenion jerked up to a sitting position. She was kneeling on the grass beside him.

"I did not hear you approach."

"That does not answer my question, young Fast."

"I like to watch you," he answered, grinning. "You run well, but I think you pump your arms too much."

"So you watch me because you like to criticize my running?"

"No, that is not what I meant." Parmenion took a deep breath, then let it out slowly. "I think you know that. I believe you are joking with me again."

She nodded. "Only a little, Parmenion."

He was exultant. She knew his name. It could only mean that she had asked about him, that she was interested in him.

"How is it you know me?"

"I saw your battle with Leonidas."

"Oh," he said, disappointed. "How so, since no women were allowed to spectate?"

"My father is a close friend of Xenophon's, and the general allowed the three girls to watch from an upstairs window. We had to take turns because we were not to be seen. You played an interesting game."

"I won," said Parmenion defensively.

"I know. I have just told you I was there."

"I'm sorry. I thought you were criticizing me. Everyone else has."

She nodded solemnly. "You didn't even need the Sciritai. Had you advanced in sixteen formation, you would still have broken through Leonidas' lines, since he reduced his strength to four."

"I know that, too." He shrugged. "But I cannot take back the move."

"Do you still have the sword?"

"Of course. Why would I not?"

"It is very valuable. You might have sold it."

"Never! It is one of the seven swords. I will treasure it all my life."

"That is a pity," she said, moving smoothly to her feet. "For I would like to have bought it."

"What need would you have of a sword?" he asked, rising to stand before her.

"I would give it to my brother," she answered.

"It would be a handsome gift. Do you object to my watching you run?"

"Should I?" she countered, smiling.

"Are you betrothed?"

"Not yet, though my father talks of it. Is this a proposal, Parmenion?"

Before he could answer, a hand grabbed his shoulder, dragging him back. Instantly he spun, his fist cracking into Leonidas' jaw and staggering him. The golden-haired Spartan rubbed his chin, then advanced.

"Stop it!" shouted Derae, but the youths ignored her, their

eyes locked together, their concentration total. Leonidas leapt forward, feinting a hook before thundering a straight right to Parmenion's face. The smaller man rolled with the blow, grabbing Leonidas' tunic and hammering his knee into his opponent's groin. Leonidas grunted with pain and doubled over. Parmenion's forehead crashed against Leonidas' face, and he sagged and half fell. Parmenion pushed him away, then saw a large jagged stone jutting from the grass. Tearing it clear, he advanced on the dazed Leonidas, wanting nothing more than to smash open his skull.

Derae leapt into his path, her open hand connecting with his cheek like a thunderclap. His fingers circled her throat, and the stone came up. . . . He froze as he saw the terror in her eyes.

Dropping the stone, he backed away. "I . . . I am sorry. . . . He . . . he is my enemy."

"He is my brother," she said, her expression as cold as the stone he had dropped.

Leonidas, recovered now, stepped alongside her. "You come near my sister again and you will answer to me with a blade in your hand."

Suddenly Parmenion laughed, but there was no humor in the sound. "That would be a pleasure," he hissed, "for we both know what blade I would carry. One that you will never own though your soul yearns for it. But fear not, Leonidas, I want nothing from you—or your family."

"You think I fear you, peasant?"

"If you don't, you should. Come against me whenever you will, you arrogant pig. But know this—I will destroy you!"

Turning on his heel Parmenion stalked from the scene.

Hermias left the training ground and loped through the streets, across the marketplace, arriving at the lake sanctuary as the girls were leaving. There was no sign of Parmenion, and he was about to duck away behind the trees when Derae saw him and waved. Smiling shyly, he stepped forward. Derae ran to him, kissing his cheek. "It is not often we see you here,

Cousin. Are you developing an interest in girls?"

Two of Derae's friends moved alongside him, touching his tunic and pretending to examine the weave.

Hermias blushed. "I am looking for my friend, Parmenion."

Her face darkened. "He was here. Now he is not," she snapped.

"Has he offended you?" asked Hermias fearfully.

Derae did not answer for a moment. Leonidas would be furious if he learned she had spoken of his defeat, yet she felt driven to talk of the incident. Linking arms with Hermias, she walked away from the other girls, and they sat down in the shade by the sanctuary lake. There she told Hermias all that had occurred.

"You cannot know what he has suffered, Derae," he explained. "For some reason—and I cannot fathom it—he is hated by all. He can do nothing right. When he wins a race, there are no cheers, even when he runs against boys from other barracks. And yet he is kind, thoughtful. They set on him in gangs, beating him with sticks. Few there are who would attempt to tackle him singly."

"But my brother would have no part in such wickedness," said Derae. "He is noble and strong; he would never run with a pack."

"I agree with you. I have always . . . respected Leonidas. But the beatings are done in his name, and he makes no attempt to stop them. The last was the evening before the game, and Parmenion was forced to hide all night upon the acropolis. You saw his bruises."

Derae picked up a flat stone and hurled it out over the lake, watching it skim across the sparkling blue water. "No one is ever hated without reason," she said. "He is obviously arrogant and lowborn. Leonidas says he is a half-breed, a mixblood, yet he struts among true Spartans, looking down on them."

Hermias nodded. "There is truth to that. But when all men are against you, all that is left is pride. He will not let them humble him. I advised him to play to lose in the game, but he would not. And look what happened! Everyone hates him even more now. What future is there for him, Derae? He is running out of money; he has no status."

"Has he no friends at all save you?"

"None. There is a girl, I think. He watches her every week. When he talks of her, he is a different man. But I do not know her name, and I doubt he has even spoken to her."

"He has spoken to her," said Derae. "He even grabbed her throat and threatened her with a rock."

Hermias closed his eyes and leaned back, resting his head on the grass. "It was you, then. I do not understand. Was he cursed at birth by some malevolent spirit? I must find him."

"I think you should avoid him, Hermias. I looked into his eyes, and there is something deadly there. My blood turned cold."

"He is my friend," answered Hermias, rising smoothly to his feet, "and I have news for him. But first I must see Leonidas. Where will I find him?"

"He said he was going to practice with spear and sword; he should still be at the training field. But do not tell him it was I who told you."

"Please, Derae, he will think Parmenion has sent me."

Derae shook her head and rose. "Very well, Hermias. Tell him you spoke to me. But be warned; he now regards Parmenion as a sworn enemy. You will find no comfort there."

Leonidas—in breastplate, kilt, and greaves—was battling against a youth called Nestus, and the training field rang with the sound of sword on shield as the two attacked one another. No wooden practice blades here; both were using the short iron stabbing swords of the *hoplite*. There was tension in the spectators as the combatants circled, seeking openings. The powerfully built Nestus was the barracks champion with the short sword, but Leonidas was cool, strong, and fast. Both youths were breathing heavily, and Nestus was cut on his upper arm, a thin trickle of blood dripping to the dust. Leonidas leapt in, but Nestus darted forward, his shield crashing against Leonidas to send him sprawling to the ground. Instantly Nestus was upon him, his blade resting against Leonidas' throat. A muted cheer went up. Leonidas grinned and rolled to his feet, discarding his shield. Embracing the other man, he congratulated him and then walked away to the shade, where water skins were hanging.

Hermias ran to him, helping him remove his breastplate.

"Thank you, Cousin," said Leonidas, wiping sweat from his face. "Damn, but he is good. I am getting closer to him, though, don't you think?"

"Yes," agreed Hermias. "You had a chance at a groin thrust. In a real battle you would have used it—and won."

"You saw that? Yes. He has a habit of raising his shield too high. What brings you here? Not to fight, surely."

"No," said Hermias, taking a deep breath. "I came to talk of Savra." He looked away from Leonidas' face, bracing himself for the anger he felt sure would follow.

"Has he spoken to you?" asked Leonidas softly.

"No. Derae told me." He glanced at Leonidas, finding the absence of anger disconcerting.

"What do you require of me?"

"An end to the beatings and the violence."

"They have nothing to do with me. I do not sanction them; I learn of them only after they have taken place. He is not popular." Leonidas shrugged. "What would you have me do?"

"Tell Gryllus and Learchus that such . . . . beatings . . . displease you."

"Why should I do this?"

"Because you are a noble man. You are not a coward, and you need no one to fight battles for you."

Leonidas chuckled. "Flattery, Hermias?"

"Yes. But I believe it is true nonetheless. They cannot beat him into submission. One day they will kill him, and for what? Because they think it would please you. *Would* it please you, Cousin?"

"Yes, it would," admitted Leonidas. "But you are right; it is base, and I will have no part in it. I will see that it stops,

Hermias; I should have done so long ago. It shamed me that he arrived at the game carrying such wounds."

"I am in your debt, Cousin."

"No," said Leonidas, "I am in yours. But know this: Parmenion is my enemy, and one day I will kill him."

For two hours Hermias searched for Parmenion, finally finding him sitting on a granite block below the statue of Athena of the Road. Hermias sat alongside him. "Why so glum, *strategos*?" he asked.

"Don't call me that! One day, perhaps, but not now."

"Your face is like thunder, Savra. Are you thinking of the fight with Leonidas?"

"How did you learn of that?"

"I spoke to Derae. I did not know she was the one you watched."

Parmenion hurled a stone into a nearby field, scattering a flock of large black and gray birds. "I hate crows. When I was a child, I was frightened of them; I thought they would fly through my window and eat my soul. I had overheard one of my neighbors saying that crows had eaten my father's eyes on the battlefield. I used to cry at night, and I could hear their wings in my mind."

"Would you rather be alone, Savra? I don't mind."

Parmenion forced a smile and put his arm around his friend's shoulder. "I don't want to be alone, Hermias, but that is what I am." Standing, he scooped up another stone, hurling it high over the field. "What is there for me here, Hermias? What can I hope to become?"

"What would you wish to be?"

Parmenion shook his head. "I do not know. Truly. Once I desired only to be a Spartan *hoplite*, bearing shield, sword, and spear. I wanted to march with the king into foreign lands, to become rich on plunder. But lately I have been dreaming strange dreams." He lapsed into silence.

"Go on!" urged Hermias. "Sometimes dreams are messages from the gods. Do you dream of eagles? They are good omens. So are lions."

"There are no animals," said Parmenion, "only men, armed for war. There are two armies on a level plain, and I am a general. The phalanxes surge forward, and the dust rises, muffling the war cries. One army is Spartan, for they are wearing blood-red cloaks. The slaughter is terrible, and I see a king lying slain. Then I awake."

Hermias was silent for a moment, then he grinned. "You are a general, you say. That is a good omen, surely. And, I would guess, a true one, for there is no one to outthink you, Savra. And with you leading them, how could Sparta lose?"

"That is the point, my friend. I am not a general in the Spartan army, and it is Sparta's king who dies."

"Hush!" whispered Hermias. "You should not say such a thing. Put it from your mind. It is not an omen at all—you were dreaming of the general's games, that is all. It has been on your mind for so long and has caused you such grief. Forget it, Savra. Do not speak of it again. Anyway, I have some news that will cheer you . . . I promise."

"Then tell it, my friend. I do need cheering."

"Leonidas spoke up for you today on the training ground, and so did Lepidus. Leonidas admitted he had played badly and that you deserved to win. Others were saying you cheated, but he spoke up for you. Isn't that wonderful?"

"I can almost hear the gods singing with joy," remarked Parmenion.

"But don't you see? It means that the beatings will end. You are free of it."

"We'll see. I'll judge it by how many attend my victory celebration."

"I do have other news that is less cheering," said Hermias sadly. "There is no easy way to say this, Savra, but there will be no victory ceremony."

Parmenion laughed grimly. "Now, there is a surprise!" His face set, he jumped down from the block and turned to look up at the stone goddess.

"What have I done, Athena, that the gods should hate me?

Am I evil? Perhaps I am. . . . But one day I will repay them for their cruelties. I swear it!"

Hermias said nothing, but he felt a sudden stab of fear as he gazed at Parmenion's face and saw the icy hatred in his eyes. He clambered down and moved to Parmenion's side.

"Do not hate me, too!"

Parmenion blinked and shook his head. "Hate you, my friend? How could I ever hate you? You have been a brother to me, and I will never forget that. Never! Brothers we have been, brothers we shall be, all the days of our lives. I promise you. Now I have to go to Xenophon's house. I will see you later. Come to my house this evening."

"I will. Take care."

"Why should I take care?" responded Parmenion. "Did you not say the war was over?"

Xenophon led Parmenion to a wide room in the eastern part of the house, where it was cool and bright. "Well?" asked the general, lounging on a divan. "Do you have the answer to Plataea?"

Parmenion nodded. "Thermopylae put thoughts of defeat into the hearts of the Persians."

"Good! Good! I am well pleased with you. I have told you that war is an art, and so it is. But the art is to win the battle before the sword is drawn, before the spears are leveled. If your opponent believes he will lose, then he *will* lose. That is what happened at Plataea. The Persians—who could not face a mere three hundred Spartans—panicked when faced with five thousand. A general must work on the hearts of men, not just his own but the enemy's."

"Does this mean that you will teach me?" Parmenion asked.

"It does. Do you read?"

"Only poorly, sir. My mother taught me, but it is not a skill that is cared about in the barracks."

"Then you must learn. I have books that must be studied,

strategies you must memorize. A general is not unlike a black-smith, Parmenion. He has many tools and must know the value and the purpose of each."

Parmenion took a deep breath. "There is a question I must ask, sir. I hope it will not offend you."

"We will not know until you ask it," replied the general, smiling.

"I am neither wealthy nor well liked. It is likely that when I come of age no senior's mess will admit me. So, sir, much as I would like to be taught by you, what is the point?"

Xenophon nodded gravely. "There is much in what you say, young *strategos*. At best you will be a first ranker, at worst a line warrior. But you have it in you to become great, to be a leader of men. I know; there is no better judge of this than I. But your future may not be in Sparta—which will be Sparta's loss. What do you desire?"

Parmenion shrugged. "Only acceptance, sir. I wish to be able to walk with my head high, having men say, 'There is Parmenion, the Spartan.'"

"That is all you wish? Come, be honest with me, *strategos*."

Parmenion swallowed hard, then his eyes came up to meet the general's piercing gaze. "No, sir, that is not all. I wish to grind my enemies into the dust, to bring them to despair. I want to be a general, like you. I want to lead men into battle." Suddenly he smiled. "I had a dream that I wish to make come true."

"You may not obtain all that you desire," said Xenophon, "but I will teach you all that I know. I will give you knowledge, but you must decide how to use it."

A servant brought them food and watered wine, and Parmenion sat and listened as Xenophon told of the march to the sea and the evils that beset the Greeks. He outlined his strategies and his successes but also talked of his failures and the reasons for them. The hours passed swiftly, and Parmenion felt like a man dying of thirst who had found the well of all life.

He could see it all so clearly—the Greeks demoralized after the battle at Cunaxa yet still holding their formation. The

Persian king, Artaxerxes, promising them safe passage through his realm and then treacherously murdering their generals, believing that without leaders the Greek *hoplites* would be easy prey to his cavalry. But the soldiers had remained steadfast. They elected new generals, and one of those was Xenophon. During the months that followed the Greeks marched through Persia, routing armies sent against them, crossing uncharted lands. The perils they faced were legion: countless enemies, the threat of starvation, ice-covered plains, and flood-ruined valleys. Yet Xenophon held them together until at last they reached the sea and safety.

"There is no warrior on earth," said Xenophon, "to match the Greek. For we alone understand the nature of discipline. There is not one civilized king who does not hire Greek mercenaries as a backbone for his forces. Not one. And the greatest of the Greeks are the Spartans. Do you understand why?"

"Yes," answered Parmenion. "Our enemies know—in their hearts—that we are the victors. And we know it in *our* hearts."

"Sparta will never be conquered, Parmenion."

"Unless there comes a foe with similar resolve—and greater numbers."

"But that will not happen. We have a country split up into city-states, each fearing its neighbor. If Athens and Thebes again joined forces against Sparta, many city-states would fear such an alliance and join with Sparta against it. Our land has a history of such disputes. Alliances made and broken, scores of disparate groups betraying one another endlessly. Never has any city achieved a complete victory. We should have conquered the world, Parmenion, but we never will. We are too busy fighting among ourselves." Xenophon rose. "It is getting late; you must return to your home. Come to me in three days. We will have supper and I will show you the books of the future."

"Do you teach your son?" asked Parmenion as he rose to leave.

Xenophon's face darkened. "I will be your teacher, and you

will ask me questions concerning strategy. You will not ask questions concerning my family!"

"I apologize, sir. I did not mean to offend."

Xenophon shook his head. "And I should not be so short-tempered. Gryllus is a troubled boy; he does not have a city. Like you he wants to be accepted, he wants to be admired. But he has no mind. His mother was a beautiful woman, Parmenion, but she also was cursed with limited intellect. It was as if the gods, having lavished beauty on her, decided that brains would be a luxury she would not need. My son takes after her. Now, we will speak no more of it."

The silence of the night covered the city as Parmenion strolled along the moonlit streets. High on the acropolis he could just make out the tall statue of Zeus and the pillars of the bronze house. He came to the wide avenue of Leaving Street and stopped before the palace, gazing out at the guards patrolling the entrance. The Cattle Price Palace, home of Agisaleus. An odd name for an abode of kings, he thought. One of Sparta's past kings had run short of money and had married the daughter of a Corinthian merchant in order to obtain a dowry of four thousand cattle. From the sale of those he had built his palace. Parmenion stared at the building, at its colossal columns and its long, sloping roof. At first he had thought that the ancient king must have had a fine sense of humor to name it so, but now he realized it was more a sense of guilt. Forced to marry a foreigner, he had left his shame for future generations to share.

A strange people were the Spartans.

The only race in Greece to take their boy children as infants and train them for war, the only race to allow their women to exercise and grow strong in order to bear warriors to continue Sparta's glory.

Parmenion moved on until he came to the street parallel to his own house. Here he stopped and scaled a high wall, his nimble fingers seeking out cracks in the mortar. Easing himself onto a tiled roof, he slid across to look down on the gate of his own small home. Hermias had said the campaign of hate was over, but Parmenion did not believe it. Keeping low to the shadows, he inched his way to the overhang of the roof and scanned the alleys below for several minutes, listening and watching.

Just as he was sure that all was clear, he saw a movement from the west and recognized Hermias running up the cobbled street. He was about to shout a greeting when five figures detached themselves from the shadows and pounced on the running youth. Parmenion saw sticks and clubs in their hands. Hermias went down to a blow that cracked against his skull. Parmenion stood and launched himself, feet first, from the roof. He landed with gruesome force on the back of a cloaked figure and heard the sickening crack of splintering bone; his victim gave a terrible scream and fell to the cobbles. Parmenion fell with him, then rolled to his feet. A stick lashed toward his head, but he ducked inside and hammered his fist into a hooded face. The hood fell back, and Parmenion recognized Gryllus. The Athenian, blood pouring from crushed lips, leapt to the attack. Parmenion stepped in close and whipped two blows to the other boy's belly before sending a hooking left to his ear. Gryllus went down hard. A club crashed against Parmenion's back, hurling him forward, but he spun on his heel and blocked the next blow with his forearms. Grabbing his opponent's cloak, he dragged him forward. Their heads cracked together, but Parmenion had dipped so that his brow crushed his opponent's nose. His attacker tore himself clear and staggered away. Parmenion scooped up a fallen club and swung it viciously as they closed in on him, smashing it into the arm of his nearest attacker. The boy he had leapt upon was lying unconscious on the ground, and Gryllus had run. Only three youths faced him now, but one of them had stumbled back with one arm hanging uselessly at his side.

Parmenion charged the other two, ramming his club forward into the belly of the first and then hurling himself at the second. He fell to the ground, his opponent beneath him, and rolled. The other youth came up with a knife in his hand, the blade shining wickedly in the moonlight.

"Now you die, mix-blood!" came the voice of Learchus. The remaining two attackers sprinted away as Parmenion rose smoothly, his club held two-handed. Learchus sprang forward, but Parmenion sidestepped, cracking the club down on the other's wrist. The dagger fell from his fingers. Parmenion gathered it and advanced.

Learchus backed away, Parmenion following, until he reached the wall.

Parmenion flicked a glance at the still form of Hermias, saw the blood oozing from a wound in the temple.

"You went too far," he told Learchus, his voice barely a whisper, his eyes gleaming. "Too far," he repeated, reaching up and pushing back the hood.

The knife plunged into Learchus' belly, ripping up into the lungs. Parmenion stepped inside, his face inches from the astonished, wide-eyed features of Learchus. "This is what death feels like, you Spartan whoreson."

"Oh, Gods," cried Learchus, sagging back into the wall. Parmenion grabbed him by the hair and hauled him back to his feet.

"Prayers will not help you now."

The breath rattled from Learchus' throat, and his eyes closed. Parmenion let the body fall, his anger disappearing. He gazed down at the corpse, then let slip the bloody dagger. Hearing Hermias groan, he ran to his side. "Are you all right?" he asked.

"My head . . . hurts."

"Let me help you."

"Your hand is injured," said Hermias, touching the blood.

"It is not mine," muttered Parmenion, pointing to the dead Learchus.

"You killed him? I don't believe it. Oh, Parmenion!"

"Let me get you inside, then I'll find the officer of the watch."

Within the hour the body had been removed, and Parmenion was escorted by Lepidus to the barracks, where the elderly general stood waiting in the dormitory doorway. Without a word the general turned and stalked up the stairs to a room overlooking the central courtyard. He sat down at a bench table and gestured to Lepidus to seat himself. Parmenion was left standing before the men. He stared at their faces in the flickering lamplight. Lepidus he knew well; the man was tough but not unfair. The general he knew only by sight as an iron-haired disciplinarian, a veteran of a score of battles. The old man glared at him.

"What do you have to say?" he asked, his voice rasping like a sword dragged from its sheath.

"Five hooded men attacked a friend of mine," said Parmenion. "What would you have me do? I went to his aid."

"You killed a fellow Spartan—a youth of good family."

"I killed a cowardly attacker who with a group of friends, armed with clubs, attacked an unarmed youth."

"Do not be insolent with me, boy!"

"Then do not patronize me, sir!"

The general blinked. His powerful fists clenched, and Parmenion felt he was about to rise and strike him down, but the old man took a deep breath and calmed himself. "Describe to me all that happened." Parmenion did so without including his final conversation with Learchus.

"Is it true," asked the general, "that you are unpopular with the other boys?"

"Yes."

"Is it also true that you have been a victim of their . . . sport before now?"

"Yes."

"Then you knew when you attacked them that they were probably hunting you, that your friend was struck by mistake?"

"Of course. Hermias is very well liked."

"So, then, had you waited until they recognized their error, there would have been no battle. They would have left. You agree?"

"I did not think of that then, though I can see you are

correct, General. But I saw my friend struck, and I went to his aid."

"You leapt upon one boy, breaking his shoulder, hit another with a club, breaking his arm, and stabbed the last, killing him. It is your fault, half-breed. You understand that? A fine boy lies dead because you did not think. Only a savage can use the excuse of lack of thought. Left to me, I would see you die for this. Now get out of my sight."

Lepidus waited until they could hear the boy padding down the stairs. Then he rose and walked to the door, pushing it closed.

"He is a disgrace," said the old man.

"No, General," said Lepidus sadly. "What happened in this room tonight was a disgrace."

"You dare to criticize me?"

Lepidus stared at the man. "As a Spartan it is my right. He went to the aid of a friend, risking himself. But he did not hesitate. You, of all men, should see that. There will be no judgment against him tomorrow. If there is, I shall speak out."

Lepidus turned and left the room. He walked out into the night and found himself drawn back to the scene of the fight. A lamp was burning in the window of Parmenion's house, and Lepidus tapped at the gatepost.

Parmenion opened the grilled gate and stepped aside for the officer. Lepidus walked into the small building and sat on the narrow bed. Parmenion offered him a goblet of water, but he waved it away.

"I want you to put from your mind what happened tonight at the barracks," said Lepidus. "And I would like you to forgive the general. Learchus was his nephew, and he loved the boy. What you did was admirable. Do you understand me?"

"Yes, sir, admirable."

"Sit down, Parmenion. Here, beside me." The boy did so. "Now give me your hand and look me in the eyes." Parmenion did as he was bade. He felt the strength in the older man's grip and saw the concern in his face. "Listen to me, boy. There are few left, it seems, who understand what being a Spartan is about. When we fight, we fight to win. We stand by our friends, we kill our enemies. The attack on Hermias was cowardly. You did well. I am proud of you."

"I did not have to kill Learchus," said Parmenion.

"Do not admit that to anyone. You understand me?"

"Yes," answered Parmenion wearily, all the events of the last few days rearing up in his mind and threatening to overwhelm him: the death of his mother, the victory at the games, the loss of Derae, and now the murder of Learchus. "I understand you."

"Listen to me. You were worried about your friend, and you took on a gang. That was courageous. And yes, you killed someone. The important—the vital—issue is, Did you enjoy killing him?"

"No," said Parmenion.

"Then do not worry about it."

Parmenion looked into Lepidus' face and nodded.

But I did enjoy it, he thought, may the gods forgive me. I wish I could have killed them all.

Tamis leaned on her staff, staring at the servant kneeling before her.

"My master urges you to come to the house of Parnas," said the man, avoiding her eyes.

"Urges? When his son lies dying? Surely you mean begs?"

"The noble Parnas would never do that but I beg you, honored one. Save Hermias," pleaded the servant, tears in his eyes.

"Perhaps I can save him, perhaps not," she answered. "But tell your master that I will ask the gods for guidance. Go now!"

Tamis turned on her heel and vanished into the dark interior of her dwelling place. The fire was burning low, but as she sat before it, the flames flickered and rose to form the face of Cassandra.

"I did not summon you," said Tamis. "Begone!"

"You must heal the boy, Tamis. It is your duty."

"Don't talk to me of duty. Learchus is dead, and I have denied the dark one a possible father of the flesh. That was my duty. Hermias is holding back the development of Parmenion. Because of their friendship he still retains, in part, a gentle soul. I did not cause Hermias to be hurt. No blame attaches to me; it was the will of the source. And now he will die, for a blood clot is in his brain. As it moves, it will kill him."

"But you can heal him," said the fire woman.

"No. When he is dead, Parmenion will become the man of iron I need."

"Can you honestly believe, Tamis, that this is the will of the source? That a boy with no evil in his heart should die?"

"Children with no evil in their hearts die all the time, Cassandra. Do not preach to me. They die in fires, in droughts, in plagues, and in wars. Does the source stop them? No. And I no longer complain about it. This is his world. If he chooses for innocents to die, then that is his right. I caused Hermias no harm even though he stood in my way. Now he is dying. I interpret that as a prayer answered."

Tamis closed her eyes and floated free of her body, rising through the low roof and drifting high above the city.

The house of Parnas stood in the east of the city, and she flew toward it, hovering in the flower-garlanded courtyard where a group of Hermias' friends had gathered. Parmenion stood alone by the far wall, ignored.

"They say he was vomiting in the night," said fat Pausias. "Then he passed out. His color is terrible. The surgeon has bled him, but to no avail."

"He is strong," said Nestus. "I am sure he will be all right." The sword champion glanced at Parmenion, then walked across to where he waited.

"What happened last night?" Nestus asked. "All I have heard is rumor."

"Hermias was attacked," answered Parmenion. "He was struck on the head by a club. He was dazed and groggy when I brought him home."

"It is said you killed Learchus. Is it true?"

"I did not know it was Learchus," lied Parmenion. "He was merely one of a group attacking Hermias."

Nestus sighed. "This is bad, Savra. Very bad. I cannot say I have ever liked you, but you know that I have never had any part in the attacks on you."

"I know that."

"If Hermias dies, the others will be arraigned for his murder."

"He will not die!" Parmenion snapped.

A movement by the gates caught Parmenion's eye, and he turned to see Derae and two of her friends enter the courtyard. She saw him but made no sign of recognition as she walked slowly to the open doors of the *andron*.

Tamis entered the main building, drawn by the girl's soul fire, which blazed like concentrated starlight.

The father of Hermias was sitting in the *andron* talking to the surgeon, Astion. He looked up as Derae entered, then stood, his face drawn and haggard. He kissed her cheek, offering her watered wine.

"Can I see him?" she asked.

"He is dying, my dear," said Parnas, his voice breaking.

"He is my friend, my dearest friend," Derae told him. "Let me go to him."

Parnas shrugged and led her to the bedroom where Hermias lay, his face as pale as the linen sheet that covered his body. Derae sat beside him, her hand moving to stroke his brow.

"No!" shouted Tamis, though none could hear her. Derae's soul fire flared, bathing Hermias in blinding light. Tamis could not believe what she was seeing: At the boy's temple the light turned gold, then red, the blood clot beneath the bone dispersing. Hermias groaned and opened his eyes.

"Derae?" he whispered. "What are you doing here? It is most unseemly."

"They told me you were dying," she answered, smiling. "But I can see that is not the case."

"I had the most terrible dreams," he told her. "I was in a place of darkness where nothing grew and no birds sang. But even now the memory fades. . . ."

"So it should, for the sun is shining outside and all your friends are gathered here."

"Parmenion?"

"He also," she said, her smile fading. "Now I will leave you to your rest."

Standing, she returned to the *andron*. "He is awake," she told Parnas, "and his color is good."

Parnas ran to the bedroom, embracing his bewildered son.

The surgeon seized Derae's arm. "What did you do?" he asked.

"I did nothing. As soon as I sat down, he awoke."

Tamis listened to the words, her anger rising. You do not know, you stupid child! You have the gift, and you do not realize it!

Furious, the seer returned to her body. The fire was dead, the room in darkness. Derae's power was a new element, and Tamis gathered her strength to walk the paths of this new future.

It was dusk when Leonidas was summoned to the rooms of the barrack senior. He had been riding along the banks of the Eurotas River for most of the day and had learned of the previous night's tragedy only upon his return, when he found Lepidus waiting for him at the stables.

The soldier had said little as they walked to the barracks, mounting the stairs to the general's rooms. Inside, seated with the senior, were two of the city's *ephors*, councillors responsible for the day-to-day organization of Sparta's rigid social, legal, and economic structure. Leonidas bowed to them both. One he recognized as Memnas, a friend of his father's. Memnas was the chief magistrate, and he headed the night watch and the militia.

The senior stood. "Your friend Learchus lies murdered," he said.

Leonidas felt the shock of the words. "Murdered? I was told he was killed in a fight," he replied.

"That is what we are to determine," put in Memnas. He was a short, slender man with a trident beard and dark hawk-like features. In the blue robes of the *ephor* he seemed a frail figure, yet he had marched with Agisaleus into Persia and had fought, so it was said, like a lion. "Be seated, young man. We have asked you here so that you may corroborate the claims of the killer."

"I was not there, sir. How can I help you?"

"Two boys—friends of yours—lie injured, one with a broken shoulder and another with a broken arm. They will say nothing of the incident save that it was a brawl. They did not see the killing blow struck. They also say that Parmenion attacked them without warning, and they deny harming Hermias."

"What would you have me do?" asked Leonidas. "I am not a militiaman, nor yet a member of the night watch."

"You are from a noble family and highly regarded in the barracks. Find out the truth and come back to us within two hours. Otherwise there will be a full—and public—inquiry that will, whatever the outcome, harm the reputation of Lycurgus barracks."

"I will do what I can, but I promise nothing," Leonidas told them.

He found Gryllus at the gymnasium; the Athenian youth's nose was swollen, his eyes bruised. Leonidas walked him to the square, finding a quiet spot lit by the torches of the oracle shrine. There Gryllus told him all he could recall of the fight.

"He murdered him, Leon!" he said, at last. "I still can't believe it!"

"You went after him at night, hooded and masked. And not for the first time, Gryllus. What did you expect? That he would greet you with flowers?"

"He killed him with his own dagger. I saw it. He backed him to a wall and then stabbed him."

"You saw it and did nothing?"

"What could I do? He is a demon—possessed. He leapt from the sky. We didn't know it was Hermias; we were just going to stop Savra from running in the trials. We did it for you, to avenge your shame!"

Leonidas' hand snaked out, his fingers circling Gryllus' throat. "You did nothing for me!" he hissed. "I have seen it in you for a long time, Athenian. You like inflicting pain, but you are not man enough to stand alone. You run with a pack, like the cowardly dog you are. Now hear this: Tomorrow you will be gone from Sparta. I care not where. If you are here, I will come after you myself and rip out your bowels with a blunt knife."

"Oh, please, Leonidas."

"Be silent! You will tell no one else of your . . . infamy. Learchus' death is on your head, and one day you will suffer for it."

Leonidas returned to the *ephors* at the appointed time.

"You have discovered the truth?" Memnas asked.

"I have, sir. A group of youths attacked Hermias, believing him to be Parmenion. The half-breed is innocent of blame; he acted to save his friend."

"And the names of the other youths?"

"That was not part of your instruction to me, sir. The ringleader—an Athenian—will be leaving the city tonight. He will not return."

"Perhaps it is better that way," said Memnas.

Two hours after dawn the five hundred youngsters of Lycurgus barracks were marched to the training ground, where file leaders ordered them into line to await the barrack senior. First- and second-year children were allowed to sit at the front, while those aged nine to nineteen stood silently to attention. All the older youths now knew of the tragedy, and not one person had spoken to Parmenion since muster.

He glanced to his left and right. The boys on either side of him had edged away, creating distance. Parmenion did not respond but stared stonily ahead, longing for the day to pass swiftly.

The children at the front stood up as the barrack senior strode into view flanked by two of the city councillors in their blue ceremonial robes. Parmenion felt panic flare within him. The blue-clad *ephors* looked grim, and he pictured them marching to him and escorting him to the execution ground. Tearing his eyes from them, he gazed at the general. In full armor the barrack senior looked even more ferocious than when Parmenion had seen him the previous night.

The old man's eyes scanned the ranks. "Many of you already know," he roared, "of the death of our comrade Learchus. The *ephors* here," he added, gesturing at the councillors, "have investigated fully and have, in their wisdom, declared the incident closed. So be it. Today the body of our departed friend is being laid out. Tomorrow we will attend the cremation. The lament will be sung by Leonidas. That is all!" He stepped back, spun on his heel, and stalked away.

Lepidus ordered the boys to stand down and then spoke for a moment or two with the *ephors* before making his way to Parmenion and leading him to one side. "That was hard on you, and you did well to be here. But there is something else. After today you will no longer be part of Lycurgus barracks. Next week you will join the Menelaus group."

"What about my mess bill here? I have just paid for the year ahead. I have no more money."

"I will loan you the sum," said Lepidus. "I wish I could give it to you, but I am not a rich man."

"No! I will not leave," argued Parmenion, fighting to control his temper. "There are no grounds. I will refuse to go."

"Life will be unbearable for you here, boy! Surely you can see that. Your presence would wreck morale. And the barracks system depends on morale. You understand that, don't you?"

"Yes, I do," answered Parmenion softly. "I would like to see the barrack senior to discuss the move."

"He does not want to talk to you," said Lepidus, aware of

a change in Parmenion but unable to pin down the exact nature of it.

"His wants are immaterial. If he does not see me, then I stay. Tell him that, Lepidus!" And Parmenion walked away without a word.

That afternoon he was summoned to the senior's rooms. The old man did not look up from his desk as Parmenion entered. "Make this swift," he snapped. Then he heard the rasp of a chair leg against the floor and looked up shocked to see Parmenion seated before him. "What do you think you are doing?" he asked.

"I am negotiating, General," answered Parmenion, meeting the other man's eyes and holding his gaze. "You want me gone? I wish to go. But there is the matter of my mess fees. Three days ago I paid over one hundred and forty drachmas to this barracks. My mother sold a one-third share in our landholding to raise that money."

"That is not a problem of mine," said the old man.

"But it is," Parmenion told him. "Since I have paid, then I will stay. You have no right to request me to leave. I have broken no rule."

"Broken . . . ? You murdered a boy!" snarled the old man, pushing himself to his feet.

"Not according to the *ephors*," answered Parmenion calmly. "Now if you wish me to leave, you will supply me with two hundred drachmas. Is that clear enough for you . . . sir?"

For almost a minute the general stared at Parmenion, his face deep crimson. Then he smiled and relaxed. "So the Macedonian blood finally rises to the surface. There's not a man in that whole country who wouldn't sell his wife to buy a sheep. Very well, *peasant*, I will give you your two hundred—much good will it do you. You may stay on in any barracks, but when you reach manhood, you will find no one willing to endure you in any soldiers' hall. You will never be a Spartan, Parmenion. *Never!*"

The youngster chuckled. "You mean that as an insult? I do not take it so. I know what I am, General, as I know what you are. I would be obliged if the money could be sent to my home before sunset."

Parmenion stood and bowed.

Within the hour he was standing before another old man, fierce-eyed and grim-lipped. Leaning back in his chair, Agenor linked his arms behind his bald head and observed the young man. "I want no deaths here," stated the officer.

"Nor I, sir."

"But I want fighters, and I want thinkers. I understand you run well."

"Yes, sir."

"Good. Find yourself a bed in the western dormitory and then report to Solon at the training field." As Parmenion prepared to leave, the man rose and waved him back. "Lepidus spoke well of you, boy. He says you have had a tough time and that you bore it well. Know this, that here you will be judged only by what we see, not by what we have heard."

"That is all I ask, sir. Thank you."

Parmenion hoisted his blanket roll to his shoulder and walked to the western wing. All the rush beds but two had blankets on them. Parmenion chose the empty bed farthest from the door and lay down. For a while he watched dust motes dancing in shafts of sunlight coming through a broken shutter. Then he closed his eyes.

A hand touched his shoulder, and he was instantly awake. There were stars in the sky, and the room was filling up with young men. He looked up at the boy who had touched him.

It was Hermias.

"What are you doing here?" asked Parmenion, rolling to his feet and embracing his friend.

"I transferred here this morning," Hermias answered. "I wouldn't want you to feel lonely."

Parmenion was truly moved. Lycurgus barracks was where the rich sent their youngsters; it was for the elite Spartiates. Parmenion had been the only poor boy enrolled there; as he was the son of a hero, part of the cost of his education was being paid by his father's battalion. For Hermias to leave the elite to join Menelaus, the smallest of barracks, was something Parmenion could hardly believe. "You should not have done this, Hermias, my friend. But I am glad you did. I cannot tell you how glad."

"It is a new beginning, Savra. A chance to forget the past."

Parmenion nodded. "You are right," he said.

But he would not forget. He would make them pay. He would live for the day when his enemies lay in the dust at his feet, staring up at him, begging forgiveness.

"That's better, Savra! I like to see you smile," said Hermias.

PARMENION settled swiftly into life at Menelaus and during the next three years, though never popular, found few of the problems that had beset him at Lycurgus. Every year he and Hermias represented their barracks in the short- and middle-distance races, but in other spheres they remained merely good students, neither excelling nor falling short of the required standard in throwing the javelin or the discus, in sword work or wrestling. Parmenion enjoyed working with the short sword, for he was fast and strong, but only when he was angry did his skill become lethal. Understanding this instinctively, he was not concerned that some youths could best him in practice. Deep in his heart he knew the outcome would be different if the battles were to the death.

But as a runner Parmenion was the finest athlete in Sparta. Twice, in interbarracks competitions, he bested Leonidas in the four-mile race but was himself narrowly beaten in the third year when Leonidas was chosen to represent Sparta in the coming Olympics.

It was a bitter disappointment to Parmenion, who had trained hard during his time at Menelaus.

"I understand your anger," said Xenophon as they sat in his courtyard one evening, "but you did the best you could. No man can ask more of himself than that."

Parmenion nodded. "But I made a tactical mistake. I tried to beat him with two hundred paces left. He was waiting for my move and hung on to me. He beat me with three strides to go."

"You beat him in the games three years ago, and he endured his shame well. Allow him his moment of glory." In his fiftieth year, the Athenian was still a handsome man, though his hair was now totally silver and thinning at the crown. He poured a goblet of wine, added water, and sipped the drink. Parmenion lived for the hours they spent together, discussing tactics and strategy, formations and battles. The youth learned when to wheel a phalanx, when to fight with a thinned line, when to extend, when to draw back, how to choose the anchor warriors who held the line together. Xenophon loved to talk, and Parmenion was happy to listen. At times he would disagree with an analysis, and the two men would argue long into the night. Parmenion always had the good sense—ultimately—to allow Xenophon to convince him, and their relationship grew. Gryllus had been sent to friends in Athens, and often Parmenion would stay with the Athenian general for days at a time, taking Gryllus' place on summer journeys to Xenophon's second home in Olympia, near the sea.

As the years passed Xenophon took to discussing modern strategy and politics with his student, and Parmenion detected a growing cynicism in the Athenian.

"Have you heard the news from Thebes?" Xenophon asked him one day.

"Yes," answered Parmenion. "At first I could not believe it. We have made a bad mistake, and I think we will rue it."

"I tend to agree," said Xenophon. Three months earlier the Macedonian king, Amyntas, had appealed to the Spartans for aid against Chalcidian warriors who had invaded Macedonia and sacked the capital of Pella. Agisaleus sent three Spartan battalions to Macedonia's aid, crushing the Chalcidians. But on their journey north one Spartan division, under the command of a general named Phoebidas, seized the Cadmea, the fortress at the center of Thebes. Since there was no war declared against Thebes and they were unconnected with the Chalcidian invaders, the action was seen by many Greeks as underhanded.

"Agisaleus should return the city to the Thebans," said Parmenion.

"He cannot," answered Xenophon. "Spartan pride would not allow it. But I fear the result. Athens has spoken out against Sparta, and I think it will not be long before we suffer another war."

"You are disappointed, my friend," said Parmenion. "Sparta has not proved a good leader for Greece."

"Hush!" said Xenophon swiftly. He lowered his voice. "You should not speak this way in public. My servants are loyal, but they are loyal to me, not to you. If one should speak against you, there would be a trial for treason. You would not survive."

"Have I spoken anything but the truth?" countered Parmenion, keeping his voice low.

"What has that to do with anything? If Sparta could govern with half the skill she displays in battle, then all of Greece would rejoice. But she cannot. That is the truth of the matter, and saying it will get you killed."

"Other people are saying it," Parmenion told him. "The talk at the barracks is of little else. There have been some bitter herbs for Spartans to swallow. They cling to power now only because the Persians support them. The descendants of the sword king playing lickspittles to the sons of Xerxes!"

"The politics of expediency," Xenophon whispered. "But let us leave this conversation for another few days. Then, when we are back in Olympia, we can ride and talk with only the land to listen to our idle treasons." The two men rose and walked to the gate. "How are your finances?" asked Xenophon.

"Not good. I sold the last share in the landholding. It will pay my mess bills until the spring."

"And then?"

Parmenion shrugged. "And then I will leave Sparta. No soldiers' hall would have me anyway; I know that. I will probably join a mercenary regiment and see the world."

"You could sell the sword of Leonidas," Xenophon pointed out.

"Maybe I will," replied Parmenion. "I will see you in two days."

The two men shook hands, and Parmenion walked out into the night. Despite the closeness of midnight he felt no fatigue, and he walked to the acropolis and sat by the bronze statue of Zeus, staring at the sky and the diamond stars. The wind was chilly now, and his light woolen *chiton* offered little protection. Closing his mind to the cold, he cast his eyes over the mountains.

The last three years had been good to him. He had grown tall and, though slender, was lean and powerful. His face had slimmed down, losing its boyish qualities, and his deep-set blue eyes now had a brooding look. Yet it was not, he knew, a friendly face or even a handsome one. The nose was too prominent and the lips too thin, making him appear older than his nineteen years.

At last, as the cold grew too much even for Parmenion, he rose to leave. Just then he saw a cloaked and hooded figure move from the bronze house and walk toward him.

"Good evening," he said. Moonlight glanced from the dagger blade that leapt into the figure's hand.

"Who is there?" came a woman's voice.

"It is Parmenion, and I am no danger to you, lady," he answered, holding out his hands and showing empty palms.

"What are you doing here? Are you spying on me?"

"Not at all. I was enjoying the stars. Why should I spy on you?"

Derae pushed back the hood, the moonlight turning her hair to silver. "It is a long time since we spoke, young Fast."

"Indeed it is," he replied. "And what brings you to the bronze house at midnight?"

"My own business," she answered, smiling to rob the words of sharpness. "Perhaps I, too, like to look at the stars."

A movement at the edge of his vision caused Parmenion to swing his head, and he saw a young man dart away behind the sanctuary to the Muses. He said nothing.

"Good night to you," said Derae, and Parmenion bowed and watched as the girl moved away to the path. It was a dangerous game she was playing. Unmarried Spartans were not allowed to mix freely with members of the opposite sex, and any liaison could end in execution or banishment. That was one reason why the young men were encouraged to take lovers among their male comrades. He found himself envying the young man who had fled and realized that he, too, would risk a great deal for the chance to spend time alone with Derae. He still remembered the lithe young body, the small, firm breasts, the narrow waist. . . .

Enough! he chided himself.

Returning home, he sat in the tiny courtyard and ate a late supper of dried fish and wine; it had cost two obols. The thought of his dwindling finances depressed him. The sale of the last share in the landholding had realized one hundred and seventy drachmas, but eighty of those had gone to pay his mess bill. Thirty more had been set aside to buy the armor he would need when he reached manhood next spring. The rest must keep him in food and clothing. He shook his head. The price of a new cloak was twenty drachmas, new shoes just under ten. It would be a long hard winter, he realized.

Entering the house, he shut the windows and lit a small lantern. By its light he took the sword of Leonidas from the cupboard by the far wall and drew it from its bronze scabbard.

It was an iron blade no longer than a man's forearm, the hilt decorated with gold wire that encircled a pommel globe of purest silver.

Xenophon had urged him many times to sell it. There were families in Sparta that would pay as much as a thousand drachmas for a blade with such an illustrious history. Parmenion slid the sword back into its scabbard; he would sooner starve than part with the only trophy of his life.

He had a dream, and the sword was part of it. He would march away to war as a mercenary, gather a great fortune and an army, and return to Sparta, humbling the city and visiting his vengeance on all the enemies of his youth. It was a foolish dream, and he knew it, but it sustained him.

More likely, he realized, he would be forced to sign on as a *hoplite* in a mercenary company and spend his days marching across the endless wastes of Persia at the whim of whatever prince had the money to hire them. And what would he earn? Seven obols a day—just over a drachma. Which could mean that if he survived twenty years with such a company, he might—just *might*—be able to buy a part share in a farm or landholding. And even then it would not be as large as the property his mother—and now he—had been forced to sell.

Parmenion pushed thoughts of his poverty from his mind. For at least the next eight weeks he could enjoy the comforts of Xenophon's estate at Olympia. Soft beds and good food, fine riding and hunting, and, with luck, a tilt at one of the Arcadian girls who tended the sheep in the low hills. He had found such a one last year; she had been plump and willing and an expert teacher for an inept city youth. He removed his *chiton* and climbed into bed, picturing her body. But he could no longer recall her face. . . . In his mind's eye the woman moaning beneath him was Derae.

One day out from the city, the small party saw a group of horsemen cantering toward them. Xenophon hoisted his spear and kicked the gelding into a run to meet them. Parmenion rode after him, while Tinus, Clearchus, and three other servants remained with the wagon.

Parmenion guided his mount alongside Xenophon. "I think it is Leonidas," he shouted. The Athenian drew rein and waited, and Parmenion could see his concern. Spartan cavalry had been sent out into the Sciritis hills after two villages were hit by raiders, renegade mercenaries who had been dismissed by the authorities in Corinth. There were said to be more than thirty men in the raiding party.

Shading his eyes, Parmenion could see Leonidas riding at the head of a large group of warriors. Behind him was his father, Patroclian. Xenophon held up a hand in greeting, and Leonidas dragged on his reins while Patroclian rode forward.

"An ill day, Xenophon," said the red-bearded Spartiate. "My daughter, Derae, has been taken."

"Taken? How?" Xenophon asked.

"She was riding alone to the east of our column; I think she must have stopped by a stream and dismounted. I have a Thracian servant who reads tracks, and he said her horse must have run clear when they surprised her. They are heading north, into the hills."

"We will join with you, of course," said Xenophon.

Parmenion swung his horse's head and cantered back to the wagon. "Hand me the bow," he ordered Tinus.

The man reached into the back of the wagon and lifted out a bow of horn and a goatskin quiver containing twenty arrows. Parmenion hooked the quiver over his shoulder and scanned the countryside. The men were heading north, Patroclian had said, but by now they would know that Derae was part of a larger group, and it would make little sense to hold to their course. To the northeast was a heavily wooded line of hills beyond which Parmenion could see a high pass that swept northward. Without waiting for the others, he heeled the mare into a run and rode for the wooded slopes.

"Where in Hades is he going?" asked Leonidas.

"I don't know, and I don't care," snapped Patroclian. "Let's ride!"

The warriors set off for the north.

Parmenion rode high into the hills, angling his mount toward the pass. The footing was treacherous here, scree and loose shale. He slowed the mare, dismounted, then led her up into the trees. On reaching safe ground, he tethered her to a bush and climbed a tall cypress tree. From its uppermost branches he scanned the surrounding hills, seeing no sign of movement save for the dust of the hunting party as it galloped north. He stayed in the tree for some time and was just beginning to face the possibility of being wrong when several black and gray crows took off from the trees some two hundred paces to his right. They seemed panicked, and he focused on the area, straining to see through the undergrowth. After a moment or two he caught the glint of sunlight on metal and heard a horse whinny. Swiftly he climbed down the tree, mounted the mare, and set off at a run for the pass.

He reached it ahead of the raiders and dragged on the reins; the mare whinnied and reared. Parmenion leapt from her back and swiftly hobbled her. Climbing to the peak of a tall, rocky outcrop overlooking the narrow pass, he slid an arrow from the quiver and notched it to the string.

His heart was beating wildly, and there was a pounding pain behind his eyes. The headaches had been worse of late, waking him in the night and leaving him nauseous and shaken. But now he had no time to be concerned with petty pain.

His reaction to the news of Derae's abduction had surprised him. She had been in his thoughts often, but he had never allowed himself to believe he could win her. Now, with the thought of her being taken from him for good, he felt a rising sense of panic and a realization that she was part of his dreams. A foolish dream! his mind screamed at him as he crouched, waiting for the raiders. Leonidas would never allow such a marriage. Marriage? He pictured Derae standing beside him at the sacred stone to Hera, her hand on his, the priestess binding their arms together with laurel leaves. . . .

Wiping his sweating palms on his tunic, he forced such thoughts from his mind and stared at the tree line. Several minutes later the first of the scouts came into view. The man was sun-bronzed and dark-bearded, wearing a Phrygian helm with a metal crest and a red eye painted on the brow. He was carrying a lance. Beside him rode a warrior wearing a wide Boeotian helm of beaten iron; he was carrying a bow in his left hand, with an arrow ready notched.

Parmenion crouched down behind a rock and waited, listening to the steady rhythmic sound of hooves on stone. Then, risking a glance, he saw the main group, numbering more than thirty, riding out behind the scouts. He could see Derae, her hands tied behind her. There was a rope around her neck, being held by a warrior on a tall gray stallion. The man was wearing silver armor and a white cloak. To Parmenion, he looked like a prince from legend.

Laris rode his stallion clear of the trees and tugged on the rope. The girl almost stumbled. He glanced back at her and smiled. What a beauty! There had been no chance yet to hear her screams, to enjoy her writhing beneath him, but that would come once they had thrown off their pursuers. Spartans! The weak-livered councillors of Corinth had all but wet themselves when he had talked of invading Spartan lands. Could they not see that the Spartans could be taken? If Thebes, Corinth, and Athens joined forces, they could destroy Sparta once and for all. But no. Ancient fears held sway. Remember Thermopylae, they said. Remember the defeat of Athens twenty years ago. Who cared about events a lifetime in the past? At best the Spartans could put fifteen thousand men in the field. Corinth alone could match half that number, and Athens make up the rest. Thebes and the Boeotian League could double the force.

Dismissed! The shame of it burned at Laris. But now he had shown them: with a mere forty men he had raided deep into Spartan lands. True, they had found little gold and the men

were unhappy, but he had proved a point. If forty could ride
into the home of warriors and emerge unscathed, what would
be the result when forty thousand marched in?

He looked up to see the scouts riding into the pass.

Suddenly an arrow flashed through the air to strike
Xanthias in the throat, and with a terrible cry he pitched from
his mount. Instantly all was chaos. Men leapt from their
horses, taking shelter behind the rocks. Laris slid to the
ground, dragging Derae down beside him.

A young Spartan stood in full view of the men.

"Release the woman!" he called, "and there will be no
further killing."

"Who speaks?" yelled Laris.

"A man with a bow," answered the warrior.

"And why should we trust your word, man with a bow?"

"Look behind you," shouted the archer. "Can you see the
dust cloud? You are trapped. If you wait, you will die. If you
advance, you will die. List your choices, if you will."

"I see no one up there with you," said Laris, rising and
drawing his sword.

"Do you not? Then it must be that I am alone. Attack me
and find out!"

"Show us your men!"

"Your time is running out, along with my patience. If you do
not have the wit to save your comrades, perhaps another man
among them will make the choice for you."

The warrior's words stung Laris. Already his men were far
from happy, and now this lone archer was questioning his
leadership.

A man rose from behind a rock. "For Athena's sake, Laris!
Let the woman go, and let us get away from here!"

The leader turned to Derae. His knife slashed the thongs
binding her hands, then he lifted the noose from around her
neck. He turned to see the Spartan riding toward him, his bow
looped over his shoulder. Laris scanned the rocks but could
see no one. He licked his lips, convinced the bowman was

alone, longing to plunge his blade into the Spartan, to see his lifeblood draining from him.

The warrior smiled at him. "I have told the others to let you pass, and you can trust my word. But I should ride fast. I do not speak for those who follow."

The men ran for their horses. Laris suppressed the urge to strike out; he could hear the hoofbeats of the Spartan force. Grabbing his stallion's mane, he leapt to the beast's back and galloped through the pass. As he had expected there was no one there—no archers, no *hoplites*, no slingers. Just rock and shale. He could feel the eyes of his men upon him. He had been tricked by one Spartan. One man had made him surrender his prize.

What would they say in Corinth?

Parmenion leaned out, taking Derae's hand and swinging her up behind him. Then he touched heels to the mare and walked the beast back into the trees.

Within minutes Patroclian came galloping toward them, followed by Leonidas and the others. Parmenion raised his hand, and the red-bearded Spartiate drew rein as Derae eased herself to the ground.

"What happened here?" Leonidas demanded, pushing his way to the front.

"Parmenion and the others blocked the pass," said Derae. "He killed one of their scouts, then negotiated to allow them through if they gave me up."

"What others?" asked Patroclian.

"Archers, I suppose," said Derae. "He threatened to kill all the raiders unless they released me."

"Where are these other men?" Patroclian enquired of Parmenion. "I would like to thank them."

"There are no others," Parmenion told him. Edging his mount forward, he rode through the group and back down the scree slope to where the wagon was waiting. Tossing the quiver and bow to Tinus, he lifted a water skin from the seat beside the servant and drank deeply.

Xenophon rode alongside. "You did well, *strategos*. We found where the trail swung east, but we would have been too late had you not blocked the pass. I am proud of you." He tossed a blood-covered arrow to Tinus. "It was a fine strike at the base of the throat, severing the windpipe and lodging in the spine. A fine strike!"

"I was aiming for the chest or belly, but I overcompensated for the gradient."

Xenophon was about to speak when he noticed Parmenion's hands begin to tremble. He glanced at the young man's face, which showed no expression, though the blood had drained from it.

"Are you well?" asked the Athenian.

"My head is pounding, and there are lights flashing in my eyes."

"We will camp here," said Xenophon. Parmenion dismounted and staggered several paces before falling to his knees and vomiting. Then he stood and sucked in great gulps of air. Xenophon brought him the water skin, and he rinsed his mouth. "You feel better?"

"I am shaking like a leaf in a storm—I can't believe it. Back there I was so calm, but now I am acting like a frightened child."

"Back there was the work of a man, a cool man. A man of iron nerve," Xenophon assured him. "This takes nothing from it."

"I feel as if there are hot lances inside my head. I have never known pain like it." Parmenion sat down, resting his back against the wagon wheel. "And the light is burning my eyes." Tinus climbed down from the wagon, holding a wide hat of straw over Parmenion's head to shade him. The pain grew, and Parmenion slipped into darkness.

Parmenion awoke several times in the night, but his head seemed filled with searing light, bringing agony and nausea.

With an effort of will he slipped back into the sanctuary of sleep. When finally he opened his eyes, the absence of pain was almost blissful. He was lying in a cool room with the shutters closed, and he could hear the low hum of conversation beyond the whitewashed walls. He sat up and saw that his left forearm was bandaged, but he could not remember being wounded.

Someone stirred in a chair across the room, and a man rose and walked over to him. He was short and slender, with wispy gray hair. He smiled.

"The pain is gone, yes?" inquired the man, his voice deep and faintly comical coming from so frail a body.

"Yes," agreed Parmenion. "What happened to me?"

"The world," said the man, sitting on the bed beside him, "is made up of four elements: earth, air, fire, and water. But it is held in harmony by the will of the gods. As I understand it, you displayed an act of rare courage. You put yourself under severe stress. This caused an excess of fire in your system, heating your blood and destroying your harmony. Hot blood coursed in your brain, causing intense pain and nausea."

"You bled me, then," said Parmenion, touching the bandage on his arm.

"I did. It is well known that this relieves the pressure. If you feel faint, I will repeat the process."

"No, I feel fine."

"Good. I will tell the general you are well. But you ought to be purged, young man; it would be safer."

"Truly, I am well. The pain has gone. I commend your skill."

The little man smiled. "In truth I am better with wounds, but I study," he confided.

"Will this happen to me whenever I face danger?"

"It is unlikely. I have known many men to suffer such head pain, but the attacks are usually rare and only accompany times of undue stress. It is common also among clerics who complain of blurred vision and dancing lights before their eyes. Opium is the best cure for this, processed to the Egyptian formula. I will leave some with Xenophon in case your pain returns."

Parmenion lay back. He fell asleep once more, and when he awoke, Xenophon was sitting beside him.

"You gave us a scare, *strategos*. The good doctor wanted to drill a hole in your skull to release the bad humors, but I dissuaded him."

"Where are we?"

"Olympia."

"You mean I have slept for a full day?"

"More than that," replied Xenophon. "It is now almost noon on the second day. I had hoped to take you hunting, but as it is the doctor says you should rest for today."

"I am well enough to ride," Parmenion argued.

"I am sure you are," agreed Xenophon soothingly, "but I will not allow it. The doctor has spoken, and we will follow his advice. Anyway, there is a guest to see you, and I am sure you will not object to spending time with her while I ride out to hunt with her father."

"Derae? Here?"

"Waiting in the gardens. Now remember, my boy, to appear feeble and wan. Elicit her sympathy."

"I need to bathe and shave."

"And to dress, let us not forget that," said Xenophon as the naked Parmenion threw back his sheet and rose from the bed.

The gardens were constructed around a shallow stream flowing from the eastern hills. White boulders had been carefully polished and placed in circles, half-buried in the soil. Around them, brightly colored flowers had been planted after the fashion of the Persians. Stone pathways had been designed to meander through groves of oak trees, and stone benches were placed in shaded hollows. There were statues from Corinth and Thebes, mostly showing the goddess Athena in full armor and one of Artemis carrying a bow. By a small man-made lake there was a series of statues portraying the twelve labors of Heracles. Usually Parmenion would sit by them, enjoying the cool breeze across the water, but not today. He found Derae sitting by the stream under the shade of a willow. She was dressed in an ankle-length *chiton* of white edged with green and gold. Around her waist and looped over her shoulders was a sea-green *chlamys*, a long, rectangular strip of fine linen, delicately embroidered. As she saw him, she stood and smiled. "Are you now well, hero?" she asked.

"Indeed I am. You are looking beautiful; your clothes are very fine."

"Thank you. But you are pale—perhaps you should rest for a while." They sat together in uncomfortable silence for several minutes until Derae laid her hand on his arm. "I wanted to thank you. I was terrified. You have no idea how I felt when you stood upon that rock and demanded my release. It was as if you were sent by the gods."

"Perhaps I was," he whispered, covering her hand with his own.

"My father was very impressed by your courage—and your initiative. I was really convinced there were men with you."

Parmenion grinned. "Xenophon taught me that victory is achieved by putting the thought of defeat into the heart of your enemy. To him goes the honor."

"But to you the glory. I like to see you smile, Savra; it makes you handsome. You do not smile enough."

Her hand was warm beneath his, and he could feel her closeness and smell the heavy scent of the perfumed oil on her hair. Her head was tilted toward him, and he could not read her eyes; the pupils were wide, her face flushed, her lips slightly parted. He found himself leaning closer toward her. She did not draw back, and his lips touched hers. Her arms encircled his neck, her body pressed in to him, and he could feel her breasts against his chest. He felt dizzy yet exhilarated. His hand slid along her shoulder and down her arm. Her hand came up to close over his fingers. For a moment only he felt disappointment, then she drew his hand down to her breast.

Then, as swiftly as it had begun, Derae ended the embrace, pulling back sharply.

"Not here! Not now," she pleaded.

"When?" asked Parmenion, battling to control his surging emotions.

"When they have gone. We will hear the horses."

"Yes . . . the horses."

They sat in unnatural silence, waiting, listening as the grooms beyond the garden wall brought out the mounts, hearing the laughter of the hunters, men boasting of their skills and others mocking with gentle humor. Then came the thunder of hooves, and quiet descended on the garden. Parmenion stood, reached out, and took Derae's hand, drawing her up to him. He kissed her again, and they walked back through the garden gate and on to the house. Back in his room Parmenion gently untied the thongs at Derae's shoulder, the white and green *chiton* falling to the floor.

Stepping back, he gazed at her upper body. Her arms and face were bronzed, but her breasts and waist were white as marble. Tentatively he reached out to touch her breast, his palm stroking gently across the raised nipple. She unfastened the brooch that held his *chiton*, and, naked now, they moved to the bed.

For a while they kissed and touched, but then Derae lay back, drawing Parmenion onto her. He groaned as he entered her and felt her legs slide up over his hips. In all his life he had never known such pleasure or dreamt of scaling such a peak of joy. It was madness, he knew, but he had no control—wished for none. Even the thought of death could not stop him now.

His passion made him want to power into her, yet he did not wish the moment to end and forced himself to move slowly, rhythmically, his eyes open, watching her face. Her eyes were closed, her cheeks flushed. He brushed his lips against hers, and her mouth opened, her tongue darting against his own. He felt himself building to a climax and slid from her.

"No," she said, pulling at him. He knelt by the side of the bed, running his tongue across her flat belly, then lifted her thigh across his shoulder. "What are you doing?" she asked, struggling to sit. He pushed her back and lowered his head between her legs. Her hair was soft, peltlike, and his tongue caressed her. She began to moan, softly at first and then louder. She shuddered against him, her hands tugging at his hair. Climbing to the bed, he entered her once more. Derae's arms circled his neck, and she clung to him with fierce strength until he, too, reached a climax.

Bathed in sweat, they lay together with arms entwined. Now that it was over, the passion spent, all Parmenion's fear came rushing back. What they had done was against the law. What if the servants had seen them walking hand in hand from the garden? And could they have failed to hear her cries or the creaking of the bed? Raising himself on his elbow, he looked down at the girl. Her eyes were closed, her face wondrous in its beauty.

He knew then that she was worth the risk, worth any risk.

"I love you," he whispered.

Her eyes opened. "I had a dream," she said. "Three days ago. I went to a seeress with it. She told me that it meant I would love only one man in my life and that he would stand and defy an army for me."

"What was your dream?"

"I dreamed I was in a temple, and all was darkness. And I said, 'Where is the Lion of Macedon?' The sun shone then, and I saw a general in a white-plumed helmet. He was tall and proud and walking with the light at his back. He saw me and opened his arms. He called me his love. That's all I remember."

"Why was there darkness? You said the sun was shining."

"I don't know. But the dream disturbed me. I should have thought of you, for you are half Macedonian. You are the Lion of Macedon from my dream."

He chuckled. "I am told Macedon has few lions," he said. "And it is not a country renowned for producing generals."

"You don't believe in my dream?"

"I believe we are destined to be together," he told her. "And I would defy an army for you."

"You already have."

"That wasn't an army, that was a rabble. But I could bless them now for bringing us together."

Leaning down, he kissed her—and his passion returned.

For five days the lovers met in secret, riding out into the hills high above the land. They saw only a few shepherd girls and spent their days wandering through the woods and making love in sheltered hollows.

For Parmenion it was a time of bliss beyond imagining. His bitterness fled from him, and he reveled in the glory of the summer sun, the clear blue skies, and the beauty of the land. The cruelties of his life seemed distant now, like the memory of winter snow. He could picture them but could not feel the icy cold of their reality.

On the morning of the sixth day his world changed. He led the chestnut mare from her stall at the rear of the white-walled house and bridled her.

Xenophon walked to him, laying a hand on his arm. "Do not ride today," he said softly.

"I need to feel the wind in my face. I will be back soon."

"I said no!" Xenophon snapped. "And if you need reminding, the mare belongs to me."

"Then I shall walk!" responded Parmenion, his face flushed with anger.

"You fool! When will you start using your mind?"

"What do you mean?"

"You know exactly what I am saying. My servants know where you are going. I know where you are going. Patroclian knows where you are going. You have conducted this affair with all the subtlety of a rutting bull."

"How dare you?" stormed Parmenion. "You have spied on me."

"What need was there for spies? You took her to your room

on the first day, and her cries echoed around the house. You meet her on hillsides and walk hand in hand, where you can be observed for miles. Patroclian would be within his rights to have you arrested and executed, but he is a man of honor and feels he owes you for your courage."

"I intend to marry her," declared Parmenion. "It is not as you think."

"As I said, Parmenion, you are a fool! Now return the mare to her stall."

"Allow me to ride out to Derae. I need to talk to her," begged Parmenion.

"She will not be there; she has been sent back to Sparta."

Parmenion's throat was dry, his belly knotted. "Sent back? I will go to see Patroclian."

Xenophon swung and lashed his open palm across Parmenion's face. The blow stung him, and he staggered. "Maybe the doctor purged you of brains," hissed Xenophon. "Will you think, man? You have violated a virgin. What will you say to her father? 'I want to marry her?' What do you have to offer? What dowry do you bring? You are a penniless student without a landholding or a farm. You have no income. All you have done is ruin the girl for anyone else."

"You make it sound vile," said Parmenion, "but it isn't."

"You don't understand, do you?" said the general sadly. "You cannot see it. Derae is pledged to Nestus, and they were to have been wed in the spring. When he hears of the shame to himself and his family—as he will, since you chose to act so openly—he will demand repayment of the dowry, and if he condemns Derae publicly, she will die."

"I will save her. She loves me, Xenophon. She is a gift from the gods to me; I know it. They will not let any harm come to her. Do not hate me for this!"

The Athenian laid his hands on Parmenion's shoulders. "I do not hate you for it, my young friend. Your life has not been particularly blessed. But listen to me and try to use that part of your mind which we have trained. Do not think of Derae. Pull your thoughts away from what you call love and think of life as it has to be lived. You have brought great shame to Patroclian and to his whole family. You have shamed me, and you have shamed yourself. Love? Love is born of caring, of compassion, of understanding. Do not talk of love but speak openly and honestly of desire. You put Derae in a position of great danger—that is not the act of a lover. You have destroyed her reputation and blighted the name of a noble line. Tell me where love appears in this scene."

Parmenion could not reply, but he led the mare back into her stall and removed the bridle. The events of the last five days seemed suddenly dreamlike and unreal. He saw now that Xenophon was right: he had shamed his friend and tarnished Derae.

He walked back out into the sunlight, but Xenophon had gone.

Parmenion wandered out into the garden, stopping by the bench where Derae had first kissed him. There had to be a way to resolve the dilemma, a way in which he and Derae could live together. He had decided months before to leave Sparta when he reached manhood, but Derae had changed all that. Now he just wanted to have enough money to marry and raise a family, to pay for his own boys to attend barracks.

For most of the day he wrestled with the problem, seeing only one solution. At last, with the sun setting, he made his way back to the house. Xenophon was sitting in the courtyard, eating a supper of figs and cheese, as Parmenion stood before him.

"I am sorry, sir. Deeply sorry for the shame I have brought you. It is a terrible way to repay the friendship you have shown me."

Xenophon shrugged. "That is life, Parmenion. Sit down and eat. Tomorrow we will ride to the sea, feel the fresh winds upon our faces."

"When we return to Sparta," said Parmenion, "I will sell the sword of Leonidas. With that money, I will be able to marry Derae."

"We have almost two months here," said Xenophon sadly, looking away. "It will give you time to think out your plans, and Patroclian time to lose his anger. Much can happen in that interval. Perhaps the servants will not talk. Perhaps Nestus will forgive her. Who knows? But if you are to grow, Parmenion—if you are to become the man you ought to be—then you must learn from this experience."

"What can I learn? Not to fall in love?"

"No, no man can do that. But you must realize that love is perilous; it affects the mind, blinding us to obvious realities. Think of Helen and Paris. They brought about the downfall of Troy. You think that is what they intended? No, they were merely lovers. You are one of the most intelligent and intuitive men I have ever met, and yet you have acted like a complete dullard. If that is what love brings, then I am thankful it has eluded me."

"It will end well," whispered Parmenion. "I promise you."

"That is still love talking. No man of intellect makes a promise he cannot keep. Now eat, and let us talk of this no more tonight."

As the weeks passed Parmenion found Xenophon's wisdom once more to be true. The longing and the love he had for Derae did not pass, but his mind cleared and he felt a deep sense of shame for the foolish way he had conducted his affair.

Had Patroclian been so minded, he could have taken the matter to the council, which would have recommended Parmenion's death to the *ephors*. There was no question of a defense; the law was specific. Any Spartan who violated a virgin was subject to death by poison or by the blade. Derae herself could be sacrificed to the death goddess, Hecate.

Now Parmenion could look back on his passion with cool logic. In truth, he could not regret their lovemaking; it had been the high point of his life and had freed him from the miseries of his childhood, exorcising bitterness and hatred. He no longer desired vengeance against Leonidas, no longer dreamed of leading an army against the Spartans. All he wanted now was to live with Derae and sire children of their love.

During the days he rode with Xenophon out into the countryside of the Peleponnese, and when the sun had fallen he ran on the hillsides, building his strength and exhausting his passions with physical effort.

At night he would sit with the Athenian general, discussing military tactics or political strategies. Xenophon was deeply distressed by Sparta's failure to provide sound leadership for Greece and gloomily predicted future disasters.

"Agisaleus cannot abide the Thebans and makes public his disdain. It is unwise. I love the man, but he is blind to the dangers. He cannot forget that it was Thebes' actions which brought him back from military successes in Persia. He cannot forgive."

"And yet," said Parmenion, "his return from Persia brought him great credit. He crushed the Thebans and restored Sparta's position."

"That is a popular Spartan view," Xenophon agreed, "but in reality the only victor was Persia."

"But they had no part in the revolt, did they?"

Xenophon laughed aloud. "Politics, Parmenion. Do not think merely of swords and campaigns. Agisaleus had invaded Persia, and he was winning. Persian gold—of which there is an unlimited supply—was sent to Thebes and Athens. With that gold they raised their armies; that is why Agisaleus was forced to come home. There was only one way he could win: He sent ambassadors to Persia, agreeing to be her vassal. Persia then abandoned Thebes and Athens and supervised the peace negotiations."

"Good strategy," said Parmenion. "No wonder the empire has ruled for so long. With a little gold, they halted an invasion."

"Better than that: the Greek cities of Asia were all given over to the Persians."

"I did not know that," Parmenion said.

"It is not taught to Spartan youngsters; it would be bad for morale. But it is a canker with Agisaleus. He knows he can never march on Persia again, for Thebes and Athens would rise against Sparta in his absence."

"Surely he could meet with their leaders. Then he could lead a joint expedition into Persia."

Xenophon nodded. "Exactly. But he never will. His hatred has blinded him. Do not misunderstand me, Parmenion. Agisaleus is a good king and a fine man, cultured and wise."

"I find it hard to understand," said Parmenion.

"Do you, now? Love and hate are very similar. Think of your own madness with Derae—did you take time to consider the perils? No. Agisaleus is the same. Mention Thebes and his face changes, and you can see his hand reaching for a sword hilt."

Servants brought them their evening meal of fish and cheese. They ate in silence for a while, but Xenophon's appetite was not good and he pushed away his plate, pouring a goblet of wine and adding a little water. He drank it swiftly and poured another.

"Perhaps Cleombrotus will make a difference," Parmenion suggested. The Spartans had always boasted two kings on the principle that one could lead the warriors into battle while the other stayed home and guided the fortunes of the city. Agisaleus had shared the kingship with his cousin, Agesopolis, but he was simpleminded and rarely appeared in public. Agesopolis' death four months before had seen the rise to power of Cleombrotus, a fine warrior and athlete.

"I doubt he will change the mind of Agisaleus," said Xenophon. "Cleombrotus is sound enough, but he lacks intellect. I fear for Sparta. *Those whom the gods would destroy, they first make proud*," he quoted.

"Surely pride is Sparta's great strength?" said Parmenion, watching with concern as Xenophon refilled his goblet without bothering to add water.

"Indeed it is, but do you know how many true Spartiates are left in the city? Fewer than two thousand. For the mess bills have risen, and the poorer Spartans can no longer afford to send their children. Think of yourself. Your mother had a good holding, but it has gone to pay for your education. It is nonsense. In ten years the number of Spartiates will halve again—how then will Sparta remain preeminent? And how long will it be before we see your strategy from the games used in reality?"

"Do not let it sadden you, Xenophon. None of it is within your power to change."

"That *is* what saddens me," the general admitted.

Not for the first time Tamis found her doubts growing. Events were moving swiftly now, and she sensed the power of the Dark God's acolytes seeking her, searching for a way to attack and destroy the one who could disrupt their plans.

But Tamis was not without power of her own, and she cloaked her soul, avoiding the spirit eyes of those who hunted, slipping by them like the unseen breeze that whispers through moonlit branches.

Learchus had died—killed by Parmenion. Tamis had not actively sought his death, though she knew part of the blame rested on her increasingly frail shoulders. All men die, she told herself. And was it not Learchus who had hidden in the alleyway ready to attack an unarmed boy? He had brought his doom upon himself.

Still the doubts nagged at her. Her prayers now were largely unanswered, and she felt alone against the servants of chaos. She could no longer summon Cassandra or any spirit of the past. The ways were no longer open to her. It is just a test, she assured herself. The source is still with me. I know it!

Surely it is better for a few to die out of their time than for many—for multitudes—to suffer?

How many times had she told herself this, repeating it like a spell against her fears? Too many, she realized. But I have gone too far to falter now.

When Learchus died, the Dark God's servants had turned

their eyes on Sparta, weaving their spells around the survivors
Nestus and Cleombrotus, watching over them. It was harder
now for Tamis to manipulate their emotions secretly, encour-
aging them to be reckless, to risk their lives.

Yet the watchers could not oversee everything, and Tamis
had waited patiently, ready to exploit even a momentary
lapse. Now it had come. The girl Derae had been publicly
denounced, her fiancé, Nestus, filled with righteous anger and
a truly Spartan lust for revenge. Only the death of the man
who had shamed him would satisfy his warrior's heart.

The watchers were furious, Tamis knew. She could feel
their anger and frustration like flames in the night. Tamis
opened the shutters of her single window and stared out over
the distant acropolis.

The first of many perils faced Parmenion now, and she was
unable to help him, just as the watchers were unable to protect Nestus. Now would be a time of swords, of strength, and
of skill. And the watchers were closing in. Soon they would
locate her, and then would come the onslaught, demons in the
night tearing at her soul or assassins in the daylight with sharp
blades to rip into frail flesh.

Turning, she gazed around the squalid room that had been
her home for so many lonely years. She would not miss it, or
Sparta, or even Greece, the home of her spirit.

Opening the door, she stepped out into the sunlight. "For
the moment, Parmenion," she said, "you are alone. Only your
own strength and courage can aid you now."

Leaning on a staff, a tattered gray cloak around her shoulders, Tamis walked slowly from Sparta. Not once did she look
back or allow a single moment of regret to touch her heart.

Back at the dwelling the temperature plummeted as a dark
shadow formed on the wall opposite the window, growing,
spreading, forming into the semitranslucent shape of a tall
woman, hooded and veiled in black.

For several moments she moved around the room, her spirit
eyes searching. Then the dark woman vanished . . .

. . . opening the eyes of her body in a palace across the sea. "I will find you, Tamis," she whispered, her voice low and cold. "I will bring you to despair."

Three days before the end of his stay in Olympia, Parmenion was surprised to see Hermias riding across the long meadow to the house. His friend usually journeyed south to the sea with his family for the hottest part of the summer, and their summer home was several hundred leagues from Olympia.

During the last year Parmenion had seen little of Hermias, for his friend had become close with the young king, Cleombrotus, and the two were often seen together in the city or riding in the Taygetus mountains.

Parmenion strode out to meet Hermias. He, too, had changed during their time at Menelaus, and at nineteen he was strikingly beautiful, with no trace yet of a beard. Once a fine runner, he no longer had the inclination to exercise hard and was rarely seen at the training ground. Hermias had grown his hair long, and Parmenion could smell the perfumed Persian oil that adorned it even before his friend jumped to the ground.

"Well met, Brother," shouted Parmenion, running forward to embrace him.

Hermias pulled back from the hug. "I have bad news, Savra. Nestus, believing the lies about you, is on his way here now. He means to kill you."

Parmenion sighed, turning to stare at the distant hills. "You must ride away," urged Hermias. "Do not be here when he comes. Tell me the truth of it, and I will try to convince him."

"The truth of it?" responded Parmenion. "What would you have me say? I love Derae. I want . . . need . . . her for my wife."

"I accept that," said Hermias, "but he believes that you ravished her. I know you would never consider such a vile act, but Nestus is blinded by rage. If you go to the hills for a while, I will speak to him."

"We made love," said Parmenion softly, "and we were

foolish. He has every right to be angry."

Hermias stood openmouthed. "You . . . it is true, then?"

"I did not ravish her! We are lovers, Hermias. Try to understand, my friend."

"What is there to understand? You behaved like . . . like the Macedonian you are." Parmenion stepped forward, reaching for his friend's arm. "Don't touch me! Nestus is a friend of mine and has been since we were children. Now he carries a shame he does not warrant. I know why you did it, Savra: it was to revenge yourself on Leonidas. I despise you for it. Take a horse and ride from here. Go anywhere. But do not be here when Nestus arrives."

Hermias strode to the gelding and vaulted to the beast's back. "I gave up much for you, Parmenion. Now I rue the day I met you. What you have done is evil, and much suffering will come of it. I loved you as a friend and a brother. But your hate was—and is—too strong."

"It is not hate," protested Parmenion, but Hermias swung the gelding's head and galloped away. "It is not hate!" shouted the Spartan. Standing thunderstruck as Hermias rode back across the meadow, Parmenion heard footsteps behind him but did not turn. Instead he watched his friend riding into the distance.

"That was sound advice," said Xenophon sadly. "Take the bay mare and ride for Corinth. I will give you enough money for the journey and a letter to a friend who resides there. He will be glad to make you a guest until you decide where you want to go."

"I cannot. It would mean giving up Derae."

"She is lost to you anyway."

"I will not accept that!" He swung on Xenophon. "How *can* I accept it?"

"Are you willing to die for your love?"

"Of course. What would you expect me to say?"

"And are you willing also to kill an innocent man for it?"

Parmenion took a deep breath, struggling for a calm that would not come. He did not know Nestus well, but the man had never been one of his enemies, had never tormented him. Now he was seeking—as any Spartan would—to exorcise his shame with the blood of the man who had dishonored him. He met Xenophon's eyes. "I cannot run, Xenophon. My life would be nothing without Derae. I know that now."

The general masked his disappointment. "How good are you with the sword?"

"Capable."

"And Nestus?"

"He was—and is—the sword champion of Lycurgus. He is powerful."

"Can you master him?"

Parmenion did not answer. "Am I evil?" he asked.

"No," answered Xenophon. "Action and reaction, my boy. I knew a man once in Persia who was asked to bring water to a dry area. He built a small dam that diverted a river, irrigating fields and saving a community. They were grateful, for he had given them life, and there were feasts and banquets in his honor. He stayed with them for several months. When he left, he came after five days to a deserted town where there were corpses and a dry stream. He had saved one community and destroyed another. Was he evil? Intention is everything. You did not set out to shame either Nestus or Derae, but now you must suffer the consequences. One of you must die."

"I do not want to kill him. I swear that by all the gods of Olympus," said Parmenion. "But, if I run, I can never claim Derae. You understand?"

"You may borrow my breastplate and helm, assuming that Nestus is geared for war. Oh, Parmenion, what has your folly brought upon you?"

Parmenion forced a smile. "It brought me Derae, and I cannot regret that—though I have lost Hermias, and he has been my friend since childhood."

"Come and eat. The body does not fight well on an empty stomach, believe me. Take honey; it will give you strength."

It was late afternoon before Nestus and his companions rode up to the house where Parmenion was sitting with Xenophon in the shadow cast by the sloping tiled roof. The Athenian rose, gestured for Parmenion to remain where he was, and walked out to meet the riders.

There were six men with Nestus but Xenophon knew only two of them: Leonidas and Hermias.

"Welcome to my home," said Xenophon.

"We seek the man Parmenion," stated Nestus, lifting his leg and jumping to the ground. He was a tall young man, broad-shouldered and lean-hipped—not unhandsome, though his beauty was marred by a hook of a nose.

Xenophon approached him. "Have the *ephors* granted permission for this duel?"

"They have," said Nestus. Reaching into his tunic, he produced a scroll and handed it to Xenophon. The Athenian opened it and read swiftly.

"Will honor be satisfied with anything but blood?" he asked, handing back the warrant.

"No. You know what he did. What choice do I have?"

"As a gentleman, none at all," said Xenophon softly. "But—and I speak not in his defense, nor even with his permission—he did not know of your involvement with the lady."

"She is no lady; she is a whore—made a whore by your half-breed houseguest."

Xenophon nodded. "Then blood it must be. However, let us act like gentlemen. You have ridden a long way, and you and your friends must be thirsty. My home is your home; I will have servants fetch refreshments."

"That will not be necessary, Athenian," snapped Nestus. "Just send Parmenion to me. I will kill him and we will be on our way."

Xenophon moved closer to the young man. "While I appreciate your anger," he whispered, "it ill becomes a gentleman to act with such rudeness."

Nestus looked into the pale blue eyes and saw the fury there. "You are correct, sir. My anger spoke, and it should not be directed at you. I thank you for your courtesy, and I am sure my friends would be glad of refreshment. For myself, with your permission, I will wait in your gardens until the time for the battle."

Xenophon bowed. "I will send cool water to you, unless you would prefer wine."

"Water will suffice." Nestus stalked off into the gardens. The other men dismounted and followed Xenophon into the house. No one looked at Parmenion, who sat silently with his eyes on Nestus seated alone on a bench by the stream.

After a few minutes Parmenion heard someone approaching from behind and looked up, expecting to see Xenophon.

"You nursed your hate well," said Leonidas, "and the arrow you sent found its mark."

Parmenion stood and faced his old enemy. "I do not hate you, Leonidas, or your family. I love Derae. What I did was wrong, and I am ashamed of my actions. But I mean to marry her."

For a moment Leonidas said nothing, his expression unreadable. "I love my sister," he said, "even though she is willful. But you are my enemy, Parmenion, and will remain so until the day of your death, which I pray will be today. You cannot stand against Nestus."

"Why must this go on?" Parmenion asked. "How can you carry this hatred when I will be wed to your sister?"

Leonidas reddened, and Parmenion saw not just anger but anguish in his eyes. "It would be unfair to speak of it now, before you fight. If you survive, then I will tell you."

"Tell me, and to Hades with fairness!"

Leonidas took a step forward, seizing the front of Parmenion's tunic. "Derae will soon be dead—can you understand that? My father had her named as Cassandra's victim, and even now she is on board a ship bound for Troy. When they get close to the shore, she will be hurled over the side. That is what you brought her to, half-breed! You killed her!"

The words cut into Parmenion like knives, and he reeled back from the blazing anger in Leonidas' eyes. Cassandra's victim! Every year a young unmarried woman was sent from Sparta as a sacrifice to the gods, to drown off the coast of Troy.

It was a penance for the murder of the priestess Cassandra after the Trojan War hundreds of years before. All major cities of Greece were obliged to send victims.

The girls were taken by ship to within a mile of the coastline of Asia, then their hands were tied behind their backs and they were thrown from the deck. There was no hope for Derae; even if she got her hands free and managed to swim to the shore, the local villagers would pursue and kill her. That was part of the ritual.

"Well, what have you to say?" hissed Leonidas, but Parmenion did not reply. He walked out into the sunshine and drew his sword, hefting it for weight. He could not answer his enemy: all feelings had vanished from him. He felt curiously light-headed and free of torment. They had taken from him the only light in his life, and he would not live in darkness again. Better for Nestus to kill him.

Xenophon approached him after a while and called Nestus to the flat ground before the house. "I have sent for the surgeon. I think it advisable to wait until he arrives before this battle commences."

"Doctors cannot help dead men," Nestus observed.

"Very true, but it is likely that the victor will also receive wounds. I would not want a second man to bleed to death."

"I do not wish to wait," declared Nestus. "Soon the sun will be down. Let us begin."

"I agree," said Parmenion. Xenophon looked at him closely.

"Very well. You both have swords, and the required number of witnesses are present. I suggest you salute one another and then begin."

Nestus drew his blade and glared at Parmenion. "There will be no salute to you, mix-blood."

"As you wish," Parmenion answered calmly. "But before we fight, I want you to know that I love Derae—even as you must."

"Love? What would you know of it? I shall remember her with great fondness, and I shall especially remember the moment when I told her father, in her presence, the price he would have to pay for my shame. She did not look pretty then, half-breed, not as she fell to her knees begging her father not to let her die."

"You asked for her death?"

"I demanded her death—as I demanded yours."

"Well," said Parmenion, feeling the heat of rising fury but holding it in check, "you had your way with her. Now let us see if you can fight as well as you can hate."

Nestus suddenly lunged. The sword of Leonidas flashed up, iron clashing on iron as Parmenion parried the thrust. Nestus slashed a backhand cut, but Parmenion blocked it.

The watchers spread out around the fighters. Xenophon had walked back to the shade of the roof, where he sat hunched forward with his chin on his hands, watching every move. Nestus, he saw, had the strength, but Parmenion was more swift. Their swords rang together, and for several minutes they circled, testing one another's skill. Then Parmenion's blade slashed down to open a shallow cut at the top of Nestus' right shoulder. Blood sprayed out, staining the young man's blue tunic. Xenophon rose and rejoined the watching group, who were cheering Nestus on and shouting advice. Nestus launched an attack, sending a stabbing lunge toward Parmenion's throat, but Parmenion sidestepped and lanced his blade into his opponent's side, the sword ripping the skin and glancing from his ribs. Grunting with pain, Nestus backed away. Blood was now flowing from two wounds, and the watching men fell silent. Parmenion feinted a cut to the head but dropped the blade down, hammering it into his opponent's left side. A rib snapped under the impact, and Nestus screamed in pain, only partly parrying a second lunge that opened the wound further. Blood now drenched his blue tunic and was coursing down his leg.

"Enough!" yelled Xenophon. "Stand back from each other!"

Both men ignored him. Stepping in close, Parmenion blocked a feeble thrust and plunged his sword into Nestus' belly. With a terrible cry Nestus dropped his blade and fell to his knees.

Parmenion wrenched his sword loose and looked down at his opponent. "Tell me," he hissed, "is this how Derae looked when *she* was upon her knees, begging for her life?"

Nestus was trying to stem the blood gushing from his belly. He looked up and saw Parmenion's eyes. "No . . . more," he pleaded.

"You came for death. You found it," said Parmenion.

"No!" shouted Xenophon as the sword of Leonidas rose and hacked down into the kneeling man's throat, severing the jugular and smashing the bones of the neck. Nestus rolled to his side.

Parmenion turned away from the corpse and focused his gaze on Leonidas. "Pick up his sword," urged Parmenion. "Come on! Take it and die like he did."

"You are a savage," said Leonidas, seeing the light of madness in Parmenion's eyes. The young Spartan strode forward and knelt by Nestus, rolling the man to his back and closing his eyes.

Xenophon took Parmenion's arm. "Come away now," said the general, his voice low. "Come away."

"Does no one else want to fight me?" shouted Parmenion. His eyes raked the group, but no one would meet his stare.

"Come away," urged Xenophon. "This is not seemly."

"Seemly?" Parmenion tore himself from Xenophon's grasp. "*Seemly?* They've killed Derae, and they've come to kill me. Where is seemly in all this?"

Xenophon turned to Leonidas. "There is a small wagon at the rear of the house—you may use it to return Nestus to his family. I suggest you leave now." He swung back to Parmenion. "Sheathe your sword; there will be no more fighting here. The battle warrant was issued, and it has been served. Further bloodshed will accomplish nothing."

"No," said Parmenion. "They came to kill me, so let them try. Let them try now."

"If you do not put away your sword and return to the house, the next person you fight will be me. Do I make myself clear to you?"

Parmenion blinked and opened his mouth to speak, but there were no words. He dropped the sword and strode to the house. Clearchus and Tinus were standing in the doorway, but they moved aside to let him pass. He sat in his room, his mind reeling. Derae was gone. At this moment she was alive somewhere out to sea, but in a matter of days she would be dead, and he would not know the hour of her passing.

The door opened, and Clearchus came in, carrying a bowl of water and a towel. "Better clean the blood off," advised the servant, "and change your tunic. What would you like for your supper?"

Parmenion shook his head. "Supper? I just killed a man. How can you ask me about supper?"

"I've killed a lot of men," said Clearchus. "What has that to do with food? He was alive. Now he's not. He was a fool; he should have listened to Xenophon and rested first. But he didn't. So . . . what would you like for supper?"

Parmenion rose and felt the tension slide from him as he looked into the old man's face. "You don't hate me, do you? Why is that? I know you did not like me when you were my judge at the games. Why is it you now befriend me?"

Clearchus met his gaze and grinned. "A man can change his mind, boy. Now, since you seem incapable of deciding what to eat, I shall prepare some fish in soured milk; it sits well on a queasy belly. Now bathe and change. You'll have a long ride tomorrow."

"Tomorrow? Where should I go tomorrow?"

"Corinth would be a good place to start, but I think Xenophon will send you to Thebes. He has a friend there, a man named Epaminondas. You'll like him."

"We have such dreams," said Xenophon as they walked together in the gardens under bright moonlight, "and sometimes I think the gods mock us. I wanted to conquer Persia, to lead a united army into the richest kingdom the world has ever seen. Instead I live like a retired gentleman. You wanted to find love and happiness; it has been taken from you. But you are young, Parmenion; you have time."

"Time? Without Derae nothing is worthwhile," answered Parmenion. "I know it deep inside my soul. She was the one. We were so close during those five days."

"I know this may sound callous, my friend, but perhaps your passion deceives you. You are not yet a worldly man, and it may be that you were merely infatuated. And there are many women in Thebes to make a man happy."

Parmenion gazed out over the man-made lake, watching the fragmented moon floating on the surface. "I shall not love again," he said. "I will never open my heart to the risk of so much pain. When my mother died, I felt lost and alone, but deep in my heart I had been expecting it and, I suppose, preparing for it. But Derae? It is as if a beast with terrible talons had reached inside me and ripped away my heart. I feel nothing. I have no dreams, no hopes. For a moment back there I was willing for Nestus to kill me. But then he told me he had ordered Derae's death."

"Not too clever of him, was it?" observed Xenophon dryly. Parmenion did not smile.

"When I killed Learchus that night, I felt a surge of joy. I gloried in his death. But today I killed a man who did not deserve to die, watched the light of life fade from his eyes. Worse, he begged me not to strike the death blow."

"He would have died in agony from the stomach wound," said Xenophon. "If anything, you ended his misery."

"That is not the point, is it?" asked Parmenion quietly, turning to face the silver-haired Athenian.

"No, it is not. You destroyed him, and it was not good to see. Also, you made enemies. No one who saw the duel will forget the way he died. But in Thebes you can make a new life. Epaminondas is a good man, and he will find a place for you."

Parmenion sank back on a marble seat. "Derae had a dream about me, but it was a false one. She dreamt she was in a temple and I came to her dressed as a general; she called me the Lion of Macedon."

"It has a good ring to it," said Xenophon, suddenly feeling the chill of the evening and shivering. "Let us go back to the house. I have some gifts for you."

Clearchus had set out the presents on a long table and Parmenion moved first to the bronze breastplate. It was simply made and not, as in more expensive pieces, shaped to represent the male chest. Yet it was strong and would withstand any sword thrust. At the center of the breast was a lion's head cast in iron. Parmenion glanced up at Xenophon. "Perhaps she was not so wrong," the Athenian whispered. Parmenion reached out and stroked his fingers across the lion's jaws. Beside the breastplate was a round helm, also of bronze and lined with leather. There were greaves, a bronze-studded leather kilt, and a short dagger with a curved blade.

"I do not know what to say," Parmenion told his friend.

"They were to have been a manhood gift. But now, I think, is a better time. There is something else which I hope will prove useful."

Xenophon lifted a leather-bound scroll and passed it to Parmenion, who opened the tiny buckles and spread the parchment. "It details my journeys across Persia and the march to the sea. I do not claim to be a great writer, but there is much that a soldier can learn from my notes, and many of my friends have asked me for copies of it."

"I will never be able to repay you for your kindness."

"Friends never need repaying; it is what makes them friends. Now prepare yourself for the journey. With luck the Spartans will forget about you as time passes."

Parmenion shook his head. "They will not forget, Xenophon. I will see to that."

"You are a man alone, and such thoughts are foolish. Sparta is the power in Greece and will remain so long past our lifetimes. Forget about vengeance, Parmenion. Even the might of Persia could not bring down Sparta."

"Of course you are correct," said the young man, embracing his friend.

But as the dawn was breaking and he rode from the estate, he thought of Derae's dream and of Thebes and the Spartan garrison there. A hostile force, hated and feared, dwelling at the center of a city of thirty thousand Thebans.

Drawing his sword, he gazed down at the gleaming blade. "I pledge you to the destruction of Sparta," he whispered. Raising the weapon high, he pointed it to the southeast, and though the city was far beyond his range of vision, he pictured the sword poised above it with the sun's harsh light turning it to fire.

"I carry the seeds of your hatred," he shouted, hurling his words to the winds, "and I know where to plant them."

Yes, he thought, Thebes is the right destination for the Lion of Macedon.

"I care nothing about omens," said the warrior, his voice shaking. "Let us gather an army and drive the cursed Spartans from the city."

The tall man at the window turned to the speaker and smiled. Allowing the silence to grow, his dark eyes raked the room. "We three," he said at last, "hold the hopes of our city in our hearts. We must not be rash." Ignoring the warrior, he locked his gaze to the sea-green eyes of the orator Calepios. "The Spartans seized Thebes because they *knew* we had not the force to oppose them. What we must consider is what *they* want from us."

"How do we do that?" Calepios asked.

"What they want is sharp swords in their bellies!" roared the warrior, surging to his feet.

The tall man moved swiftly to him, dropping his voice. "Why not get closer to the window, Pelopidas? For then you could let the whole city hear you!"

"I'm sick of this constant talk," Pelopidas replied, but he

lowered his voice. "It offends me that we allow the Spartans to strut around Thebes."

"You think you are the only man who finds it so?" the tall man asked him.

Their eyes met. "I am sorry, my friend," said the warrior, "but it knots my belly and clouds my mind. Speak on."

"We must decide what the Spartans desire—and do the opposite. But we must use stealth and cunning, and we must learn patience."

The tall man moved back to the window, staring out over the city and the hill upon which the Cadmea stood, its high walls patrolled by Spartan soldiers.

"It seems to me," said Calepios, "that the Spartans desire what they have always desired—conquest. They want to rule. Agisaleus hates Thebes. Now he has us."

"But does he have what he *wants*?" queried the tall man. "I think they are hoping we will rise against them and attack the Cadmea. If we do that, spilling Spartan blood, they will descend upon us with a full army. They will sack the city, maybe even destroy it. And we have no force with which to oppose them."

"There are other cities," said Pelopidas. "We could ask for help."

"Cities full of spies and loose mouths," snapped the tall man. "No, I suggest we organize ourselves. You, Pelopidas, should leave the city. Take to the open country. Gather to yourself warriors and move north, selling your services as mercenaries in Thessaly or Illyria or Macedonia—it does not matter where. Build a force. Prepare for the day when you are summoned back to Thebes."

"And what of me?" Calepios asked.

"The pro-Spartan councillors now lord it over the city. You must become part of their ruling elite."

"I will be hated by the people," the orator protested.

"No! You will never speak about the Spartans in public, neither to criticize nor to praise. You will devote yourself to working among Thebans, helping and advising. You will invite no Spartans to your home. Trust me, Calepios; we need a strong man at the center, and your abilities are respected by all. They will need you—even as we need you."

"And what of you, Epaminondas?" asked the warrior.

"I will stay in the city, and slowly I will gather supporters for the cause. But remember this: It is vital that the Spartans find no excuse to send an army into our lands—not until we are ready."

The door to the *andron* opened, and Calepios leapt from his seat as a servant entered and bowed.

"Sir," he said to the tall man, "there is a Spartan to see you."

"Do they know?" whispered Calepios, his face reddening.

"Is he alone?" Epaminondas asked.

"Yes, sir. He has a letter from the General Xenophon."

"Show him to the eastern room; I will see him there," said the tall man. "Wait here for a little," he told the others, "then leave by the rear alleys."

"Be careful, my friend," warned the warrior. "Without you we are nothing."

Epaminondas leaned back in his chair, his dark eyes fixed to the young man's face. "And how is the general?" he asked, his fingers drumming on the desk before him.

"He is well, sir. He sends you greetings, and I have a letter for you."

"Why did he send you to me, Parmenion? I am merely a private citizen in a city ruled by . . . others. I can offer you little."

The younger man nodded. "I understand that, sir. But Xenophon said you were a soldier of great skill. I think he hoped you would find me a place in the army of Thebes."

Epaminondas chuckled, but there was little humor in the sound. He stood and walked to the window, opening the shutters. "Look up there," he said, pointing to the citadel on the hill. "There is the Cadmea. It is garrisoned by Spartans like yourself; there are no Thebans there."

"I am no Spartan," replied Parmenion. "I was despised as a mix-blood, part Macedonian, but were I a Theban, I would be seeking a way to . . . persuade the Spartans to leave."

"Would you, now?" responded the Theban, a red flush spreading across his thin, pockmarked cheeks but his voice remaining cold. "There are few men who would attempt such an action. For myself, as I said, I am a private citizen and have little interest now in matters martial."

"Then I shall trouble you no further, sir," said Parmenion. Leaving the letter from Xenophon on the desk, he bowed and walked to the door.

"Wait, man!" called Epaminondas, not wishing his unwelcome visitor to see his other guests as they left. "You are a stranger in the city, and you can stay in my home until we can find suitable lodging for you. I will have a servant prepare you a room."

"That will not be necessary. I have no wish to remain where the welcome is so grudging."

"I see you are a plain speaker, so let me be equally frank. I have no great love for Spartans, be they friends of Xenophon or no. But you are a stranger in a strange city. Finding good lodgings will take time. I urge you to reconsider, and," he added, forcing a smile, "I will even apologize for my crusty behavior."

At the smile Parmenion appeared to relax. "I, too, must apologize. I am out of place here, and I feel awkward."

"We shall start again, then, Parmenion. Come, sit and take some wine while I read this letter."

Returning to his couch, the Theban unrolled the parchment and read of the duel with Nestus and the need for Parmenion to seek his fortune in another city. "Why did you fight this man, or is it a private matter?" he asked at last.

"He was betrothed to a girl. I, too, was in love with her."

"I see. What happened to her?"

"She was sacrificed as Cassandra's victim."

"What a barbarous people we are," said Epaminondas. "It amazes me how easily we criticize the peoples of other races, calling them barbarians, while still we practice obscene blood sacrifices."

"The gods require them," Parmenion said.

"There are no gods," responded the Theban. "It is all a grand nonsense, yet they have their uses."

"How can something that does not exist have a use?" asked the younger man.

The Theban smiled. "There are two doors leading from this room, Parmenion. If I told you that one door was guarded by a lion and that the other leads to a paradise, which door would you open?"

"The paradise door."

"Exactly. The lion does not exist, but it helps me make sure you open the door I require. It is very simple. Soldiers tend to believe in gods and oracles, but in my experience any prophecy can be turned to advantage."

Parmenion felt uneasy with this casual blasphemy and changed the subject. "Xenophon told me you once fought alongside the Spartan army."

"Three years ago. I was twenty-five then and a lot more naïve. Thebes and Sparta were allies against the Arcadians. I was given ten gold pieces by Agisaleus, who told me I fought well—for a Theban."

"The line broke," said Parmenion, "but you and Pelopidas locked shields and stopped their advance. When Pelopidas was struck down, wounded in seven places, you stood over his body and protected it until the Spartans came up to support you."

"You know a great deal about me," said Epaminondas, "while I know little about you. Was Xenophon your lover?"

"No, friends only. Is it important?"

Epaminondas spread his hands. "Only insofar as I must trust his judgment. He says you are a gifted *strategos*. Is he right?"

"Yes."

"Excellent, no false modesty. I cannot abide a man who

cloaks his talents." The Theban rose. "If you are not tired from your long ride, we will walk around the city and become acquainted with your new home."

Epaminondas led Parmenion through to the front of the house and out onto the wide main street heading south to Electra's Gates. Parmenion had ridden through those gates only an hour before, but now he stopped to examine the reliefs carved in the stone gateway. The figure of a man, hugely muscled, was shown attacking a beast with many heads. "Heracles' battle with the Hydra," said the Theban. "It was carved by Alcamenes. There is more of his work to the northwest."

Together the two men walked around the walls of Thebes, through the marketplaces, passing houses built of white marble and other smaller dwellings of sun-dried clay bricks painted white. Everywhere there were people, and Parmenion was struck by the variety of color in the clothing and in the decoration on house walls. The streets also were paved and decorated with mosaics, unlike the hard-packed earth of Sparta's roads. Parmenion stopped and stared at a woman sitting on a low wall. She wore a dress of red edged with gold, and silver pendants hung from her ears. Her lips were impossibly red, her hair a gold he had never seen.

She saw him and rose smoothly. "A gift for the goddess?" she inquired.

"What gift?" asked Parmenion. She giggled, and Epaminondas stepped in.

"He is a stranger to Thebes; doubtless he will give the gift on another day." Taking Parmenion's arm, he steered the young man away from the girl.

"What gift did she desire?"

"She is a priestess of the temple of Aphrodite, and she wanted to bed you. It would have cost forty obols. One obol goes to the temple, the rest to the priestess."

"Incredible!" whispered Parmenion.

They walked on and made their way slowly through the

crowds thronging the market stalls. "I have never seen so much waiting to be sold, so many trinkets and items of little value," remarked Parmenion.

"Little value?" replied Epaminondas. "They are pleasing to look at or to wear. There is value in that, surely. But then, I am forgetting you are a Spartan; you like to live in rooms with one chair made of sharp sticks and a bed with a mattress of thorns."

"Not quite," responded Parmenion, smiling. "We occasionally allow ourselves the treat of sleeping naked on a cold stone floor!"

"A Spartan with a sense of humor. No wonder you were unpopular with your fellows."

At last they came to the twin statues of Heracles and Athena, standing at the southern base of the Cadmea. They were shaped from white marble and were over twenty feet high. "Alcamenes' greatest achievement," said the Theban. "When you and I are dust and forgotten by history, men will marvel at his workmanship."

"They are so real, like frozen giants," said Parmenion, lowering his voice.

"If Athena did exist, I would think she would be pleased with his creation. It is said that the model was a priestess of Aphrodite, but then, with a body like that it is hardly surprising."

"I wish you wouldn't blaspheme," said Parmenion. "Have you ever considered the possibility that you might be wrong? The Spartans are very religious, and they have never lost a land battle where the foe had equal numbers."

"I like you, Parmenion, and I ask you to consider this: Sparta is the only city to retain a regular army, magnificently trained, superbly disciplined. Could that be the reason they win battles?"

"Perhaps it is both."

"Spoken like an ambassador," said the Theban with a broad smile. He led Parmenion to an open square where seats and tables had been placed beneath canvas awnings to block the sun. They sat at an empty table, and a young boy wandered over and bowed.

"Bring us some water and a few honey cakes," ordered Epaminondas. As they ate, he questioned Parmenion about his life in Sparta and the full story behind his departure. He listened in silence as the Spartan talked of his life and of his love for Derae.

"Falling in love is like gripping a sword by the blade," said the Theban. "You have it in your hand, but at great cost. We stopped sending victims for Cassandra more than thirty years ago. Athens abandoned the vile practice ten years since. It makes no sense."

"It placates the gods," said Parmenion with the ghost of a smile.

"I'll not worship any being who demands the blood of innocence," responded the Theban. He gazed up at the citadel on the acropolis; it was surrounded by a high wall on which Parmenion could see sentries walking. "So, young *strategos*, merely for the sake of debate, how would you retake the Cadmea if you were a Theban?"

"I would not bother. I would take the city."

"You would conquer Thebes in order to save it?"

"How many citizens live in or around this city? Twenty thousand? Thirty?" asked Parmenion.

"More, but I do not know the exact number," replied the Theban, leaning forward and lowering his voice.

"And how many Spartans in the garrison?"

"Eight hundred."

Parmenion lifted his goblet and drained his water. "Is there a well there?"

"No."

"Then I would encourage the citizens to rise up and besiege the Cadmea—starve the Spartans into submission."

"And what would happen when the Spartans drew their swords and opened the gates? There would be panic; the crowd would flee."

"If they *could* open the gates," Parmenion agreed. "But

what if they were secured from the outside? Then there would be no way out unless the soldiers lowered themselves by ropes. I don't think I can recall a battle where a phalanx advanced by dropping down on the enemy."

"Interesting," said Epaminondas, "merely as a theoretical strategy, of course. But I like you, young man, and I think it likely that we shall become friends. Now let us move on; there are many things to see."

"It is a wonderful city," said Parmenion later as the two men returned to Epaminondas' white-walled home. A servant brought them platters of cheese and bread, and they sat on a first-floor balcony, enjoying the cool of the shade below the towering Cadmea.

"You have not seen one-tenth of it," Epaminondas told him. "Originally the Cadmea was the city, and Thebes grew up around its base. Tomorrow we will see the theater, and I will show you the grave of Hector and the great north gate."

"With respect, I would sooner see the training ground. My muscles ache from the ride, and I would like to run."

"Then it shall be as you say."

That night Parmenion slept in a room at the top of the house, and a cool easterly wind blew in through the open window. He dreamed of an ancient temple with huge, broken columns. An old woman was there, lying on a pallet bed beside an altar; he took her hand and gazed down into her blind eyes. It was a curious dream, and he awoke in the depths of the night feeling calm and strangely refreshed.

Lying back, he thought of Nestus and the terrible fear in the man's eyes and remembered with sorrow the look on Hermias' face as he had swung around with the bloody sword in his hands. Hermias was his friend no longer; worse, Parmenion had seen in him the beginnings of hate.

Through all the years of his childhood Hermias had been his one ally, loyal and steadfast. It hurt the young Spartan that such a gulf should have come between them. But that is yet another price I must pay, he thought, to achieve my revenge.

Revenge. The word stirred in him like a living thing—writhing, growing, dissolving the memories of the dream and the calm that followed it. Revenge will be neither simple nor swift, he told himself. I must bide my time, learn the ways of this new city, seek out the rebels who hate the Spartans as I do. But I must act with care. His thoughts turned to Epaminondas. Here was a man to cultivate—a great warrior but also a thinker. Parmenion rose from the bed and drew the sword of Leonidas from its scabbard, the moonlight reflecting on the blade and turning it to silver. A longing began in him then to plunge the blade again and again into the hearts of his enemies, to see it dripping with their blood. Do I have the patience? he asked himself. How long can I wait?

Xenophon's words echoed in his mind: "The good general—if he has a choice—does not engage in battle until he is sure he can win, no more than a warrior will charge into the fight with a piece of iron ore. He will wait until the armorer has forged from it a blade with a killing edge."

Parmenion drew in a deep, calming breath and sheathed the sword. "You are right as always, Xenophon. And I miss you. I will bide my time." Returning to his bed, he dozed for a while, cascading images flowing through his mind: the general's games, his mother's death, Derae running on the training ground, Derae lying beneath him in the oak grove, Nestus dying, drowning in his own blood.

And he dreamed he was walking on a dark hillside beneath a crimson sky. A white tree was growing there, its trunk made up of gaping skulls obscenely wedged together. Swords and spears, gripped by skeletal hands, were its branches, and the fruits of the tree were severed heads, dripping blood to the ground. Where the gore touched the earth, dark flowers grew, the blooms in the shape of faces. A cold wind moaned across the flowers, and Parmenion seemed to hear a thousand distant whispers sighing, "Spare me! Spare me!"

A shadow moved upon the hillside, and the Spartan swung to see a hooded figure rise up before the tree. "What do you

*wish for, young warrior?" came a woman's voice from within
the hood.*

"Blood and vengeance," he replied.

"You shall have it," she told him.

Parmenion awoke to the dawn and joined Epaminondas on
the lower terrace for breakfast. The Theban was wearing a
simple tunic of gray-green that made his pale, pockmarked
face seem sallow and unhealthy. But his dark eyes were bright
and his smile open and friendly as Parmenion joined him.

"You mentioned a run, Parmenion. Are you an athlete?"

"I am fast and should have represented Sparta in the Olympics. But I made a mistake in the final race and was edged out
by Leonidas."

"Interesting. There is a man in Thebes who runs with great
speed. He is a Spartan from the citadel: his name is Meleager."

"I have heard of him. Leonidas beat him by ten paces a year
ago."

"You think you could beat him?"

Parmenion broke bread and dipped it into a bowl of onions,
soft cheese, and oil. "Unless he has grown wings."

"How much money do you have?" Epaminondas asked.

"I signed over my house to Xenophon, in return for which
he gave me a hundred and eighty drachmas and the bay mare.
It will not last long."

"Indeed it will not. Does Meleager know of you?"

Parmenion shrugged. "He will know of my name, but what
has this to do with the money I hold?"

"Here in Thebes we wager on races. If you could beat
Meleager—and no one else has—you could triple, perhaps
quadruple your money."

Parmenion leaned back in his chair. No one wagered in
Sparta; it was considered vulgar. But it would be a fine way
to extend his finances. At present he had barely enough
money to see him through to the spring. If he did quadruple
the amount, he would be able to eke out a careful existence for

at least two years. But what if you lose? he asked himself. Races were tough, the runners using elbows and shoulders to barge their way through. Then there was the danger of being tripped or falling. Nothing was certain in competition.

"I will think on it," said Parmenion.

The Iolaus training ground was bordered by oak trees to the north and west. To the east was the shrine to Artemis of the Glory, a high-columned temple dedicated to the goddess of the hunt, and to the south was the legendary grave of Hector, the mighty Trojan warrior slain by Achilles during the war with Troy.

As Parmenion stretched the muscles of his thighs and groin prior to his training run, he gazed at Hector's tomb. It was of marble, decorated with raised reliefs, carvings that showed his valiant battle with the Greek hero. Parmenion had always felt a great admiration for Hector. Most Spartans spoke of Achilles, for he was the victor, and yet it seemed to Parmenion that Hector had shown the greater courage. An oracle had warned Hector that to fight Achilles would mean death, for his opponent was invincible. During the ten-year Trojan War both men had studiously avoided single combat. And then, one bright morning, Hector had seen Achilles riding toward him in a bronze chariot, his armor—caught in the sunlight— seeming to blaze with white fire. The two men had met on the field of combat—and Hector won. He struck down Achilles with a terrible blow to the neck and watched his nemesis writhe in his death throes.

What a glory for Hector, what a weight lifted from his heart! Now he would see his baby son grow to manhood; now he would know again the peace that the oracle had stolen. He knelt by the body and tore the white-plumed helmet from the head—only to find himself gazing down on the dead face of Patroclus, Achilles' lover. Hector staggered back, shocked, confused. He ran to a Greek prisoner. "What is the meaning of this?" he demanded. "Why was Patroclus wearing Achilles' armor?"

The man could not meet Hector's fierce eyes but looked

down. "Achilles has decided to return home. He will fight no more," he said.

Oh, but he would. Hector knew that. In killing Patroclus he had hastened his own doom. Leaping into his chariot, he galloped his horses back into the city of Troy and waited for the challenge he knew must come.

Within the hour Achilles was at the gates. . . .

Parmenion finished his exercises and walked to the tomb, laying his hand upon it. "You went out to meet him, Hector," he said. "That was bravely done. And you died as a man should, facing his enemy."

The bones of Hector had been brought from the ruins of Troy and buried in Thebes because of another oracle that said, "Thebans in the city of Cadmos, your country shall have innocent wealth if you bring out of Asia the bones of Hector. Carry them home and worship the hero by the decree of Zeus."

The Thebans had obeyed. Every year, according to Epaminondas, they declared a holy day for Hector and a great celebration was held at the training ground, where men and women danced and drank in honor of the Trojan. And wealth had followed, in trade with Athens in the south and the exporting of goods north to Thessaly and Macedonia, to the Illyrians and the Thracians. Thebes was awash with coin.

Parmenion sucked in a deep breath and began to run. The track was hard-baked clay, formed in a great oval that skirted the training ground. Five circuits represented a mile. He loped easily around the circuit, examining the ground. The races all began and ended at the shrine to Artemis, so he stopped on the last curve before the finish and knelt to examine the track. Here it was more concave, the clay powdery on the surface. This was no surprise, for the runners would kick for home and over the years the track had taken more punishment here. A man could slip and fall at this point if he was not wary. He would need to come wide on this last bend . . . but then, so would Meleager.

Parmenion continued his run for almost an hour, increasing

his speed in short, lung-bursting sprints before dropping back to an even pace. Finally he jogged to where Epaminondas lay in the shade of a spreading oak.

"You run well," said the Theban, "but I saw no evidence of great speed. Meleager is faster."

Parmenion smiled. "I don't doubt that he is. But speed comes from strength, and the middle distance is a fine race for robbing a man of that. Will you wager on me?"

"Of course; you are my guest. It would be impolite not to do so. However, do not put all your money on yourself, Parmenion." The Spartan laughed.

"When can I race him?"

"There will be games in three weeks. I will put your name forward. What shall we call you?"

"I was known as Savra in Sparta."

"Lizard?" queried Epaminondas. "No, I don't think so. We need something Macedonian." He looked up, and there, through the trees, was the stone lion dedicated by Heracles. "There," said the Theban. "We will keep it simple and call you Leon. You run like a lion, with your short bursts of speed."

"Why not keep to Parmenion? This smacks of trickery."

"Smacks of? It *is* trickery, my friend. Or perhaps it would soothe our consciences if we called it strategy. You almost won a place in the Spartan team for the coming Olympics. If we let that be known, no one will bet against you . . . and then you will earn no money. As it is—if you win—the gold you gather will be mostly Spartan."

"I need money," Parmenion agreed, grinning.

"And there you have it," replied Epaminondas. "The victory of expediency over principles. And long may it remain so."

"You are very cynical," Parmenion observed.

The Theban nodded. "Indeed I am. But then, that is the lesson life teaches to those with eyes to see. No one is above price, be it money, or fame, or power."

"You think you have a price?"

"Of course. To free Thebes, I would sacrifice anything."

"There is no dishonor in that," argued Parmenion.

"If you truly believe that, then you have a lot to learn," the Theban answered.

During the weeks leading up to the race Parmenion had run hard for two hours every day, building strength and stamina. Now, with only a day left, he had eased up on his training, merely loping around the track, gently stretching his muscles. He had no wish to start the race feeling tired. As Lepidus used to say, "Never leave your strength on the training ground, gentlemen." Finishing his run, he bathed in the fountain by the shrine to Artemis. As usual he wandered through the city during the afternoon. Thebes continued to fascinate him with her complexity and color, and he was dazzled by the skills shown in her construction—she made Sparta seem like a collection of peasant houses thrown together during a storm.

The public buildings here were awesome, colossal pillars and beautiful statues, but even the private homes were well built, not of sun-dried brick but of stone shaped into polygons for close fitting. The windows were large, allowing greater light, and the inner walls were decorated with paintings or hangings of brightly colored wool. Even the poorer homes in the northern quarter were handsomely roofed with terra-cotta tiles and had skillfully carved shutters, while many courtyards boasted their own fountains.

His own home in Sparta had been modest, but not more so than many other dwellings: the floors of hard-packed earth, the walls of clay and rushes covered with lime mortar. But even Xenophon's home, which Parmenion had seen as splendid, had nothing to rival the house of Epaminondas. Every floor of the eight-room building was stone-studded, decorated with mosaics of white and black stone set in circles or squares. The main room, the *andron*, was split-leveled with seven couches for the guests. And there was a bathroom with a water cistern inside the house!

Thebes was quite simply the most exciting place Parmenion had ever seen.

Toward dusk he would find a table at one of the many

dining areas near the square and order a meal. Servants would carry food to him on flat wooden trays: a fresh loaf, a dish of soured cream, herbs and olive oil, followed by spiced fish. He would sit out under the starlight, ending his meal with sweet honey cakes and feeling as if the gods themselves had invited him to Olympus.

It was only later, when alone in his upper room, that memories of Derae would steal upon him, bringing pain and clutching at his heart. Then he would rise from his bed and stare balefully out over the sleeping city, his thoughts bitter. Dreams of revenge grew inside his soul, building slowly like a temple of hate within him.

They would pay.

Who will pay? asked a still small voice.

Parmenion pondered the thought. It was Leonidas who was his enemy, yet the whole of Parmenion's life had been scarred by rejection, by the hated use of "mix-blood." He had been welcomed nowhere save at the home of Xenophon. No one in Sparta had made him feel he belonged, not even Hermias.

They will all pay, he told himself: the whole city. There will come a day when the very name Parmenion will bring a wail of anguish from ten thousand throats.

And in this way Parmenion cloaked the hurt of Derae's death.

Epaminondas spent little time with Parmenion in the days before the race. Every evening he would visit friends in distant parts of the city, going out early and arriving home late. He was cool during this time, though not unfriendly, but Parmenion took to wandering the city, learning its roads and streets, orienting himself.

On most days he saw Spartan soldiers walking through the marketplaces or sitting at the dining areas. Their voices were loud and pompous, he felt, and the manner of the soldiers was arrogant. In his calmer moments Parmenion knew this was untrue; they were merely unwelcome strangers in a foreign city. But his hatred was growing now, and he could rarely look upon the soldiers without feeling its dread power.

On the night before the race Epaminondas invited him to the *andron*, and the two men reclined on couches and discussed the contest.

"Meleager likes to wait at the shoulder of the leader, then strike for home from a hundred paces," said the Theban.

"That suits me well," responded Parmenion.

"He has a friend who runs with him, dark-bearded, short. In three races, when it looked as if Meleager could be beaten, this man tripped and fell in front of the leader, bringing him down."

"Meleager should have been disqualified."

"Perhaps," Epaminondas agreed. "On the second occasion at least. But he is a Spartan, and Theban objections count for little. I have managed only odds of three to one. How much money will you wager?"

Parmenion had given great thought to the race. At four to one he could have afforded to hold back some coin. But now? He lifted the pouch from his belt and handed it to the Theban.

"I have one hundred and sixty-eight drachmas. Wager it all."

"Is that wise?"

Parmenion shrugged. "It would be nice to have choices. If I lose, I will sell the bay mare and seek employment in a mercenary company. If not? Then I will be able to hire rooms."

"You know you are welcome to stay with me."

"That is kind, but I will be a burden to no man."

The training ground was packed with people when the two men arrived early the following morning, and tiered seats had been set at the center of the field. Parmenion was restless as he waited for the races to begin. There was a boxing tourney first, but it was a sport that did not interest him, and he wandered to the grave of Hector and sat in the shade of an oak tree.

The middle race was new to the Greeks, and pride of place still went to the *stadia*, a sprint of two hundred paces. In many cities, Xenophon had told him, training groups did not have oval tracks and runners were forced to move up and down the *stadia* distance, turning around poles set in the earth. But the Persians loved the longer-distance races, and gradually they had caught the interest of spectators in Greece. Part of the appeal, Parmenion knew, was born of the wagers. If a man was to bet on a runner, then he liked to watch a longer race where his excitement could be extended.

For a while he dozed, then was woken by a roar from the crowd as the final boxing match ended with an earsplitting knockout. Parmenion rose and went in search of Epaminondas, finding the Theban at the northern end of the ground, watching the javelin throwers.

"It is a good day for running," said Epaminondas, pointing up at the sky. "The clouds will make it cooler. How do you feel?"

"There's some tightness in the neck," admitted Parmenion, "but I am ready." Epaminondas pointed to a spot some thirty paces away, where a tall, clean-shaven man was limbering up. "That is Meleager," he said, "and beyond him is his friend—I believe he is called Cletus."

Parmenion watched them closely. Meleager was stretching his hamstring by lifting his leg to a bench and bending forward. Then he eased the muscles on both sides of the groin. Cletus was loping up and down, swinging his arms over his head. Meleager, Parmenion saw, was tall and lean, ideally built for distance running. He watched the man for some time; his preparation was careful and exact, his concentration total.

"I think it is time you began your own preparations," said Epaminondas softly, and Parmenion came to with a jerk. He had been so engrossed with Meleager that he had almost forgotten he was to race him. He smiled guiltily and ran down to the start. Stripping off his *chiton* and sandals, he put himself through a short stretching routine, then ran gently for several minutes until he felt the stiffness leave his muscles.

The runners were called to the start by an elderly man with

a short-cropped white beard. Then, one by one, the twelve racers were introduced to the crowd. There were seven Thebans running, and they received the loudest cheers. Meleager and Cletus were given shouts of encouragement by a small Spartan contingent. But Leon, the Macedonian, was greeted only by polite applause.

Once more in line, the runners watched the starter. He raised his hand.

"Go!" he yelled. The Thebans were the first to sprint to the front, the line of runners drawing out behind them. Meleager settled down alongside Cletus in fourth place, Parmenion easing up behind them. The first five of the twenty laps saw no change in the leadership. Then Parmenion made his move. Coming smoothly on the outside, he ran to the front and increased the pace with a short punishing burst of half a lap, opening a gap of some fifteen paces between himself and the second man. At a bend he risked a glance behind him and saw Meleager closing on him. Parmenion held to a steady pace, then put in a second burst. His lungs were hot now, and his bare feet felt scorched by the baked clay. The clouds parted, brilliant sunshine bathing the runners. Sweat coursed down Parmenion's body. By lap eleven Meleager was still with him despite four bursts of speed that had carried Parmenion clear. Slowly, inexorably, the Spartan had reeled him back. Meleager did not panic. Twice more he pushed ahead; twice more Meleager came back at him.

Parmenion was beginning to suffer, but, he reasoned, so, too, was Meleager. On lap sixteen Parmenion produced another effort, holding the increased pace for almost three-quarters of a lap, and this time Meleager was left some twenty paces adrift. He had misread the surge and expected Parmenion to falter. Now he began to close the gap. By the nineteenth—and last—circuit Meleager was only six paces behind.

Parmenion dared not look back for it would break his stride pattern, and late in the race that could cost him. He was coming up now to the back markers, ready to lap them. Two were Thebans, but ahead he saw Cletus. The man kept glancing back, and Parmenion sensed what was coming. The Spartan would fall in front of him, dragging him down, or would block him as Meleager swept past.

He could hear panting breath just behind him, and as Parmenion closed on Cletus, he guessed Meleager's plan. The Spartan racer was trying to move alongside him, boxing him in and forcing him into the back of the man ahead. Anger swept through Parmenion, feeding strength to his limbs.

He injected more speed until he was just behind Cletus.

"Make way on the outside!" he yelled, and at the same moment he cut inside to his left. The Spartan tripped and fell to his right, crashing into Meleager. Both men tumbled to the ground, and Parmenion was clear, racing into the final lap. The crowd was on its feet now as he ran to the finishing line.

It didn't matter to them that he was Leon, an unknown Macedonian. What mattered was that two Spartans had rolled in the dust by his feet.

Epaminondas rushed to his side. "The first victory for the Lion of Macedon," he said.

And it seemed to Parmenion that a dark cloud obscured the sun.

Parmenion set out his winnings on the stone courtyard table, building columns of coin and staring at them with undisguised pleasure. There was 512 drachmas, a king's ransom to a Spartan who had never before seen such an amount in one place, let alone owned it.

There were five gold coins, each worth twenty-four drachmas. He hefted them, closing his fist around them, feeling the weight and the warmth that spread through the metal. The four hundred silver drachmas he had built into twenty columns like a miniature temple.

He was rich! Spreading the gold coins on the table, he stared down at the handsome, bearded head adorning each of them. They were Persian coins, showing the ruler Artaxerxes with a bow in his hand. On the reverse was a woman holding a sheaf of corn and a sword.

"Will you stare at them all day?" Epaminondas asked.

"Yes," replied Parmenion gleefully. "And tomorrow!"

The Theban chuckled. "You ran well, and I took great pleasure over the way you tricked Cletus. How they must be suffering now. Meleager will have beggared himself to settle his debts."

"I don't care about him," said Parmenion. "Now I can afford to rent a home and perhaps even hire a servant. And today I shall go to the marketplace and buy myself a cloak and several tunics—and a pair of fine sandals. And a bow. I must have a bow. And a hat! perhaps one of Thracian felt."

"I have rarely seen a man so happy with his fortune," Epaminondas told him.

"But then, have you ever been poor?" Parmenion countered.

"Happily that is a state I know little of."

The two men spent the afternoon in the main marketplace, where Parmenion bought a cloak of sky-blue wool, two tunics of fine linen, and a pair of calf-length sandals. He also allowed himself one extravagance—a headband of black leather, finely woven with gold wire.

Toward dusk, as they were making their way back to Epaminondas' house, the Theban suddenly cut off to the left down an alley. Parmenion touched his friend's sleeve. "Where are we going?"

"Home!" answered Epaminondas.

"Why this way?"

"I think we are being followed. Do not look back!" he snapped as Parmenion started to turn. "I do not want them to know we have spotted them."

"Why would we be followed?"

"I do not know. But when we turn the next corner—run!"

The alley twisted to the right, and as soon as they were out of sight, the two men ran along the path, cutting left and right through the narrow streets until they reached an alley at the back of Epaminondas' home. The Theban halted at the mouth of the alley and glanced out. Four men were sitting on a low wall at the rear of the house. They were armed with daggers and swords, whereas Parmenion and the Theban were without weapons. Swiftly the Theban ducked back out of sight.

Epaminondas took another circuitous route to the front of the house. Here, too, a group of armed men waited.

"What do we do?" queried Parmenion.

"We have two choices: either we brazen it out or we go elsewhere."

"Who are they?" the Spartan asked.

"Scum, by the look of them. If I had my sword, I would not hesitate to confront them. But who do they want? You or me?" Epaminondas leaned against a wall. There were only two reasons why the men could be waiting. One, the authorities had found out about the small group of rebels who met at the home of Polysperchon; two, Meleager had learned of Parmenion's true identity and had paid these rogues to exact revenge. Neither thought was comforting, but on the whole Epaminondas hoped it was the latter.

"Show me more routes to the house," said Parmenion softly.

"For what reason?"

The Spartan grinned. "So that I can lead them on a chase. Trust me, Epaminondas. Much of my early life was spent in this way, being hunted, chased, beaten. But not this time, my friend. Now show me the alleys and back roads."

For almost an hour the two men wandered through the twisting alleys between the houses until Parmenion had memorized various landmarks. Then they returned to the opening at the rear of the house.

"Wait here," said Parmenion, "until they have left. Then you can get your sword. And mine, too."

The Spartan ran back into the maze of buildings, emerging

from an alley some forty paces to the left of the waiting group. One of them looked up and nudged the man beside him. The group stood.

"Are you the man Parmenion?" asked a stocky, redheaded warrior.

"Indeed I am."

"Take him!" the man yelled, drawing a sword and rushing forward.

Parmenion turned on his heel and sprinted for the alley, the four attackers in pursuit. Epaminondas darted across the open ground to the rear of the house and hammered on the door. A servant opened it, and the Theban moved through to the *andron*, gathering up his sword. He sent the servant to Parmenion's room to fetch the sword of Leonidas and, armed with two blades, ran back toward the street.

"Where are you going, master?" called the servant fearfully.

Epaminondas ignored him.

All was quiet at the rear of the house, and Epaminondas waited, his mind calm, his body ready. There would be little point in entering the maze of alleys; better to wait until Parmenion brought the pursuers to him. Finding his mouth to be dry, he allowed himself a wry smile. It was always this way before a battle: a dry mouth and a full bladder. Then he heard the pounding of feet and saw Parmenion race into view with the four men just behind him. The young Spartan sprinted forward, holding out his hand. Epaminondas tossed him his sword; Parmenion caught it deftly and swung to face the attackers.

The men halted their charge and stood back, uncertain.

"We have no quarrel with you," the red-bearded leader told Epaminondas. The Theban cast his eyes over the man, taking in his grease-stained tunic and his matted beard. The man's forearms were crisscrossed with scars.

"You have been a soldier, I see," said Epaminondas. "You have fallen a long way since then."

The man reddened. "I fought for Thebes—precious good it

did me. Now stand aside, Epaminondas, and let us deal with the trickster."

"In what way have you been tricked?" Epaminondas asked.

"He ran under the name Leon when in fact he is the Spartan racer Parmenion."

"Did you lose money?" asked the Theban.

"No, I had no money to bet. But now I have been paid, and I will honor the agreement. Stand aside!"

"I think not," said the Theban. "And it is an ill day when a Theban soldier takes blood money from a Spartan."

"Needs must," shrugged the man, and suddenly he ran forward with sword raised. Parmenion moved in to meet him, blocking the blow and hammering his left fist into his attacker's face. His opponent staggered back. Parmenion leapt into the air, his right foot cracking into the man's nose and hurling him from his feet. The other three men remained where they were as the red-bearded leader snatched up his fallen sword and rose unsteadily.

"There is no reason for you to die," Parmenion told him.

"I took the money," said the man wearily, and moved in to attack once more, stabbing out his sword for a belly lunge. Parmenion blocked it with ease, his left fist lancing into the man's jaw and dropping him to the ground.

Epaminondas suddenly charged at the other three men, who broke and ran. Parmenion knelt by his unconscious opponent. "Help me get him inside," he told Epaminondas.

"Why?"

"I like him."

"This is insane," said Epaminondas, but together they hauled the body back into the house, laying him on one of the seven couches in the *andron*.

A servant brought wine and water, and the two men waited for the red-bearded man to come round. After several minutes he stirred.

"Why did you not kill me?" he asked, sitting up.

"I need a servant," Parmenion answered.

The man's green eyes narrowed. "Is this some jest?"

"Not at all," the Spartan assured him. "I will pay five obols a day, the payment to be made every month. You will also have a room and food."

"This is madness," said Epaminondas. "The man came to kill you."

"He took money, and he tried to earn it. I like that," said Parmenion. "How much were you paid?"

"Ten drachmas," the man answered.

Parmenion opened the pouch at his side and counted out thirty-five silver drachmas. "Will you become my servant?" he asked. The man gazed down at the coins on the table; he swallowed, then nodded. "And what is your name?"

"Mothac. And your friend is right—this *is* madness."

Parmenion smiled and scooped up the coins, handing them to Mothac. "You will return the ten drachmas to the man who hired you; the rest is your first month's pay. Get a bath and buy a new tunic. Then gather what possessions you have and return here tonight."

"You trust me to return? Why?"

"The answer is not difficult. Any man prepared to die for ten drachmas ought to be prepared to live for twenty-five a month."

Mothac said nothing. Turning on his heel, he left the room.

"You will never see him again," said Epaminondas, shaking his head.

"Would you care to wager on that?"

"I take it the wager is thirty-five drachmas. Correct?"

"Correct. Is it acceptable?"

"No," conceded Epaminondas. "I bow to your obviously superior understanding of the human species. But he will make a terrible servant. Tell me, why did you do this?"

"He is not as those others. They were cowardly scum; he at least was prepared to fight. But more than that, when he knew he could not win, he came forward to die rather than take money falsely. That sort of man is rare."

"We must agree to differ," said Epaminondas. "Men who would kill for ten drachmas are not rare enough."

* * *

The man called Mothac left the house. He felt dizzy and nauseous, but anger gave him the strength to keep going. He had not eaten in five days and knew this was the reason the Spartan had defeated him so easily. Give back the ten drachmas? He had paid that to the doctor for the drugs that would nurse Elea back to strength. He wandered into an alley and leaned against a wall, trying to summon up the energy to return home. His legs started to give way, but he grabbed a jutting stone on the wall and hauled himself upright.

"Don't give in!" he told himself. Drawing in a great breath, he started to walk. It took almost half an hour to reach the marketplace, where he purchased fruit and dried fish. He sat in the shade and ate, feeling strength soaking into his limbs.

The Spartan was a fool if he expected him to come back. "I will be no man's servant. Not ever!"

He felt better for the food and pushed himself to his feet. The Spartan had shamed him, making him look weak and foolish. Three miserable blows and he had fallen. That was hard to take for a man who had stood against Arcadians and Thessalians, Chalcideans and Spartans. No man had ever laid him low. But lack of food and rest had conspired to see him humbled.

Still, now he had thirty-four drachmas and three obols and with that he could buy food for two months. Surely in that time Elea would recover. Returning to the marketplace, he bought provisions and began the long walk home, deep into the northern quarter where the houses were built of sun-dried brick, the floors of hard-packed earth. The stench of sewage flowing in the streets had long since ceased to cause him concern along with the rats that ran across his path.

You've come down a long way, he told himself, not for the first time.

Mothac. The name had sprung to his lips with an ease he found surprising. It was an old word from the gray dawn of time. Outcast. It is what you are. It is what you have become.

He turned into the last alley beneath the wall and entered

his tiny house. Elea was in the bedroom asleep, her face calm. He glanced in and then unwrapped the food, preparing a platter with pomegranates and sweet honey cakes.

As he worked he pictured her smile, remembering the first day he had seen her, during the dance to Hector. She had been wearing a white *chiton*, ankle-length, her honey-colored hair held by an ivory comb. He had been smitten in that moment, unable to drag his eyes from her.

Six weeks later they were wed.

But then the Spartans had taken the Cadmea and pro-Spartan councillors controlled the city. Her family had been arrested and sentenced to death for treason, their estates confiscated. Mothac himself had been named as a wanted man and had sought the refuge of anonymity in the poor quarter of the city. He had grown his beard thick and changed his name.

With no money and no hope of employment, Mothac had planned to leave Thebes and join a mercenary company. But then Elea had fallen sick. The doctor diagnosed lung fever and bled her regularly, but it seemed only to make her grow weaker.

He carried the platter into her room and laid it beside the bed. He touched her shoulder . . . she did not move.

"Oh, blessed Hera, no!" he whispered, turning her onto her back. Elea was dead.

Mothac took her hand and sat with her until the sun set, then stood and left the house. He walked through the city until he reached the main square, his eyes unseeing, his thoughts random, unconnected. A man grabbed his arm. "What happened, my friend? We thought they had killed you."

Mothac pulled clear of his grip. "Killed me? I wish they had. Leave me alone."

He walked on down long avenues, through winding streets and alleyways, with no thought of a destination, until at last he stood before the house of Epaminondas.

With nowhere else to go, he strode up to the wide doors and rapped his fist on the wood.

A servant led him to the Spartan, who was sitting in the courtyard drinking watered wine. Mothac forced himself to bow to his new master. The man looked at him closely, his clear blue eyes seeming to gaze into Mothac's soul.

"What is wrong?" the Spartan asked.

"Nothing . . . sir," replied the Theban. "I am here. What do you require of me?" His voice was dull and lifeless.

The Spartan poured a goblet of wine and passed it to Mothac. "Sit down and drink this."

Mothac dropped to the bench and drained the wine at a single swallow, feeling its warmth spreading through him.

"Talk to me," said the Spartan.

But Mothac had no words. He dipped his head, and the tears fell to his cheeks, running into his beard.

Mothac could not bring himself to speak of Elea, but he would long remember that the Spartan did not force questions upon him. He waited until Mothac's silent tears had passed, then called for food and more wine. They sat together, drinking in silence, until Mothac became drunk. Then the Spartan had led his new servant to a bedroom at the rear of the building, and here he had left him.

With the dawn Mothac awoke. A new *chiton* of green linen was laid out on a chair; he rose, washed, and dressed, then sought out Parmenion. The Spartan, he was told by another servant, had gone to the training ground to run. Mothac followed him there and sat by the grave of Hector watching his new master lope effortlessly around the long circuit. The man moved well, thought Mothac, his feet scarcely seeming to make contact with the earth.

For more than an hour Parmenion continued to run, until sweat bathed his body and his calf muscles burned with fatigue. Then he slowed and jogged to the grave, waving to Mothac and smiling broadly.

"You slept well?" he asked.

Mothac nodded. "It was a good bed, and there is nothing like wine for bringing a man sweet dreams."

"Were they sweet?" asked Parmenion softly.

"No. You are a fine runner. I never saw better."

Parmenion smiled. "There will be a better man somewhere; there always is." He began to ease his way through more stretching exercises, pulling gently at the muscles of his calves by leaning forward against the stone of the grave.

"Are you going to run again?" Mothac asked.

"No."

"Then why are you exercising?"

"The muscles are tight from the run. If they are not stretched, they will cramp; then I would not be able to run tomorrow. I was pleased to see no assailants waiting this morning," he added, changing the subject.

"They will be back," said Mothac. "There are people determined to see you dead."

"I do not think I will ever be an easy man to kill," answered Parmenion, stretching out on the grass. "But that could be arrogance speaking."

"You have not asked me who hired me to kill you," said Mothac.

"Would you tell me?"

"No."

"That is why I did not ask."

"Also," added the red-bearded servant, turning his head away, "you had the good grace not to question my tears. For that I thank you."

"We all carry grief, my friend. Someone once told me that all the seas are but the tears of time, shed for the loss of loved ones. It may not be true, but I like the sentiment. I am glad you came back."

Mothac smiled ruefully. "I am not sure why I did. I had not intended to."

"The reason does not matter. Come, let's get back and enjoy breakfast."

As they reached the last corner, Parmenion held out his arm, stopping Mothac. Leaning out, the Spartan peered down the street. Once more there were armed men at the front of the house, and Parmenion's lips thinned as anger swept over him, but he crushed the rising fury and took a deep breath. "Go out to them," he told Mothac, "and explain that you have just seen me running at the training ground and that no one else was around. It will not be a lie, after all."

The red-bearded Theban nodded and then ran out to the waiting men. Parmenion ducked down behind a low wall and waited as they pounded past him; then he rose and walked to where Mothac waited.

"Let us eat," said Parmenion.

Epaminondas had left the house the night before but had not yet returned. His servants were unable or unwilling to say where he had gone, so Parmenion and Mothac sat down to breakfast without waiting for the master of the house.

"Should I not be with them?" asked Mothac as the servants brought food from the kitchens.

"Not yet," answered Parmenion. "We should get to know one another. Have you ever been a servant?"

"No," Mothac admitted.

"And I have never had one."

Mothac chuckled suddenly and shook his head.

"What is amusing you?" asked Parmenion.

The Theban shrugged. "I had servants once. I can probably instruct you in how to care for them."

Parmenion smiled broadly. "I could do with instruction. I have very few belongings, so caring for my clothes will not strain you. My diet is . . . Spartan? My needs are few. But I do need someone I can trust and someone I can talk to. So let us begin by giving you a better title—you will be my companion. How does that sound?"

"I have been in your service only one day and already I am promoted. I see the prospects are good with you. But will you allow me one more day before I join you? There is something I must finish."

"Of course." Parmenion looked at him closely. "Is this . . . business . . . something I can help you with?"

"No. I will settle it."

The two men finished their breakfast, and Mothac left the house and walked back to the main square and onto the Lane of the Dead. He paid twelve drachmas to an elderly man and gave him directions to his home.

"I will be there at sunset," he told the undertaker. "Make sure the mourners wail loudly."

"They are the best," the man promised him.

Mothac returned home and changed into an old *chiton*: it had once been red but had faded to the pink of a dawn sky. He waited for an hour before the women arrived. There were three of them, all dressed in mourning gray. He left them to prepare Elea, then strapped on his sword belt and dagger and strolled back to the square.

Elea was gone. Nothing could bring her back now, but he hoped she would find happiness on the other side, reunited with her parents. But he would miss her and would never forget her. Some men, he knew, married several times when their wives died. But not Mothac.

Never again, he decided, as he sat waiting for the night. When I travel to the other side, it will be to find Elea and to enjoy eternity beside her.

The sun sank in splendor, and the stars illuminated the sky. Torches were lit and placed in brackets set on the walls. Lanterns were hung from ropes, and servants began to carry tables out into the square, ready for the diners. Mothac stood and faded back into the shadows, waiting patiently. The hours passed, and it was approaching midnight before the Spartan, Cletus, made his way to a table and sat down to eat. Mothac knew the cause of Cletus' hatred of Parmenion. The racer Meleager had been unable to settle all his debts and had been sent home in disgrace. Without Meleager to help him, Cletus would soon run short of money and be forced to give up the life of pleasure he now enjoyed.

All Cletus now wanted—desired above all else—was to

revenge himself on the Spartan traitor who had tricked them.

Mothac could understand his desire for revenge.

He waited until the Spartan had finished his meal, then followed him on the long walk to the Cadmea steps. As the Spartan began to climb the winding path, Mothac glanced around. There was no one in sight. Softly he called Cletus by name and then ran up alongside him.

"Have you good news for me, man?" the Spartan asked.

"No," answered Mothac, ramming his dagger into the man's neck, driving it deep above the collarbone. Cletus fell back, scrabbling for his sword. Mothac struck him viciously in the face, then wrenched his knife clear, severing the jugular. Blood spouted from the wound, but still Cletus tried to attack, swinging his sword desperately. Mothac leapt back. The Spartan fell and began to writhe in his death throes.

Mothac ran from the pathway and back to his home, removing his bloodstained *chiton* and washing himself clean. Dressed once more in the new tunic bought for him by Parmenion, he returned to the house of Epaminondas.

It would not take long for the hired killers to find out that their paymaster was dead.

When he entered the house, he found Parmenion lounging on a couch in the *andron*.

The Spartan looked up at him. "You concluded your business?"

"I did . . . sir."

"To your satisfaction?"

"I would not call it satisfaction, sir. Merely a necessary chore."

When Epaminondas brought the news of Cletus' murder to Parmenion, the Theban seemed genuinely distressed by the killing.

"I thought you had no love for Spartans," said Parmenion as they strolled through the gardens at the base of the great statue to Heracles.

Epaminondas glanced around. There were few people in

the gardens, and none within earshot. "No, I have not, but that is not the issue. I trust you, Parmenion, but there are plans in progress that must not be thwarted. The Spartan officer commanding the Cadmea has called for an investigation. He is also said to be requesting more troops from Sparta, for he fears the murder may be the opening move in a revolt."

"Which it was not," said Parmenion, "for if it was, you would know of it."

Epaminondas looked at him sharply, and a blush spread over his pockmarked features. Then he smiled. "You have a keen mind; thankfully it is allied to a curbed tongue. Yes, I am one who seeks to free Thebes. But it will take time, and when it is close, I will seek your advice. I have not forgotten the plan you outlined."

They halted by a fountain that spouted from the arms of a statue of Poseidon, the sea god. Parmenion drank from the pool below it, then both men sat on a marble seat beneath a canvas awning.

"You must be more careful," advised Parmenion. "Even the servants know you are engaged in secret meetings."

"My servants can be trusted, but I take your point. I have no choice, however. We must meet to plan."

"Then meet in daylight," Parmenion suggested.

The two friends walked back along the avenue by Electra's Gates, but Epaminondas, instead of walking on to his house, turned left down a shaded alley, stopping by an iron gate. He pushed it open and beckoned Parmenion inside. There was a narrow courtyard with high walls festooned with purple blooms. Beyond this was a paved section, roofed by climbing plants growing between crisscrossed twine. Epaminondas led the Spartan into the house beyond. There was a small split-level *andron* containing six couches and with two doors, one leading to a kitchen and bathroom, the other to a corridor with three bedrooms.

"Whose house is this?" asked Parmenion.

"Yours," the Theban answered with a broad grin. "I placed

three thousand drachmas on your race. This house was a mere nine hundred. I felt it would suit you."

"Indeed it does, but such a gift? I cannot accept it."

"Of course you can—and you must. I won ten times what this building cost me. Also," he added, his smile fading, "these are dangerous times. If I am arrested and you are still my houseguest, then they will take you also."

Parmenion lounged on a couch, enjoying the breeze from the main window and the scent of flowers growing in the courtyard. "I accept," he said, "but only as a loan. You must allow me to pay for the house as and when I can."

"If that is what you desire, then I agree," said Epaminondas.

Parmenion and Mothac moved in the following morning. The Theban bought provisions in the market, and the two men sat in the courtyard, enjoying the early morning sunshine.

"Were you seen when you killed Cletus?" asked Parmenion suddenly.

Mothac looked into his master's blue eyes and considered lying. Then he shook his head. "There was no one nearby."

"Good, but you will never again take such an action without speaking to me first. Is that understood?"

"Yes . . . sir."

"And I do not require you to call me that. My name is Parmenion."

"It was necessary, Parmenion. He ordered your death. As long as he lived, you were in danger."

"I accept that, and do not take my criticism as ingratitude. But I am the master of my own fate. I neither want nor expect any man to act for me."

"It will not happen again."

During the next eight months Parmenion raced twice and won both times, once against the Corinthian champion, the second time against a runner from Athens. He still competed under the name Leon, and few wagered against him, which meant that his winnings were not huge. For his last race he had wagered two hundred drachmas to win fifty.

That night, as usual after a tough race, Parmenion stretched his tired legs with a gentle midnight run on the moonlit racetrack. As well as easing his muscles, he found in this quiet time a sense of peace, almost contentment. His hatred of Sparta was no less powerful now, but it was controlled, held in chains. The day of his vengeance was coming closer, and he had no wish to hurry it.

As he passed the grave of Hector, a shadow moved from the trees. Parmenion leapt back, his hand clawing for the dagger in the sheath by his side.

"It is I, Parmenion," called Epaminondas. The Theban stepped back into the shadows of the trees. Parmenion walked to the grave and sat down on the marble seat.

"What is wrong, my friend?" he whispered.

"I am being followed again, though for now I have lost them. I know you come here after races, and I need your help."

"What can I do?"

"It is only a matter of time before I am taken. I want you to prepare a strategy to retake the Cadmea. But also there are letters I need carried to friends in other Boeotian cities. You are Spartan; you can travel without scrutiny. You have business interests across Boeotia. No one will think it strange if you travel to Thespiae or Megara. Will you help?"

"You know that I will. You must bring the letters here, wrapped in oilskin. You can leave them behind this seat, covered with stones. No one will see them. I run here almost every day. I will find them."

"You are a good friend, Parmenion. I will not forget this." Epaminondas faded back into the shadows and was gone.

Eleven times during the next four months Parmenion rode across Boeotia, carrying letters to rebels in Tanagra, Plataea, Thespiae, and Heraclea. During this time he saw little of Epaminondas but heard, through Mothac, of increasing unrest among Thebans. In late summer two Spartan soldiers were stoned by a mob close to the marketplace and were rescued only when a contingent of armored warriors ran to their aid from the Cadmea.

The crowd backed away as the soldiers arrived, but the mood was still ugly. Drawing their swords, the Spartans charged the mob, their blades slicing into those unfortunates at the front. Blind panic overtook the Thebans, and they scattered in terror. Parmenion, at the marketplace to purchase new sandals, saw women and children trampled as the crowd fled. One young woman tripped and fell directly in front of the advancing Spartan line. Sprinting from the shop doorway, Parmenion hauled the woman to her feet and carried her back to the relative safety of the shop. Two Spartan soldiers ran after him.

"I am a Spartan," said Parmenion as their swords came up. Blood was dripping from the blades and battle lust shone in the eyes of the warriors, but Parmenion stood his ground, meeting their gaze.

"What statue overlooks Leaving Street?" asked one of the soldiers, touching his bloodied blade to Parmenion's chest.

"The statue of Athena," he answered, pushing aside the sword. "Now ask me how many bricks there are in the Cattle Price Palace."

"You keep bad company," the soldier said. "Make sure you know where your loyalties lie."

"I know where they lie, Brother, have no fear of that."

The soldiers ran back to the street, and Parmenion turned to the woman. Her lips were stained blood-red, her eyelids painted in the three colors of Aphrodite: red, blue, and gold. "You are a priestess?" he asked.

"No, I am a shepherd boy," she snapped.

"I am sorry. It was a foolish question."

Stepping forward, she pressed herself against him. "Do not be sorry. For forty obols I can make you very happy." Her hand slid under his tunic, but he pushed her away and left the shop. Bodies lay in the street, but the troops had moved on.

That night he thought again of the priestess, of her warm

hand on his thigh. As the moon rose high over the city, he made his way to the temple, finally finding her in a small room on the second floor. She smiled wearily when she saw him and was about to speak when his hand came up and gently touched her lips.

"Say nothing," he said coldly. "I require your body, not your voice."

As the months passed he made many visits to the young priestess with the red hair. But his passions were soon spent, and usually he left feeling sad and ashamed. It seemed to him that sex with any woman was a betrayal of the love he had known with Derae. Yet he returned week after week to the redhead, whose name he never bothered to ask.

His money dwindled as the odds on his races shortened, but at the start of his third year in Thebes he won against a Thessalian named Coranus, the middle-race victor of the Olympic Games, where he had narrowly beaten Leonidas of Sparta. The odds against Parmenion were five to one, and he wagered all he had. The race was close, Parmenion finishing a mere arm's length in front of the Thessalian, and then only because his opponent stumbled in the powdery dust at the last bend. It was a lesson well learned. Never again would he wager everything on a single gamble.

Two days later came the news Parmenion had feared for almost three years. Mothac ran into the courtyard. "Epaminondas has been arrested, along with Polysperchon. They have been taken to the Cadmea for torture."

BOOK TWO

ORDERING Mothac to stay at the house, Parmenion headed for the west of the city and the home of the councillor Calepios. An elderly servant led him to a small room with three couches and asked him to wait. After several minutes another servant entered, bowed, and led the Spartan along a corridor to an elaborately decorated *andron*, the walls covered with Persian rugs and hangings, the floor boasting a colorful mosaic showing Heracles slaying the Nemean lion.

There were nine couches set around the room, and two servants stood by, holding pitchers of wine and water, as the master of the house reclined, apparently reading from a large scroll. Calepios looked up as Parmenion entered and adopted the expression of a man pleasantly surprised to see an old friend. Parmenion was not fooled by the scene; there was tension in the air, and Calepios' eyes showed fear.

"Welcome to my house, young Leon," said the councillor, tossing aside the scroll and rising. He was not a tall man, yet he was imposing in a subtle way. His eyes were deep green under shaggy brows, and his beard was carefully curled in the Persian fashion. But it was his voice that gave him power, deep and vibrant. "To what do I owe this pleasure?"

"May we talk alone?" asked Parmenion.

"We are alone," said Calepios, unconsciously betraying his noble birth. For him, servants were as much a part of the house as tables and couches.

Parmenion flicked a glance at the wine carriers, and Calepios waved the men away. As the doors closed, the councillor beckoned Parmenion to the couch beside him, and both men sat.

"How close are your plans to fruition?" asked Parmenion.

"Plans, my boy? What do you mean?"

"We have little time, sir, for playing games. Polysperchon and Epaminondas have been arrested. But then, you know this. You are gambling that they will say nothing of your involvement in the plan to retake the Cadmea. Now I ask again, how close are you?"

Calepios' green eyes locked to Parmenion's face, and his own features tightened. "Epaminondas trusted you," he said softly, "but there is no way I can help you. I don't know what you are talking about."

Parmenion smiled. "Then perhaps the man who was with you a moment ago can offer us some advice." He turned his head and looked back over his shoulder to a long embroidered curtain. "Perhaps you would like to come out, sir, and join us."

The curtains parted, and a tall man stepped into view. He was broad-shouldered and slim-hipped, and his bronzed arms showed many scars. His face was square-cut and darkly handsome, his eyes so deep a brown that they appeared black. He smiled grimly. "You are observant, Parmenion," commented the newcomer.

"Even an accomplished drinker does not have two pitchers of wine and two servants by his side," said the Spartan. "And this couch still retained the heat from your body. You are Pelopidas?"

"Observant and sharp-witted," said Pelopidas, moving to a

nearby couch and reclining on his side. He picked up a goblet of wine and sipped it. "What would you have us tell you?"

Parmenion looked at the man who had fought side by side with Epaminondas, suffering seven great wounds and yet surviving, the man who with only thirty companions had fought off two hundred Arcadians in a pitched battle. Pelopidas looked like exactly what he was: a peerless fighter, a man made for war. "A long time ago Epaminondas asked me to prepare a plan to take the Cadmea. I have done so. I was merely waiting for him to announce the time; it can be brought into operation within a day. But it depends on the resources available."

"I take it you mean men," said Pelopidas.

"Exactly. But men who understand discipline and the necessity for timing."

"We have more than four hundred men in the city, and within minutes of a general insurrection there will be thousands of Thebans on the streets, marching on the Cadmea. I think we can kill a few hundred Spartans."

"My plan involves no killing of Spartans," said Parmenion.

"Are you mad?" Pelopidas asked. "These are Spartan warriors. You think they will give up without a fight?"

"Yes," answered Parmenion simply.

"How?" put in Calepios. "It would be against all tradition."

"First," said Parmenion quietly, "let us examine the alternatives. We can storm the Cadmea and perhaps take it. By killing the Spartans we give Agisaleus no choices. He will bring the army to Thebes and retake the city, putting to death all who had a part in the insurrection. You will have no time to gather an army of your own. The retaking of the Cadmea in those circumstances would be the worst folly."

"You speak like a coward!" snapped Pelopidas. "We can raise an army, and I do not believe the Spartans are invincible in battle."

"Neither do I," said Parmenion, holding his voice at an even pitch. "But there is a way to retake the Cadmea without a battle."

"This is all nonsense," said Pelopidas. "I'll listen to no more of it."

"It must be fascinating," said Parmenion quietly, as the warrior rose, "to have a body like a god without a mind to match it."

"You dare insult me?" stormed Pelopidas, the color draining from his face as his hand reached for the dagger at his side.

"Draw that blade and you die," Parmenion told him. "And after you Epaminondas will die, and Thebes will remain in chains or be destroyed utterly." Holding to the man's gaze, Parmenion rose. "Understand this," he said, his voice shaking with repressed emotion. "My entire life is devoted to one dream—the destruction of Sparta. For years I have been forced to wait for my vengeance, learning patience while the talons of rage tore at my soul. Now the first moment of my revenge is close. Can you imagine how much I want to see the Spartans in the Cadmea slain? How my heart cries out for them to be humbled, cut down, their bodies thrown out to feed the crows? But there is no point to petty vengeance when the greater dream lives on. First we free Thebes, then we plan for the great day. Now, Pelopidas, be silent and learn."

Swinging away from the warrior, he turned to Calepios, outlining his plan and watching the man's every expression. The councillor was intelligent, with a keen mind, and Parmenion needed his support. Choosing his words with care, the Spartan spoke quietly, answering every question Calepios put to him. Then he turned to Pelopidas.

"What now is your view, warrior?" he asked.

Pelopidas shrugged. "Sitting here, it sounds good, but I don't know how it will work in reality. And I still think the Spartans will bring an army."

"So do I," agreed Parmenion, "but they may not fight. I think Agisaleus will seek the support of Athens. The Spartans took the Cadmea three years ago because pro-Spartan dissidents in the city invited them here. They have always argued that they are guests—friends. It makes a lie of that if—when asked to leave—they return to do battle."

"What do you require?" asked Calepios.

"First, a doctor, or an herbalist, and also the name of the man who supplies provisions to the Spartans. Next, you must prepare a speech to be delivered in the main square tomorrow an hour before dusk."

"And what of me?" Pelopidas asked.

"You will kill every pro-Spartan councillor," said Parmenion, dropping his voice.

"Sweet Zeus!" whispered Calepios. "Murder? Is there no other way?"

"There are five of them," Parmenion said. "Two are good orators. Leave them alive and Sparta will use them as the lever to bring down the insurrection. After the Cadmea is taken, the city must be seen to be united. They must die."

"But one of them, Cascus, is my cousin. I grew up with him," said Calepios. "He is not a bad man."

"He has chosen the wrong side," stated Parmenion, shrugging his shoulders, "and that makes him bad. For Thebes to be free, the five must die. But all Spartan soldiers outside the citadel must be taken alive and brought to the Cadmea."

"What then?" asked Pelopidas.

"Then we will free them," answered the Spartan.

Mothac was awakened by a hand pushing at his shoulder. "What in Hades?" he grumbled as he sat up, pushing away the insistent hand.

"I need you," said Parmenion.

Mothac glanced out of the window. "But it is not dawn yet." He scratched at his red beard, then rubbed the sleep from his eyes. Swinging his legs from the bed, he rose unsteadily and reached for his *chiton*. "What is happening?"

"Freedom," answered Parmenion. "I will await you in the *andron*."

Mothac dressed and splashed his face with cold water. He had downed several goblets of unwatered wine before retiring, and now they were reminding him of his stupidity. He belched, took a deep breath, then joined Parmenion in the small *andron*. The Spartan looked tired; dark rings were showing under his eyes.

"We are going to free Epaminondas today, but first there are many matters to be resolved. Do you know the man Amta?"

"The meat merchant in the southwestern quarter. What of him?"

"You will go to the surgeon Horas and collect from him a package of herbs. You will take them to Amta; there you will be met by a tall warrior, dark-bearded. He will tell you what must be done."

"Herbs? Meat merchants? What has this to do with freeing Epaminondas?"

Parmenion ignored the question. "When you have accomplished your task, you will accompany the warrior. He is a known and wanted man. He must not be taken; therefore, he will use you—and others—to take messages across the city. Do as he bids, whatever the request."

"You are talking of revolt," said Mothac, his voice dropping to a whisper.

"Yes. Exactly that."

"What of the officers of the watch? There are more than two hundred soldiers patrolling the city."

"Theban soldiers. Let us hope they remember that. Now go. We have little time, and there are people I must see."

Mothac took his dark green cloak and swung it around his shoulders. "Take a sword and a dagger," Parmenion advised him, and he nodded.

Minutes later he was at the house of Horas the physician, where a man was waiting in the shadowed doorway. He was tall and skeletally thin. Mothac approached him and bowed. "Greetings, Doctor. You have a package for me?"

The man glanced nervously at the darkened street, his eyes flicking from side to side. "There is no one but me, I assure you," said Mothac.

"This package did not come from me. You understand that?"

"Of course."

"Now use it sparingly. Sprinkle it carefully over the meat. Try not to get it on your fingers, but if you do, then wash them with care."

"It is poison, then?" whispered Mothac, surprised.

"Of course it is not poison," snapped the physician. "You think I became a doctor so that I could kill people? It is what the lords asked for: purgatives and vomiting powders. Now get you gone from here. And remember, I have no part in this!"

Mothac took the package and headed toward the north of the city. As he turned a corner near the *agora*, a soldier stepped out in his path.

"Where are you going, friend?" he asked. Three other soldiers of the watch came into view.

"I am heading home, sir," answered Mothac, smiling. "Is there trouble?"

"You are well armed for an evening's stroll," the man observed.

"It pays to be careful," Mothac told him.

The soldier nodded. "Pass on," he said.

When Mothac arrived at the home of Amta the butcher—a large building set close to the slaughter yard and warehouse—he halted at the main gates, searching the shadows for the man he was to meet.

"You are Mothac?" came a voice from behind him. Mothac dropped the package and whirled, scrabbling for his sword. Cold iron touched his throat.

"I am," he replied. "And you?"

"I? I am none of your concern. Pick up the package and let us awaken our friend."

The gate was not locked, and the tall warrior eased it open, then the two men crept across the courtyard and into the house beyond. All was in darkness, but moonlight was shining through an open window, and they could make out the staircase by the eastern wall. Mothac followed his nameless companion up into the second story to a bedroom facing east, where the man opened the door and stepped inside. In a broad bed on a raised platform lay a fat man, snoring heavily. The warrior moved alongside him and laid a hand on his shoulder. The snoring ceased, and Mothac saw Amta's eyes flick open. The warrior's knife rested on the fat man's quivering jowls. "Good morning," said the warrior with a smile. "It will be a fine day."

"What do you want?"

"I want you to show that you love Thebes."

"I do. All men know that."

"And yet you supply food to the Spartan garrison."

"I am a merchant. I cannot refuse to sell my merchandise. I would be arrested, called a traitor."

"It is all a question of perspective, dear Amta. You see, we are going to free Thebes. And then *we* will call you a traitor."

The fat man eased himself to a sitting position, trying not to look at the knife poised above his throat. "That would be unfair," he protested, his voice regaining composure. "You could not accuse every man who deals with Spartans or all shop owners and merchants—yes, and even whores would be under sentence. Who are you?"

"I am Pelopidas."

"What do you require of me?" the fat man asked, fear returning with the sweat that suddenly appeared on his face.

"What time do you prepare the meat for the garrison?"

"An hour before dawn. Then my lads pull it up to the Cadmea on a cart."

"Then let us be about our business," said Pelopidas, sheathing his dagger.

"What has my meat to do with freeing Thebes?"

"We have some herbs with us to add to the flavor."

"But if you poison them, I'll get the blame. You can't!"

"It is not poison, fool!" hissed Pelopidas. "Would that it were! Now get out of that bed and take us to your storeroom."

Three hours after dawn Parmenion still had not slept. He waited at the entrance to the smithy, his mind whirling with thoughts that became problems and problems that became fears.

What if?

What if the Spartans saw that the meat was doctored? What if Pelopidas was caught salting the water? What if the news of the plot leaked out?

Parmenion's head was pounding, and the early-morning sunshine hurt his eyes; feeling nauseous and unsteady, he sat down in the roadside. Ever since the day he had rescued Derae he had suffered periodic head pain, but during the last two years the bouts had increased in both regularity and intensity. At times even his Spartan training could not help him overcome the agony, and he had taken to drinking poppy juice when the attacks became unbearable. But today there was no time for the sleep of opium, and he tried to ignore the pain.

The smith, Norac, came walking into the street minutes later. He was a huge man, wide-shouldered and bull-necked. Parmenion rose to greet him. "You're early, young man," said Norac, "but if you think to arrange speedy work, forget it. I have a full order book."

"I need twenty iron spikes by midday, each one the length of a man's forearm," Parmenion told him.

"You are not listening, my young friend. I cannot take any more work for this week."

Parmenion stared into the man's deep-set brown eyes. "Listen to me, Norac. You are said to be a man who can be trusted. I am sent by Pelopidas. You understand? The watchword is *Heracles*."

The smith's eyes narrowed. "For what purpose do you need the spikes?"

"To nail shut the Cadmea gates. We also need men to wield the hammers."

"Hera's tits, boy! You are not asking much, are you! You'd better come inside."

The smithy was deserted. Norac walked to the forge, adding tinder to the hot ashes inside and blowing the flames to life. "The spikes will be no problem," he said. "But how do we hammer them home without the Spartans falling upon us?"

"Speed and skill. Once the crossbar is in place, six men will run to the gates." Parmenion walked to the far wall, lifting a spear haft from a stack awaiting iron heads. Standing the haft on its end, he drew his dagger, slashing two cuts into the wood. "That is the height and thickness of the crossbar. The gates are oak, old, weathered, and thick as the length of a man's hand. Could you pierce one in six strikes?"

Norac flexed his prodigious muscles. "Aye, boy, I could. But most others will need seven or eight."

Parmenion nodded. "You can double the speed by having four men with hammers at each gate. But the timing is vital. The moment of greatest danger will come when the crowd is marching upon the Cadmea—it is then that the commander will consider sending out an armed force."

"I'll see the deed done," promised Norac, and Parmenion smiled.

"The gates are usually shut at dusk. Bring the spikes to the house of Calepios by midday, no later. And have eleven strong men with you."

Parmenion left the smithy and walked slowly to Calepios' home. The statesman was eating breakfast and asked Parmenion to join him, but the Spartan refused. "Have you heard from Pelopidas?" he asked.

"Not yet. You look dreadful, man; your face has lost all color. Are you ill?"

"I am fine. Merely tired. The word about your speech must be spread through the city. We need as many people as possible to hear it."

"You said that last night. It is all in hand, my friend."

"Yes, of course." Parmenion filled a goblet with water and sipped it.

"Go inside and sleep for a while," advised Calepios. "I will wake you when Pelopidas returns."

"Later. How many men will be watching the city gates? No one must leave until Thebes is ours."

"There will be ten men per gate. Have no fears; everything is as you planned it."

"Some people will bring bows to the Cadmea, hoping for a chance to loose an arrow at a Spartan. All but our own men must be disarmed. There must be no unplanned assault."

Pelopidas and Mothac entered the courtyard, and Parmenion stood. "Well?" he asked.

"Mothac and I delivered the food. As you thought, we were left to ourselves in the storeroom. I salted the water barrels; there were ten of them. We ran out of salt for the last barrel, and I thought of urinating in it, but instead we tipped it over on the floor."

"Good! Well done," said Parmenion, sinking back to his seat. "Then we are ready. Have you planned your speech?" he asked Calepios.

"Yes," answered the statesman, "and I will deliver it at the *agora* just before dusk. There will be a great crowd. Now will you get some rest?"

Parmenion ignored his plea and turned to Pelopidas. "What of the councillors?"

The warrior sat down on the bench seat alongside Parmenion. "The gods are with us, Parmenion. I am told they will all be at a celebration at the house of Alexandros. They are gathering there at midday; they will eat and drink and then send out for whores. We will kill them all save Calepios' cousin, Cascus."

"No!" snapped Parmenion. "All must die!"

"Cascus is no longer in the city," said Pelopidas, swinging his eyes to Calepios. "By a strange stroke of luck he left two hours ago for his summer estate near Corinth."

Parmenion's fist slammed to the tabletop, and his eyes locked to Calepios' face. "You warned him. You put everything in jeopardy."

The statesman shrugged and spread his hands. "I do not deny asking him to leave the city, but I did not betray anyone. I told Cascus of a dream I had had for three nights, that he died. I told him I had been to the seeress about it and she had said he had to make a pilgrimage to the shrine of Hecate at Corinth. All men know how religious Cascus is. He left immediately."

"It was foolish, Calepios," Parmenion told him. "If we do retake the city, then Cascus will run to the Spartans and they will use him as a figurehead to march upon us. You may have doomed us all."

The statesman nodded his head. "I have no defense to that. But Cascus is of my blood and very dear to me. And in his own way he cares for Thebes as much as any of us. But there is nothing I can do to change my actions, and if there were, I would refuse so to do."

Parmenion's head felt as if it were ready to explode. He drank more water and then walked into the house, seeking to escape the brightness of the courtyard.

Mothac followed him. "I have seen marble statues with more color than you," said Mothac as Parmenion slumped onto a divan. "I think you need some wine."

"No," said Parmenion as his stomach surged. "Just leave me for a while. I'll get some sleep."

Fierce waves pounded at a jagged coastline while monsters of the deep with serrated teeth glided around the slender figure of the girl as she struggled to free her hands. Parmenion swam through the waves, battling to reach her before the dark sea dragged her down.

A huge creature slid by him, so close that its dorsal fin rubbed against Parmenion's leg, but a colossal wave caught the young man's body, lifting him toward the heavens. At its tip, he almost screamed as he tumbled down into the trough. His head went under the water, and he found he could breathe there. Derae's body was floating beneath him; he dived down and ripped the cords from her wrists, dragging her to the surface.

"Live! Live!" he screamed. The monsters circled them, cold opal eyes staring at the lovers. Derae regained consciousness and clung to Parmenion.

"You saved me," she said. "You came for me!"

* * *

Mothac shook him awake, and Parmenion opened his eyes and groaned not just at the pain flaring within his skull but for the loss of Derae and his dream. He sat up. "Is it midday?"

"Yes," answered Mothac. Parmenion rose. Pelopidas was still in the courtyard, and with him was the smith, Norac, and eleven burly men. Four had huge, long-handled hammers.

"Good enough for you, *strategos*?" asked Norac, lifting an iron spike the length of a short sword.

"You did well," Parmenion told him, "but I would like to see your hammer men at work."

"I brought extra spikes," said the smith, "for just that purpose." Two men hoisted a thick section of timber, standing it against the far wall, while a third man held a spike in place. Moving to one side, Norac gestured to one of the hammer men to take his place on the other. The smith hefted his hammer, then swung it viciously, the head thundering into the spike. As the hammer bounced clear, the second man swung; after the first strike the holder released his grip and ducked clear. Three strikes later, the spike was deeply embedded.

"Work on it," said Parmenion. "It needs to be faster."

Calling Pelopidas to him, he walked to the *andron*. "The celebration you mentioned at the house of Alexandros—will there be guards?"

"Yes. They are not popular men," Pelopidas answered.

"How many guards?"

"Perhaps five, perhaps twenty. I don't know."

"Outside or inside the house?"

"Outside. It is a private orgy," said Pelopidas with a wide grin.

"I will meet you at the house of Alexandros. We will make a plan when we have seen how many guards are present."

After Pelopidas had gone, Calepios went to his room to rehearse his speech, leaving Parmenion in the *andron*. The Spartan was lost in thought for some time but then became aware that he was not alone. Turning his head, he saw the

Spartan seeress, Tamis, standing by the table leaning on a staff.

Tamis gazed at the young Spartan, glorying in the power of his soul fire, sensing his pain, admiring the courage he showed in resisting its power.

For a moment he stared at her, disbelieving.

"Well," she said, "will you offer me a seat, young Spartan?"

"Of course," he answered, rising to guide her to the table, where he poured her a goblet of water. "How are you here, lady?"

"I go where I will. Are you set now upon leading this insurrection?"

"I am."

"Give me your hand."

Parmenion obeyed, and she covered his palm with her own. "With each heartbeat a man has two choices," she whispered. "Yet each choice makes a pathway, and he must walk it wherever it takes him. You stand, Parmenion, at a crossroads. There is a road leading to sunlight and laughter and another road leading to pain and despair. The city of Thebes is in your hands, like a small toy. On the road to sunlight the city will grow, but on the other road it will be broken, crushed into dust and forgotten. These are the words I am ordered to speak."

"Which road, then?" he asked. "How will I know it?"

"You will not until long after you have walked upon it."

"Then what is the point of telling me?" he snapped, pulling his hand clear of hers.

"You are a chosen man. You are Parmenion, the Death of Nations. A hundred thousand souls will you send to the dark river, screaming and wailing, lamenting their fate. It is right and just that you should know your choices."

"Then tell me how to walk the road to sunlight."

"I will, but like Cassandra before me, my words will not alter your path."

"Just tell me."

"Walk from this house and bridle your mare. Ride from this

city and journey across the sea to Asia. Seek out the shrine to Hera of the Book."

"Ha! I see it now," said Parmenion. "You witch! You are Spartan, and you serve them. I will not listen to your lies. I will free Thebes, and if a city is to fall to ashes, then it will be Sparta."

"Of course," she said, smiling, showing rotted teeth and blood-red gums. "The Death of Nations speaks, and his words will be heard by the gods. But you misjudge me, Parmenion. I care nothing for Sparta or her dreams, and I am happy with the path you have chosen. You are important to me—to the world."

"Why should I be important to you?" he asked her, but she shook her head.

"All will be revealed in time. You have pleased me today; your mind is sharp, your wits keen. Soon you will become the man of iron, the man of destiny." Her laughter was like wind through dead leaves.

Parmenion said nothing, but his fingers strayed toward the dagger at his side.

"You will not need that," she told him softly. "I am no threat to you and will speak to no one of your plans."

The Spartan did not reply. He was not about to risk the life of Epaminondas on the word of a Spartan witch! The dagger slid clear. . . .

"Parmenion!" called Calepios from the doorway. "I am torn over the conclusion to my speech. Will you listen to the ending?"

For a moment only, Parmenion's attention was diverted. He glanced back to Tamis . . . but she had gone. Lurching to his feet with dagger in hand, he swung around. But of Tamis there was no sign. "Where did she go?" he asked Calepios.

"Who?"

"The old woman who was here a moment ago."

"I saw no one; you were dreaming. Now, listen to this ending. . . ."

Parmenion ran to the door. Outside in the courtyard the smith and his men were hammering at the spikes, and the courtyard gates were locked.

Parmenion listened to Calepios' speech, which sounded pompous and lacking in credibility. But he said nothing, his mind locked to the words of Tamis. Had she been real or an illusion born of pain? He had no way of knowing. Complimenting the statesman on his speech, he left the building and walked in the bright sunshine toward the house of Alexandros. The man was a poet and an actor. According to Calepios, he excelled at neither profession but made his name among the nobility for organizing exquisite orgies. His home was close to the Homoloides, the great north gate, and overlooked the hills leading to Thessaly. Parmenion found the house and sat on a wall some sixty paces from the front gates. From here he could see four guards in breastplates and helms, carrying lances, and could hear the sound of music and laughter from within. But there was no sign of Pelopidas. Leaning his back against a cool stone wall, he ran through the plans once more.

There is nothing more you can do, he told himself. It is out of your hands.

But this was advice he could not take. In the years since Derae had been taken from him, thoughts of vengeance against the Spartans had filled his mind. Now the day was here, and the beginning of his revenge was close. But where was Pelopidas?

If the councillors were not killed, they would flee to the Spartans, and even if the Cadmea was taken, Agisaleus or Cleombrotus would lead an army to regain it. Silently he cursed the Theban warrior. Arrogant, stupid man!

Slowly time passed. The guards continued to pace outside the gates, and the laughter from within grew more raucous. Seven priestesses of Aphrodite arrived, dressed in colorful *chitons* and wearing veils beneath gilded and bejeweled combs. The guards stepped aside to allow them in. Parmenion closed his eyes against the pain in his skull; the plan was complex enough without having to rely on men like Pelopidas.

A cool wind touched his face, bringing momentary relief from pain. He sat up, aware of a difference, a change. The guards still paced, and all seemed to be as it was. Then he realized there was no sound, no music or laughter.

So, he thought, the orgy has begun.

But where in the name of Hades was Pelopidas?

An hour passed. Soon it would be time for Calepios to make his speech, to lift the crowd and set them marching on the Cadmea. With a last muttered curse against unreliable Thebans, Parmenion stood and began the long walk to the *agora*. A noise from behind made him turn to see the gates of Alexandros' home opening, the priestesses emerging into the sunlight. They began to walk toward Parmenion. Ignoring them, he continued on his way, but as he turned a corner, he heard the sound of running feet and a hand fell upon his shoulder.

"Leave me be!" snapped Parmenion.

"Not even a word of greeting?" came a male voice. Parmenion stared at the tall, veiled priestess, who pulled the veil clear and grinned at him. The face he saw was handsome and beardless, the lips stained red, the eyes painted.

"Get away from me. I want nothing from you!" said Parmenion, lifting a hand to push the man from him. Powerful fingers closed on his forearm with a grip of iron.

"Do you not recognize me? It is I, Pelopidas!" The warrior chuckled and used the veil to rub away the paint and the stain on his lips. "You are not the only *stratēgos*, my friend."

Parmenion swung his gaze over the rest of the group as they divested themselves of female clothing. Each of them was armed with a hidden dagger, and only now did the Spartan see the bloodstains on the brightly colored garments. "You did it!" he cried.

"They are dead," Pelopidas answered. "So is the poet Alexandros, which, if you ask me, is no loss to anyone."

Leaving their disguises in the alley, the group ran to the *agora*, where a huge crowd was gathering. Pelopidas and his comrades moved in among the people, leaving Parmenion standing below the great steps leading to the temple of Poseidon. The crowd was many thousands strong by the time Calepios appeared from within the temple to walk slowly down the steps. The crowd roared his name, and he seemed genuinely surprised at the ovation. He raised his hands for silence. Parmenion realized he was dreading this moment, fearing the effect Calepios' pompous speech would have on this excited mob.

The statesman stared down at the crowd for several moments, then his voice boomed out. "It is a long time, my friends, since I spoke with you. But I have always believed that if a man has nothing good to say, then let him remain silent! Our friends and allies, the Spartans, were invited here three years ago by councillors and *ephors* of Thebes. I opposed that decision! I opposed it then. I oppose it now!" A huge cheer went up, but Calepios waved his hands and stilled the crowd. "Why, asked the councillors, should the Spartans not occupy the Cadmea? Were they not our friends? Are they not the leaders of Greece? What harm is there in having guests within the city? What harm?" he bellowed. "What harm? A Theban hero, praised by Agisaleus himself, now languishes in a cell, his body tortured, his flesh flayed. And why? Because he loves Thebes. Are these the actions of friends? *Are* they?" he shouted.

"No!" roared the crowd.

Parmenion could scarcely believe his ears. Gone was the pomposity, and though he had heard the words before, they now seemed fresh and vibrant. And in that moment Parmenion learned of the magic of the great orator. Timing and delivery alone were not enough; there was in Calepios a charisma, a power that made his green eyes see not just a crowd but every single man, his voice touching every heart.

"I shall go to the Cadmea," said Calepios. "I shall go and say to the Spartans, 'Free our friends and leave this city. For you are not welcome here.' And though they drag me to a dungeon, though they flay me with their whips of fine wire, I will continue to oppose them with all the power of my soul and all the courage of a Theban heart."

"Kill the Spartans!" yelled a voice from the crowd.

"Kill them?" answered Calepios. "Yes, we could. We are thousands, and they are few. But you do not kill unwelcome guests; you thank them for coming, and you ask them to leave. I shall go now. Shall I go *alone*?"

The answer was deafening, the single word rising from the crowd like a rolling peal of thunder. *"No!"*

Calepios walked from the steps, the crowd opening before him and following him as he strode up the long path to the Cadmea.

From his hiding place in the boulders some thirty paces from the Cadmea walls, Norac watched the Spartans push shut the gates. His hands were sweating, and he dried them on his tunic. Around him the others waited nervously.

"Suppose they open the gates before the spikes bite through?" asked a man to his left.

"Keep that thought in mind when you wield the hammer," advised the smith, "and also remember that Epaminondas is in that citadel now, undergoing torture. And he has your name in his head as well as mine."

"I think I can see the crowd," whispered another man. Norac risked a glance over the top of the boulder.

"That's them," he agreed. "Now let us do our part." The group sprinted out from their hiding place and ran to the gates. A sentry on the battlements saw them and shouted, but before he could loose a shaft, they were safe under the overhang of the gate tower. Norac held the marked spear haft against the left-hand gate. "There!" he ordered. A spike was held in place. Norac pointed out the second impact point, and the hammer bearers looked to the smith. "Now!" he shouted, swinging the weapon.

The clanging ring of iron on iron brought a chorus of shouts from beyond the gates. "What in Hades is happening?" someone bellowed.

"There's a crowd gathering, sir," answered a soldier from the ramparts.

"Five formation!" yelled the officer. "Prepare to attack. Open the gates!" Beyond the walls Norac could hear the pounding feet of the Spartan soldiers as they ran to form a fighting square.

The smith's hammer thundered into the spike, driving it through the gate and into the crossbar beyond. He ran to his left, barging aside the other wielders, whose spike was only halfway through. Stepping back, Norac swung with all his strength, and the head of the spike disappeared into the weathered oak.

"The bar won't move, sir," shouted a Spartan soldier, and Norac grinned as he heard them heaving at the nailed beam.

And the crowd surged up toward the citadel. . . .

Calepios marched forward ten paces, lifting his arms to halt the surging mob. On the walls above, a Spartan archer leaned out and loosed a shaft that pierced a man's shoulder. The crowd moved back.

Calepios' voice thundered above the noise of the mob. "Is this how friends treat one another? Are we armed? Have we offered violence?"

The wounded man was carried back down to the city, but there were no more shafts from the Cadmea. "Where is your general?" shouted Calepios. "Fetch him here to answer for this atrocity."

A Spartan in an iron helm leaned over the battlements. "I am Arimanes," he called. "The soldier who loosed the shaft will be punished for it, but I ask you now to disperse or I will be forced to send out my men against you."

"You will send out no one," shouted Calepios, "save the Thebans you have locked in your cells."

"Who are you to order me?" called Arimanes.

"I am the voice of Thebes!" Calepios replied to a cheer from the crowd.

Mothac made his way to Parmenion's side. "The western gates are secure," he said with a smile. "They have no way out."

Just then the crowd parted, and a group of Theban soldiers marched into sight. In their midst were eight Spartans, bruised and bloody, their hands bound.

Pelopidas greeted the Theban officer with a salute. "Take them to the Cadmea wall," he ordered. The officer bowed and waved his men on.

Calepios strode forward. "Take back your soldiers," he yelled to Arimanes, "for if they remain here, I fear for their lives."

"Open the gates!" shouted the Spartan leader as the crowd roared with laughter.

"I think you should lower some ropes," Calepios told him. Beyond the walls the crowd could hear the sounds of men still battling to move the crossbar, and they laughed and jeered at the unseen Spartans.

"By the gods, you will pay for this, you scoundrel!" bellowed Arimanes.

"I think the gods are with us," replied Calepios. "By the way, I understand there is sickness within the garrison. Can we offer you the services of a physician?"

Arimanes replied with an obscene curse and then disappeared from view. Minutes later, ropes were lowered from the walls and the captured Spartan soldiers climbed to the ramparts. The crowd remained until dusk, then most of them returned to their homes. But Pelopidas had organized a hard core of rebels to remain stationed before the gates, and Calepios had a tent pitched where, he told the joyous mob, he would wait until the Spartans accepted his invitation to leave.

Parmenion, Mothac, and Pelopidas waited with him. "So far it has all gone as you said, *strategos*," Calepios told Parmenion. "But what now?"

"Tomorrow you will offer to send a conciliator into the Cadmea. But we will discuss that later tonight—if I return."

"You do not need to do this," Mothac pointed out. "The risk is too great."

"The Spartans do not like surrendering prisoners," said Parmenion. "They may decide to kill Epaminondas. I cannot take the risk. Meanwhile, my friends, bring up more timber and order Norac to seal the gates tight. They could saw through those crossbars in less than an hour."

"You really believe you can rescue Epaminondas? How?" asked Pelopidas.

"In Sparta I had another name; they called me Savra. And tonight we will see if the *lizard* can still climb walls!" Dressed in a black full-sleeved shirt and dark Persian trews and with a coiled rope over one shoulder, Parmenion waited until a cloud obscured the moon before running silently to stand below the walls. His face blackened with earth, he edged along the wall to the east, where the ground fell away and the wall towered over a sheer drop of more than two hundred feet.

At this point, he reasoned, the walls could not be scaled by a besieging force and therefore were unlikely to be as well patrolled. Reaching up, he found the first of the narrow cracks between the four-foot-square blocks of gray stone and hooked his fingers into it.

Are you still the lizard? he wondered.

The cracks between the blocks were tiny and shallow, but Parmenion hauled himself up, his bare feet seeking out footholds, his fingers tracing the blocks, finding points where the ancient stone had worn away, leaving grooves and projections.

Inch by inch he scaled the wall, his fingers tired, his feet sore. Only once did he glance down: The ground far below shimmered in the moonlight, and his stomach heaved. There had been no buildings this high in Sparta, and he realized with a sudden burst of panic that he feared heights. Transferring his gaze to the stone of the wall, he took several deep breaths and then looked up. The parapet was still some thirty feet above him.

His foot slipped!

Like steel pins his fingers dug into the stone as he scrabbled for a foothold.

Calm yourself, his mind told him. But his heart was hammering as he hung above the awesome drop. Letting his body go limp, he slowly eased his right foot onto the stones, carefully seeking a crack. His arms were aching now, but he was calm once more. Levering himself up, he advanced with care until he hung just below the parapet.

He closed his eyes, listening for any sound: a soldier's breathing or the light footfalls of a patrolling sentry. But there was nothing. Hooking his hand over the parapet, he swiftly hauled himself to the battlements and crouched in the shadows. Twenty paces to his left a Spartan soldier was leaning over the wall, staring out at the mob. To his right was a stairway leading down to the courtyard.

Stealthily he crossed the ramparts and glided down the stairs, keeping to the moon-shadowed wall.

The Cadmea was a honeycomb of buildings. Now a citadel, it had originally been the old town of Cadmos, the modern city of Thebes growing around its base. Many of the older buildings were derelict, and Parmenion shivered as he ran through deserted alleyways, feeling the ghosts of the past hovering in empty homes and gaping windows.

At the sound of marching feet, he ducked into a doorway. A rat scuttled over his bare foot, and he could hear other rodents close by. Forcing himself to remain statue-still, he waited as six soldiers marched past the ancient building.

"As weak as dog's piss," muttered one of the soldiers. "We should saw through the beam and crush the bastards."

"It's not his way," said another. "He's probably hiding under his bed now."

One of the men groaned and knelt by the side of the road, vomiting. Two of the others helped the stricken man to his feet. "Better, Andros?"

"Fourth time tonight. My guts won't take much more."

The men moved away, and Parmenion continued toward the west, seeking out the governor's residence. According to Pelopidas, the old dungeons were below the building. Arimanes had his rooms on the second floor, the first being used as an eating hall for the officers.

Parmenion waited in the shadows of the building opposite, watching for sentries, but there were none. Swiftly he ran across the open ground, entering a doorway and finding himself in a torch-lit corridor. The sound of conversation came from the dining hall.

"Well-cooked meat is the answer to loose bowels," he heard a man say.

Not this time, thought Parmenion grimly. Opposite the dining hall was another doorway with spiral stairs leading down. He ran to it and began the descent to the dungeons. There were no torches on the stairs here, but he could see flickering light below.

Moving with care, he reached the bottom stair and risked a glance into the dimly lit corridor beyond. To the right was a row of dungeons, to the left a table at which sat two guards; they were dicing for copper coins. Parmenion cursed. One guard he could have silenced, but unarmed as he was, two were beyond him.

Think, man! Be a *strategos*!

Listening to the men as they gambled, he waited for a name to be used. He felt isolated and in danger, trapped as he was on the stairs. If anyone should come from above, he was finished.

The men gambled on. "You lucky pig, Mentar!" said one of them at last.

Parmenion moved back up the spiral stairs to crouch in the darkness. "Mentar?" he called. "Come up here!"

The man muttered an obscenity, and Parmenion heard his chair scrape back across the stone floor. Mentar reached the stairs and started to run up them two at a time, but Parmenion reared up before him, smashing his fist into the man's chin. Grabbing the soldier by the hair, Parmenion rammed his head into the wall. Mentar sagged in his arms.

Lowering the unconscious soldier to the steps, Parmenion moved back to the dungeon corridor. The second man was sitting with his back to the stairs, whistling tunelessly and rolling dice. Moving behind him, Parmenion hammered a blow to the man's neck; the guard fell forward, his head bouncing against the tabletop.

The dungeon doors were thick oak, locked by the simplest means—a wooden bar that slid across the frame. Only two of the doors were locked in this way: Polysperchon was in the first. Parmenion entered the dungeon to find the Theban asleep; his face was bruised and bloody, and the room stank of vomit and excrement. The Theban was small, and Parmenion hauled him to his feet, pulling him out to the corridor.

"No more," he pleaded.

"I am here to rescue you," whispered Parmenion. "Take heart!"

"Rescue? Have we taken the Cadmea?"

"Not yet," Parmenion answered, opening the second door. Epaminondas was awake but in an even worse state than Polysperchon. His eyes were mere slits, his face swollen almost beyond recognition.

Parmenion helped him to the corridor, but the Theban sank to the floor, his legs unable to take his weight. In the torchlight Parmenion gazed down at his friend's swollen limbs: the calves had been beaten with sticks.

"You'll not be able to climb," said Parmenion. "I'll have to hide you."

"They'll search everywhere," muttered Polysperchon.

"Let us hope not," Parmenion snapped.

Within the hour the Spartan was once more running alone through the deserted streets. Climbing the rampart steps, he tied his rope to a marble seat and then clambered to the wall.

"You there!" shouted a sentry. "Stop!"

Parmenion leapt over the ramparts and slid down the rope, his hands burning. Above him the sentry ran to the rope, hacking at it with his sword. It parted and sailed over the wall.

Far below Parmenion grabbed for a handhold, his fingers hooking into a crack just as the rope went slack. Carefully he climbed down and returned to the tent of Calepios.

"Well?" asked the orator.

"They are safe," whispered Parmenion.

At dawn inside the citadel Arimanes sat doubled over, clutching his belly. He had lost count of the number of times he had vomited during the night, and now only yellow bile filled the bowl at his side. Of more than seven hundred and eighty men under his command, five hundred were so stricken that they could not walk, and the rest moved around like walking wounded, their faces gray, their eyes lifeless. If the Thebans decided to attack today, he realized, his force would be overpowered within minutes.

An aide knocked at his door, and Arimanes struggled to his feet, stifling a groan. "Come in," he said, the effort of speaking making his stomach tremble.

A young officer entered; he, too, looked white. "We have searched the entire Cadmea. The prisoners must have escaped."

"Impossible!" shouted Arimanes. "Epaminondas could hardly walk, let alone climb. And only one man was seen going over the wall."

"There is nowhere left to search, sir," the man told him.

Arimanes sank back to his couch. Surely the gods had damned him. He had planned to execute the traitors as a warning to the mob that Sparta would not be threatened. Now he had no prisoners and commanded a force too weak to defend the walls.

A second officer entered the room. "Sir, the Thebans want to send a man in to discuss . . . the situation."

Arimanes tried to think, but logical thought was difficult when bowels and belly were in revolt. "Tell them yes," he ordered, staggering back into the latrine and squatting over the open pipe.

He felt a little better then and returned to his couch,

stretching himself out on his side with knees drawn up. He had not wanted this commission, hating Thebes and all its depravities, but his father had insisted that it was an honor to command a Spartan garrison no matter where it was stationed. Arimanes ran a slender hand through his thinning blond hair. What he would not give for a drink of cool, clean water. Damn those Thebans to Hades and the fires therein!

Minutes later the officer returned, ushering in a tall young man with dark hair and closely set blue eyes. Arimanes recognized him as the runner Leon the Macedonian, by all accounts a mix-blood Spartan. "Sit down," he whispered.

The man stepped forward, holding out a stone flagon. "The water is clean," said the messenger.

Arimanes took it and drank. "Why did they pick you?" he asked, holding on to the flagon.

"I am half-Spartan by birth, sir, as perhaps you know," said Parmenion smoothly, "but I live in Thebes now. They thought that, perhaps, I could be trusted."

"And can you?"

The man shrugged. "It seems an easy task. There is no need for deceit."

"What are their plans, man? Will they attack?"

"I do not know, sir. But they have killed all pro-Spartan councillors."

"What did they tell you to say?"

"That they will promise safe conduct for you and your men to the edge of the city. They have set tents there with fresh food and a physician who has an antidote to the poison you have taken."

"Poison?" whispered Arimanes. "Poison, you say?"

"Yes. It is a disgusting ploy—typical of Thebans," said Parmenion. "It is slow-acting but will kill within five days. That is why, I suspect, they have not attacked before now."

"Can they be trusted, do you think? Why should they not slay us as soon as we . . . we . . . ?" He could not bring himself to say the word "surrender." "As soon as we leave," he said at last.

"They have heard," said Parmenion, edging forward and lowering his voice, "that Cleombrotus has two regiments north of Corinth. He could be here in three days. I think they will let you go rather than risk the king marching upon them."

Arimanes groaned and doubled over. His mind reeled with pain, and nausea made him gag. The messenger picked up an empty bowl and held it while the officer vomited, then Arimanes wiped his mouth with the back of his hand. "They will give us an antidote?"

"I believe the man Calepios can be trusted," said Parmenion soothingly. "And after all, there is no disgrace in leaving the city. Sparta was invited to have a garrison here, but now the city has changed its mind. It is for kings and councillors to work out a solution. Soldiers merely obey the orders of the great; they do not create the policies."

"True," Arimanes agreed.

"What shall I tell the Thebans?"

"Tell them I agree. It will take us time to saw through the crossbar on the gate, but then I will march my men from the city."

"Sadly, sir, the gates are out of the question. In their excitement the mob have nailed them shut with timbers. Calepios suggests that you descend by ropes, twenty men at a time."

"Ropes!" snapped Arimanes. "You want us to leave by *rope*?"

"It shows how much the Thebans fear you," said Parmenion. "Even in your weakened state they know a Spartan force could crush them. It is a compliment of sorts."

"Curse them to the fires of Hades! But tell them I agree."

"A wise choice, sir. And one you will not regret, I am sure."

Two hours later, as the last of the Spartans left the Cadmea, Parmenion waited as Norac and the others stripped the timbers from the gates, sawing through the crossbar beyond. The gates swung open.

Pelopidas ran into the courtyard, raising his fists in the air. "They are beaten!" he bellowed, and the crowd cheered. Turning to Parmenion, he grabbed the Spartan by the shoulders. "Now tell me where you hid our friends."

"They are in the dungeons still."

"But you said they were freed!"

"No, I said they were safe. The Spartans were bound to search the Cadmea, but I hoped they would not consider such a bizarre hiding place. I merely moved them to a cell at the far end of the corridor. Take a doctor with you, for Epaminondas has been harshly treated."

As Pelopidas and a dozen men ran to the governor's house, Mothac approached Parmenion. "What will happen to the Spartan commander?" he asked.

"They will execute him," answered Parmenion. "Then they will march on Thebes. We still have much to do."

That night, as the sound of riotous celebration filled the air, Parmenion opened the gates of his home, staggered into the courtyard, and collapsed in the doorway of the *andron*. Mothac found him there in the early hours of the morning and carried him to the master bedroom.

Three times in the night Parmenion awoke, on the third occasion to find Horas the physician looming over him. The doctor cut into Parmenion's arm with a small curved knife. The Spartan tried to struggle free, but Mothac helped Horas hold him down. Once more Parmenion passed out.

His dreams were many, but one returned again and again. In it he was climbing a winding stair, seeking Derae. As he struggled on, the stairs behind him disappeared, leaving a dark abyss. He walked on toward a room within which he knew Derae was waiting, but then he stopped. For the abyss was growing, and he realized with dawning horror that he was drawing it with him. If he opened the door to the room, the abyss would swallow it. Not knowing what to do to save his love, he stepped from the stair and fell, plunging into the darkness of the pit.

Mothac sat beside the bed, looking down at the pale face of his unconscious master. Against the advice of the physician, the Theban had opened the shutters of the window to see

Parmenion's features more clearly. The Spartan looked gray under his tan, his eyes sunken and his cheeks hollow. When Mothac placed his hand on Parmenion's chest, the heartbeat was fluttering and weak.

During the first two days Parmenion had slept, Mothac was unconcerned. Each day he helped the physician, Horas, bleed the Spartan, trusting in Horas, who explained that the retaking of the Cadmea had drained Parmenion of strength and he was merely resting.

But now, on the fourth day, Mothac no longer believed it.

The flesh was melting away from Parmenion's face, and there was no sign of a return to consciousness. Filling a goblet with cool water, Mothac lifted Parmenion's head, holding the goblet to his lips. The water dribbled from the sleeping man's mouth, and the Theban gave up.

Hearing the gate below creak open, he walked to the door. Horas entered the house, climbing the stairs to the bedroom, where he unrolled his pack of knives. Mothac looked hard at the tall, thin physician; he did not like surgeons but envied them their knowledge. Never would he have believed he would ever defy such a skilled and clever man. But today he knew there would be no further bloodletting, and he stepped over to the physician.

"Put away your knife," he said.

"What's this?" inquired Horas. "He needs bleeding. Without it he will die."

"He's dying anyway," said Mothac. "Leave him be."

"Nonsense," said Horas, lifting a skeletal hand and attempting to push Mothac aside. But the servant stood his ground, his face reddening.

"I had a wife, master physician. She, too, was bled daily, until she died. I'll not see Parmenion follow her. You said he was resting, recovering his strength. But you were wrong. Now you can go." He glanced down at the doctor's hand, which still rested against his chest.

Horas hastily removed his hand, replaced his knife, and rolled his pack. "You are interfering in matters you do not understand," he said. "I shall go to the justices and have you forcibly removed from this room."

Mothac grabbed the man's blue tunic, hauling him close. All color drained from his face, and his eyes shone like green fire. Horas blanched as he gazed into them.

"What you will do, Doctor, is go away from here. If you take any action that results in the death of Parmenion, I will hunt you down and cut out your heart. Do you understand me?"

"You are insane," Horas whispered.

"No, I am not. I am merely a man who keeps his promises. Now go!" And Mothac hurled the physician toward the door.

After the man had gone, Mothac settled down in the chair beside the bed. He had no idea what to do, and a sense of rising panic set his hands trembling.

Surprised by his reaction, he looked down at Parmenion's face, aware for the first time how much he loved the man he served. How curious, he thought. Parmenion was in many ways a distant man, his thoughts and dreams a mystery to Mothac; they rarely talked of deep matters, never joked with one another, never discussed their secret longings. Mothac leaned back and gazed out of the window, remembering the first night he had come to the house of Epaminondas, the death of Elea like a hot knife in his heart. Parmenion had sat with him silently, and he had felt his companionship, felt his caring without the need for words.

The three years he had served Parmenion had been happy ones, to his amazement. Thoughts of Elea remained, but the jagged sharp edges of hurt had rounded, allowing him at least to recall the times of joy.

The creaking gate cut through his thoughts, and he rose, drawing his dagger. If the doctor had brought back officers of the watch, then he would see what it meant when Mothac made a promise!

The door opened, and Epaminondas entered. The Theban's face was swollen, his eyes dark and bruised. He walked slowly to the bedside and looked down at the sleeping man.

"No better?" he asked Mothac.

The servant sheathed his blade. "No. I stopped the physician bleeding him; he has threatened to go to the justices."

Epaminondas eased his tortured body into a chair.
"Calepios tells me that Parmenion suffered terrible pains in
the head."

"It happens sometimes," Mothac told him, "especially after
races. The pain was intense, and on occasion he would almost
lose his sight. Parmenion told me only a month ago that the
attacks were increasing."

Epaminondas nodded. "I had a letter from a friend in
Sparta; his name is Xenophon. He was Parmenion's mentor
for several years, and he witnessed the first attack. The physician then believed there was some growth in Parmenion's
skull. I hope he does not die. I would like to thank him. I could
not have taken much more . . . punishment."

"He won't die," said Mothac.

Epaminondas said nothing for a while, then he looked up at
the servant. "I was wrong about you, my friend," he admitted.

"It does not matter. Do you know of anyone who could help
him?"

Epaminondas rose. "There is a healer, an herbalist named
Argonas. Last year the Guild of Physicians sought to have him
expelled from the city; they say he is a fraud. But a friend of
mine swears Argonas saved his life. And I know of a man,
blinded in the right eye, who can now see again. I will send
the physician here tonight."

"I have heard of the man," said Mothac. "His fees are
huge. He is fat and wealthy and treats his servants worse than
slaves."

"I did not say he was pleasant company. But let us be
honest, Mothac. Parmenion is dying: I cannot see him lasting
another night. But do not concern yourself with thoughts of
fees; I will settle them. I owe him much—all of Thebes owes
him more than we can repay."

Mothac gave a dry, humorless laugh. "Yes, I have noted
how often Calepios and Pelopidas have come to see how he
fares."

"Calepios has obeyed Parmenion's last instruction," Epaminondas told him. "He has gone to Athens to seek their aid against Spartan vengeance. And Pelopidas is training *hoplites*, trying to build an army in case Cleombrotus comes against us. Stay here, with Parmenion. I will send Argonas. And Mothac . . . get some food inside you and rest awhile. It will not help your master if you fall sick."

"I am as strong as an ox. But you are right. I will get some sleep."

It was dusk before Argonas arrived at the small house. Mothac had fallen asleep in the courtyard, and he awoke to see an enormous figure, swathed in a red and yellow cloak, looming over him.

"Well, fellow, where is the dying man?" Argonas asked, his voice deep, seeming to echo from within the vastness of his chest.

Mothac rose. "He's in the bedroom upstairs. Follow me."

"I need to eat something first," said Argonas. "Fetch me some bread and cheese. I'm famished." The fat man sat down at the courtyard table. For a moment Mothac stood and stared, then he turned and strode to the kitchen. He sat and watched as Argonas devoured a large loaf and a selection of cheese and dried meat that would have fed a family of five for a full day. The food simply disappeared with little evidence of chewing. At last the doctor belched and leaned back, stroking crumbs from his glistening black beard. "And now a little wine," he said. Mothac poured a goblet and passed it across the table. As Argonas reached out, his pudgy fingers curling around the goblet, Mothac noted that each finger boasted a golden ring set with a gem.

The doctor drained the wine at a single swallow and then rose ponderously. "Now," he said, "I am ready."

Following Mothac to the bedroom, he stood looking down at Parmenion in the lantern light. Mothac was standing in the doorway, watching the scene. Argonas had brought no knives, and that at least was a blessing. The physician bent over the bed and reached down to touch Parmenion's brow; as his fingers brushed against the burning skin, Argonas cried out and stumbled back.

"What is wrong with you?" asked Mothac.

Argonas did not reply at first, and his dark eyes narrowed as he looked down on the dying man. "If he lives, he will change the world," whispered the physician. "I see the ruins of empire, the fall of nations. It might be better to leave him."

"What's that? Speak up, man, I can't hear you!" said Mothac, moving to stand beside the physician.

"It was nothing. Now be silent while I examine him." For several minutes the fat man stood in silence, his hands gently moving over Parmenion's skull. Then he walked from the room. Mothac followed him to the courtyard.

"He has a cancer," said Argonas, "at the center of his brain."

"How can you tell if it is within the skull?"

"That is my skill," responded Argonas, sitting at the table and refilling his goblet. "I traveled inside his head and found the growth."

"Then he will die?" asked Mothac.

"That is by no means certain, but it does look likely. I have a herb with me that will prevent the cancer from growing; it is from the plant sylphium, and he must take an infusion from the herb every day of his life from now on, for the growth will not disappear. But there is something else, and that I cannot supply."

"What?" asked Mothac as the fat man lapsed into silence.

"When you . . . travel . . . inside a man's head, you see many things—you feel his hopes, his dreams, you suffer his torments. He had a love—a woman called Derae—but she was taken from him. He blames himself for her loss, and he is empty inside, living only by clinging to thoughts of revenge. That kind of hope can sustain a man for a while, but revenge is a child of darkness, and in darkness there is no sustenance."

"Can you say it simply, physician?" asked Mothac. "Just tell me what I can do."

"I do not believe you can do anything. He needs Derae . . .

and he cannot have her. However, on the slender chance that it may prove useful—and to earn my fee from Epaminondas—I will prepare the first infusion. You will watch and observe me closely. Too much sylphium can kill—too little, and the cancer will spread. It may help, but without Derae, I do not think he will survive."

"If you are the mystic you claim," sneered Mothac, "how is it you cannot speak to him, call him back?"

The fat man shook his head. "I tried," he said softly, "but he is in a world he has created for himself, a place of darkness and terror. In it he battles demons and creatures of horror. He could not hear me—or would not."

"These creatures you speak of—could they kill him?"

"I believe that they could. You see, my red-bearded friend, they are demons he has created. He is fighting the dark side of his own soul."

The abyss was swirling around him as he slashed the sword of Leonidas through the throat of a man-sized scaled bat with wings of black leather. The creature spouted blood that drenched Parmenion like lantern oil, making the sword difficult to hold. He backed farther up the low hill. The creatures flew around him, keeping away from the shining sword, but the abyss lapped at his feet, swallowing the land. He glanced down to see distant fires within the pit far below, and he felt he could hear the screams of tormented souls.

Parmenion was mortally tired, his head ablaze with pain.

Wings flapped behind him, and he swiveled and thrust out his sword, plunging it deep into a furred belly. But the creature was upon him, its serrated teeth tearing at the flesh of his shoulder. He threw himself back, wrenching his sword clear and hacking the head from the demon's neck. Emptiness swallowed the land beneath his legs, and Parmenion slithered to the edge of the abyss. Rolling to his stomach, he scrambled clear and ran to the brow of the hill.

All around him, like an angry sea, the pit beckoned, closing on him slowly, inexorably.

Above him the bats circled.

Then he heard the voice.

"I love you," she said. And light streamed from the dark sky, curving into a bridge to heaven.

Mothac stood outside the temple grounds, waiting for the woman. She had two worshipers with her, and he knew he would be here for some time. There was a fountain nearby, and he sat watching the starlight in the water of the pool below it.

Finally the men left, and he made his way to the temple entrance, cutting left into the corridor where the priestesses rented their rooms. He knocked at the door of the farthest chamber.

"Wait a moment," came a weary voice, then the door opened. The redhead produced a bright smile from the recesses of memory.

"Welcome," she said. "I was hoping a *real* man would come to worship."

"I am not here to worship," he told her, pushing past her. "I wish to hire you."

"You contradict yourself," she said, the painted smile fading.

"Not at all," he rejoined, sitting down on the broad bed and trying to ignore the smell of the soiled sheet. "I have a friend who is dying—"

"I'll not bed anyone diseased," she snapped.

"He is not diseased, and you will not have to bed him." Swiftly Mothac told her of Parmenion's illness and the fears outlined by Argonas.

"And what do you expect me to do?" she asked. "I am no healer."

"He comes to you each week, sometimes more than that. You may have seen him at the training ground. His name is Parmenion, but he runs as Leon the Macedonian."

"I know him," she said. "He never speaks, not even to say

hello. He walks in, hands me money, uses me, and leaves. What could I do for him?"

"I don't know," admitted Mothac. "I thought perhaps he was fond of you."

She laughed then. "I think you should forget him," she said, moving to sit beside him, her hand resting on his thigh. "Your muscles are tense, and your eyes are showing exhaustion. It is you who need what I can give." Her hand slid higher, but he grabbed her wrist.

"I have no other plan, woman. Now I will pay you for this service. Will you do it?"

"You still have not said what you require," she answered.

He looked into her painted eyes and took a deep breath. "I want you to wash the lead and ocher from your face. I want you to bathe. Then we will go to the house."

"It will cost you twenty drachmas," she said, holding out her hand.

He reached into his pouch and counted out ten drachmas. "The rest when you have completed the task," he said.

An hour later, with the moon high over the city, Mothac and the priestess entered the house. She now wore a simple white ankle-length *chiton*, a blue *chlamys* around her shoulders. Her face was scrubbed clean, and to Mothac she looked almost pretty. He led her to the bedroom and took her hand. "Do your best, woman," he whispered, "for he means much to me."

"My name is Thetis," she said. "I prefer it to *woman*."

"As you wish, Thetis."

He closed the door behind him, and Thetis walked to the bedside and let her *chiton* and shawl slip to the floor. Pulling back the sheet, she slid alongside the dying man. His body was cold. Reaching up, she touched the pulse point at his neck; the heart was still beating, but the pulse was erratic and weak. She snuggled in close to him, lifting her right leg across his thighs, her hand stroking his chest. She felt warmth being drawn from her, but still he did not stir. Her lips touched his cheek, and her hand moved farther down his body, caressing his skin. Her fingers curled around his penis, but there was no response. She kissed his lips softly, touching them with her tongue.

There was little more she could do now. Thetis was weary after a long day, and she considered dressing and claiming her ten drachmas. But she gazed down once more at the pale, gaunt face, the hawk nose, and the sunken eyes. What had the servant said? That Parmenion had lost his love and could not forget her? You fool, she thought. We all suffer lost loves. But we learn to forget; we teach ourselves to ignore the pain.

What more could she do?

Laying her head on the pillow, she put her mouth to his ear.

"I love you," she whispered. For a moment there was no response, but then he sighed, a soft, almost inaudible escape of breath. Thetis tensed and began to rub her body against him, her fingers stroking the flesh of his inner thighs and loins. "I love you," she said, louder now. He groaned, and she felt his penis swell in her hands.

"Come to me," she called. "Come to . . . Derae."

His body arched suddenly. "Derae?"

"I am here," she told him. He rolled to his side, his arms drawing her to him, and kissed her with a passion Thetis had not experienced in a long time. It almost aroused her. His hands roamed across her body . . . searching . . . touching. She looked into his eyes; they were open yet unfocused, and tears were streaming from them.

"I missed you," he said. "As if they'd torn my heart from me."

She drew him onto her, swinging her legs over his hips and guiding him home. He slid into her and stopped; there was no sudden thrust, no pounding. Gently he dipped his head and kissed her, his tongue like moist silk upon her lips. Then he began to move, slowly, rhythmically. Thetis lost all sense of time passing, and despite herself, arousal came to her like a long-lost friend. Sweat bathed them both, and she felt him building to a climax, but he slowed once more and slid from her. She felt his lips on her breasts, then her belly, his hands on her thighs, his tongue sliding into her, soft and warm and probing. Her back arched, her eyes closed; she began to shudder and moan. Her hands reached down, holding his head to her. The climax came in a series of intense, almost painful spasms. She sank back to the bed and felt the heat of his body as he moved upon her—within her—once more. His lips touched hers, their tongues entwining, then he entered her. Unbelievably Thetis felt a second orgasm welling, and her hands pulled at his back, feeling the tension in his muscles as he drove into her with increasing passion. The spasms were even more intense than before, and she screamed but did not hear the sound. She felt the warm rush of his climax, then he slumped over her.

For a moment Thetis lay still, his dead weight upon her. Gently she pushed him to his back, seeing that his eyes were now closed. For a moment only she wondered if he had died, but his breathing was regular. She felt the pulse at his neck, which was beating strongly.

Thetis lay quietly beside the sleeping man for some minutes before silently rising from the bed. She dressed and returned to the courtyard, where Mothac sat, nursing a goblet of wine.

"Drink?" he asked, not looking up.

"Yes," she answered softly. Pouring herself a goblet of wine, she sat opposite the Theban. "I think he will live," she told him, forcing a smile.

"I guessed that from the noise," he answered.

"He thought I was Derae," she said. "I wish I was."

"But you are not," he said harshly, rising and scattering the ten drachmas on the table before her.

She scooped up the money and looked at the Theban. "I did what you wanted. Why are you angry with me?"

"I don't know," lied Mothac, forcing himself to be civil. "But thank you. I think you should go now."

He opened the gate for her and then returned to his wine, which he downed swiftly, pouring another. Then another. But still Elea's face floated before him.

THE TEMPLE, ASIA MINOR,
379 B.C.

THE priestess stared at the open gate and the lush green fields beyond, focusing on the roses that grew up and over the linteled opening, red and white blooms that filled the air with a heady scent.

This time I will escape, Derae told herself. This time I will concentrate as never before. Steadying herself, she walked slowly forward, her mind holding to a single thought.

Pass the gateway. Walk in the fields.

Each step was taken with care as her bare feet touched the paved path. Roses were growing on either side of her, beautiful blooms of yellow and pink.

Don't think of the flowers! The gate! Concentrate on the gateway.

Another step.

Birds flew above her, and she glanced up to see their flight. They were eagles, flying together, banking and gliding on the thermal currents. Such grace. The priestess returned her gaze to the roses beneath the gate. Mindful of the thorns, she plucked a bloom and held it to her nose; she stared around the garden, seeing the old man who cared for the plants; he pushed himself wearily to his feet and approached her.

"That one is almost dead," he told her. "Take a bloom that is still to open. Then, if you put it in water, it will fill your room with perfume."

"Thank you, Naza," she said as he cut two blooms and placed them in her hand. She walked back up the path to the temple, pausing in the doorway.

Then, as she remembered, Derae closed her eyes and a single tear forced its way through closed lids, spilling to her cheek. There was no escape through the gateway . . . just as there was no escape from the window of her room. She could lean out and enjoy the sunshine or see the distant mountains, but as soon as she attempted to climb from the room, she would find herself sitting at her bed, her thoughts confused.

It had been this way for three years, three lonely, soul-aching years.

She recalled the first day when she had opened her eyes and seen the old woman sitting by her bed. "How do you feel, child?" the woman asked.

"I am well," she had answered. "Who are you?"

"I am Tamis. I am here to teach you."

Derae had sat up, remembering the ship and her hands being bound behind her, men picking her up and throwing her over the side . . . the sudden shock of the cold water, the terrible struggle to be free of her bonds as she sank beneath the waves. But then there was nothing save a strange memory of floating high in the night sky toward a bright light.

"What will you teach me?"

"The mysteries," answered the woman, touching her brow. And she had slept again.

She had discovered the spell of the gateway on her third day as she walked in the garden alone. Approaching it to look at the runes carved in the old stone, she had found herself back in the white-columned temple.

Twice more she tried, then Tamis had seen her. "You cannot leave, my dear. You are the priestess now; you are the heir to Cassandra."

"I don't understand—not any of this," said Derae.

"You were the victim. The legend says that any girl who successfully survives the sacrifice and reaches the temple becomes the priestess until the next victim is similarly successful. You knew that."

"Yes, but . . . they bound my hands. I do not remember coming here."

"But you *are* here," Tamis pointed out. "And therefore I will instruct you."

Day by day the old woman had tried to teach Derae the mysteries, but the girl seemed incapable of understanding. She could not free the chains of her soul and soar her spirit into the sky, nor could she close her eyes and enter the healing trance. Simple tasks like holding a dead rose and willing it to become once more a fresh, budding bloom were beyond her.

At the end of the first year Tamis took her to a small study at the rear of the temple. "I have thought much about your lack of talent," said the old woman, "and I have researched the origins of the legend. You surrendered a gift a long time ago: you allowed a man to violate you. This has caused your powers to be buried deep. In order to bring them forth, you must now be prepared to give another gift."

"I do not want to be a priestess," protested Derae. "I do not have these gifts. Just let me go!"

But Tamis continued as if she had not heard her, her words striking Derae like sharp knives. "I watched you heal Hermias when his skull was crushed! That is when I knew you were the one to follow me. You can do it, Derae—but only by surrendering another gift. You know what is needed; why do you persevere with this defiance?"

"I will not do it!" stormed the girl. "Never! You will not take my eyes!"

Tamis had shrugged and had patiently continued with the lessons. By the third year Derae showed small signs of success. She could stand in the garden and will sparrows to fly to her hand, and once she healed Naza of a cut to his arm, placing her fingers over the wound and sealing it so that there was no scar.

At night she still dreamed of escape, of running into the hills, hiding in the distant woods, and somehow finding her way back to Sparta—and Parmenion.

But it would not be today, she realized, staring at the open gateway and the fields beyond. Slowly she walked between the temple pillars to the open altar, where she laid the roses Naza had given her.

"When will you learn, child?" asked Tamis.

The girl looked around. "I did not know you had returned."

The old woman approached the priestess, laying her hand on the girl's shoulder. "It must be as it is. Try to accept it: you are chosen."

"I don't want it!" cried the girl, brushing Tamis' hand from her shoulder. "I *never* wanted it."

"You think that I did? Wanting it is not part of the gift. You have it or you do not."

"Well, I do not. I speak no prophecies; there are no visions."

Tamis took the girl by the arm and led her back into the garden to sit beside a white-walled pool. "There are men and women who will die today," said the old woman softly. "They do not wish to. All of them will have works that are left undone, or children, or husbands or wives. They have no choice—as you have no choice. The days of the Dark God are close, my dear, and I will be dead. Someone must follow me. Someone of courage and spirit. Someone who cares. It was always to be you."

"Are you deaf, Tamis? I have few gifts!"

"They are there, but they have been pushed deep. You will find them when you give your own gift to the Lord of All Things, when you give up your sight."

"No!" said the girl. "You cannot force me! I will not do it!"

"No one is going to force you. That would destroy all I have worked for. It must be your own decision."

"And if I do not?"

"I don't know, child. I wish that I did."

"But you can see the future. You are a sorceress."

Tamis smiled. Leaning forward, she cupped her hand in the water of the pool and drank. "Life is not so simple. There are many futures. The life of a single person is like a great tree: every branch, every twig, every leaf is a possible future. Years ago I looked at my own deaths—it took almost a year to track them all down, and at the end I realized there were still thousands to be seen. Now the end is close, and I know the day. But yes, I have seen you take up the challenge and refuse it, and I have seen you both win and lose. But which is it to be?"

"Will I be able to speak to the gods?" questioned the priest-ess.

Tamis was silent for a moment, then she sighed. "I am patient, Derae, but time is becoming precious. I have waited three years for you to realize there is no going back. But now is the time for a different course. I may be wrong, but I will tell you the truth—all of it, though it will be painful. Firstly, there are no gods as you think of them. The names we know—Zeus, Apollo, Aphrodite—all were once men and women like you and I. But that is not to say there are no gods at all. For beyond the myths there are real forces of light and darkness, of love and chaos."

"And which do you serve?" the priestess asked.

Tamis chuckled. "Do not seek to annoy me, girl. If I served the chaos spirit, I would have taken your gift by force!"

"But that is how you hold me here. I am not free to leave."

"As I said, nothing is simple. But I hold you not out of hate but out of love. You see, my dear, you cannot leave this place—ever. And that is not my doing."

"Then who is my jailer? Who holds me here?" asked the priestess.

"Your death," Tamis answered.

"What does that mean?" she asked, suddenly fearful.

"I am sorry, Derae, but you died when they threw you

overboard. I found your body by the rocks, I carried you here and brought you back. That is why you cannot leave."

"You are lying! Tell me you are lying!"

Tamis took the girl's hand. "If you left this temple, your body would decay in seconds, your flesh peeling away, corrupt and worm-filled, and your bleached bones would lie on the grass not ten paces from the gateway."

"I do not believe you. It is a trick to keep me here!"

"Think back to the day, your hands bound, your lungs filling with salt water, your struggles weakening as you sank."

"Stop it!" shouted Derae, covering her face with her hands. "Please stop it."

"I will not apologize, for it cost years of my life and all my power to bring you back. Naza helped carry you here. Speak to him if you disbelieve me."

"Sweet Hera, why did you tell me this? I have lived here for three years, waiting for Parmenion to come for me, praying, hoping. And now you dash all my hopes."

"Then you believe me?"

"I wish that I did not," answered Derae, "and now I will never see Parmenion again. Why did you not let me die?"

"You will see him," insisted Tamis. "He is the reason I saved you. Once you have learned the mysteries, your soul will be free to fly anywhere in the world—into the past or the many futures. But it will take time for you to learn all the mysteries . . . perhaps years."

"What do years matter to the dead?"

"In this temple you are not dead. You will age, as do all of us, and finally your body will give out and your soul will fly free. When it does, I will be waiting for you. I will show you paradise."

Derae stood and leaned over the pool, gazing down at her reflection, seeing the red-gold of her hair and the flush of health on her cheeks. Swiftly she looked away. "Why was I chosen?"

"Because you love Parmenion."

"I don't understand."

"The Dark God is coming, Derae. Not today, not this year, but soon. He will be born in the flesh, and he will grow into a man. All the world will fall to him, and chaos will reign. There will be rivers of blood, a mountain of dead. He must be stopped."

"And Parmenion can destroy him?"

"That is the question that torments me, Derae. It is why I need you. When first I saw the shadow of the Dark God, I prayed to the source for a way to defeat him. I saw Parmenion then and heard his name echo across the vaults of heaven. I thought he would be the sword to strike the chaos spirit. But since then I have realized that he is also linked to the Dark God, and I have followed the paths of his futures. He is the Death of Nations, and he will change the world."

"I cannot believe that of Parmenion," protested Derae. "He is gentle and kind."

"In some ways, yes. But since your . . . you left him . . . he has become filled with bitterness and hate. And that serves the chaos spirit. If I were more sure, I would see him dead. But I am not sure." Tamis drank again from the pool, then rubbed her weary eyes. "You see a rabid dog about to kill a baby, what do you do?"

"You kill the dog," answered Derae.

"But if you know the future and you know that the babe will grow into an evil destroyer who will bring the world to blood and fire?"

"You let it kill the baby?"

"Indeed, but what if the destroyer is due to sire another babe who will rebuild the world and bring peace and joy for a thousand years?"

"You have lost me, Tamis. I don't know. How can anyone answer such a question?"

"How indeed?" whispered the old woman. "I cling to my first prayer, when the source showed me Parmenion. He is a man torn, pulled toward darkness, yearning for the light. When the Dark God comes, he will either serve him or help destroy him."

"Can you destroy a god?" Derae asked.

"Not the spirit. But he will come in the flesh, in the guise of a man. And *that* is where his weakness will lie."

Derae took a deep breath. "I want to help you, Tamis, I really do. But is there a way I can develop my . . . powers . . . without giving the gift you require?"

"We do not have the time," answered Tamis sadly. "It would take perhaps thirty years."

"Will there be pain?"

"Yes," admitted Tamis, "but it will be short-lived, that I promise you."

"Show me Parmenion," said Derae. "Then I will give you my answer."

"That might not be wise."

"It is my price."

"Very well, child. Take my hand and close your eyes."

The world lurched, and Derae felt she was falling into a great void. She opened her eyes . . . and screamed. All around her were stars, huge and bright, while far below her the moon floated in a sea of darkness. "Do not fear, Derae. I am with you," came the voice of Tamis, and Derae calmed herself. Colors blazed around her, and she found herself floating above the night-shrouded city of Thebes, gazing down at the colossal statues of Heracles and Athena. Closer they flew until they came to a house with a small courtyard.

A redheaded man was sitting at a table, but from above came the sounds of a couple making love. Still closer they came, passing through the walls of the bedroom.

"I missed you," Parmenion told the woman beneath him. "As if they'd torn my heart from me."

"Take me back," whispered Derae. "Take me home. You may have my gift; you may take my eyes."

Mothac opened the package from Argonas and ran his fingers through the shredded leaves and stalks within. Filling a large goblet with boiling water, he added a handful of the leaves, and a pungent aroma—sweet, almost sickly—filled the kitchen.

Parmenion was awake upstairs, but he had said nothing or even turned his head when Mothac looked in on him. Stirring the infusion with a wooden spoon, Mothac strained off the leaves and stalks floating on the surface and climbed the stairs. Parmenion had not left the bed. He was sitting up and staring out through the open window.

Mothac moved to the bedside. "Drink this," he said softly. Without a word Parmenion accepted the brew and sipped it. "Drink it all," Mothac ordered, and the Spartan silently obeyed.

Mothac took the empty goblet, placing it on the floor beside the bed. "How is the pain?" he asked, taking Parmenion's hand.

"It is receding," answered the Spartan, his voice distant.

"You have been asleep for five days. You missed the celebrations—they were dancing on the *agora*. You should have seen them."

Parmenion's eyes closed, and his voice was a whisper. "She came to me, Mothac. From beyond death she came to me. She saved me on the hill of sorrow."

"Who came to you?"

"Derae. She was still young and beautiful." Tears welled in Parmenion's eyes. "She freed me; she took away the pain."

Mothac bit back the truth as the words surged up in his throat. "Good," he said at last. "That is good. Now it is time for you to leave that bed and get some air into your lungs. Here, let me help you." Taking Parmenion's arm, he gently pulled his master to his feet.

Parmenion stumbled, then righted himself. Mothac took a clean white *chiton*, helped Parmenion dress, and then guided him down to the courtyard.

The sky was overcast, but the day was warm, a fresh breeze blowing. Mothac brought Parmenion a meal of figs and dried fish and was relieved when the Spartan ate it all.

In the days that followed Parmenion's strength flowed back

into his wasted limbs. Argonas came twice to the house, examining the Spartan's skull and pronouncing with satisfaction that the cancer was sleeping.

But still Parmenion did not venture from the house. He slept often and took little interest in the affairs of Thebes. Each day he drank the infusion prepared by Mothac, ate a light breakfast, and dozed until after noon. Concerned by Parmenion's lethargy, Mothac sought out Argonas.

"Do not be worried," the fat man told him. "It is the sylphium; it is also a strong sleeping potion. But his body will become used to it, and that effect will lessen."

Epaminondas did not visit during this time. Mothac informed Parmenion that the Theban was organizing a new city council with other members of the rebel conspiracy, while the warrior Pelopidas had gathered to him almost five hundred young Theban men and was training them for the war that was almost certain to follow. Parmenion listened to the news without expression, venturing no opinions and asking no questions.

A month after the retaking of the Cadmea, Parmenion heard cheering in the streets and sent Mothac to inquire as to the cause. The Theban returned within minutes. "An Athenian force has arrived," he said. "They have come to help us against the Spartans."

"That seems unlikely," offered Parmenion. "The Athenians are in no position to make war against Sparta; they have few land forces, and Sparta has three armies that could march on Athens almost unopposed. Go and find out more."

Mothac was delighted as he ran from the house. Parmenion's voice had been sharp, authoritative, and Mothac felt like a man who had just seen the first rays of spring sunshine after a long winter. It took him two hours to locate Epaminondas, who was returning from a meeting in the Cadmea. The Theban leader looked weary, his shoulders slumped, his eyes dull.

"Parmenion is asking about the soldiers," said Mothac, moving alongside the man as he pushed his way through the crowds.

"They are mercenaries," Epaminondas told him. "Calepios bought their services in Athens. How is Parmenion?"

"As he once was," said Mothac, and Epaminondas brightened.

"I'll come back with you. I need to talk to him."

A thunderstorm burst over the city as the three men reclined on couches in the *andron*, lightning flashing like the spears of Ares. Epaminondas lay back, resting his head on an embroidered cushion and closing his eyes. "There is a great deal of meaningless debate at present," he said. "It is beginning to look as if removing the Spartans was simplicity itself compared with planning a coherent policy. There are some who want to hire mercenaries to defend the city, others who talk of meeting the Spartans in the field. Still more dither and wait for Athens to come to our aid. Calepios says the Athenians are happy with our revolt and promise us everything—except real support. They are overjoyed to see the Spartans humbled, but they will do nothing to help us."

"And what of the Spartan army?" asked Parmenion.

"Cleombrotus has seven thousand men near Megara—two days' march from us. So far he has done nothing. Cascus is with him; we should never have let him escape. Calepios has much to answer for in that regard, blood kin or no. Cascus is telling all who will hear him that the Theban revolt is masterminded by a treacherous group of exiles and that the people do not support them. He is urging Cleombrotus to march on Thebes and is assuring him that the Theban people will rise against the rebels."

"Then why have the Spartans not marched?" asked Mothac.

"Agisaleus is ill. Some say he is dying, and the omens are not good. I hope he does die."

"Pray he does not," put in Parmenion. "As long as he remains sick, the Spartans will do nothing. If Agisaleus dies, Cleombrotus will feel compelled to show his strength to the Spartan people. And you are not ready for war."

"What do you advise, my friend?"

"Your choices are limited," Parmenion told him. "There are Spartan garrisons all through Boeotia—north, south, east, and west of Thebes. Until those garrisons are removed you have no chance to succeed. But you cannot remove them while Spartan armies are poised to invade. Not an easy problem to solve."

Epaminondas sat up and rubbed his eyes. "We have allies in Thessaly, but they alone cannot give us victory. Worse, if we ally ourselves to any strong power, we will merely be exchanging masters."

"Where are the strongest Spartan garrisons?" asked Parmenion.

"Orchomenus in the north, Tanagra to the west, Aegosthena to the south. We have men in each of them, trying to inspire a rebellion, but—wisely—the rebels are waiting to see how we fare. We are caught like dogs chasing our tails. In order to win, we need support from other cities, but these cities wait to see if we can win before joining us. We need a victory, Parmenion."

"No," said the Spartan. "That is not possible—yet. My advice to you is to avoid any pitched battle with Cleombrotus. You would be crushed."

"We will be crushed anyway should he march against us."

Parmenion was silent for a moment, his eyes fixed on a point high and to the right on the northern wall. Slowly he lifted his hand, rubbing at his jaw. Mothac grinned, and Epaminondas waited expectantly.

"It could be," said Parmenion at last, "that Cascus' escape will work for us. If he has convinced the Spartans that the Theban people are ready to rise against us, then it is unlikely that Cleombrotus will attack the city; he will ravage the land around us in the hope that a show of strength will cause a counterrevolt. Winter is almost here, and with it the rains. Most of the Spartan army will return home. It is then we will strike."

"And where should we attack? And with what force?" queried Epaminondas.

"Athens," answered Parmenion with a broad smile. "And we will use the Spartan army."

Day by day tension within the city mounted. Arguments broke out in public places as to the wisdom of expelling the Spartans. Fear was almost palpable, yet still the Spartan army remained at Megara, two days' march to the southeast. News from the surrounding countryside was bleak. At the small city of Thespiae, northeast of Thebes, a group of rebels besieged the acropolis, where Spartan troops were garrisoned. The Spartans marched out among them, killing twenty-three men and routing the mob. At the cities of Tanagra and Aegosthena troublemakers were rounded up and arrested, while in Plataea two suspected rebels were executed after a traitor told of their plotting.

Pelopidas marched from Thebes with a force of four hundred men to aid the rebels at Tanagra. Hopes were high when the warriors marched through the Proitian gates, but eight days later they were back, having been waylaid in the mountains by a Spartan force. Forty-one men were dead, twenty-six wounded. It was a bitter reverse, and yet Pelopidas emerged from the debacle with credit, for when surrounded he had gathered his men to him and charged the Spartan ranks, breaking clear and killing four Spartans single-handedly. The Thebans had sought refuge in the mountains, and the Spartans had let them go, not wishing to lose men in the narrow passes with daylight fading.

The Athenian mercenaries were sent to Erythrae, along with two hundred Theban *hoplites*, to aid the rebels there, but no word was heard from them and fear grew among the Theban people. Epaminondas proved himself a capable public speaker, but the rebels missed the oratorical skills of Calepios, who remained in Athens.

As winter moved inexorably on and the rains began, news came from the south that Agisaleus had recovered from his fever.

And the Spartan army moved north.

* * *

Parmenion seemed unconcerned and during the days sat reading Xenophon's story of the march into Persia. As the shortest day of winter approached, Mothac walked into the *andron*, removed his rain-drenched cloak, and poured himself a goblet of watered wine.

"It will all be over in days," said the servant sourly. "The mood in the streets is full of despair. When the Spartans come, the people will surrender without a fight."

"*If* the Spartans come," replied Parmenion, putting aside the scroll.

"How can you remain so calm?" Mothac snapped.

"By using my mind—and not my emotions," replied Parmenion. "Listen to me. Sparta's armies are not trained for sieges; they prefer battle on an open plain. A phalanx cannot climb a wall. I do not believe Cleombrotus will attack the city; he will hope that our forces can be lured out, and he will seek to prevent supplies coming into Thebes."

Mothac was unconvinced, and ill fortune continued for the beleaguered Thebans. The Athenian mercenaries had been beaten back from Erythrae, and Cleombrotus marched through Aegosthena and Plataea, his army now almost in sight of Thebes.

Pelopidas wanted to gather a force to attack them, but cooler counsel prevailed. Then came the news Parmenion had been hoping for. With winter making maneuvers more difficult, Cleombrotus split his army and marched south, back through Aegosthena, Megara, and Corinth, leaving a large force at Thespiae under the command of the General Sphodrias.

Parmenion sought out Epaminondas and Pelopidas. "Now is the time to act," he said. "By spring Agisaleus will be fit to command the army, and that *will* lead to an attack on Thebes."

"What can we do?" Pelopidas asked. "My stomach turns at the thought of sitting idle. But what choices do we have?"

"We must capture a messenger, a Spartan rider."

"One messenger! This is your plan?" snorted Pelopidas. "This will bring about Spartan defeat?"

Parmenion looked into the man's dark eyes and chuckled. "The time will come for warriors like yourself—trust me, Pelopidas. This single man is like the stone that starts the landslide. But it is vital that he be taken; he must be stripped of armor and clothing, his body buried where it will not be found. Everything he carries must be brought here."

"It sounds easy enough," Pelopidas muttered.

"Then I will make it more difficult. The killing must not be seen: his disappearance must remain a mystery."

"Well, at least his messages may prove useful," the Theban said.

"Not even that," said Parmenion. "The Spartans must have no idea that we have intercepted them."

"Then would you kindly outline the point of this exercise?" asked the Theban.

Parmenion glanced at Epaminondas, who nodded. "I shall take the place of the messenger," said Parmenion, "and ride to Sphodrias at Thespiae. But this is to be known only by us three."

"It will be as you say," promised Pelopidas. "I will send out riders to watch all roads to Thespiae."

Parmenion walked back through the night-cloaked city. He felt tense and excited, and as he passed the temple to Aphrodite he remembered the redheaded priestess. Stopping by the marble fountain, he gazed at the temple, feeling the stirrings of desire deep in his loins. Checking his money sack, he strolled into the temple precincts and along the corridor. The hour was late, but lantern light could be seen under the woman's door; he put his ear to the wood, listening for sounds of movement, but there were none, and he knocked softly. He heard the creaking of the bed as she rose. The door opened.

He held out his money and was surprised to see her smile. "I am happy you are recovered," she said.

"I do not wish you to speak!" he snapped. The smile froze on her lips, then her cheeks darkened.

"Take your money and go!" she said, slamming the door in his face. For a moment Parmenion stood shocked; then he backed away and returned home to the cold comfort of his bed. The meeting with the woman had disturbed him. She knew he required her to say nothing; he had been with her scores of times. He would pay her, satisfy his lust, and leave. It was a simple business. Why, then, had she broken the rules?

As he had stood in the doorway, her perfume had washed over him, filling his senses. And in her face, as he reprimanded her, there had been shock, surprise, and a hurt he could not understand. He felt an almost physical need to seek her out and apologize. But for what? How had he offended her?

At last he dropped into a troubled sleep and dreamed of Derae.

Parmenion awoke three hours later and climbed to the flat roof to watch dawn illuminate the city. He turned his gaze southwest to the towering peaks of Mount Cithaeron and the mountains beyond. This is a beautiful land, he thought, yet we squabble over it like children.

He sat in the sunlight, thinking back to his days with Xenophon.

"Greece can never rise to full glory," the general had told him, "for we are not a complete nation and we have no national view. We have the finest soldiers in the world, the best generals, and we are supreme on the sea. Yet we are like the wolf pack; we rend and tear at each other while our enemies gloat."

"But the wolves always find a leader," Parmenion had pointed out.

"Yes," Xenophon agreed, "and there the comparison ends. Greece is composed of scores of city-states. Even a man of greatness from—let us say—Athens would not be able to bind Greece together. The Spartans would envy and fear him, the

Thebans likewise. They would not see him as a Greek but as an Athenian. The hatreds are too deeply ingrained, and they will not be overcome—at least not in my lifetime. So what *do* we see? Persia controls the world, and she uses Greek mercenaries to do it—while here we live in a country with beautiful mountains and poor soil. Everything we need we import from Egypt or Asia, paying the Persians handsomely for each transaction."

"What if one man were to lead a united force against the Persians?" asked Parmenion.

"He would need to be a colossus among men, a demigod like Heracles. More than that, he would have to be a man without a city, a Greek. And there are no such men, Parmenion. I had hoped Sparta would take the lead, but Agisaleus cannot forget his hatred of Thebes. The Athenians learn with their mothers' milk to hate Spartans. Thebans and Corinthians loathe Athenians. Where, then, can Greece find a leader?"

"What would you do?"

"If I were a god, I would lift the nation from the sea and shake her so that all the cities fell to dust. Then I would gather the survivors and tell them to build one great city and call it Greece."

Parmenion chuckled. "And then the Athenian survivors would take the northern part of the city and call the district Athens, while the Spartans would take the southern part. Then each would decide that their neighbor's district was more precious than their own."

"I fear you are right, my boy. But set against my despair, there is a good side to the situation."

"And what is that?" Parmenion asked.

"There will always be a demand for good generals."

Now Parmenion smiled at the memory and climbed down from the roof. Mothac brought him a goblet of the sylphium brew, which he drank swiftly. He had experienced no head pain since the night of Derae's miracle, and his body felt strong once more.

"I need to run," he told Mothac.

But the training ground was packed with warriors practicing with sword and shield. Pelopidas was roaring out orders, and several officers were moving among the men, offering advice or encouragement. Parmenion stood and watched for some minutes, then Pelopidas saw him and ran to where he stood.

"They are coming along well," said the Theban. "Good men, proud men."

"Given time, you will have a fine force here," said Parmenion, choosing his words with care. "But how much close formation work do you plan?"

"We always conclude with a formation run. But the men prefer more open combat; it makes them competitive."

"Indeed it does, my friend, and you are quite right. Yet, as I am sure you are aware, when they meet the Spartans, it will be in close formation. If they are spread like this, they will be cut to pieces."

"Would you be willing to help train the men?" Pelopidas asked.

"It would be an honor," answered Parmenion. The Theban took his arm and led him out onto the field.

"Splendid attack!" shouted Pelopidas as a swordsman blocked a thrust and hammered his shoulder into his opponent, knocking him from his feet. The man grinned and saluted with his wooden blade.

"What is the man's name?" asked Parmenion as they walked on.

"I don't know. Do you want me to find out?"

"No," answered Parmenion softly. Pelopidas gathered the men together, forming them in a huge semicircle around Parmenion.

"This is the man who planned the retaking of the Cadmea," he roared. "This is the *strategos* who climbed the walls and rescued Epaminondas." The men cheered loudly, and Parmenion reddened; his heart pounded, and irrationally he felt the onset of fear. Pelopidas spoke easily to the soldiers, and it was obvious that he was much admired, but Parmenion had never before addressed such a group, and his nerves were in tatters. "He will be training you in close formation maneuvers so that the next time we meet the Spartans we will close around them like an iron fist!" Pelopidas turned to Parmenion. "Do you wish to say anything to the men?"

"Yes," said Parmenion. There were several hundred men seated around him, their eyes upon him. He could feel those eyes pressing on his soul, and his legs felt weak, almost unable to support him. "Close formation fighting . . ." he began.

"We can't hear him!" someone called from the back. Parmenion took a deep breath.

"Close formation fighting is about brotherhood," he shouted. "It is about understanding and caring. It is about putting the good of all above what is good for one." He paused to take a breath.

"What is he talking about?" asked a man in the front row. A ripple of laughter spread back through the ranks, and anger flared in Parmenion's heart.

"Stand up!" he bellowed, his voice ringing with authority. The soldiers obeyed instantly. "Now form a complete circle with me at the center," he told them, striding to the middle of the training field. The soldiers rose and trooped after him.

"Who is the best swordsman here?" he asked them as they formed a great circle, many ranks deep.

"Pelopidas!" they shouted.

"And the worst?" This was greeted by silence until a young man raised his hand. He was slender to the point of emaciation.

"I am not very skilled—yet," he said, "but I am getting stronger." More laughter followed this admission.

"Let both men come into the circle," said Parmenion.

Pelopidas rose and walked with the young man to stand beside the Spartan. "May I say something?" the Theban general asked Parmenion, who nodded. "Some of you men," began Pelopidas, "laughed when our friend—and brother—Callines admitted his shortcomings with the blade. His admission took courage." His angry eyes raked the men.

"Courage," he repeated, "and a man with that kind of courage will improve. And you will help him, as we will all help each other. The cause of Thebes is sacred to me, and every man who aids Thebes is sacred to me. We are not just men playing a game of war; we are a sacred band, bound to one another in life and death. Let there be no more sneering." He stepped back and turned to Parmenion. "I am sorry, *strategos*; please continue."

Parmenion allowed the silence to grow. The words of Pelopidas had surprised him, but the sentiments were good.

"You have heard something today," said Parmenion at last, "that you should burn into your hearts. Because in days to come, when you are old, your hair gray and your grandchildren playing at your feet, you will hear men say with pride, 'There he is. He was one of the sacred band.' And you will look up and see young men gaze at you with awe and envy." Once more he let the silence swell. "Now, let us have two more swordsmen, good men of talent and speed."

When the four men were standing ready, holding their swords and shields of bronze, Parmenion walked to Pelopidas. "Your sword, sir." Mystified, Pelopidas handed the wooden blade to the Spartan, who turned to the young man beside the Theban general. "Your shield, sir." The man surrendered it. Parmenion dropped the weapons at the inner rim of the circle and repeated the maneuver with the other pair. "We have here," he told the bewildered watchers, "an example of close formation fighting. Four men with only two swords and two shields. The shield bearer must protect the swordsman but has himself no weapon with which to attack. The swordsman must protect the shield bearer though he has no shield to defend himself. Each man in the pair must depend on the other. Now to battle, if it please you, gentlemen."

Pelopidas and the slender Callines advanced together. The opposing swordsman launched a sudden attack. Pelopidas blocked the blow with his shield, and Callines lunged, but his strike cracked against the shield of his opponent. The warriors circled each other but could find no openings. After several

minutes the enemy pair dropped back for a whispered conference, then advanced once more, the swordsman suddenly
moving to the right, seeking to outflank Pelopidas. Ignoring
him, Pelopidas darted for the shield bearer, hurling himself at
the man. Their shields met with a clash, and Pelopidas' opponent was hurled from his feet. Callines ran forward, touching
his sword to the fallen man's throat. Pelopidas swung as the
swordsman came up behind him, and only the rim of his shield
deflected the blow. Callines came to his aid. Pelopidas parried
a thrust, then swung his shield into his opponent's sword arm,
pushing it back. Callines leapt, his blunt sword ramming into
the man's groin, and the warrior fell to the earth with a groan.

"What you just saw," said Parmenion, moving to the center
of the circle and hauling the man to his feet, "was your worst
swordsman killing two opponents. That, in essence, is the
secret of the phalanx. Ordinary men, well trained, can prove
magnificent in battle. But great warriors become invincible.
You will be invincible!"

For two hours Parmenion worked the men, until Pelopidas
called a halt and allowed the training to end. Taking Parmenion's arm, he led him to the shade by the grave of Hector.
"You did well, my friend. Very well indeed," said the Theban.
"You gave us a name, an inspired name. From today we are
the Sacred Band."

"No," answered Parmenion. "The name was yours; you
coined it when you spoke up for young Callines. But it is
fitting, and it does no harm for warriors to feel bonded. You
are a fine leader."

"Enough compliments," said Pelopidas. "I feel uncomfortable with them. Now tell me why you asked the name of the
first swordsman you saw?"

Parmenion smiled. "It is not I who should know his name—
it is you. A general is like a craftsman who knows the name
and merits of each of the tools he possesses. The men look up
to you; they admire you for your courage and your strength.
As a general you cannot make a friend of every man, for that

might lead to lax discipline. But speak to each by name and they will fight the better for you—and for Thebes."

"But will we beat the Spartans?" asked Pelopidas.

"If any man can, you will," Parmenion assured him.

Derae opened her eyes, but the darkness was total. She could feel the warmth on the right side of her face and knew that the sun was up, and she wept for her loss.

Blindness. The fear of humans from the dawn of time: helpless against the whims of nature, the cruelty of savage beasts.

Her last sight had been of Tamis looming above her, the copper vial in her hand with steam rising from the bubbling contents within. Then the touch of fire on her open eyes and the scream of agony that followed the kiss of acid.

She heard the door open and felt the bed shift as Tamis sat beside her. "Lie still," said the old woman, "and listen to me. Hold your body still and think of a blue sky and a long stem of gold. Can you do that?"

"Yes," answered Derae weakly.

"Picture the stem of gold against the blue and see the tip swell and grow—bending, twisting, becoming a loop joined back to the stem like a huge needle of gold. Do you have it in mind?"

"I do. Gold against blue," Derae whispered.

"Now, below the loop, like the cross-guard of a Persian sword, two further stems grow from the gold. Hold it in your mind, the blue and the gold. Tell me what you feel?"

"I feel as if warm air is blowing inside my head."

"Good. Now soar!" ordered Tamis. Derae felt all weight fall from her, as if chains of lead had parted. She floated—and opened her eyes. The ceiling was close, and she rolled her spirit, looking down to see herself lying on the pallet bed with Tamis beside her. The old woman looked up. "Now you can see," Tamis told her, "and you have discovered one of the secrets of the source. A gift to him is returned manifold. You are free, Derae. Free to fly and free to learn. Go! Travel like the eagle and see all that you desire. But look not to the future, my child, for you are not ready."

Derae's soul sped from the temple, glorying in the sunlight, moving up through clouds and across the ocean. Far below her she saw the mainland of Greece, its rearing mountains and arid plains. Tiny triremes were anchored in the bay near Athens, and fishing boats bobbed on the waters around them. Southwest she flew to Sparta, hovering above her old home, seeing her mother and her sister in the courtyard.

Sorrow swept over her; she did not wish to see them like this; rather, she desired to see what *was*. The scene blurred and shifted, and she watched herself running from the gateway, down to the meadow where the girls could exercise, while on a nearby hilltop she saw the boy Parmenion lying on his belly, waiting for a glimpse of her.

The scenes were painful, but she could not resist following them through. She watched again his rescue of her and their first day of passion in the summer home of Xenophon. She could not bear to see her death, so she remained with Parmenion, observing with horror as he destroyed Nestus.

Then she followed his journey to Thebes and his brief, passionless encounters with Thetis the whore. Anger flared in her. How could he? she wondered.

Yet, despite her anger, she felt pride when he planned the retaking of the Cadmea and watched, astonished, as he collapsed and was carried to his bed. She saw Mothac's concern, his anger at the physician, and, at the last, his desperate pleading with the whore, Thetis. And this time she watched the complete scene, hearing Parmenion whisper her name in his sleep.

He was delirious and thinking of her!

Joy flooded her. She wanted to reach out and touch him, to tell him she was alive and she cared for him. But cold reality came to her like the breath of winter. I am not alive, she realized. And I can never have him.

She urged time on—seeing him run on the training field, floating close to him, her spirit face mere inches from his own. Reaching out, she tried to stroke his dark hair, but her fingers moved through his skin and the skull beyond, his thoughts tumbling into her mind.

As he ran he was thinking of the days in the mountains, before their secret was out, of making love in the meadows and holding hands beneath the trees.

She withdrew from him, for his bitterness touched her like the acid that had destroyed her eyes. Her joy evaporated, and she returned to the temple and a world of darkness. Tamis helped her dress.

"What did you learn?" asked the old woman.

"Love is pain," she answered dully. "What will you teach me today?"

"I will teach you to see," Tamis told her. "Spirit eyes are far more powerful than the orbs you have lost. Concentrate. You have loosed the chains of your soul, and you float now inside the cloak of your body. At any time you may draw aside that cloak like a veil. Try it. The gold and the blue."

Derae focused on the looped stem and rose. "Not too far," shouted Tamis, catching the falling body and lowering it to the floor. "You must retain control of yourself. Come back!" The priestess returned to her body and climbed to her feet. "It will take practice," said Tamis, "but merely move your spirit head forward while holding your body still." Derae tried. For a moment it seemed to work, she could see and yet still feel her body. But then dizziness overcame her and she stumbled into Tamis, who held her upright.

"It will come," Tamis promised. "But each step is a victory. And now we must work. You must learn. We must identify all your weaknesses."

"Why?"

"You have joined the eternal war, Derae, and you now have a deadly enemy. The Dark God will also be testing you, seeking a way to destroy you."

"That is a frightening thought," Derae admitted.

"As it should be, for when the crucial moment of conflict comes, I will be dead and you will be alone."

Parmenion paused at the top of the ridge and gazed down on the tents of the Spartan army. They were set out in a long rectangle along the valley floor close to the city of Thespiae. Swiftly he counted the tents. There were five lines of fifty, with each tent housing ten warriors: two thousand-five hundred fighting men, not counting those billeted in the city.

Parmenion stroked the neck of the black gelding, then touched heels to the beast's flanks, urging him on. Now came the danger, but to his surprise Parmenion felt a sense of rising excitement along with his fear. This, he realized, was what brought joy to life, the exquisite sensations of fear and exhilaration combining to sharpen the mind and thrill the senses. It was as if the past years in Thebes were without color. He glanced up at the sky and the drifting clouds, feeling the mountain air soaking into his lungs.

This was life!

Down there was Hecate, goddess of death, her dark dagger drawn, ready for him to make one mistake, one slip that would cost him his life.

Parmenion chuckled, tightened the chin strap on his leather helmet, and began to hum an old song his mother had taught him. The gelding's ears pricked up, and he tossed his head at the sound. He was a fine beast; Pelopidas had said that he had almost outrun the pursuers, but a lucky arrow had taken the rider in the base of the skull, toppling him to the ground. The gelding had halted its run then, turning to nuzzle at the corpse on the earth.

The man's armor fitted Parmenion well, save that the breastplate was a little large. But the greaves and metal-studded kilt could have been made for the slender Spartan. The cloak was of fine wool, dyed red and held in place by a golden brooch that Parmenion replaced with one of bronze.

Such a brooch would be recognized and would lead to questions, he reasoned.

The rider's papers had been taken to Thebes, where Epaminondas opened the dispatch and read it. It dealt with supplies and the need to isolate Thebes, but at the close it mentioned Athens and the need for vigilance. Epaminondas handed the scroll to a middle-aged scribe with prematurely white hair. "Can you duplicate the style of script?" he asked.

"It will not be difficult," said the man, peering at the dispatch.

"How many lines can we add above the king's signature?" queried Parmenion.

"No more than two," the scribe told him. Parmenion took the script and read it several times. It concluded with the words: *"The traitor Calepios is hiring mercenaries in Athens. Be vigilant."* Then there was a gap before the signature *Cleombrotus*.

Parmenion dictated a short addition to the scroll, which the scribe carefully inserted. Epaminondas read the words and smiled grimly. " *'Be vigilant and advance upon the Piraeus, destroying any hostile force.'* If this succeeds, Parmenion, it will mean war between Athens and Sparta."

"Which can only be good for Thebes," Parmenion pointed out.

"There are great dangers for you in this," said the Theban softly. "What if you are recognized, or your message disbelieved? Or if there is a password? Or . . ."

"Then I will be dead," snapped Parmenion. "But it must be done."

Now, as he rode down toward the tents, Parmenion felt his fear swell. Three soldiers on sentry duty barred his way on the road; they were men from the Sciritis hills and not Spartiates. They saluted as he approached, clenched fists on their breastplates of leather. He returned the salute and tugged on the reins.

"I seek the general Sphodrias," he said.

"He is in the city; he stays at the house of Anaximenes the *ephor*. You ride through the main gate and head for the temple of Zeus. There is a tall house with two slender trees alongside the gates."

"Thank you," said Parmenion, riding on.

The city was smaller than Thebes, housing a mere twelve thousand inhabitants. Thespiae was a city of tradesmen, specializing in chariots and the training of horses. As Parmenion entered, he could see many small pastures holding fine herds. He rode until he reached the house with twin trees, then he dismounted and led the gelding to the front of the white-walled building. A male servant ran to take the horse's reins, and a second servant, a young girl dressed in white, bowed and bade him follow her into the house.

Parmenion was taken through to a large *andron* where several Spartan officers were sitting and drinking. The servant moved to a burly figure with a rich red beard, who rose and stood with hands on hips, scrutinizing Parmenion, who bowed low and approached.

"Well, who are you?" snapped Sphodrias.

"Andicles, sir. I have dispatches from the king."

"Never heard of you. Where's Cleophon?"

"He had a fall from his horse, broke his shoulder, sir. But he is determined to ride with the king this evening and be at his side during the battle."

"Ride? Battle? What are you talking about, man?"

"My apologies, sir," said Parmenion, handing the general the leather cylinder. Sphodrias pulled out the scroll within and opened it. As he did so, Parmenion glanced at the other officers, his eyes falling upon a young man dicing at a window table. His stomach turned: The man was Leonidas.

"There's nothing about numbers here," muttered Sphodrias. "How many of the enemy are there? Where are they camped? I can't just march into Athenian territory and butcher the first men I see in armor."

"There are said to be five thousand of them," said Parmenion swiftly. "Three thousand *hoplites*, the rest cavalry. It is rumored that they are being paid with Persian gold."

Sphodrias nodded. "You can always expect treachery from Athenians. But we'll have to march all night to surprise them. I don't doubt they have scouts out. You will stay by my side while I brief my officers. They may have questions."

"With respect, sir," said Parmenion, struggling to keep his voice calm, "the king has ordered me to return at once with your plans, so that he can link with you on the Thriasian plain."

"Very well. I'll order my scribe to draft an answer."

"That will not be necessary, sir. If you are to march all night, I will advise the king to meet you between Eleusis and Athens."

Sphodrias nodded and returned his attention to the scroll. "Curious dispatch. It starts by talking of supplies and ends with the invasion of Athens. Still, who am I to argue, eh?"

"Yes, sir," replied Parmenion, saluting. His eyes flicked to Leonidas, who had stopped playing dice and was watching him intently. Parmenion bowed and swung back to the door, marching out into the yard beyond; once there, he ran behind the house to the stables. The gelding had been brushed and combed, and the lionskin shabraque was laid carefully over a rail. Parmenion draped it over the beast's back, smoothing out the folds before grasping the horse's mane and vaulting to his back.

He could hear the sound of pounding feet and kicked the gelding into a run, galloping past the running figure of Leonidas.

"Wait!" shouted the man.

The gelding thundered out onto the main avenue, where Parmenion slowed him until they reached the main gates. Then he allowed the horse his head, riding at speed toward the mountains.

Glancing back, he saw two horsemen galloping from the city. The gelding was breathing hard as they topped a rise, and Parmenion had no choice but to slow down. Even so he took the horse along narrow paths and treacherous trails where he guessed the riders would not follow.

He was wrong. As he made camp in a cave high on a ridge, he heard the sound of walking horses on the scree outside. He had a fire blazing, and there was no way to disguise his presence.

"Come inside, there's a warm fire," he called, keeping his voice cheerful and bright. Moments later two men entered the cave. One was tall, his beard dark and heavy, the other slender but well muscled. Both wore swords and breastplates.

"Leonidas wished to speak with you," said the bearded man. "What is your name, friend?"

"Andicles. And yours?" asked Parmenion, rising.

"And what of your family?" continued the man. "Where do you live?"

"By what right do you question me, Sciritai?" stormed Parmenion. "Since when do slaves badger their masters?"

The man's face burned crimson. "I am a free man and a warrior, and Spartan or no, I'll take no insults!"

"Then offer none!" snapped Parmenion. "I am a messenger of the king, and I answer to no man. Who is this Leonidas that he should send you to question me?"

The slender man moved closer. "By all the gods, Leonidas was right! It is you, Parmenion!"

Parmenion's eyes narrowed as he recognized the man; it was Asiron, one of the boys who had taunted him at Lycurgus barracks ten years before.

"There is obviously some mistake here," he said, smiling.

"No," said Asiron. "I'd stake my life on it."

"Yes, you have," replied Parmenion, drawing his sword and slashing it swiftly across Asiron's throat. The man hurled himself back from the gleaming blade, but blood was already gouting from the wound in his neck.

The Sciritai leapt to his left, drawing his own sword and grinning wolfishly. "Never killed a Spartan yet," he hissed, "but I always wanted to."

The Sciritai attacked with blinding speed. Parmenion parried and jumped back, his right forearm stinging. Glancing down, he saw a line of blood oozing from a narrow cut. "I think I'll take you a slice at a time," said the Sciritai. "Unless you'd like to surrender and throw yourself on my mercy."

"You are very skillful," Parmenion told him as they circled one another. The Sciritai smiled but said nothing. He launched an attack, feinted with a belly thrust, and then slashed his sword toward Parmenion's face. The blade sliced agonizingly close to Parmenion's throat, the tip opening the skin of his cheek.

"A slice at a time," repeated the Sciritai. Parmenion moved to his left, putting the fire between them; then, sliding his foot forward into the blaze, he flicked burning branches into the Sciritai's face. His opponent stumbled back, oiled beard aflame. Parmenion ran in close, slamming his sword into the man's groin. The Sciritai screamed and lashed out, but Parmenion ducked and wrenched his blade clear. As bright arterial blood gushed from the wound, drenching the Sciritai's leg, Parmenion moved back, waiting for him to fall. Instead, the Sciritai charged him. Parmenion blocked a vicious cut, but the man's fist cracked into his chin, sprawling him to the cave floor; he rolled as the man's iron blade clanged next to his head, sending a shower of sparks into the air. The Sciritai staggered, his blood pooling on the floor by his feet.

"By the gods," he muttered thickly. "I think you've killed me, boy."

He sank to his knees, dropping his sword.

Parmenion sheathed his own blade and caught the man as he toppled sideways. Lowering him to the ground, he sat beside the warrior as his face grew ever more pale.

"Never . . . got to . . . kill a . . . Spa . . ." His eyes closed, his last breath rattling from his throat. Parmenion rose and walked to Asiron. The man had hit his head on the cave wall as he had jumped back from Parmenion's wild cut. His throat was bleeding, but the cut was not deep and already the blood was clotting. Removing the man's sword belt, he bound his hands behind him and then rebuilt the fire. His right foot was blistered from the flames, and he removed his sandals, hurling them across the cave. It took more than an hour for Asiron to wake: at first he struggled against his bonds, then he sat back and stared at Parmenion.

"You treacherous dog!" he hissed.

"Yes, yes," said Parmenion wearily. "Let us have all the insults first. Then we can talk."

"I have nothing to say to you," answered Asiron, his eyes flicking to the body of the Sciritai and widening in shock. "Gods, I never believed he could be bested with a blade!"

"All men can be bested," said Parmenion. "What did Leonidas say to you?"

"He thought he recognized you but could not be sure. He sent me and Damasias to intercept you."

Parmenion nodded. "Not sure . . . that is good. Then even now the Spartan army is marching upon its old enemy. I wonder if they are singing battle songs of glory. What do you think, Asiron?"

"I think you are a misbegotten and vile creature."

"Is that any way to speak to an old friend who has decided not to kill you?"

"You'll get no thanks from me."

Parmenion chuckled. "Do you remember the night before the general's games when you and Learchus and Gryllus attacked me? I spent that night hiding upon the acropolis, dreaming of the day when I could repay you all. But then, children are like that, aren't they—full of fantasies? As you sit here I have sent the Spartan army to invade Athens. My heart is glowing."

"You make me sick! Where is your loyalty? Your sense of honor?"

"Honor? Loyalty? Why, I think that was thrashed out of me by good Spartan gentlemen like yourself, who pointed out that I was a Macedonian, not a Spartan at all. For whom should I express my loyalty?" His voice hardened. "To the people who killed the woman I loved? To the city that made me an outcast? No, Asiron. I left you alive for a simple reason. I want you to tell Leonidas that it was I who organized the retaking of the Cadmea and I who set Sparta at war with Athens. And more, my old, dear friend. It will be I who will see Sparta destroyed, her buildings razed, her power at an end."

"Who do you think you are?" Asiron asked with a dry, humorless laugh.

"I'll tell you who I am," answered Parmenion, the words of Tamis echoing in his mind. "I am Parmenion, the Death of Nations."

Soon after dawn Parmenion released Asiron and rode for Thebes. The cuts on his face and arm were healing fast, but his right foot was burned and blistered, leaving his mood grim as he cantered to the city gates. An arrow flashed by him, then another. Swinging the gelding's head, he galloped out of range. Several horsemen rode out toward him, swords drawn. Parmenion wrenched off the Spartan helmet and waited for them.

"It is I," he yelled, "Parmenion!" The horsemen surrounded him, and he recognized two of the men as members of the Sacred Band. They began to question him, but he waved them away and steered his mount into the city to report to Epaminondas.

Four days later Parmenion was awakened at midnight by shouting outside his home. Rising from his bed, disgruntled and annoyed, he threw a cloak around his naked frame and moved down the stairs, meeting Mothac as he emerged to the courtyard. "I'll crack his skull, whoever he is," muttered the Theban as the pounding on the gate began. Mothac pulled open the gate, and Pelopidas ran in, followed by Epaminondas. The drunken Theban warrior grabbed Parmenion around the waist, hoisting him into the air and swinging him round.

"You did it!" yelled Pelopidas. "Damn your eyes, you did it!"

"Put me down, you oaf! You're breaking my ribs."

Pelopidas released him and turned to Mothac. "Well, don't just stand there gaping, man. Get some wine. This is a celebration!"

Mothac stood his ground. "Shall I break his face?" he asked Parmenion.

The Spartan laughed. "I think not. Better fetch the wine." He turned his gaze to Epaminondas. "What is going on?"

"A messenger arrived an hour ago from Calepios in Athens. Sphodrias and his army appeared to the north of the city at dawn three days ago. They ravaged some villages and advanced on the Piraeus. An Athenian force went out to meet them, the Spartan ambassador with them, and Sphodrias was forced to withdraw. By all the gods, I wish I'd seen it," said Epaminondas.

"But what happened then?" snapped Parmenion.

"Let me tell him," urged Pelopidas. His face sported a lopsided grin, and his joy was almost childlike.

Epaminondas bowed to him. "Continue," he said, "noble Pelopidas!"

"The Athenians were not happy. Oh, no! Their council met, and they have decided to send—sweet Zeus, I love this—they have decided to send five thousand *hoplites* and six hundred cavalry for the defense of Thebes. Five thousand!" he repeated.

"It is wonderful news," said Epaminondas, accepting the goblet of wine from Mothac. Pelopidas staggered into the *andron* and stretched himself out on a couch.

"It is not an end in itself," said Parmenion quietly, "but it is a good beginning. What has happened to Sphodrias?"

"He has been summoned back to Sparta, with his army. Boeotia is free—except for the garrisons."

"So," whispered Parmenion, "Sparta and Athens are now at war. We should be safe—at least until next spring."

Epaminondas nodded. "And now other cities in Boeotia will seek to rid themselves of Spartan garrisons. Pelopidas is leading his Sacred Band out into the countryside tomorrow to aid the Tanagra rebels. I think we could win, Parmenion. I really do."

"Do not tempt the gods," advised Mothac.

Epaminondas laughed aloud. "A long time ago I was told I

would die at a battle in Mantinea. This frightened me greatly, for the seer was the renowned Tamis and beloved of the gods. So you can imagine how I felt when, with Pelopidas, I found myself fighting at Mantinea against the Arcadians. We were surrounded, and Pelopidas went down. I stood my ground, ready to die. But I did not die. And why? Because there are no gods, and all prophecies can be twisted to mean anything the hearer desires. Tempt the gods, Mothac? I defy them. And even if they do exist, they are far too interested in changing their shapes and rutting with anything that moves to care what a lonely mortal thinks of them. And now I think I should collect Pelopidas and guide him home." He took Parmenion's arm suddenly, the smile fading from his face.

"Once more you are our savior, my Spartan friend. I cannot tell you how grateful I am. One day I will find a way to repay you."

Pelopidas was asleep on the couch, but Epaminondas shook him, hauling him to his feet and steering him to the gates. Immediately the drunken Theban launched into a marching song, and the two men walked off into the darkness.

During the months that followed Parmenion settled back into private life, spending his time training *hoplites*, running, and reading. Occasionally he would attend parties or celebrations as a guest of Epaminondas or Calepios, who had returned in triumph from Athens. But mostly he kept to himself, taking his horse and riding into the countryside, exploring the hills and valleys surrounding Thebes.

By the spring of the following year hopes were high in the city that the Spartan menace had been overcome and that the old Boeotian League could be re-formed. Pelopidas and the Sacred Band had been instrumental in helping the rebels of Tanagra and Plataea expel the Spartan garrisons, and there was even talk of the great king of Persia granting the Theban request for autonomy from Sparta.

Then came fearful news. Agisaleus had gathered an army of eleven thousand *hoplites* and two thousand cavalry and was marching to crush the rebellion. The next night Mothac returned from visiting the grave of Elea, tending the flowers planted there. It was late, and he walked home in darkness, his thoughts somber. As he reached the narrow street before the house of Parmenion, he saw a figure in the shadows leap and scale the wall. He blinked and focused his eyes on the spot, but there was nothing to be seen. Then a second figure scrambled over the wall to Parmenion's home.

Mothac felt a chill sweep over him. Swiftly he ran for the gate, pushing it open. "Parmenion!" he bellowed. As he raced across the courtyard, a dark figure leapt from the shadows, cannoning into him. Moonlight glinted on a knife blade that slashed by his face. Mothac rolled and came to his feet, blocking a thrust and hammering his fist into the man's face. The assassin fell back. Mothac threw himself at the man, making a wild grab for the knife wrist. He missed, and the blade plunged home into his left shoulder. His knee jerked up into the man's groin, bringing a grunt of pain, then Mothac's hands were on the assassin's throat. Hurling himself forward, he cracked the man's skull against the courtyard wall. The assassin went limp, but three times more Mothac smashed the man's head to the stone. Blood and brains fell onto his hands, and he let the corpse sink to the ground.

"Parmenion!" he shouted again.

The assassin Gleamus cursed softly as he heard the servant call out, then ran up the steps to the upper floor bedroom where the traitor slept. Pausing outside the door, he listened, but there was no sound from within. Was it possible that the Spartan had not heard the cry?

Perhaps, but Gleamus had practiced his trade for almost twenty years in Egypt and Persia, Athens and Illyria, and he had survived by always using his wits, leaving nothing to chance.

For days now he had watched the house, observing the movements of the traitor, gauging the man. His prey was a warrior. He moved well, smoothly, his eyes alert. But the weakness was in the house. There was only one exit from the bedroom unless the man wished to leap to the courtyard below, where he would surely break bones.

The plan had already gone awry, but there was still time to collect the bounty offered by Agisaleus. Gleamus considered his next move. The man beyond the door could be awake. If so, where would he be? The previous day, while no one was present, Gleamus had searched the building, memorizing the details of the bedroom. There was nowhere to hide. The room was small. So there were few options for the man within. If awake, he would be standing either to the left of the door or to the right. Behind him Aris and Sturma were moving up the stairs. But he would not need them. This was a kill he could make alone. It would show them he was still the master.

Lifting the catch, he hurled open the door, which crashed against the left wall. In that moment he saw the bed was empty, and with a savage cry he leapt forward, his knife slashing to the right, where the traitor had to be. The blade slammed against the wall.

Momentarily stunned, Gleamus stood still, his gaze scanning the moonlit room. The traitor was gone! It was impossible. He had seen the man enter. There was nowhere else for him to be!

A shadow moved above him. He spun, his blade coming up. But he was too late. The traitor's sword slammed down past his collarbone, plunging deep into his lungs. Gleamus grunted and fell back, his dagger clattering to the floor. Even as life fled from him, his assassin's mind could not help but admire the ploy. The Spartan had climbed to the lintel stone above the door.

So simple, thought Gleamus.

The wood of the floorboards was cool against his face, and his mind wandered. He saw again his father's house on the isle of Crete, his brothers playing on the hillsides, his mother singing them to sleep with songs of gods and men.

Blood bubbled into his throat, and his last thoughts returned to the Spartan. So clever. So cle . . .

❖   ❖   ❖

Parmenion dragged his sword clear of the corpse and stepped from the doorway. A blade sliced toward his face. The Spartan's sword flashed up, blocking the cut, his left fist cracking into the man's chin, sending him back into a third assassin on the stairs. Both men stumbled. Feet first, Parmenion leapt at them, his right foot thundering against the first man's chin. The two assassins were hurled to the foot of the stairs. Parmenion vaulted over the balcony, dropping to the *andron* below. Both assassins regained their feet and advanced on him.

"You are dead now, mix-blood," muttered the first.

The two men moved apart, coming at the Spartan from both sides. Parmenion launched a sudden attack at the man on the right, then spun on his heel, his sword cleaving the throat of the man on the left as he darted in. The assassin fell, blood gouting to the Persian rugs covering the stone floor. The last assassin moved warily now, and sweat shone on his bearded face.

"I am not easy to kill," said Parmenion, his voice soft.

The man edged back toward the door. Mothac loomed up behind him, ramming a dagger through his lungs.

The assassin crumpled to the floor.

Mothac staggered in the doorway, then stumbled outside to sit at the courtyard table, the bronze hilt of a knife jutting from his shoulder. Parmenion lit two lanterns and examined the wound.

"Pull the cursed thing out," grunted Mothac.

"No. It is best where it is for the moment. It will prevent excessive bleeding until we get a physician." He poured Mothac a goblet of unwatered wine. "Do not move around," he ordered. "I will come back with Argonas."

Mothac reached up and grabbed Parmenion's arm. "I appreciate that you want to move quickly," he said, forcing a grin. "But it might be better if you dressed first."

Parmenion smiled, his face softening. "You saved my life, Mothac. And almost lost yours. I will not forget it."

"It was nothing. But you could at least say you'd do the same for me."

Two hours later, with Mothac asleep, the knife removed, the wound bandaged, Parmenion sat with Argonas, watching the fat man devour a side of ham and four goblets of wine, followed by six sweet honey cakes. Argonas belched, then lay back on the couch, which creaked under his weight.

"An interesting life you lead, young man," said Argonas. "Impersonating Spartans, fighting assassins in the dead of night. Is it safe to be around you? I wonder."

"Mothac will be as he was?" asked Parmenion, ignoring the question.

"The wound passed through the fleshy part of the shoulder, where he is well muscled. It is not a round wound and will therefore heal more easily. I have applied fig-tree sap, which will clot the blood. He will be in some discomfort for several weeks, but the muscles will knit and he should be recovered by the summer."

"I am very grateful to you. Mothac means much to me."

"Yes," agreed Argonas, stroking his oiled beard, "good servants are hard to come by. I myself had a Thracian body servant, a wonderful man who anticipated my every need moments before I realized the need was there. I have never found another like him."

"What happened to him?" inquired Parmenion, more from politeness than out of genuine interest.

"He died," said Argonas sadly. "He suffered a brain growth—like yours—but he was a man who never spoke of his troubles, and when he finally collapsed, it was too late to prevent his death. Never forget, my friend, to take the sylphium brew. Such deaths are painful to see and worse to suffer. I must say that your servant found a novel cure for you. I would use it myself, but already I am in trouble with my peers."

"I thought it was the sylphium that healed me," said Parmenion.

"Indeed it was. But first you had to be brought back in order to drink it. He is a thoughtful man and a clever one. If ever he should think of leaving your service, I would be delighted to acquire him."

"Yes, yes, but what did he do?"

"You don't remember?"

"For pity's sake, Argonas! If I remembered, why would I ask you?" snapped Parmenion, his irritation growing.

"He brought your favorite whore to your bed: a priestess. It seems that the will to live is considerably strengthened in a man who is aroused to copulation."

"No," whispered Parmenion, "that is not how it was. It was Derae who came to me."

Argonas heaved himself upright, his dark eyes showing concern. "I am sorry, Parmenion," he said. "I have not spoken wisely. Put it down to a lack of sleep and an excess of wine. Perhaps it was both women: Derae in the spirit, the priestess in the flesh."

Parmenion scarcely heard him. He was seeing again the priestess in the doorway, her smile, the smell of her perfume, the anger and sorrow in her eyes, the slamming of the door.

"Have you thought about why assassins should seek to kill you?" asked Argonas.

"What? No, I cannot think of a reason. Perhaps they were merely robbers."

"Robbers without pockets or sacks? I think not. Well, I must leave. I will come back tomorrow to check Mothac's wound and receive my fee."

"Yes. Thank you," said Parmenion absently.

"And walk with care, my friend. Whoever hired these men can always hire more."

Two days later the senior officer of the city militia visited Parmenion. Menidis was almost seventy years of age and had been a soldier for more than half a century. For the last ten years he had headed the small militia force operating within the city, responsible for patrolling the streets after dark and manning the great gates of Thebes.

"The men were foreigners," said Menidis, his sharp gray eyes peering at Parmenion from under thick white brows. "They arrived in the city four days ago, passing through the Proitian gates. They said they had recently traveled from Corinth and were interested in purchasing Theban chariots. My belief is that they came from Sparta." The old soldier waited to see what effect this had on the young man before him, but Parmenion's face was impassive. "The part you played in freeing us of Spartan domination is well known," he continued. "I believe the men were hired to kill you."

Parmenion shrugged. "They failed," he said.

"This time, youngster. But let us assume for a moment that they were paid by a rich nobleman. Such men are easy to find. Sadly, so too are you."

"You suggest I leave Thebes?"

The old man smiled. "What you do is a matter for you. I could have men guard you wherever you go and watch over you while you sleep. The lord Epaminondas has requested— at the very least—that we set a sentry outside your gates. But still there will be times when you walk in crowded avenues or pause at market stalls or shops. A dedicated killer will find you."

"Indeed," agreed Parmenion, "but I am in no mood to run. This is my home. And I do not want your guards here, though I thank you for the offer. If an assassin is to kill me, then so be it. But I will not be an easy victim."

"Had it not been for your *Theban* servant," Menidis pointed out, "you would have been the simplest victim. A sleeping man offers little resistance. However, it is your choice and you have made it." The soldier stood and replaced his bronze helm, securing the strap at the chin.

"Tell me something," asked Parmenion. "I sense you do not care much whether they succeed or fail. Why is that?"

"You are very astute, and I believe in honesty at all times, so I will tell you. That you chose to betray your own city and aid Thebes gives me cause to be grateful to you. But you are still a Spartan, and I despise Spartans. Good day to you."

Parmenion watched the old man depart, then shook his head. In a curious way the words of Menidis caused him more concern than the attack. He strolled up to Mothac's room, where the servant was cursing as he tried to nurse his injured arm into a *chiton*.

"Let me help you," said Parmenion, "though Argonas insisted you stay in bed for a week."

"Two days felt like a week," Mothac snapped.

"Do you feel up to walking?"

"Of course! Do I look like a cripple?" Parmenion looked into the man's face, reading the anger in his eyes. Mothac's cheeks were flushed almost as red as his beard, and he was breathing heavily.

"You are a stubborn man. But let it be as you say; we will walk." Parmenion armed himself with sword and dagger, and slowly they made their way to the gardens at the western slope of the Cadmea, where fountains were placed to cool the breeze and flowers grew all year. The two men sat close to a shallow stream, beneath a yellowing willow, and Parmenion told the Theban about his conversation with Menidis.

Mothac chuckled. "He doesn't mellow with age, does he? Two years ago he arrested two Spartan soldiers, cracking their skulls for them. He claimed they were molesting a Theban woman of quality, which was complete nonsense. Theban women of quality are not allowed on the streets."

"In that—if in nothing else—you lag behind Sparta," said Parmenion. "There women walk as freely as men, with no restrictions."

"Disgraceful," Mothac observed. "How, then, do you tell them from the whores?"

"There are no whores in Sparta."

"No whores? Incredible! No wonder they are so anxious to conquer other cities."

"While we are on the subject of whores, Mothac, tell me about the night you brought one to my bed."

"How did you find out?"

"It does not matter. Why did you not tell me?"

Mothac shrugged, then winced as his shoulder flared. He rubbed at the wound, but that only made it worse. "You were convinced it was a miracle. I wanted to tell you the truth, but . . . but I didn't. No excuses. I am sorry; it was all I could think of. Yet it worked, didn't it?"

"It worked," agreed Parmenion.

"Are you angry?"

"Just a little sad. It was good to feel that Derae came back to me, if only in a dream. Perhaps Epaminondas is right and there are no gods. I hope he is wrong. When I look at the sky, or the sea, or a beautiful horse, I like to believe in gods. I like to feel there is some order, some meaning to existence."

Mothac nodded. "I know what you mean, and I do believe. I have to. There is someone waiting for me on the other side; if I didn't believe that, I would cut my throat."

"She died on the day you came to me," said Parmenion. "Her name was Elea."

"How did you know?"

"I followed you on the first day. I saw the funeral procession. When you went off—as it turned out, to kill Cletus—I walked to the grave to pay my respects."

"She was a wonderful woman," said Mothac. "She never complained. And I still see her face whenever I close my eyes."

"At least you had more than five days," whispered Parmenion, rising. "Let us return. I think you are more tired than you look."

Suddenly a man stepped from the shadows behind them. Parmenion's sword slashed into the air, and the man leapt back, lifting his hands, his mouth hanging open in shock.

"I have no weapon! No weapon!" he screamed. Behind him stood a child of around seven years, clutching his father's cloak.

"I am sorry," said Parmenion. "You startled me." Sheathing his sword, he smiled down at the child, but the boy started crying.

"You are more concerned than you look," said Mothac as the two began the long walk home.

"Yes, it frightens me to know that a knife, or a sword, or an arrow could come from anywhere. Yet if I leave Thebes, I will be as I was when I came here—virtually a pauper. I have money in several merchant ventures, but I have still to pay Epaminondas for the house."

"Better to be poor and alive," said Mothac, "than rich and dead."

"But better still to be rich and alive."

"You could join the Sacred Band. Pelopidas would be delighted to have you, and even the doughtiest assassin would have difficulty in getting close to you."

"That is true," Parmenion agreed, "but I will serve under no man—save perhaps Epaminondas. He and I think alike. Pelopidas is too reckless, and it does not pay to be reckless when facing the Spartans."

"You still believe we do not have the strength to go against them?"

"I *know* it, Mothac; it is not a question of belief. No, we must stall them, refuse open battle. The time will come. But we must have patience."

Leucion had slept badly, his dreams full of anxiety and frustration. He woke early, his mood foul, while the other nine warriors still slept.

Curse the whore! thought Leucion as he stirred the ashes of the fire, at last finding a glowing ember and adding dry leaves and twigs to bring the blaze to life. She had talked of love, but when his money ran out, she had laughed at him, ordering him from her house. Cursed Persian whore! The battles were over, the mercenaries disbanded. We were welcomed by cheering crowds and flowers strewn in our path, he remembered, but dismissed in the night with a handful of coins and not a word of thanks.

They all look down on us, he realized. Persians. Yet where

would they be without us, fighting their miserable battles? Barbarians, all of them. He opened the pouch at his side, pulling clear his last coin. It was gold, heavy and warm. On one side was stamped the face of the great king, on the other a kneeling archer with bow bent. The Persians called them darics, after Darius the Great. But to the Greek mercenaries they were archers and the single reason why so many Greek warriors fought in Persian wars.

"No Greek is impervious to Persian archers," Artabazarnes had told him during a drinking bout. Then the Persian had laughed, the sound mocking. He had wanted to smash the leering grin from the Persian's face.

Leucion sat now before the fire, his anger burning brighter than the flames. Pendar awoke and joined him. "What troubles you?" asked his friend.

"This cursed country," Leucion told him.

"Your mood was fine yesterday."

"Well, this is today!" snapped Leucion. "Wake the men and let us push on. It is a ten-day ride to the city."

"You think they'll take us on?"

"Just do as I ask!" roared Leucion. Pendar backed away from him and woke the men as Leucion rubbed his fingers through his short black beard. It was matted now, and he longed for a vial of perfumed oil . . . and a bath. Lifting his breastplate into place, he settled the shoulder guards and strode for his horse.

Mounted at last, the men rode across the green hills, their armor glinting in the morning sun. Topping a rise, they gazed down on a series of small villages and a distant temple with white columns, beyond which lay the shimmering sea.

Leucion tugged on the reins, riding toward the nearest village. His head was pounding now, and he squeezed his eyes shut against the pain.

Curse you, whore, to a worm-ridden death!

As they neared the village, he glanced at the temple. Riding high on the hills, they could see over the white walls of the temple garden. A young woman was walking there, her red-gold hair reflecting the sunlight, her body slim, breasts pressing against the filmy gown she wore.

A scene came to his mind: the woman writhing beneath him, begging him to stop, pleading with him, his knife at her throat, the blade slipping into the skin, the blood gushing from her. . . .

Kicking his horse into a run, he galloped for the rose-covered gateway.

Even as he approached, he realized that the others would never stand for him murdering the girl before they had enjoyed her. No, he would have to be patient. His thoughts surprised him, for he had never before considered there to be pleasure in murder. In fighting, yes; in war, obviously. How curious, he thought. Dragging on the reins, he leapt from the horse's back and strode through the gateway. The girl was kneeling by a rosebush. Her head came up.

She was blind. For some reason this made his arousal more fierce, his sense of power soaring.

He heard the other men dismounting and halted, watching the girl. Her beauty was considerable, more Greek than Persian, but Leucion did not care what nationality she was.

"Who are you?" she asked, her voice soft yet deeper than he had expected, her accent betraying her Doric origins. Spartan or Corinthian, he thought, which delighted him. He would not have felt as content with the prospect of raping an Athenian woman.

"Why do you not speak?" she asked, no trace of fear yet in her voice. But that would come, he knew. Slowly he drew his knife and advanced toward her.

"What are you doing?" cried Pendar.

Leucion ignored him and moved close to the woman. Even above the scent of the roses he could smell the perfume of her hair. Reaching out, he took hold of her gown at the shoulder and slashed through it, pulling the remnants clear of her body. She stumbled back naked, and now the fear showed.

"Stop this!" Pendar shouted, running forward and grabbing

Leucion's arm. Before he could stop himself, the warrior swung and plunged his blade into his friend's chest. "Why?" whispered Pendar, falling against Leucion and sliding to the ground, his blood smearing Leucion's bronze breastplate. For a moment Leucion hesitated, confused; then he shook his head and swung to the other men. "You want to take her?" he asked them.

"Why not?" answered Boras, a thickset Thracian. "She looks tender enough." The men advanced on the naked girl, Leucion in the lead with his bloody knife raised. The priestess stood her ground. She lifted her hand, and Leucion felt the knife writhe in his grasp. Glancing down, he screamed. He was holding a viper whose raised head was drawn back with fangs poised for the strike. He threw it from him, hearing it clatter to the stones.

"What's the matter with you, man?" asked Boras.

"Did you not see it? The snake?"

"Are you mad? You want her first or not? I'll not wait for long."

A low growl came from behind them.

A beast stood in their midst. It had the head of a lion, the body of a bear, huge shoulders, and taloned paws. Swords flashed into the air as the warriors attacked the creature, which offered no resistance as the blades cleaved its massive frame. It fell, covered in blood, and became their comrade Metrodorus.

"She's a witch!" shouted Boras, moving back from her.

"Yes, a witch," the blind woman told them, her voice almost a hiss. "And now you will all die!"

"No!" came another voice, and Leucion saw an old woman struggling along the pathway. Easing past the swordsmen and kneeling beside the dead Metrodorus, she placed her hands on his wounds and began to chant. Clouds seemed to race across the sky, then freeze in place. The wind at first howled but then died, and the silence was eerie. Leucion glanced up to see an eagle hanging motionless in the sky, wings spread. The chanting continued, and the men watched as Metrodorus' wounds closed. A shuddering breath shook his frame, then a groan.

"See to the other one," the sorceress told the blind girl.

"They are killers! They deserve to die!" she shouted.

But the old woman ignored her, and the young priestess moved to the body of Pendar, laying her hand over the chest wound. Leucion watched in silent amazement as the wound closed. Pendar awoke and gazed up at the blind healer.

"Did they harm you?" he asked her. She shook her head. "Am I dying?"

"No. You are well," she told him.

Leucion stood dazed and blinking in the sunlight. The wind picked up, and the eagle continued its flight as he stumbled to Tamis. "I don't know . . . I have never . . ." But the words would not come.

Pendar rose and took his friend's arm. "Are you well now, Leucion?"

Suddenly the leader began to weep. "You know me, Pendar. I would never . . . do such a thing."

Tamis turned to Derae but said nothing. The young priestess' stepped forward, taking Leucion by the hand. "Go from here to Tyre," she said coldly. "There you will find what you seek."

"I am sorry," he told her.

"Nothing happened of any importance," Derae assured him.

Pendar gathered up Derae's dress and wrapped it around her, tying the torn pieces together.

"And you, Pendar, should return to Athens, where your family has need of you."

"I will, lady," he promised.

After the men had gone, Tamis walked to the pool and splashed cold water to her face. Derae sat beside her.

"Why did you stop me?" asked Derae.

"You touched Leucion; you know why he came. The chaos spirit was working within him."

"But I could have killed him."

"And who would have won, Derae? Who would gain the victory? The Dark God cares nothing for Leucion. He knew the man could not destroy you; it was *you* he was seeking to test. We cannot use his weapons. Every small victory gained that way leads to a future defeat. I know; I have killed men. Leucion will find love and happiness in Tyre. He will raise sons, good men, proud men. But he will never forget this day."

"Nor shall I," said Derae with a smile. Tamis could sense her pleasure, and for a fleeting moment she merged with her, touching her soul like an unheard whisper. The Spartan woman was recalling with satisfaction how the men had fallen upon their comrade. She was relishing the memory of power.

Tamis pushed herself to her feet and returned to her room. She was tired and failed to see the black shadow forming on the wall behind her as she sat down on the bed. As she poured a goblet of water and sipped it, talons slid from the wall at her back—long and curved. The water touched an edge of rotting tooth, and Tamis grunted and rose. The sun moved from behind a cloud, and a shaft of light shone through the window, casting the shadow of talons on the bed. Tamis whirled as the claws slashed for her face. Her arm came up, light blazing from her fingers to become a glowing shield of gold. The talons raked across it, and the wall shimmered, a huge head pushing clear of it as if the stone were no more solid than smoke. The demon's skin was scaled, its teeth pointed. Slowly it emerged into the room, its enormous arms and taloned hands reaching for the old seeress.

"Begone!" thundered Tamis, pointing at the creature. But the light was fading from her hands, and she knew that she had used too much of her power on the slain man.

The demon lunged at the shield, which split in two and vanished from sight. Talons hooked into Tamis' robes, and she was dragged across the stone floor toward the gaping hole where once the wall had been.

The door opened. . . .

A blazing shaft of light smote the demon in the chest. Fire

and smoke leapt from the beast, and a terrible cry filled the room. The talons tore free of Tamis, and the creature swung on Derae.

The Spartan woman waited until the demon was upon her, then threw out both arms. Lightning lanced from her fingers. The creature was punched from his feet; he tried to rise, but blue light encircled him, chaining his huge arms and legs.

Derae moved forward, standing over the beast. "Begone," she whispered. A wind blew up, sucking the demon back through the wall, which shimmered before becoming stone once more.

"You . . . did . . . well," said Tamis, clutching the side of the bed and hauling herself to her feet.

"What was the . . . thing?"

"A night hunter. Our enemies have breached the spell I placed over the temple. You must help me form another."

"Do you know who our enemies are?"

"Of course. The leader of them is Aida."

"Can we not attack them?"

"You do not listen, Derae. We cannot use their weapons."

"I am not convinced," said Derae. "How can we fight them when all the weapons are theirs?"

"Trust me, child. I have no answers that would convince you. Just trust me."

Lying back on the bed, Tamis closed her eyes, unable to look at the young priestess. Twice today the Spartan had tasted the joys of power. . . .

And Tamis could almost hear the Dark God's laughter as she fell into an exhausted sleep.

Thetis wandered through the narrow streets to her home in the south of the city, her season at the temple of Aphrodite completed. Once home, she scrubbed away the paint and the ocher and threw the shimmering gown and bright, filmy *chlamys* to a corner. Pulling on a white cotton gown, she stretched herself out on a couch and stared at the soiled garments.

Tomorrow she would burn them and would never again visit the temple of Aphrodite. Unlike many of the other girls Thetis had spent her earnings wisely, investing with three merchants engaged in the spice trade and one from Thespiae who bred and trained war-horses.

Thetis was now financially secure. The house had cost 980 drachmas, and she had also hired a maidservant, a Thessalian girl of fifteen who lived in a small alcove at the rear of the kitchen.

From now on life would be without care, without sweaty hands groping at her, without the grunts of the worshipers in her ear.

Without Damon, she found herself thinking. She closed her eyes and settled back, hugging an embroidered cushion to her belly.

Without Damon. . . .

How could someone so young and athletic have died in such a manner, collapsing on a training field after a race? The surgeon said he had a weakness in the heart. Yet he was so strong, his body carrying no fat, his muscles firm and as finely chiseled as those of Heracles. No, he had no weakness of the heart, Thetis knew. He had been struck down by the gods who were jealous of his beauty, and Thetis had been robbed of the only love she would ever know.

For a while she dozed on the couch, then rose and wandered to the kitchen, where she ate some bread and cheese, washing it down with cool water. The servant girl, Cleo, was snoring softly in her bed, and Thetis moved silently about the room so as not to wake her.

Her hunger satisfied, she returned to her couch. The clothes on the floor caught her eye, and she realized she could not wait to burn them. Taking the small, curved knife she carried for protection, she slowly ripped the garments into tiny pieces until the floor around her couch looked as if it were strewn with flower petals.

Six years of her life had been spent wearing those garments, six long years filled with faceless, nameless men. Bearded or unbearded, fat or thin, young or old, all desired the same service.

She shook her head as if to dislodge the memories, and Parmenion's face loomed in her mind. She had thought of him often in the months since she had brought him back from the dead. It was the contrast, she realized, between the silent rutting animal he was with her and the caring, considerate lover she had seen on that one night as he dreamed of . . . what was her name? Derae?

So physically unlike the powerful Damon yet possessing the same qualities of tenderness and understanding of her needs. No, not *her* needs, she reminded herself: Derae's needs.

Taking up the cushion, she held it to her and fell asleep once more, waking with the dawn. Beyond the kitchen Cleo had filled a bath with heated water, and Thetis climbed in, soaking her skin and washing her short, thickly curled red hair. When she stood, Cleo wrapped a warm towel around her, patting her dry. Then the servant smeared perfumed oil on Thetis' body, scraping it clean with a round-edged knife of bone.

Thetis put on an ankle-length *chiton* of blue-dyed linen and wandered to the courtyard. It was long and narrow but caught the early-morning sunshine. Beyond the gates she could hear people moving on the streets and the distant hammering from the forge of Norac the smith. She sat in the sun for an hour and then walked inside, taking up an embroidery she had begun three years before. It was a series of interwoven squares and circles with shades of green, brown, and yellow. Working on it calmed her mind.

Cleo came to her. "There is a man to see you, mistress."

"A man. I know no men," she answered, realizing as she said it that it was the truth. She had coupled with hundreds, perhaps thousands of men, and not one did she know.

"He asks to speak with you."

"What is his name?"

The girl blushed and ran to the courtyard, returning within moments. "Parmenion, mistress."

Thetis took a deep breath, composing herself. "Show him in," she said, "then leave us."

"Leave you, mistress?" queried Cleo, surprised.

Thetis smiled. "If I need you, I will call out."

Thetis returned to her embroidery as the girl led Parmenion to her. She glanced up, her face stern.

"Please be seated," she said. "Cleo, fetch some water for our guest."

"That will not be necessary," said the man, seating himself on the couch opposite. They sat in silence until Cleo had left, pulling the door shut behind her.

"I do not welcome uninvited guests to my home," said Thetis. "So I would appreciate it if you would state your business swiftly."

"I came to apologize," began Parmenion.

"For what?"

The man suddenly smiled sheepishly; it made his face more boyish, less stern, she thought. "I am not sure, but I know it is necessary. You see, I did not know it was you who brought me back that night."

"I was paid for it," she snapped, battling to control an anger she could scarcely understand.

"I know that," he said gently. "But I felt . . . feel . . . I have caused you pain. I would not wish that."

"You would like to be friends?" she asked.

"I would—very much."

"My friendship cost forty obols," she told him, rising and tossing aside the embroidery, "but no longer. Now, please leave. You can find many friends at the temple, and the price remains the same."

"That is not what I meant," he said, pushing himself to his feet. "But it will be as you say." He walked to the door and turned to face her. "I value friendship highly," he told her. "Perhaps it is because in my life I have very few friends. I know you were paid for what you did, but even so you saved my life. That is a debt I will carry. Should you ever have need of me, I will be there. No question. Whether you wish it or not, I am your friend."

"I do not need friends, Parmenion, but if ever I am short of forty obols, I will think of you."

After he had gone, she sank down to the couch and lifted the embroidery. Cleo came to her, kneeling at her feet. "Your hands are trembling, mistress."

"He is not to be allowed in here again. The next time he calls, you will stop him at the gate. Do you understand?"

"At the gate. Yes, mistress."

But the days passed and Parmenion did not call again, and for some curious reason this only served to make Thetis more angry with the young Spartan.

As spring progressed Thetis found her new life increasingly oppressive. When a priestess, she had been able to walk the streets day or night. But no Theban woman of quality would ever be seen unaccompanied save at the marketplace, and the house that had been Thetis' dream fast became a comfortable prison. Cleo brought news daily, but mainly her conversation revolved around the latest clothes, or perfumed oils, or jeweled necklaces. The girl took little notice of the movements of the Spartan army as it entered Boeotia. All Thetis could gather was that the Spartan king, Agisaleus—having forced a passage for his troops through the passes of Mount Cithaeron in the south—was ravaging the countryside and that Epaminondas had fortified a ridge outside Thebes with five thousand Athenian *hoplites* and three thousand Thebans.

Not that it mattered to Thetis whether the Spartans won or lost. It seemed to her that whatever the city of origin, the grunts in her ear were always the same.

But the war was affecting her investments, the Spartans having confiscated the last shipment of opium as the carts passed through Plataea. Thetis lost almost six hundred drachmas and was now relying on Asian spices coming in through Macedonia to keep her profits high.

Thoughts of her finances left her thinking of the temple.

Nothing would make her go back to that way of life again, she promised herself.

Then Parmenion's face came to her mind.

Curse him, she thought. Why does he not call?

With Agisaleus unwilling to assault the ridge defended by Athenians and Thebans and Epaminondas refusing battle on the open plain, the war entered a stalemate, the Spartans marching through Boeotia, sacking small towns and villages and bolstering their garrisons but leaving Thebes unscathed.

Then Agisaleus, tiring of a war of attrition, marched toward the city. He had in mind to storm the Proitian gates and raze Thebes to the ground. The less hardy of the city dwellers fled, packing their belongings into carts or wagons.

One wagon contained the physician Horas with his wife and three children. The eldest child, Symion, complained of a severe headache as the wagon moved on into the night, heading for Thespiae. By dawn the boy had a raging fever, and glands in his throat and armpits had swollen to three times their size. Red patches formed on his skin, and he was dead by noon. That afternoon Horas himself felt the onset of fever and delirium.

An advance scouting party from the Spartan army found the wagon. The officer looked inside, then backed away swiftly.

"The plague," he whispered to his aide.

"Help me!" croaked Horas, struggling to climb from the wagon. "My wife and children are sick."

"Stay where you are," shouted the officer, signaling a bowman forward. "Where are you from?"

"Thebes. But we're not traitors, sir. We are sick. Help us, please!"

The officer gave a signal to the bowman, who shot an arrow through Horas' heart. The physician fell back into the wagon.

"Burn it," the leader ordered.

"But he said there was a woman and children inside," argued his aide.

The officer rounded on the man. "Then you climb in and put them out of their misery!"

The soldiers gathered brushwood and piled it around the wagon. Within moments the dry wood roared into flame, and as the screams were beginning, the soldiers marched back to report the encounter to Agisaleus.

The plague started in the poorest quarter of the city but spread swiftly. Fearing the army would become affected, the councillors ordered the city gates to be shut and barred. No one was allowed out of or into the city. A mob attacked the guards at Electra's Gates but was turned back by bowmen on the walls commanded by the old warrior Menidis.

Within a week more than a fifth of Thebes' thirty thousand population endured the symptoms of glandular swelling and ugly, inflamed red swirls that appeared on face and arms. The death toll rose, and scores of carts were pulled through the city streets every night to collect the dead whose bodies had been placed in alleys beyond house gates.

Mothac succumbed to the sickness on the ninth day, and Parmenion helped him to his room before running to the house of Argonas. The physician was not there; his servants told Parmenion he was visiting the sick in the north of the city. The Spartan left a message for him and returned home. Food was now scarce, but he bought some dried meat and stale bread in the marketplace for a sum four times its worth and prepared a broth for Mothac.

Argonas arrived at dusk. The flesh of his face was sagging, and his eyes were dark-rimmed. He examined Mothac, then took Parmenion aside.

"The fever will burn strongly for two days. It is important to take the heat from the skin. Bathe him hourly in warm water, but do not dry him. Allow the heat of his body to evaporate the water; this will cool him. He will then suffer intense cold, and he must be wrapped in warm blankets until the fever rises once more. Then repeat the procedure. Make sure he drinks plenty of water. Add a little salt—not too much or he will vomit. If the swellings begin, wait until they split and weep, then apply honey."

"Is that all that can be done?"

"Yes. I ran out of herbs four days ago."

"Sit down and have some wine," invited Parmenion, moving to the jug on the kitchen shelf.

"I have no time," Argonas replied, heaving himself to his feet.

Parmenion took him by the shoulders. "Listen to me, man. If you go on in this way, you will collapse; then you will achieve nothing. Sit down."

Argonas sank back to the chair. "Most of the physicians got out before the gates were shut," he said. "They recognized the symptoms early. There are too few of us now."

"Why did you not leave with them?"

Argonas smiled. "That's what everyone would expect. Fat Argonas, who lives for money: look at him run! Well, I do like money, Parmenion. I enjoy a life of pleasure and gluttony. I was born poor, a peasant in a foreign land. And I decided a long time ago that I would taste the good things and revel in luxury. But that does not make me less of a physician. You understand?"

"Drink the wine, my friend, and *revel* in a little cheap broth."

"Not cheap anymore," said Argonas. "Prices are rising very fast."

"How bad is the plague?" Parmenion asked, ladling broth into a deep bowl and placing it before the fat man.

"Not as bad as the one that struck Athens. There are probably eight thousand people in Thebes who have the symptoms, but curiously, many of them stop short of developing the plague. It is deadly in children and the old, but the young and strong seem able to fight it off. Much depends on the swellings. Armpits only and there is a chance; if it spreads to the groin, death soon follows." Argonas spooned the broth into his cavernous mouth, then rose. "Time to go. I will call on Mothac tomorrow evening."

Parmenion saw him to the gate and watched the fat man make his way down the narrow alley, stepping over the bodies laid out in rows.

Mothac was sweating heavily when Parmenion returned, but his lips were cracked and dry. Lifting the Theban's head, he forced cool water between his lips and then bathed him as Argonas had directed. For two days Mothac scarcely moved. In his delirium he called out for Elea and wept. On the third day large swellings appeared in his armpits, and he lapsed into a near coma. Parmenion was exhausted, but still he stayed by day and night at Mothac's bedside. The swelling under the left arm turned purple, and as Argonas had warned, it split, oozing watery pus. Parmenion smeared honey on the wound and covered Mothac with fresh blankets.

The following morning, as he slept in a chair beside the bed, he heard a rattling at his gate. Rubbing the sleep from his eyes, Parmenion stumbled to the courtyard to see the servant girl, Cleo.

"It is my mistress," cried Cleo. "She is dying."

Parmenion took the girl to Mothac and ordered her to sit by him, instructing Cleo on how to bathe the sleeping man. Then he took his cloak, armed himself with sword and dagger, and carefully made his way to the house of Thetis. Corpses lay everywhere, and the marketplace was deserted.

Thetis was lying on her bed, lost in a fever sleep. Pulling back the sheets, Parmenion examined the woman's naked body. There were swellings under both armpits and in the groin. Wrapping her in a blanket, he lifted her into his arms and began the slow walk back to his own house.

On the way two men who were pulling a cart piled high with bodies called out to him: "We'll take her." He shook his head and staggered on. His muscles were burning with fatigue as he carried her into his courtyard and through to the *andron*, where he laid her on a couch. Together he and Cleo manhandled his bed down the stairs and into the room alongside Mothac. "It will be easier to look after them both in the same room," Parmenion told Cleo. "Now go back to the house and gather what food there is and bring it here."

With the girl gone, Parmenion bathed Thetis, applying honey to a seeping sore under her right arm. He felt her pulse, which was fluttering and weak, then sat beside her, holding her hand. After a while her eyes opened.

"Damon?" she whispered through dry lips.

"No, it is Parmenion."

"Why did you leave me, Damon? Why did you die?"

"It was my time," he told her, his voice gentle and his hand squeezing hers. "Rest now. Gather your strength—and live."

"Why?" came the question, and it cut into him like a jagged blade.

"Because I ask you to," he told her. "Because . . . I want you to be happy. I want to hear you laugh again."

But she was asleep once more. Soon she began to shiver, and Parmenion wrapped her in a warm blanket and hugged her frail body, rubbing her arms and shoulders, willing heat into her.

"I love you, Damon," she said, her voice suddenly clear. Parmenion wanted to lie as once she had lied for him. But he could not.

"If you love me, then live," he said. "You hear me? *Live!*"

Time passed swiftly for Derae. Every day she learned new skills, healing the sick of the surrounding villages who were carried into the temple on makeshift stretchers. She mended the broken leg of a farmer, stroked away the weeping, cancerous sore on a child's neck, and gave sight to a blind adolescent girl who had traveled with her father from the city of Tyre. Word spread throughout the Greek cities of Asia that a new healer had come among them, and day by day the lines lengthened outside the temple.

Tamis had been gone for several months, but she returned late one evening to find Derae sitting in the garden, enjoying the cool of the night air. Already there were people sleeping in the fields beyond, waiting for their chance to see the healer.

"Welcome home," greeted the younger woman.

"They will be a never-ending source of exhaustion for you," said Tamis, gesturing to the fields. "They will come from all over the empire, from Babylon and India, from Egypt and Cappadocia. You will never heal them all."

"A blind child asked me why I did not heal myself."

"And what did you tell her?" asked Tamis.

"I told her that I did not need healing. It was true; it surprised me. You look weary, Tamis."

"I am old," snapped Tamis. "One expects to feel weary. But there is something I must do before I leave again. Have you seen Parmenion while I have been away?"

Derae blushed. "I like to watch him. Is that wrong?"

"Not at all. But as yet you have seen no futures. However, now is the time to walk the many paths. Take my hand."

Their souls linked, the two women sped to the city of Thebes and the house of Parmenion. It was shrouded in darkness, and the sound of wailing came from the streets around the dwelling.

"What is happening?" Derae asked.

"The plague has come to the city," answered Tamis. "Now watch!"

Time froze; the air shimmered. Derae saw Parmenion staggering out into the courtyard, his face mottled and red, his throat swollen. He collapsed, and she tried to go to him, but Tamis held her. "You cannot interfere here," she said, "for this is the future. It has not yet occurred. Just as we cannot change the past, neither can we work in the days yet to be. Keep watching!" The scene blurred, re-forming to show Parmenion dying in his bed, dying in the street, dying at the home of Calepios, dying on a hillside. Finally Tamis returned them both to the temple, groaning as she reentered her body to find her neck stiff and aching.

"What can we do?" asked Derae.

"I can do nothing at the moment. I am too tired," said Tamis. "But tell me, do you feel strong enough to use your power at such a distance?"

"Yes."

"Good. But first let me ask you this: How would you react to Parmenion taking a wife?"

"A wife? I . . . I don't know. It hurts me to think of it, but then, why should he not? He thinks me dead—as indeed I am. Why do you ask?"

"It is not important. Go to him. Save him if you can. If you cannot deal with the plague, return for me. I will rest now and gather my strength."

Derae lay back and loosed her soul.

Thebes glistened below her. She flew to Parmenion's home, but he was not there. Mothac lay sick, a young girl beside his bed wiping the sweat from his face with a damp cloth. Derae rose high above the house, her eyes scanning the deserted streets. Then she saw him, staggering under the weight of the woman he carried.

She recognized the whore Thetis and watched as Parmenion brought her home and tended her, listened as the woman spoke of her love in a fever sleep. Derae floated close to Parmenion, laying her hands within his head, his thoughts flowing into her mind. He was willing the woman to live. Derae relaxed her mind, merging with Parmenion, flowing with his blood through veins and arteries.

The plague was within him, tiny and weak but growing even as she observed it. Focusing her concentration, she hunted the pockets of corruption, destroying them until, at last satisfied, she pulled back from him. The woman was dying, huge swellings under her jaws, in her armpits and her groin.

But Parmenion was safe. Derae soared into the night sky and hovered there, confused and uncertain. Parmenion wanted the woman to live. Did he love her? No, his thoughts were not of love but of debts unrepaid. Yet if Derae saved her, he might grow to love her, and she would lose him a second time.

It is not as if I am killing her, Derae rationalized. She is dying anyway. I am not to blame. She wanted to fly back to the temple but could not. Instead she returned to the bedroom and merged with Thetis.

The hunt was monumentally more difficult. The plague was everywhere, rampant and deadly. Three times Thetis' heart shuddered and almost failed. Derae revitalized exhausted glands, feeding energy to the woman, then continued her work, battling the disease. For a long time the plague had the better of her, multiplying faster than she could destroy it. She drew back to the heart, cleaning the blood as it pumped through, filling it with power. The danger area, she realized, was in the groin, where the swellings had burst and were oozing poison-filled pus. Here she accelerated the healing powers of the tissue. Hours fled past. Derae was faint with exhaustion as she finally rose from the body.

She began her journey back to the temple, but her mind was groggy and she found herself floating over an unknown palace in which a woman was screaming. Derae tried to concentrate.

"He is born!" someone cried, and a great cheer went up from the army of men outside the palace.

A dark cloud swept up toward her, opening like a colossal mouth. She saw fangs the length of a tall man, and a purple tongue, forked and swollen. She was powerless to resist.

A spear of lightning slashed into the mouth just as it loomed beneath her.

"Take my hand!" cried Tamis.

But Derae lost consciousness.

She awoke in her own room at the temple, sensing Tamis beside her. "What was it?" she asked.

"You were lost in the future. You saw the dark birth."

"I am tired, Tamis. So . . . tired."

"Then sleep, my child. I will protect you for a little while yet."

Cleo returned with enough provisions for three frugal days, and combined with the food Parmenion had stored, there was enough for a week.

The days dragged by. Argonas no longer called, and Parmenion learned from a collector of the dead that the fat man had suffered the fate of thousands, his body consumed by the plague. Mothac grew stronger, the red swirls disappearing, the swellings abating, but he was weak, needing to sleep often. Cleo worked tirelessly, bathing her mistress, changing soiled sheets, cooking and cleaning. Parmenion scoured the city for food, but even the horses and dogs had long since been slaughtered.

Then, like a spent storm, the plague began to wither away. Fewer and fewer bodies were left for the collectors, and the gates were opened to allow a convoy of food wagons to enter the blighted city. Parmenion fought his way through the mob that surrounded the convoy and emerged with a haunch of beef and a sack of dried cereal.

At home Cleo cooked some of the meat and spoon-fed it to Thetis, who was now more lucid. The two men carried her bed upstairs to Parmenion's room to give her more privacy, while Cleo slept on a couch in the *andron*.

By the end of summer the city had almost returned to normal. More than four thousand people had perished in the plague, but as Calepios pointed out, this was a fraction of those who would have died or been enslaved had the Spartan army sacked the city. Fearing the plague, the Spartans had marched from Boeotia without a battle, and allied troops had now secured the passes over Mount Cithaeron against them. News also came from Tegyra that Pelopidas and the Sacred Band had routed a Spartan division that outnumbered them two to one and had killed Phoebidas, the Spartan responsible for the taking of the Cadmea four years earlier. The defeated soldiers were not Spartan regulars but mercenaries from the city of Orchomenus, yet even so a day of celebration was declared in Thebes and the sounds of laughter and song drifted to the room where Thetis lay. She was still very weak, her heartbeat ragged and irregular, but the distant laughter cheered her.

Parmenion entered, bearing a tray of food and drink. Setting it down, he sat beside her. "You have more color today," he said. "Mothac managed to find some fresh honey cakes. An old friend of mine swore they gave strength to the weary."

Her green eyes rested on his face, but she said nothing. Instead she reached out and took his hand, tears falling to her cheeks.

"What is wrong?" he asked her.

"Nothing," she replied.

"Then why are you weeping?"

"Why did you do this for me?" she countered. "Why did you not let me die?"

"Sometimes there are no answers," he told her, lifting her hand to his lips and kissing her palm. "You are not Derae, as I am not Damon. But our lives have crossed; the lines of our destinies are now entwined. I no longer have great faith in distant gods, but I believe in the Fates. I believe we were meant to be together."

"I do not love you," she said, her voice barely above a whisper.

"Nor I you. But I care for you. You have been on my mind constantly since I discovered the truth about the night you brought me back. Stay with me, Thetis. I cannot promise to make you happy, but I will try."

"I will not marry you, Parmenion, but I will stay. And if we are happy, so be it, we will remain together. But know this: one day you may awake to find me gone. If that happens, promise me you will never try to find me."

"I promise," he said. "Now eat and regain your strength."

The man stood in the moonlight at the gates of Parmenion's house. There was no one in sight as he carefully slid his knife into the crack at the center of the gates, easing up the wooden bar beyond. The gate opened, the bar sliding at an angle toward the ground, but before it could thud against the stone, he rammed his knife blade into the wood, jamming it in place until he could slip through and lower it carefully to the court-yard. Returning the knife to its sheath, he walked toward the closed door of the *andron*.

Something cold touched his neck, and a hand clamped to his

shoulder. "Were I you, I would stand very still," warned a voice by his ear.

"I have a message for Parmenion," whispered the man.

"The knife at your throat is very sharp. Put your hands behind you."

The man obeyed, standing quietly as his wrists were lashed together. Then he was led into the darkened *andron* and watched as his red-bearded captor lit three lanterns. "You would be Mothac?"

"I would. Sit down." Mothac pushed the man to a couch. "Parmenion!" he called. Moments later a tall, slender man, thin-faced, with piercing, pale blue eyes, entered the room. He was carrying a gleaming sword.

"Clearchus!" cried Parmenion, tossing aside the sword and smiling broadly.

"The very same," grunted Xenophon's servant.

"Untie him," ordered Parmenion. Mothac slashed his knife through the leather thongs binding the man, and Clearchus rubbed at his wrists. His hair was whiter and thinner than the young Spartan remembered, the lines on his face deeper, like knife cuts in leather. "An odd time to be calling," Parmenion commented.

"My lord asked me to make sure I was unobserved." Reaching into his thick woolen shirt, Clearchus produced a scroll, which he handed to the young Spartan.

Parmenion put it aside and sat facing the older man. "How does the general fare?"

Clearchus shrugged. "He's a sad man. He writes now. Many things—horsemanship, tactics, the state of Greece. He spends hours every day with his scribes. I cannot recall the last time he went riding or hunting. And he has grown *fat*." Clearchus almost spit the last word, as if even forming it offended his mouth.

Parmenion reached for the scroll, then noticed Mothac still standing by, his knife in his hand. "It is all right, my friend.

This is Clearchus, a companion of the general Xenophon. He is trustworthy."

"He is a Spartan," muttered Mothac.

"Beware, child, lest I crack your skull for you," snapped Clearchus, reddening.

"Once upon a time perhaps, Grandfather," retorted Mothac. Clearchus lurched to his feet.

"Stop this, both of you!" ordered Parmenion. "We are all friends here—or we should be. How long have you been in Thebes?"

"I arrived this evening," answered Clearchus, casting a murderous glare at Mothac. "I visited friends in Corinth, then bought a horse and rode here through Megara and Plataea."

"It is good to see you. Would you like some food and drink?"

Clearchus shook his head. "I will be leaving once you have given me an answer for my lord."

Mothac bade Parmenion good night and wandered back to his room, leaving the two Spartans together. The younger man opened the scroll and sat close to a lantern.

Greetings, friend [he read], the years move on, the seasons gathering pace, the world and its troubles drifting further from me. And yet I see matters more clearly than when young, and with increasing sadness.

There was a young man in Sparta who killed another in a duel over a woman. The dead boy's father still grieves and has hired assassins to seek out the killer, who no longer resides in Sparta. I understand that four assassins were slain by the boy, who is now a man. But others may follow.

I hope that you are well and that your life is happier than that of the Spartan boy who lives now far from home. I think of that boy often. I think of his courage and his loneliness.

At worst may the gods smile on you, at best may they ignore you.

There was no signature.

Parmenion looked up into the weather-beaten face of the old servant. "You risked much to bring this to me, Clearchus. I thank you."

"Do not thank me," said the old man. "I did it for the general. I liked you, boy. But that was a long time ago, before you became a traitor. I hope the assassins find you before you can play any more of your deadly games."

"None of you will ever see it, will you?" said Parmenion, his voice icy. "You Spartans think of yourselves as demigods. You take a child and you torment him all his life, telling him he is no Spartan, then accuse him of treachery when he takes you at your word. Well, here is a thought for you, Clearchus, and all your foul breed: After I tricked Sphodrias, I was caught by a Sciritai warrior. He had fought for you for years; he had been raised to fight for you. And as we drew swords against one another, he told me he had always wanted to kill a Spartan. You are hated not only by Thebes and Athens but by the very people who fight alongside you."

Clearchus opened his mouth to reply, but Parmenion raised his hand.

"Say nothing, servant!" he hissed. "You have delivered your message. Now begone!"

For a moment only the old man glowered at him, then backed away and vanished into the darkness.

Mothac stepped into view, still carrying his knife. "Do not let it concern you," he said gently.

Parmenion gave a bitter laugh. "How would you recommend I do that? After the assassins came, Menidis told me he couldn't care less whether I lived or died. That's the Theban view of me, Mothac: I am a Spartan traitor. And it cuts me to the bone to be called so."

"I think we should get drunk," Mothac suggested.

"It is not exactly the answer I was looking for," Parmenion responded.

"It is the best I have."

"Then it will have to do," said the Spartan. "Fetch the jug."

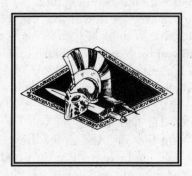

THETIS awoke early. Her dreams had been good, her sleep restful. She stretched her arms and rolled on one side, gazing at the sleeping man beside her. Reaching out, she gently brushed back a lock of hair from his forehead. He sighed but did not wake.

The last six years had been good to them both. Parmenion at twenty-nine was in his prime and had won races in Corinth, Megara, Plataea, and even Athens. His face was sharper now, the prominent nose more hawklike, his hair slowly receding. But his smile was still boyish, and his touch gentle.

Good years . . .

At first he had noticed her discontent at being virtually housebound and had come to her one morning from the marketplace, where he had purchased a dark *chiton*, knee-length sandals, a pair of Persian-style trews in light linen, and a felt hat. "Put these on," he told her.

She had laughed then. "You want me to dress as a man? Are we in need of such devices?"

"No," he replied with a grin. "But I will teach you another way to ride."

It was an adventure she had enjoyed more than she would ever have thought possible. Still weak after the plague, she had sat high upon a chestnut mare and had ridden through the city, her felt hat covering her hair and the loose *chiton* disguising the curves of her body. Once in the hills, she had discovered the joys of the gallop, the wind in her hair, the impossible speed.

They had made love in a high meadow, shaded from the afternoon sun by the branches of a tall cypress, then splashed naked in a cold mountain stream. The recollection of that day shone with clear light in her memories. "When I am gone," he said, "you will be able to send Mothac to fetch the horses and continue to ride. There is freedom here and no one to question you or frown at the lack of dignity shown by a woman of quality."

"Gone?" she queried. "Where will you go?"

"Epaminondas has decided it is time to set about freeing Boeotia. We will be taking troops to captive cities and aiding their rebellions. We must secure the land against Sparta."

Early one morning, some five weeks later, Thetis awoke to see Parmenion standing beside the bed. He was dressed in a bronze helm with baked leather cheek guards and a breastplate showing the head of a roaring lion. His sword was strapped to his side, the scabbard resting against a kilt made of bronze-edged leather strips.

"It is today, then?" she said.

"Yes."

"You could have told me last night."

"I did not want to burden you. I will be gone for perhaps a month, maybe two." She nodded and turned her back to him, closing her eyes and pretending to sleep.

For days she fretted, imagining him riding to his death. "I will not fall in love with him," she promised herself. "I will not cry over his corpse as I did with Damon."

But her fears grew as the news of skirmishes and sieges

reached the city. The Spartan garrison at Thisbe, formed mainly from mercenary units from the city of Orchomenus, had marched out to confront the Theban force. A short battle had followed, before the mercenaries were routed; it was reported that seventeen Thebans were dead. One by one the cities fell, mostly without bloodshed, the beleaguered Spartan garrisons agreeing to leave after being granted safe conduct back across the Peloponnese. But still there was no news of Parmenion.

Six weeks to the day since she had refused to say good-bye, he walked into the courtyard. She saw him from the upstairs window and stopped herself from running down to meet him. Instead she walked slowly, and they met on the stairs. His helmet was dented in two places, his breastplate gashed, the lion's head showing a deep groove.

"Did you miss me?" he asked, untying the chin strap and removing the helmet.

"A little," she conceded. "Are you home for good?"

"No, I ran out of sylphium. I ride back tomorrow."

Back in their room she helped him remove his breastplate and shirt. Only then did she see the vivid red scar on his upper right bicep. "It did not bleed much," he said, trying to reassure her. "It was a mercenary who got too close. Epaminondas killed him."

"I do not want to know the details," she snapped. "I will have a bath prepared."

They had made love that night, but Thetis could not relax and Parmenion's needs were too urgent. The following morning he was gone again.

As the months passed, Epaminondas, Calepios, and others gradually re-formed the old Boeotian League, launching it in Thebes after a general assembly attended by councillors from all the freed cities. The meeting was democratic, and hopes were high for the year ahead.

Parmenion, released for the autumn from military duties, was less sure of the future. On one of their rides he confided to Thetis his fears.

"It is less democratic than it appears," he said as they sat in the high meadow they had come to consider their own private place. "Thebes can veto any decision and directly controls the votes of Thespiae, Plataea, and Tanagra."

"Why is that a problem?" countered Thetis. "Thebes is a great city, and all our councillors value freedom and care about the rights of others. You heard Calepios' speech. The new federal state of Boeotia will have no dictators."

"I heard it, and I hope it proves true. But an old friend once told me that society is like a spear point—wide at the base, pointed at the tip. Democrats believe you can reshape it, removing the point. But as if by magic, it will grow again. There will always be kings, Thetis, and if not kings, then dictators. It is the nature of man to strive to rise above others, to impose his will on all."

"There is no one like that in Thebes," she said. "Maybe in ancient times, yes, but this is the modern world, Parmenion. It does not have to be like that anymore. Epaminondas will never be a dictator, nor Pelopidas. Nor you. I think you worry too much."

And the years appeared to prove her right. Five years after the retaking of the Cadmea, a peace agreement was reached between Athens and Sparta that allowed Thebes and the Boeotian cities the right of self-government.

Thetis remembered that autumn well. Epaminondas had come to the house, accompanied by Calepios, to discuss with Parmenion the terms of the settlement. Against all tradition the Spartan had stopped Thetis as she was leaving the room and signaled for her to sit beside him.

The two Thebans had looked astonished. "It saves me going over everything twice," Parmenion told them. "She will only insist on hearing it all after you have gone."

"But . . ." stuttered Calepios. "She . . . a woman . . ."

"Is this the great orator?" asked Parmenion, struggling to look serious. "Come now, Calepios, you have known Thetis for years. It should not be difficult to speak in front of her."

"It is not a question of difficulty," snapped Calepios, "but one of decorum. I know you Spartans have curious ideas about women, but here in Thebes we prefer to maintain civilized standards. Such matters as we are to discuss would both bore and confuse dear Thetis."

"I am sure Calepios is right," said Thetis, rising, "and I am grateful for his kindness in thinking of me." She had swallowed her anger and retired to her rooms. Later Parmenion gave her a full account of the meeting, but not before his own anger had been unleashed.

"You should have stayed!" he stormed. "Your advice would have been valuable."

"You do not understand, *strategos*. The meeting would not have gone ahead; Calepios would have left. You cannot flout tradition—not in Thebes. Now tell me how *you* view the peace talks."

"Athens is short of money, and Sparta is all but bankrupt," Parmenion told her. "Therefore, all we have won is a little breathing space. The war is not over, but we will use the time wisely."

"How much time?"

He had shrugged. "Two years, three. But this issue will not be decided without a battle, and that means Thebes against Sparta, for Athens is mainly a sea power."

"The Spartans are only men like other men," she had pointed out.

"Perhaps, but they have never lost a major battle against a foe of equal numbers. And whatever happens, we cannot yet match their strength."

"You will think of something, my love; you are the *strategos*." She said it lightly, but he had brightened, his smile returning.

Now Thetis shook her head clear of memories and rose from the bed. Parmenion moaned in his sleep but did not wake as she dressed and moved downstairs, where Mothac was preparing breakfast.

The Theban smiled as he saw her. "Another fine day," he said as she entered the kitchen. There were gray hairs in

Mothac's red beard, and his hair was thinning at the crown. Thetis shivered. It was all very well lying in bed reliving memories, but it had the effect of highlighting the passing of time.

Cleo had long since left, wedded to the son of Norac the smith, and Thetis now helped Mothac in the work of the household.

"You should take a wife," she said suddenly as they sat in the courtyard enjoying the early-morning sunshine.

"I had a wife," replied Mothac. "I don't want another. But I would have liked a son."

Thetis found her good mood evaporating, and Mothac's hasty apology did nothing to alter the downward slide of her emotions. They finished their breakfast in silence, and Mothac went back to the kitchen to prepare Parmenion's daily infusion of sylphium.

A son. The one gift she could never give to Parmenion.

She had long known she was barren, having never suffered the monthly periods of bleeding endured by all other women. But only since she had lived with Parmenion had the knowledge turned to bitterness. Parmenion never spoke of it, and this cheered her, but she knew that all men reached a point in their lives where they desired an heir.

She heard Parmenion approaching but did not turn. His hands touched her shoulders, his lips kissing the back of her neck.

"Good morning, lady," he said.

She smiled. "You sleep later and later," she chided. "I think you are becoming old and lazy."

"I was with Calepios until almost dawn."

She looked into his face. "Is it war again?"

"I don't know. Epaminondas is going to Sparta to meet with Agisaleus."

"Is that wise?" she asked.

"There is to be a meeting of all the cities. Agisaleus has promised safe conducts, and Athens will be represented. It may bring lasting peace."

"But you do not think so?"

"I cannot make up my mind. My fear is that Athens and Sparta will reach agreement, leaving Thebes standing alone. If that is the case, then Agisaleus will feel free to lead his forces into Boeotia, and this time we will have to face him."

"Thebes against Sparta," she whispered.

"To the death," he said.

"And is that what you want?" she asked suddenly.

"What do you mean?"

"You hate the Spartans. Would you really desire peace?"

Parmenion smiled. "You are an astute woman, Thetis. But you are right. I do not want peace. These years have been hard, but I am close now to my dream. One day the Spartans will come—and I will have my vengeance."

"And then?" she pressed.

"What can I say? I have lived so long with no other dream; I can see nothing beyond the humbling of Sparta. They have taken so much from me, and they shall pay in blood and shame for every moment of it."

"Either that or you will die," she pointed out.

"One or the other," he agreed.

Parmenion called a halt to the combat training, and the warriors of the Sacred Band sheathed their swords. In full battle armor, they were sweating heavily. Some sank to the hard-baked clay of the training ground, others wandering to the shade near the grave of Hector.

"Do not be so swift to relax, gentlemen," called Parmenion. "Ten circuits should be enough to stretch those tired muscles."

A groan went up, but the men began to run. Parmenion was about to join them when he saw a young boy sitting beneath the trees watching the training intently. The youngster was around thirteen years of age, with dark, tightly curled hair and a face that, given time, would be exceedingly handsome. But it was his expression that touched a chord in Parmenion. The face was still, the emotions masked, and Parmenion remembered his own boyhood long ago, the trials and suffering he had endured in Sparta.

He strolled across to where the boy sat. "You are studying the art of war?" he asked.

The boy stood and bowed. He was not tall but sturdily built. His dark eyes fixed to Parmenion's face. "It is good to study the ways of foreigners," he said, his voice soft.

"Why is it good?"

"One day we may be enemies. If so, I will know how you fight. If we are friends or allies, I will know whether you can be relied upon."

"I see," said Parmenion. "You are a wise young man. You are a prince, perhaps?"

"Indeed I am. A prince of Macedonia. My name is Philip."

"I am Parmenion."

"I know. I have seen you run. Why is it you compete under a Macedonian name?"

Parmenion sat down, beckoning the boy to join him. "My mother was Macedonian," he told him. "It is a tribute to her. You are a guest in our city?"

The boy laughed. "You do not need to be coy, Parmenion. I am a hostage against the good behavior of Macedonia. But life here is good, and Pammenes takes fine care of me. It is better, I think, than being back in Macedonia. There I would probably be killed by an anxious relative."

"Harsh words, young prince."

"Harsh but true," said the boy. "I am one of many brothers and half brothers, all of whom have some right to the throne. It is not our way to leave rivals alive. I can see the logic of it, I suppose."

"You seem to be taking your plight with great calmness, young prince."

"What else can I do?"

Parmenion smiled. "That is not a question I can answer. I am not a prince."

"No," agreed Philip, "and I do not wish to be one. Nor would I want to be a king. Certainly not in Macedonia."

"What is wrong with Macedonia?" queried Parmenion. "I have heard it is a beautiful land, full of rolling plains and fine forests, mountains and pure streams."

"So it is, Parmenion. But it is also a land surrounded by strong enemies. To the west there are the Illyrians of King Bardylis: tough, doughty warriors. To the north there are the Paionians: tribesmen who love nothing better than to ride south for plunder. To the east there are the Thracians: good horsemen, fine cavalry. And to the south there are the Thessalians and the Thebans. Who would want to be king of such a country?"

Parmenion did not reply. The boy's eyes were sorrowful, his mood dark, and there was nothing the Spartan could say. In all probability the lad was right. Once back in Macedonia, his life would be worth little. The thought depressed Parmenion.

An uncomfortable silence developed, and Parmenion rose to leave. The Sacred Band was still toiling around the circuit, and the Spartan turned to the young prince. "I learned a long time ago never to give in to despair. Fortune may be fickle, but she loves a man who tries and tries again. I think you have a strong mind, Philip. You are a thinker, a planner. Most men just react to circumstances, but thinkers create the circumstances. If there are relatives who wish to see you dead, then make them love you. Show them you are no threat. Show them you can be useful. But more than anything, boy, you must become a hard man to kill."

"How do I do that?"

"By staying alive. By thinking of all the ways your enemies will come at you. By preparing for them. Despair is the brother of defeat, Philip. Never let it touch you."

The boy nodded, then pointed to the runners who were staggering to a halt on the tenth circuit. Parmenion strode out to meet them. "I think that will be all, gentlemen," he said. "Be here tomorrow one hour after dawn."

"Have a heart, Parmenion," called one youngster. "Three days in a row?"

"I have no heart," he said. "I am a man of stone. One hour after dawn, if you please."

Turning back to the trees, he saw that the boy had gone. Parmenion sighed. "May the gods favor you, Philip of Macedon," he whispered.

For three weeks the peace conference at Sparta seemed likely to end all thoughts of war. Trade agreements were negotiated and signed, border disputes argued over but finally settled. Epaminondas was treated like an honored guest and twice dined with King Agisaleus.

Pelopidas returned to Thebes in the fourth week, regaling Parmenion with stories of the geniality that surrounded the conference.

"I think Agisaleus has resigned himself to losing his power over us," said Pelopidas. "There was a representative of the great king there, a golden-haired Persian with a curled beard. You should have seen the clothes he wore: I swear to Zeus, he had more jewels sewn into his coat than stars in the sky! He positively shimmered whenever he entered the room."

"Did he speak?" asked Parmenion.

"He opened the conference, bringing us all the greetings and blessings of the great king. He said the king was happy that his children were to become reconciled, one to the other."

"Speaking of kings, what of Cleombrotus?"

"He has not been present," Pelopidas answered. "It is said he is ill. But I'll tell you this; Sparta is an appalling city. I don't know how you could stand the smell. All the waste flows to the streets, and the flies are thicker than smoke. An ugly place, fit for an ugly people."

"Ill?" queried Parmenion. "With what?"

"They did not say, but it could not have been very serious, for they seemed unconcerned by his absence. You know, when you told me that Spartan women were allowed to walk in the open, I really did not believe you. But you were right. They were everywhere. And some of them even stripped part naked and ran in the meadows. I'll say this; I don't know how such an ugly race of men could ever sire such beauties. There was one woman, with hips like—"

"I know about the women," said Parmenion patiently. "I lived there. I am more concerned with Cleombrotus; he is strong as an ox and would not have missed the conference willingly. What proof did you have that he was in Sparta at all?"

"Where else would he be?"

"What about the army? How many soldiers did you see?"

"Agisaleus ordered the army south for maneuvers. He said the conference would proceed more amiably without the constant clashing of Spartan shields, which some might take as a covert form of persuasion."

"So," said Parmenion. "We have both the battle king and the army lost from sight. Does that not suggest something to you, Pelopidas?"

The Theban warrior got up from the couch and walked to the window. Outside the sun was shining in a clear sky. He swung back toward Parmenion and smiled. "You think they plan some treachery? I doubt it. If they wanted to invade, they could do so without long-drawn-out jabbering and debate and the endless signing of treaties."

"I agree," Parmenion concurred. "But there is a taste to this that does not sit well on the tongue. How many men could we muster in, say, two days?"

"Hypothetically? Three thousand from Thebes, maybe a thousand from the federation."

"Not enough if Cleombrotus and the army marched north instead of south. When is the conference now due to end?"

"Ten . . . no, nine days from now. It will conclude with the signing of a full agreement between the Athenian Alliance, Sparta, and Boeotia. Then there will be two days of celebration."

"And how many men can we bring to the field in nine days?"

"Gods, Parmenion, are you obsessed with Sparta? We could

not consider bringing together an army at this time. If we did and word reached the conference, how would it be seen? We would be accused of aggressive behavior, and the treaty would come to nothing. Why must you look for treachery at every turn? Perhaps the Spartans have come to terms with the reemergence of Thebes."

"How many men?" pressed Parmenion. "Hypothetically."

Pelopidas filled his goblet with watered wine and returned to his couch. "Perhaps seven thousand—if we could get cavalry from Thessaly. But I'll be honest with you; Jason of Pherae is as great a cause for fear as the Spartans, perhaps greater now. His Thessalian cavalry already numbers twenty thousand men, and he has at least twelve thousand *hoplites*. I think it is to the north that we must look with trepidation. The Spartans are out of it."

Parmenion said nothing but sat quietly staring at a point high on the wall, his right hand stroking his chin. After a time he turned his gaze on Pelopidas. "There are two points to consider here, my friend. If you are right, then we have nothing to fear. If my fears are confirmed, then all we have fought for will be taken away from us. So let us assume for a moment that I am right and the Spartan army is closer to us than is thought. Where would they be? How would they be planning to enter Boeotia? We still have a force overlooking the passes of Mount Cithaeron. They would see the Spartans and raise the alarm, yet it is unlikely they would try crossing the Corinthian Gulf, since we now have the twelve battle triremes at Creusis. Where, then, Pelopidas? You know the territory." Parmenion moved to a chest by the far wall, pulling clear a map of central Greece etched on cowhide. He sat beside Pelopidas, dropping the hide into the Theban's lap.

Pelopidas drained his wine. "I'll play the game with you, Parmenion, though you are wrong this time. But let me think. We hold the southern passes and all entries from the Peleponnese. We could pin down a Spartan army for months. And as you say, they could not cross the gulf without a sea battle—unless, that is, they crossed much farther north, say, here at

Agion," he said, stabbing the map. "Then they would head for Orchomenus and Lake Copais. They would be able to draw allies from the city, strike southwest through Coronea and Thespiae to Thebes herself, and, coming from the north, would bar all help from reaching us from Thessaly."

"Exactly my point," said Parmenion. "Most of our troops are south, guarding the passes. But who do we have in the north?"

"Chaireas with a thousand *hoplites*, mostly from Megara and Tanagra. Good fighting men. Solid. They are based at Thespiae."

"Send riders to Chaireas, ordering him north to blockade the passes at Coronea. If I am wrong, we can say that Chaireas was merely taking his troops through maneuvers."

"Sometimes," said Pelopidas, "I do not enjoy your company. My father used to tell stories about dark demons who stole the souls of little boys. Afterward I would lie in my bed unable to sleep, even though I knew the bastard was only trying to frighten me. I never liked the man. But now you have made me nervous." He sighed. "I will do as you suggest, but when you are proved to be wrong, you will give me your new black gelding. How does that sound?"

Parmenion chuckled. "Agreed. And if I am proved to be right, you will give me your new shield?"

"But I sent to Corinth for that shield. It cost me twice what any reasonable man would pay for a horse."

"You see," observed Parmenion, "already you are beginning to consider I may be right."

Pelopidas grunted. "What I will do," he said, "is ride your gelding up and down outside your gates every morning. Then you will see the cost of your obsession with Sparta."

A week later came disquieting news, though not from the north, where Chaireas had marched to Coronea and fortified a ridge. Calepios returned from Sparta and went straight to the home of Pelopidas. The Theban general heard him out, and both men sought Parmenion. They found him on the racetrack, pounding out the miles in an effortless lope. Pelopidas waved, beckoning the runner to them.

Parmenion masked his irritation and joined them; he did not like his daily run to be disturbed or interrupted. Nevertheless he bowed politely to Calepios; the orator returned the bow, and the three men sat at the new marble bench by the grave of Hector.

"There has been an unusual turn of events," said Calepios. "We were preparing to sign the treaty of peace, when Epaminondas noticed that the word 'Boeotian' had been changed to 'Theban.' He asked why this was so, and Agisaleus told him that Thebes—and not the Boeotian League—was currently the power north of the Peleponnese. Epaminondas reminded him that he was the representative of the league, not merely of Thebes. But the Spartans remained firm. Either Epaminondas signed for Thebes or he did not sign. All others have already signed, Parmenion. Epaminondas asked for a further three days to consider the matter and report back to the league. That is why I am here. What is Agisaleus planning? Why would he do such a thing?"

"To separate us from Athens. If all cities sign save Thebes, then we are outcasts. Sparta could march against us without fear of attack from Athens."

"The Athenians would never allow it," said Calepios. "They have been with us from the start."

"Not quite," Parmenion pointed out. "It needed a Spartan invasion to spur them on. But they must be starting to see the Boeotian League as a possible threat. The Athenians have long coveted the title of leaders of Greece. If they sit back and watch Thebes and Sparta rip each other to shreds, who prospers but them? They can gather the pieces."

"Therefore," said Pelopidas, "we should sign. What difference does it make?"

Parmenion laughed and shook his head. "A great warrior you may be, Pelopidas, but avoid the area of politics. If Epaminondas signs, it will be a message to all democrats in

Boeotia that Thebes has declared herself the ruler of all. It would sunder the league. It is a clever ploy. Agisaleus is as cunning as ever."

"What, then, is this all about?" asked Pelopidas. "Will he sign or will he not?"

"He cannot," said Parmenion. "If he did, it would mean a slow, sure death for the league. Instead, we must muster the army. Agisaleus will come now for sure."

"We cannot just *muster the army*," put in Calepios. "We are a democracy. First the seven elected Boeotian generals must be summoned; that is part of the constitution. And one of those generals is Epaminondas."

"A rule devised by idiots," snapped Parmenion. "What will you do, Pelopidas? You are one of the seven."

"I will order the Sacred Band to re-form and gather what *hoplites* I can from Thebes and the surrounding areas. All we can do now is alert the other cities and *request* troops. We cannot order them."

"A wondrous beast is democracy," said Parmenion.

It was almost dawn when Parmenion left for home, walking the deserted streets and avenues, past the fountains and the moonlit statues. He moved with care, avoiding narrow alleys, his hand on his sword hilt. As he crossed an open square, he saw a dark, hooded figure sitting by a walled pool. Anxiously he cast his eyes around the square, but there was no one else in sight or any hiding place behind which an assassin could lurk. Parmenion walked on.

"No greetings for an old friend?" came the dry voice of Tamis as he sought to pass. He stopped and turned; the old woman raised her head and smiled.

"Are you human or spirit?" he asked, feeling the chill of the night breeze on his skin.

"I am Tamis," she replied.

"What is it you require of me? Why do you haunt me, woman?"

"I require nothing, Parmenion. I am an observer. Are you content?"

"Why should I not be? And give me no more of your false prophecies. Thebes still stands—despite your words."

"I did not say she would fall in a day," said Tamis wearily, "and my prophecies are never false. Sometimes I wish they were. Look at you, young and in your prime, feeling immortality in your veins. You look at me and you see a walking corpse seeking a suitable grave. You see wrinkled skin and ruined teeth. You think that is me? You think this is Tamis? Look again, Parmenion," she said, rising and pushing back the hood. For a moment she was bathed in moonlight so bright that he could not bear to look upon her, then it cleared. Standing before him now was a young woman of breathtaking beauty, her hair gold, her lips full, her eyes a brilliant blue yet warm and more than friendly. Then the image faded, and he saw her skin dry out and sag, her shoulders bow, and her waist thicken. His mouth was dry. "You are a sorceress!" he whispered.

Her laugh became a cackle, and she sank back to her seat. "Of course I am a sorceress," she told him, her voice edged with sorrow. "But what you saw was once real. There is not one old woman in all the world who would not understand. One day, Parmenion, perhaps you, too, will be old, your skin dry and mottled, your teeth loose in your jaws. But inside you will be as you always were, except that you will find yourself trapped in a decaying shell."

"I have no time for this. What do you want of me?"

"Is your hatred still strong?" she asked. "Do you still require the death of Sparta?"

"I desire to see Thebes free of Spartan influence, that is all."

"You told Asiron you were the Death of Nations."

"How could you know that?" Suddenly he laughed. "A foolish question to ask of a sorceress. Or a Spartan spy. Yes, I told him. But that was years ago. Perhaps your prophecies worried me then. They do not now. Was it you who told Epaminondas he would die at Mantinea? Was that another falsehood?"

"Yes, it was I. But that is between the great man and myself. Do you love Thetis?"

"I don't know why I am bothering to talk to you," he said. "I am weary. I need sleep." He swung away from her and began to walk across the square.

"Do you love her?" she called softly. He stopped, the question echoing in his mind, then slowly he turned.

"Yes, I love her. Though not as I loved—and still love— Derae. Is there a reason for the question? Or are we playing another game?"

"I asked you once to ride from the city, to seek a destiny at the shrine to Hera in Troy. You did not heed me. You will not heed me now. But yet I say it to you: Do not go home. Ride from Thebes tonight."

"You know I will not."

"I know," she told him, and in her voice he heard a depth of sadness that struck him worse than a blow. He opened his mouth to speak, to find some gentle words of parting; but she moved away swiftly, pulling her hood over her head.

The sky was brightening with the predawn as he arrived at the gate of his house. He yawned and raised his fist to rap at the wood, knowing that Mothac would awaken instantly and raise the bar. Then he saw that the gate was ajar. Irritation flared. Ever since Clearchus had entered so easily, Parmenion had insisted that at night the gate should be both chained and barred; it was not like Mothac to forget such an order. Parmenion put his hand to the gate, then hesitated. The meeting with Tamis had unsettled him. In all probability Mothac had merely consumed too much wine and had fallen asleep waiting for him.

His unease remained, and with a whispered curse he moved to his right until he stood beneath the lowest part of the wall. Hooking his fingers over the edge, he hauled himself up, carefully avoiding the pots and jars he had placed along the top for an unwary intruder to send crashing. Silently he moved two of them aside, making room to ease his body onto the wall. Scanning the courtyard below, he saw two armed men waiting, one on either side of the gates. Lowering himself back to the alley, he drew his sword. His mouth was dry, his heart hammering, but, taking several deep breaths, he calmed himself and crept to the gates. He had one advantage, he knew: the assassins expected to surprise their victim. He crashed his shoulder into the left-hand gate, which flew open. The first assassin was smashed to the ground as Parmenion leapt to his right, his sword cleaving the second man's neck. The first man rose groggily; his sword had been knocked from his hand, but he scrabbled for a knife. Parmenion's blade plunged into his chest.

The assassin sagged against Parmenion, who ripped clear his sword, pushing him away. With a groan the man fell face first to the courtyard; his leg twitched, and his bowels opened, the stench filling the air. Parmenion ran toward the *andron*, throwing open the door.

"Welcome," said a tall Spartan. "Put down your sword or the woman dies." His left hand was on Thetis' throat, but in his right was a short dagger, the point held to the woman's side.

Thetis stood very still. She had awoken in the night to hear a scuffle in the courtyard below. Seizing a dagger, she had run down to find four men standing over the body of Mothac. Without thinking, she hurled herself at them. One of them made a grab for her, but she twisted and rammed the dagger deep into his groin. A fist cracked against her cheek, spinning her to the ground; then they were on her, pinning her arms and tearing the dagger from her hand. The man she had stabbed was lying very still, his blood spreading across the courtyard. One man dragged her back into the *andron*, while the others pulled the bodies into the kitchen.

"You slut!" stormed the man who held her. "You killed him!" He backhanded a blow that knocked her from her feet, then advanced on her with her own dagger.

"Leave her!" commanded the leader, a tall man dressed in a dark green *chiton* and riding boots.

"But she killed Cinon!" protested the other.

"Watch the gates! When he enters, kill him. Then you can do as you will with the woman."

And the long night had begun. Thetis was determined that when she heard Parmenion, she would shout a warning. But the first sound was of the gate crashing open, followed by the screams of the dying.

Now Parmenion stood in the doorway, blood on his clothes, a terrible fury in his eyes.

"Put down your sword or the woman dies."

She saw the indecision in Parmenion, watched his sword hand slowly drop. "Don't!" she cried. "He will kill us both anyway."

"Be silent, whore!" ordered the Spartan.

Parmenion's sword fell to the floor. "Now kick it over here," ordered the assassin, and Parmenion obeyed. The Spartan flung Thetis against a wall and advanced on Parmenion.

"Your time has come, traitor!" the man hissed.

Parmenion edged into the *andron*, circling away from the knifeman. "Who sent you?" he asked, his voice calm.

"I serve the king and the cause of the just," the man replied. Suddenly he leapt, the knife flashing for Parmenion's belly. Parmenion sidestepped to the left, throwing a punch that glanced from the man's chin. The knife slashed by his face, cutting the skin of his shoulder.

Thetis' head had cracked against the wall, and a thin trickle of blood was flowing from a narrow gash in her temple. Her vision was blurred, but she crawled across the floor, gathering Parmenion's sword. Slowly she rose. Nausea swept through her. She saw Parmenion grappling with the assassin, whose back was to her. Running forward, she plunged the sword into the Spartan. He tried to turn, but Parmenion held him by the knife wrist.

Thetis fell back against a couch, the room spinning around

her madly. She saw the two men struggling, the gleaming
sword jutting from the assassin's back. Parmenion threw his
weight against the killer, hurling him at the wall. The sword
hilt hit the stone, driving the blade deeper into the Spartan's
back. Blood bubbled from the man's mouth. Parmenion
jumped aside as the assassin tried one last desperate lunge
with his dagger. The man's eyes closed, and he toppled to the
floor.

Parmenion ran to Thetis, lifting her to the couch. "Are you
all right?" he asked, his hands cradling her face.

"Yes," she answered weakly. "Mothac . . . in the kitchen."

Parmenion rose, dragging his sword clear of the dead Spartan. With the bloody blade in hand he moved through the
house to the kitchen. Two bodies lay on the floor. Stepping
over the first, he knelt by Mothac, touching his fingers to the
man's throat. There was a pulse! Parmenion ripped away
Mothac's bloodstained shirt to reveal two wounds, one high in
the chest and the other over the left hip. The blood flow from
the chest was slowing, but the bleeding from the hip showed
no sign of abating. Parmenion had seen battlefield surgeons at
work, and he pinched the flesh over the cut, drawing the skin
together and holding it tight. He sat for some minutes with
blood seeping through his fingers, but at last it began to slow.

Mothac groaned. "Lie still," ordered Parmenion, gently
releasing his hold. Blood still ran from the wound, but only as
a trickle.

Returning to the *andron*, he found Thetis asleep. Leaving
her, he ran to the home of Dronicus, the physician who had
replaced Argonas. The man was an Athenian and notoriously
brusque, but his skill was without question, and like Argonas
before him, he had little use for the practice of bleeding. He
was bald and beardless and so short as to appear deformed.

The two men heaved Mothac onto his bed, then Dronicus
plugged the wounds, using wool smeared with sap taken from
fig-tree leaves. He covered the plugs with woolen pads soaked
in red wine, holding them in place with bandages of white
linen.

Parmenion returned to the *andron* and knelt beside Thetis, lifting her hand and kissing her fingers.

She awoke and smiled. "Why is it so dark?" she asked him. "Can you not light a lantern?"

Sunlight was pouring in through the window, and Parmenion felt a touch like ice on his soul. He passed his hand across her face, but her eyes did not blink. He swallowed hard. "Dronicus!" he called. "Come quickly!"

"What is the matter?" asked Thetis. "Light a lantern for me."

"In a moment, my love. In a moment."

"Is Mothac well?"

"Yes. Dronicus!"

The doctor moved to Thetis' side. Parmenion said nothing but passed his hand once more over her face. Dronicus reached out and touched the wound at Thetis' temple, gently pressing it. She groaned. "Is that you, Parmenion?" Her voice was slurred now.

"I am here," he whispered, holding her hand.

"I thought we were going to die, that all our happiness would be ended. And then I thought: That is the price for the years we had. The gods do not like us to be happy for too long. I know this sounds strange, but I realized I had no regrets. You brought me back to life, you made me smile and laugh. But now . . . we have . . . won again. And there will be more years. Parmenion?"

"Yes?"

"I love you. Do you mind my saying that?"

"I don't mind," he whispered. He glanced at Dronicus, but the man's expression was unreadable. "What is wrong?" Parmenion mouthed the words without a sound.

Dronicus rose but gestured for Parmenion to remain. The doctor walked out into the courtyard and sat in the sunshine.

"Do you love me?" asked Thetis, her voice suddenly clear.

Parmenion found his throat swelling, tears burning at his eyes. "Yes," he said.

"I can't . . . hear . . . you. Parmenion? Par . . ." Her breath sighed away.

"Thetis!" he shouted, but she did not stir. Her eyes stared at him. Dronicus returned silently and pressed her eyelids closed. Taking Parmenion by the arm, he led the dazed Spartan out into the sunlight.

"Why? There was only a small wound."

"Her skull was crushed at the temple. I am sorry, Parmenion. I do not know what else to say. But take comfort that she did not suffer; she did not know she was dying. And try to remember what she said about your life together. Few people know such happiness."

Parmenion ignored him. He sat down at the courtyard table and stared at the purple flowers growing by the wall. He did not stir even when Menidis and a squad of Theban soldiers arrived to clear away the bodies of the assassins. The elderly officer sat opposite him.

"Tell me what happened," he said.

Parmenion did so calmly, mechanically. He did not even notice when Menidis stood and walked away.

Pelopidas found him there at dusk. The Theban general sat beside him.

"I am sorry for your loss," he said. "Truly. But you must rouse yourself, Parmenion. I need you. Thebes needs you. Cleombrotus is in the north with twelve thousand men. Chaireas and his men have been slaughtered, and the road to Thebes is open."

Epaminondas sat alone on the ridge, gazing down at the Spartan army camped on the plain of Leuctra, a day's march east of Thebes. Slowly he undid the chain strap on his simple iron helmet and removed it, laying it on the stony slope as he sat watching the distant camp fires.

As the breeze gusted and veered, he could hear laughter from the Spartan camp and hear the whinnying of their horses picketed beyond the fires.

Tomorrow loomed in his mind like the half-remembered monsters of his childhood dreams. For more than fifteen of his thirty-seven years Epaminondas had worked, conspired, risked his life in the service of Thebes to free the city he loved from Spartan rule. And he had come so close.

So close . . .

Now he faced an army of twelve thousand men—twice the combined Boeotian force—and the future of Thebes hung like a fragile jewel, suspended over a fiery abyss.

In Sparta he had allowed himself to dream of golden days. Agisaleus had been convivial—even friendly—and the negotiations had moved smoothly ahead . . . until that bitter moment when he had seen the change to the treaty of peace. And then Epaminondas had been caught like a fish in the net. To sign would mean the end of Boeotia. Not to sign would herald a new invasion.

Drawing in a deep breath, he closed his eyes, trying to concentrate on the advice of his generals, but all he could see was the Spartan army, the finest fighting men in all of Greece—all the world.

He thought of Parmenion's plan, but dismissed it from his mind.

Hearing a sound from behind, he looked up to see the Thespian general, Ictinus. The man was young and slender, his iron armor polished to shine like silver. Epaminondas said nothing. Ictinus irritated him, but as the elected representative of Thespiae, he had to be tolerated.

"We will not engage them in open battle, will we, Epaminondas?" asked Ictinus. "My men are concerned. Not for their lives, of course, which they would willingly give . . . willingly give. But . . . it would be folly. Tell me you are not considering this course."

"I am considering all possibilities, sir, and I shall present my views to the seven at the agreed time. Now, if you will leave me to think."

"Yes, yes. But we could hold the ridge? Yes. That would be good, sound strategy, I think—"

"I will see you in an hour, Ictinus, with the other Boe-otarchs," snapped Epaminondas. The man bowed and walked away, but almost immediately the Theban general thought he heard him return. "For the sake of the gods!" he stormed. "Will you leave me alone?"

"You need a drink," said Pelopidas, smiling broadly and thumping the back of Epaminondas' breastplate.

"I am sorry. I thought it was that fool Ictinus."

"Whatever happens tomorrow, my friend, I think your strategy should ignore the Thespians. They will run if the Spartans so much as shout at them."

"Which leaves us with around five and a half thousand fighting men—against twelve thousand. Good odds, don't you think?"

Pelopidas shrugged. "I do not care how many there are. Tomorrow we crush them." He hawked and spit on the rocks. "I like Parmenion's plan."

Epaminondas closed his eyes for a moment. "He has been deranged since Thetis was murdered. I cannot consider it. To gamble all we have on a single move, to risk annihilation? Do not take this wrongly, Pelopidas, but would you attack a lion with a brooch pin?"

"Why would a lion have a brooch pin?" asked Pelopidas, grinning.

Epaminondas chuckled. "If all the men were like you, I would not hesitate to follow Parmenion's advice. But they are not, Pelopidas. You are . . . special, perhaps even unique. I cannot take the risk."

"Ask yourself why," Pelopidas suggested.

"You know why. All we have worked for is at risk."

"That is not an answer, and you know it. Either the strategy is a good one or it is not. You cannot plan a battle on anything else. Are you saying that if nothing rested on the outcome you would try the plan?"

"Perhaps I am." Epaminondas laughed. "But the truth is that I am frightened out of my wits."

"Think on this: If Parmenion had not realized the Spartans

were planning to invade, you would have had no army to block the passes at Coronea. Even so, they captured Creusis and our precious triremes. That dealt a blow to our pride—and to our credibility. The league is tottering. If we do not deliver a crushing blow, we will be finished anyway. Thebes will fall. And this time Agisaleus has promised to raze the city, selling every man, woman, and child into slavery. I would not want to live to see that. Would you?"

Epaminondas pushed himself to his feet. His right knee ached, and he rubbed warmth into it. "Even if I did agree," he said, "we would never be able to convince the other Boeotarchs."

"I have already convinced Bachylides of Megara. With you, that makes three of the seven. We could carry the vote, I am sure of it."

"Such a tactic has never been tried," argued Epaminondas.

"Oh, but it has," said Pelopidas, straight-faced. "Parmenion told me he once won a game with it in Sparta."

For a moment Epaminondas stood and stared at his lifelong friend, then he began to laugh. Pelopidas joined in, and the sounds of their merriment echoed through the silent camp.

It was close to noon before the Spartans and their allies marched out into the center of the plain, taking up their battle formation, challenging the Boeotians to confront them.

Epaminondas looked to his right and watched his army preparing to march. On the extreme right were the Thespians under Ictinus, forming their phalanx behind Parmenion and the four hundred horsemen. At the center the Sacred Band, and behind them javeliners and archers. Epaminondas himself stood in the fifth rank of the Theban contingent, four thousand strong, well armored with breastplates and helms, metal-edged leather kilts, and bronze greaves to protect the shins. Each man carried a large bronze-rimmed shield of leather-covered wood. Epaminondas drew his short stabbing sword and hitched up his shield, his voice ringing out.

"Forward! For Thebes and glory!"

The army began to move.

The Theban general tried to swallow, but his mouth was dry. He could feel his heart beating like a ragged drum, and such was his tension that his legs trembled as he sought to keep pace with the men at either side. From here there was no going back.

The arguments had raged long into the night, not helped by a curious accident. As Epaminondas had sat down in the tent to address the seven generals, his chair had collapsed beneath him, sprawling him to the floor. At first only nervous laughter greeted him, but then Ictinus said, "It is a bad omen, Epaminondas. Very bad." The other Boeotarchs had looked nervous.

"Yes, it is an omen," snapped Epaminondas, rising. "We are commanded not to sit idle but to stand like men." Then he had outlined the battle plan.

"You cannot have thought this through," said Ictinus. "The Spartans are deadly. If we must attack, then let us hit their left, where the Orchomenans stand. Smash their allies and isolate Cleombrotus."

"And what do you think Cleombrotus will be doing while we march upon his left?" Epaminondas asked. "I'll tell you: He will wheel the regiments and crush us. No, I propose to strike at the head of the snake."

The debate had continued until just before dawn. Bachylides of Megara and Pelopidas had supported him, but it was not until they convinced Ganeus of Plataea that they won a majority.

Now, as he marched down the long slope to the plain, Epaminondas could not help but worry at the decision. For many years he had plotted and planned, risking his life to free the city he loved. But now, if he was wrong, the city would be destroyed—the statues broken, the homes razed—and the dust of history would blow over the deserted Cadmea. His hand was sweating as he gripped his sword, and he could feel rivulets of perspiration running down his back.

A quarter of a mile ahead the Spartans waited silently, their forces spread out in a great crescent. To the right the Spartan battle king, Cleombrotus, in gold-embossed armor, could be clearly seen surrounded by his bodyguard.

Slowly the distance between the armies closed, until at two hundred paces Epaminondas called a halt. The Spartan right was facing him, while in the center the enemy archers and slingers were preparing their weapons. Glancing nervously to the enemy left, he saw six hundred Spartan cavalry galloping along the enemy front to take up a position at the center, in front of the archers.

Now everything depended on Parmenion. Epaminondas lifted his sword high into the air.

Led by Parmenion, the Theban cavalry kicked their horses into a gallop, heading straight for the enemy left. Dust swirled around them, and the thunder of hooves filled the air. But behind the cavalry the Thespians, led by Ictinus, turned and fled from the field. "Curse you, coward!" screamed Epaminondas.

"We'll do it without them, General," said the man along-side him.

"That we will," Epaminondas agreed, tearing his gaze from the fleeing men and switching it to Parmenion as he galloped at the head of the Theban cavalry.

Parmenion's mind was strangely calm as he led the four hundred horsemen. Dust rose in a choking cloud, but he was ahead of it, the black stallion moving at ferocious speed toward the enemy. He had no thought of victory or defeat. In the night he had dreamed of Thetis and of Derae, and in his haunted sleep he had seen Leonidas and endured his mocking laughter. All he desired now was to come face to face with the Spartan, to cleave and cut, to crush and kill.

With the enemy left locking shields and preparing to withstand the charge, Parmenion dragged on the left-hand rein, turning the stallion. Behind him the Theban cavalry also swerved, angling now toward the Spartan horsemen waiting at the center of the line. Parmenion dipped the point of his lance and located his target, an officer in a long red cloak sitting on a gray horse.

Too late the Spartan cavalry realized they were to bear the brunt of the first charge. Their officers yelled orders and tried to countercharge, but the Thebans were upon them, screaming battle cries, lances smashing men from their mounts. Parmenion's spear glanced from the officer's breastplate to plunge into his jaw and on through his brain. The man was lifted from his horse's back, the weight of his body snapping the spear shaft. Parmenion threw the broken weapon aside and drew the sword of Leonidas.

All was milling chaos now, the Spartan cavalry forced back into the ranks of archers, slingers, and javeliners. Unarmored men fell beneath the hooves of panicked mounts, and the enemy center fell back in confusion.

A cavalryman slashed his sabre toward Parmenion's head. Parmenion swayed away from the cut and plunged his own sword into the man's neck.

An enormous dust cloud obscured the front of the battle lines now, and the air was thick and choking.

At the rear of the Spartan ranks on the right, Leonidas watched the attacking cavalry swerve and strike the center. At first he was unconcerned, for the javeliners and archers were hardly significant; as always, the battle would be won by the Spartan phalanx. But something stirred deep in his memory, a cold, whispering thought that he could not quite grasp. In some strange way he felt as if he had fought in this battle before, the enemy cavalry striking the center. He swung his gaze to the front and the swirling dust cloud.

And remembered. . . .

At that moment the battle king, Cleombrotus, saw moving shapes within the dust and realized that the Thebans were advancing on him. He was exultant. He had expected the Boeotians to fortify the ridge and dare him to attack them, but for them to have the temerity to advance on him was a gift he had not anticipated.

"Rear four ranks right spear, right flank!" he bellowed. The warriors, Leonidas among them, moved smoothly to the right, thinning the Spartan line to twelve deep and preparing to encircle the advancing enemy.

In a moment of icy terror Leonidas saw again the sand pit at the home of Xenophon, the massed ranks of the enemy smashing the thinned Spartan line. "No!" he screamed. "Sire!" But his voice was lost as the Theban battle cry went up, the sound like rolling thunder.

Inside the dust cloud Pelopidas and the Sacred Band ran in front of the advancing Thebans, taking up a position at the head of the charge. "Death to the Spartans!" shouted Pelopidas.

"Death! Death! Death!" roared the army, and they began to run.

Eighty shields across and fifty ranks deep, the Thebans smote the Spartan front line like an ax blade against timber. The first two Spartan ranks buckled and fell beneath the stabbing swords, the phalanx sliced open by the weight of the charge.

The Spartans bravely tried to re-form, but no army twelve deep—no matter how courageous—could hope to contain an enemy with fifty concentrated ranks. Unable to lock shields, Spartan warriors were cut down where they stood.

At the head of the charge Pelopidas powered into the Spartan ranks, Callines beside him. A sword lanced toward Pelopidas' head, but Callines blocked it with his shield, stabbing his own sword deep into the Spartan's groin. The phalanx moved on, slowing now but still advancing. Pelopidas was stabbing and hacking, oblivious to the many small cuts that bled freely on his arms and legs.

Behind him Epaminondas, at the center of the phalanx and not yet brought into the fighting, peered through the dust, locating the Spartan king, Cleombrotus, who was fighting alongside his bodyguard a little to the right of the main advance.

"Pelopidas!" shouted the Theban general. "To your right! Your right!"

Pelopidas heard him even through his blood lust and

glanced around. He saw Cleombrotus and began to fight his way toward the Spartan king. Callines moved alongside him, the two men protecting one another and fighting as a team. Behind them the Sacred Band also altered the line of advance, homing in on the Spartan battle king.

On the right Leonidas forced himself to the front of the two Spartan ranks ordered out to encircle the Thebans. Seeing the enemy closing on Cleombrotus, he ordered the men to close ranks. "The king! The king!" he bellowed. The Spartans surged forward, desperately trying to reach the beleaguered monarch. "Fall back, sire! Fall back!" yelled Leonidas.

Cleombrotus, realizing the danger, could not bring himself to retreat in the face of Thebans. "Stand firm," he told his bodyguard. "They will break upon us like the sea against stone."

Parmenion and the cavalry had pushed deep into the enemy center, the lightly armored archers fleeing before them. The Spartan cavalry had been routed. Parmenion swung left to see the Theban battle line slowing as it sought to turn and crush Cleombrotus. His eyes flickered to the Spartan right, where he saw that Leonidas had gathered two ranks to him and was forcing a path to save his king.

"Thebans to me!" shouted Parmenion. There were only fifty riders within hearing distance—the others were chasing down the fleeing archers—but the men galloped to him. "Follow me!" Parmenion cried, kicking his heels to the stallion and charging the Spartan line.

The Spartans had tried to lock shields against the Theban phalanx, but they were more open on their left, and the attacking horsemen cleaved the ranks.

The move surprised the Spartans, who tried to turn and defend themselves. But this only weakened the front of the line, allowing Pelopidas and the Sacred Band to hammer through.

Cleombrotus cursed. His sword stabbed out, cleaving the teeth of an advancing man and piercing him to the brain. Another Theban, then another, fell to the battle king.

A scream came from beside him, and he twisted in time to see his lover and companion, Hermias, fall, his throat slashed open. A dark-bearded warrior with a death's-head grin leapt at him. Cleombrotus parried a thrust, then a second. But Pelopidas crashed his shield against the king, forcing him back, then dropped to his knees to ram his blade through Cleombrotus' groin. Still the king tried to fight, but his life-blood drained away, and with it his strength. His shield arm dropped, and the Theban's sword smashed his jaw to shards.

As the king fell, the Spartan center buckled. Leonidas and his men finally forced their way to the front, gathering up the dead king and fighting a rear-guard action back toward the defensive line of their night camp.

At last the battle petered out. Isolated groups of Spartan warriors were surrounded and destroyed, but Leonidas gathered the remnants into a strong defensive position on a nearby ridge. The Spartan allies, seeing the fall of Cleombrotus, fled the field without a fight.

The Thebans gathered around Pelopidas and Epaminondas, hoisting them to their shoulders and carrying them around the battlefield, their cheers echoing to the Spartan lines.

Parmenion, his horse dead, walked slowly over the battlefield, looking down at the twisted corpses. More than a thousand Spartiates had died for the loss of two hundred Thebans, but at that moment those figures meant nothing to him. He was dazed and emotionless. He had seen the battle king fall to Pelopidas, but worse, he had watched the Theban kill Hermias moments before. Parmenion knelt by the body, looking down at the face of a man and seeing the face of the boy who had befriended him.

He remembered the night when they had sat by the statue of Athena of the Road, when he had learned there would be no victory celebration after winning the games.

"I will make them all pay!" he had promised. *And Hermias had touched his arm.*

"Do not hate me too, Savra!"

"Hate you, my friend?" he had answered. "How could I ever hate you? You have been a brother to me, and I will never forget that. Never! Brothers we have been, brothers we shall be, all the days of our lives. I promise you."

He closed the dead eyes and rose to his feet. The surgeons were coming onto the battlefield now, moving to the wounded Thebans. Most of these men would die, Parmenion knew, for physicians with the skills of Argonas or Dronicus were rare. He gazed around him. There to the left lay Callines, the man who had admitted to being a poor swordsman. Farther away was the body of Norac the smith. Later he would hear of the other dead, like Calepios the orator and Melon the statesman. He looked down at his hands, which were covered in blood, drying now to a dull, scabby brown.

Crows were already circling above the plain.

He recalled the general's games, the cleanly carved soldiers in the box of sand. No blood there, no stench of open bowels. Just a child's game fought without pain in the sunshine of another age.

"I will repay them all," he had promised Hermias.

And he had. But at what price? Hermias was dead, as Derae and now Thetis were dead.

Sparta was finished, her invincibility gone. Now other cities dominated by Sparta would rise against her, and she would fade away, her power a memory. Not immediately, he knew; there would be other Spartan victories. But never again would they rise to rule Greece.

"I am the Death of Nations," he whispered.

"Or the savior of them," suggested Epaminondas.

Parmenion turned. "I did not hear you. You won, my friend. You won a famous victory. I hope Thebes proves a better ruler than Sparta."

"We seek to rule no one," said Epaminondas.

Parmenion rubbed at his tired eyes. "It will be thrust upon you, General. In order to be safe, you will carry the battle to

Sparta and humble her. Then the Athenians and their allies will fear you and will come against you. Rule or die: they are the choices you have."

"Do not be so glum, Parmenion. This is a new age, when we do not have to repeat the follies of the past. The Spartans will send an ambassador to ask permission to remove their dead; you will receive him."

Parmenion shook his head. "Listen to me," said Epaminondas softly. "You have carried your hate for too many years. With this victory you can bury that hate forever. You can be free. Do this for me."

"As you will," agreed the Spartan, his mind empty, his emotions drained. All his adult life he had dreamed of this moment, but now it was here, he felt dead inside. Thetis had asked him what he would do once his vengeance was complete. He had no answer then; he could find none now. He gazed around at the silent corpses. Where, he wondered, was the joy of victory? Where was the satisfaction?

Three hours later, with dusk approaching, a Spartan rider cantered into the Theban camp.

Leonidas was led to a tent where Parmenion waited.

"I knew it was your plan," said Leonidas. "How does it feel to have defeated the army of your homeland?"

"You are here to concede defeat," Parmenion told him coldly, "and to ask permission to remove your dead. I give you that permission."

"You do not wish to gloat?" Leonidas asked. "I am here, Parmenion. Mock me if you will. Tell me how you promised this. Tell me how fine it makes you feel."

"I cannot. And if I could, I would not. You almost held us. With a mere twelve ranks you almost turned the battle. Had Cleombrotus fallen back to link with you, you could have held. There has never been an army so disciplined, or so brave, as that of Sparta. I salute your dead, as I salute the memory of all that was great in Spartan history." He poured two goblets of wine, passing one to the stunned Spartan. "A long time ago," he continued, "your sister wanted to buy you a gift. I

would not sell it. But now is the time for it to be returned."
Unbuckling his sword belt he passed the legendary blade to
Leonidas, who stared down at it disbelievingly.

Then Leonidas sat on the pallet bed and drained his wine
at a single swallow. "What is it that we do to one another?"
asked the Spartan. "You won the games fairly. I said it then,
and I will say it now. I never asked those boys to beat you.
Indeed, I did not know it was happening. And I wish that you
had married Derae. But events propel us, Parmenion. Our
souls are but leaves in a storm, and only the gods know where
we will come to rest. We are enemies, you and I; the Fates
have decreed that. But you are a man of courage, and you
fight like a Spartan. I salute your victory." He stood and
returned the empty goblet. "What will you do now?"

"I shall leave Thebes and travel. I will see the world, Leonidas."

"As a soldier?"

"It is all that I have—all that I know."

"Farewell, then, Parmenion. If we meet again, I will do my
utmost to kill you."

"I know. May the gods walk with you, Leonidas."

"And with you . . . *strategos*."

Tamis was confused as her spirit eyes watched Parmenion
return the legendary sword. That was not how it was meant
to happen. The hatred between the two men should have
been strengthened—all the futures showed it so. For a moment only her confusion threatened to become panic, but she
brushed her doubts aside. What did it matter? Three of the
chosen were dead. Only one remained.

And with him there was time. All kinds of accidents could
befall a fourteen-year-old hostage living in Thebes.

Surely he would prove less of a threat than Cleombrotus,
the mighty battle king of the Spartans. The boy was not even
from a civilized city, born and bred as he was in the forests and
hills of Macedonia.

He would probably be murdered like his father. Such was

the fate of those close to the throne in backward nations, the king eliminating all possible rivals.

No, Tamis decided, there was nothing to fear from Philip of Macedon.

BOOK THREE

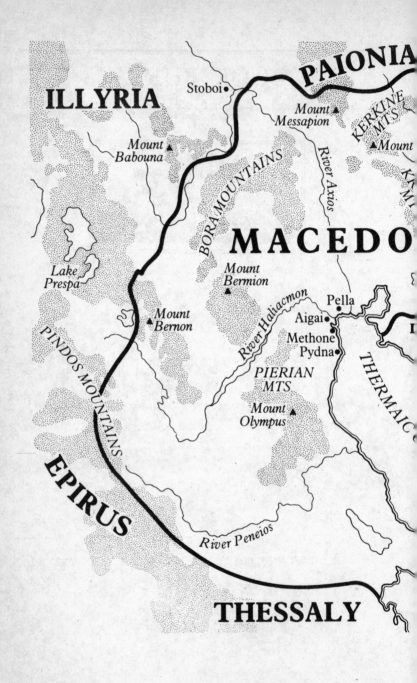

THRACE

River Nestos

River Augites

River Strymon

IA

Amphipolis

THASOS

S OF THE
ALCIDEAN
LEAGUE

Stageira

Akanthos

hos

SAMOTHRACE

LIMNOS

Macedonian border
circa 359 BC

THEBES, AUTUMN, 371 B.C.

Philip of Macedon watched the cheering crowds as the flower-garlanded heroes of Leuctra marched through the streets. It had been an unbelievable victory. Never before had the Spartan army been defeated in such a manner. It was both impossible and somehow wonderful, even to a Macedonian. Philip could understand the irrepressible joy of the multitudes for they were celebrating an event few of them had believed credible: the Spartans crushed by a smaller force.

There was music from the streets, and Philip longed to leave the silent house and join them, to dance and forget his own private torments.

But Pammenes had told him to wait for a visitor.

The Theban had been unable to meet his eyes, shifting nervously as he spoke. Fear and anger had flared in Philip at that moment, but he masked both emotions until Pammenes had left. Moving back from the window, Philip poured himself a goblet of water and considered the problem.

He had heard nothing from his brother Perdiccas for two

months, so the present fear was hardly new. Perdiccas was three years older than Philip and therefore closer to the throne. He would be the first to die. So Philip wrote to him constantly, and to his cousins and nieces, asking about the royal horse herds, inquiring after the health of relatives. When the letters from Perdiccas stopped, Philip's sleepless nights had begun, as he waited for the day of the assassin. Now it was here. They would not kill him while he was in Thebes, he reassured himself, for that would be bad manners. Idly he touched the dagger at his belt. Little use that would be. Though strong, Philip was a mere fourteen years old and no match for any but the clumsiest adult warrior. And they would send no one clumsy.

"What shall I do, Crosi?" he asked the ghost of the old man. There was no answer, but whispering the name aloud helped ease his tension. He remembered the night of the knives, the old man moving silently into his bedroom with a short sword in his hand. Philip had been ten then. Crosi had led him to a shadowed corner of the room, ordering him to hide behind a couch.

"What is happening?" Philip asked.

"Blood and death," replied the old man. "But I will protect you, boy. Have no fear."

Philip had believed him. At ten a child had faith in the fully grown. Crosi had sat on the couch, sword in hand, and they had waited until the dawn. No one came.

Philip had crouched in the cold, wrapped in a blanket, too frightened to ask the nature of the peril. As the sun cleared the distant Crousian mountains, Crosi had relaxed.

"Come out, boy," he said, taking Philip's hand and drawing him forth. He put his arms around the prince and hugged him briefly. "Last night," he said, "your father died. Ptolemaos now rules in Macedonia."

"But . . . Father is so strong! He can't be dead!"

"No man can withstand a dagger in the heart, Philip."

"Who did it? And why?"

"These are questions I will not answer, boy. But for now—I hope—your danger is past.'"

"Uncle Ptolemaos will look after me," said Philip, but even at ten he saw the angry look in Crosi's eyes just before the old man stood and turned away. He did not fully understand it then, but now he remembered it clearly. Now he knew the answers, though no one had ever voiced them.

Ptolemaos had killed King Amyntas. Uncle Ptolemaos, who within three months had married Philip's mother, Eurydice, and buried her a year later beside her murdered husband. Philip's parents had been cold toward their youngest son, but even so the boy had loved them, worshiping his father and doing all in his power to please him.

The following year had seen Philip's boyhood washed away in the acid of intrigue and sudden death. Philip's eldest brother, Alexander, had been found murdered at his summer home in Aigai, killed by unknown assailants. Three adult cousins died mysteriously.

Then had come the Theban demand for hostages, following a short, bitter month of conflict between the Macedonian army and a force led by Pelopidas, the great Theban warrior. The Macedonians had been crushed. Ptolemaos sent twelve hostages—including Philip—to Thebes, and for the first time in months the young prince felt safe.

They had not let Crosi come with him, and the old man had died of a fever the previous spring. Philip still mourned him and prayed that his ghost would be allowed to walk alongside him until his own assassination. Then, maybe, together they could journey into the lands of the dead.

The sound of footsteps on the stairs jerked Philip's thoughts to the present. He stood and found his legs trembling.

A tall warrior in full armor and white-plumed helm entered the room. The man was not old, perhaps eighteen, but his eyes were pale and cold.

He bowed. "Good morning," he said. "I am here to accompany you home, Philip."

"Do you bring letters?" he asked, proud that his voice did not betray his terror.

"Yes, sir. I have one from your brother Perdiccas."

"He is well?"

"He is alive, sir, though he has suffered a fever from which he is now recovering. My name is Attalus. I hope we can be friends."

Philip nodded. "Lifelong friends, I do not doubt," he said, his dark eyes holding to the pale snakelike gaze of the warrior. The man blinked, and Philip smiled. "Do not concern yourself, Attalus. I do not judge you."

"I am not here to kill you, sir," the warrior told him. "My orders are explicit: I am to take you to the capital. Nothing more."

"Then let us walk for a while," said Philip suddenly, striding past the astonished Attalus. The two of them wandered out into the streets, easing their way through the crowds that gathered on the thoroughfares and onto the *agora* where Epaminondas was scheduled to speak. The general had been delayed by the throng, but the people were unconcerned. They sang and danced and drank; the strength of their happiness was almost as intoxicating as the wine. Philip felt better out here in the open, but glancing at Attalus, he saw that the same could not be said of the tall warrior. Philip took his arm and led him into a deserted side street. Once there, he drew his dagger and held the point to his own breast.

"What are you doing?" asked Attalus.

Philip took the other's hand and held it to the hilt. "If you have to kill me, you can do it here. No one will see you, and you could say that I was slain by a Theban. It would make it so much more simple for you."

"Listen!" hissed Attalus. "I am the king's man. I do as he bids. Had he told me to kill you, then I would do it. But you are to return with me to Pella. How can I convince you?"

"You just did," Philip told him, returning the dagger to its sheath. His heart was beating wildly, and he grinned. "These are dangerous days, Attalus."

"They are certainly strange," agreed the young man with a tight smile. His teeth were too prominent, like marker stones, thought Philip. And he has the eyes of a killer. Remembering Parmenion's advice, he took the warrior by the arm and smiled warmly. "I like you," he said. "So if Ptolemaos ever decides to have me killed, request that he send someone else. No man should be slain by a man he likes."

"I'll try to remember that."

The journey back to Pella was slow and surprisingly pleasant as they rode along the line of the Pindos mountains, angling northeast to the city at Aigai. Attalus proved an interesting if unamusing companion, and Philip found himself admiring the man's single-minded ambition. As they rode, he learned of events in the kingdom. The Paionians had raided from the north, but Ptolemaos had smashed their army, forcing their king to agree to a yearly tribute of two hundred talents. Macedonian joy was short-lived, however, as the Illyrian army of King Bardylis had defeated Ptolemaos two months later at a battle near the Prespa Lakes in the west. For this defeat Ptolemaos had agreed to pay Bardylis a yearly tribute of two hundred and fifty talents.

"There are too many wolves seeking their meat in too small a sheep pen," said Attalus, and Philip nodded. It was not that northern Greece was truly small, but with Illyria, Macedonia, Paionia, and Thrace all boasting armies and countless independent cities like Olynthus and Amphipolis employing large mercenary forces, no one king could take control of the area.

Crosi used to say that northern Greece was a mercenary's paradise. Never short of employment, he could grow rich on the proceeds of blood and violence and then buy himself a quiet farm in the more civilized south.

Everywhere Philip and Attalus rode, there were signs of the frontier nature of the north. Towns were walled, settlements stockaded, single farms or lonely houses unheard of. People gathered together, never knowing when an enemy would descend on them with hot hearts and cold iron.

"It is a land for men," said Attalus as they journeyed high

in the Pierian mountains, their cloaks drawn tightly around them against the bitterness of the north winds of autumn.

"Men need wives and children," said Philip. "Children need education. Farmers need to be able to farm in peace. Macedonia is a rich land, with the finest timber in all of Greece. The land should yield tremendous riches. Yet it does not. For men must needs become warriors and forget the earth and its treasures. There should be a more profitable way."

"Perhaps one day you will be king," said Attalus softly. "A great king, maybe. Then you could conquer the Illyrians and the Thracians and see your dream fulfilled."

"I have no wish to be king," said Philip. He smiled suddenly. "And remember to report that to Ptolemaos!"

PELLA was a growing city. Philip's father, Amyntas, had borrowed heavily in order to bring architects from the south, planning avenues and temples and enlarging the palace. The richer Macedonian nobles were also encouraged to move to the capital, building homes in the hills and bringing with them servants who needed cheaper housing. This influx of new residents brought with it merchants and tradesmen, and the city flourished.

Philip stood at the window of his palace bedchamber staring out over the marketplace beyond the high walls of the gardens. He could hear the stallholders shouting out prices, enticing custom, and wished he could walk from the forbidding palace and mingle with the crowds.

But it was not to be. Ptolemaos made it clear that he did not wish his young nephews to venture far from his sight, claiming that he was worried for their safety. This surprised Philip, since he did not seem quite as concerned for his own son, Archelaos, who was allowed to ride and hunt and go whoring whenever the mood took him. Philip had no liking for Archelaos and despite Parmenion's advice could not bring himself to attempt to win over the boorish young man.

Archelaos was a younger version of his father: the same hook of a nose, the same cruel mouth and jutting chin. Philip found it hard enough being pleasant toward his murderous uncle without having to abase himself before the heir to the throne. He said as much to his brother Perdiccas as the older youth lay in his sickbed.

"There would be little point in trying to win him over," whispered Perdiccas, the effort of speaking sapping his strength. "Archelaos is a pig; he would take any overture as a sign of weakness and do his best to exploit it. I hate the man. Do you know what he said to me last spring? He said that even if Ptolemaos lets me live, the first order he will give upon his own coronation will be for my death."

"We could flee the country," said Philip. "You are nearly seventeen. You could become a mercenary, and I could be your servant. We could gather an army and come back."

"Dream on, little brother. I cannot shake off this fever. I feel weak as a two-day colt." He began to cough, and Philip brought him a wine cup filled with water. Perdiccas raised himself on one elbow and drank. Unlike his dark, almost swarthy brother, Perdiccas was golden-haired, and before his illness men had marveled at his beauty. But now his skin was stretched and tight, the color pale and unhealthy. His eyes were red-skimmed and dull, his lips the blue of the consumptive. Philip looked away. Perdiccas was dying.

Philip sat for some time with his brother, then wandered back to his own rooms. Food had been left for him on silver platters, but he was not hungry. He had felt sick that morning and had vomited painfully for an hour until at last only yellow bile came away. Now he drank a little water and lay back on his couch. Barking from the garden awoke him, and he remembered that the hound, Beria, had recently produced a litter. Sitting up, he wrapped the cold meat of his supper inside a linen towel and carried it to the gardens, where he sat for some time playing with the black puppies and feeding them scraps of food. They clambered over him, licking and mock biting. It lifted his mood, and he returned to his rooms. A servant came to collect the platter. He was a kindly old man named Hermon, white-bearded, with keen blue eyes under shaggy brows.

"You are feeling better, I hope, young lord?"

"Yes, thank you."

"That is good, sir. Would you like some sweet honey cakes? They are freshly made."

"No, Hermon. I think I will sleep now. Good night to you."

Philip's dreams were troubled, and twice he awoke in the night. The dogs were howling at the moon, and a whistling wind was shaking the shutters. Finally the howling began to annoy him, and he threw a cloak around his shoulders and strode down to the gardens. His room was the worst in the palace: close to the kennels and facing north, enjoying no sunshine, prey to the bitter north winds of winter. The gardens were cold, the blooms colorless and ethereal under the moonlight. Philip found Beria sitting by the wall, her howls high and heartrending. Around her lay the bodies of her six pups, black and lifeless. Philip knelt by them; the ground was stained with their vomit. Taking Beria by the collar, he pulled her away from the tiny corpses, then knelt hugging her great black head to his breast, stroking her ears. She whined piteously and pulled to return to her babies.

"They've gone, my lovely," he told her. "You come with me; we'll stay together, you and I."

The mastiff followed him up the stairs but padded to the window, howling once more. Philip tugged her collar and let her stretch out on the bed. Then he lay beside her with his arm around her, and she slept with her head resting on his breast.

As he lay there restless, he remembered the scraps of food he had fed to the puppies.

And thought of kindly old Hermon with the pale blue eyes. . . .

* * *

Philip lay awake through the night, his anger overwhelming his fear. Poison was not a new way of eliminating enemies, but why not use the age-old method? The assassin's blade—it was swift and sure. The answer came easily: Ptolemaos was not popular with the army, having been defeated by both Bardylis in the west and Cotys, the king of Thrace, in the east. His only success had come against the weak Paionians of the north.

As with all kings, Philip knew, Ptolemaos ruled by consent. The rich Macedonian nobles desired a man who could increase their fortunes; they wanted a king who could bring them glory. What else was there in life for a warrior people? And now they were no longer prepared to tolerate the seemingly endless—and obvious—murders of potential rivals. Ptolemaos was attempting to tread carefully.

Philip suddenly thought of Perdiccas. Of course! He, too, was being slowly poisoned.

But what to do? Who to trust? The answer to the second question was easier than the first. Trust no one. Rising from his bed, he crept across the room, anxious not to awaken the mastiff. Out in the corridor he moved silently through the palace, down the narrow stairway to the kitchens; there were meats there, and fruit, and he ate his fill. Then he filled a small sack with provisions and carefully made his way to the room of Perdiccas. His brother was asleep, and he woke him, gently pressing a hand to the young man's shoulder.

"What is it?" asked Perdiccas.

"I have brought you some food."

"I am not hungry, Brother. Let me sleep."

"Listen to me!" hissed Philip. "You are being poisoned!"

Perdiccas blinked, and Philip told him of the dead pups. "Anything could have killed them," said Perdiccas wearily. "It happens all the time."

"You may be right," whispered Philip. "But if you are, you will lose nothing by playing my game. If you are not, then your life will be saved."

He helped Perdiccas sit up and waited as his brother slowly ate a little beef and cheese. "Fetch me some water," asked

Perdiccas. Philip filled a cup from a pitcher on the nearby table . . . then stopped. Walking to the window, he emptied both cup and pitcher.

"We can trust nothing we do not fetch ourselves," he said. Once more he left the room, filling the pitcher from a barrel in the kitchen.

"No one must know we suspect them," said Philip upon his return. "They must think we are eating the food they give us."

Perdiccas nodded. His head fell back to the pillow, and he slept.

For four days Philip continued his nightly visits to his brother, and slowly the color returned to Perdiccas' features. On the morning of the fifth day Hermon arrived at Philip's rooms, bearing a tray of cheese and figs and a fresh pitcher of water.

"How did you sleep, my lord?" he asked, his smile kindly.

"Not well, my friend," Philip told him, keeping his voice low and tired. "I cannot seem to recover from this vomiting. And my strength is not good. Should I see a doctor?"

"That is not necessary, lord," said Hermon. "These . . . minor stomach ailments occur in autumn. You will recover soon."

"Thank you. You are very kind to me. Will you join me for breakfast? There is too much there for me."

Hermon spread his hands. "Would that I could, lord, but my duties are not yet completed. Enjoy your meal. I would advise you to force yourself to eat; only in this way will you rebuild your strength."

When he had gone, Philip put on a long blue cloak and, carrying the pitcher hidden within its folds, walked swiftly to the servants' halls and the rooms of Hermon. He knew the old man would be with Perdiccas, and he entered his quarters. A fresh pitcher of water stood by the window. Leaning out over the sill, the youngster saw that the gardens below were deserted and emptied Hermon's pitcher, refilling it from his own.

On the following morning a different servant brought the

prince's breakfast. "Where is my friend, Hermon?" Philip asked.

"He is unwell, sir," said the man, bowing.

"I am sorry to hear that. Please tell him I hope he recovers soon."

That afternoon Perdiccas rose from his bed. His legs were weak, but his strength was returning. "What are we to do?" he asked his younger brother.

"This cannot go on," Philip said softly. "They will soon realize we are no longer taking the poison. Then, I fear, it will be the knife or the sword."

"You mentioned running away," offered Perdiccas. "I think I am nearly strong enough to join you. We could head for Amphipolis."

"Thebes would be better," said Philip. "I have friends there. But we cannot wait too long—another three days at most. Until then you must stay in your bed and tell any who ask that you are feeling weaker. And we will need coin and horses."

"I have no money," said Perdiccas.

"I will think on it," Philip promised.

Hermon knelt before the three men, glancing up nervously into the hawklike eyes of Ptolemaos. "They must be very strong to withstand the powders, sire, but I will increase the doses. The older one will be dead in three days, I promise you."

Ptolemaos turned to Attalus. "I should have listened to you," he said, his voice deep and sepulchral.

"It is not too late, sire," replied Attalus. "Perdiccas is weak. I could smother him in his sleep. No one would be the wiser."

"And Philip?"

Attalus hesitated.

"I'd like to kill him," said Archelaos suddenly. "It would give me pleasure."

His father laughed. "I do not know what it is about the boy that you detest. He is personable enough. But let it be so. You kill him—but not tonight. Let Perdiccas die first. Philip can wait a week or so." He swung to Attalus. "You say that no one will suspect if the boys are smothered? Is there no sign?"

"None, sire."

Ptolemaos gestured to his son, then whispered in his ear. The tall prince nodded and made as if to leave the room. Then suddenly he sprang upon Hermon, pinning his arms behind him.

"Show me!" ordered the king. Attalus took hold of an embroidered cushion and covered Hermon's face, pressing the material hard against the old man's nose and mouth. The victim struggled weakly for a while, then his legs twitched and gave way, the stench of open bowels filling the room. Attalus lifted the cushion clear of the old man, and Archelaos let go of the body, which sank to the floor. Ptolemaos leaned over it, staring hard into the dead face. "I don't like the expression," he said. "He doesn't look like someone who died in his sleep."

Attalus chuckled and knelt by the body, pushing shut the mouth and closing the dead eyes. "Yes, that is better," whispered the king. "Good. Let it be done."

As the evening approached, Attalus sat in his rooms, sipping watered wine. He did not want to be drunk for this evening's work, yet his impulses urged him to drink the flagon dry. He prided himself on having an ordered mind and pushed away the wine cup. What is the matter with you? he asked himself. The answer came swiftly. He did not feel comfortable with the thought of Philip's death, though he could not think why. It was not as if he liked the boy; Attalus did not like anyone. And yet I do not wish to see him dead, he realized. The whole business was becoming disturbing. Ptolemaos was a fool; he was ruthless enough, but there his talents ended. Archelaos was no better. If anything, he had less talent than his father. Unrest was growing. Many of the nobles now stayed away from the palace, and the morale of the army was low. If Ptolemaos should fall, then his favorites would be dragged down with him, and Attalus had no wish to win a place among the fallen.

But what do I do? he wondered.

Attalus found his mood darkening along with the sky. He had no choice. Not yet. First kill Perdiccas, then find the leading Macedonian dissident and be ready to switch horses when the days of blood drew near. He cursed—and reached once more for the wine.

He waited until midnight and then walked silently along the deserted corridors, coming at last to the oak doors of Perdiccas' rooms. He could see light beneath the door and pushed his ear against the wood. There were voices within, though he could make out no words. He cursed softly and was about to leave, when the door was pulled open and he found himself facing Philip. The boy looked shocked, his hand flicking toward his dagger.

"There is nothing to fear," said Attalus, easing past him and into the room. The older prince was sitting on a couch, eating bread and cheese; he looked stronger than Attalus had ever seen him. The warrior turned to Philip. "I was looking for you," he lied easily, "but you were not in your rooms. I thought you might be here."

"Why should you seek me out in the night?" asked Philip, suspicious.

"There is a plot to kill you," said Attalus, "but then, you know that. Hence the midnight feast. No wonder the poisons failed to take effect. But that is by the by. Ptolemaos has ordered me to kill your brother tonight. You are to die next week."

Attalus heard the rasping whisper of an iron blade hissing from a scabbard and swung to see Perdiccas advancing with a sword. He had not realized how tall the prince was or sensed the power in him.

"That is not necessary," he said, his voice low. "I am not here to obey the order; I am here to warn you."

"Why should I believe you?" countered Perdiccas, holding the point of the blade to Attalus' throat.

"Wait!" urged Philip as he saw his brother tense for the thrust. "Let us not be rash! I believe him."

"Thank you," whispered Attalus, slowly reaching up and pushing the blade from his skin. "The question is, What do we do? I would suggest riding from the palace and heading for Amphipolis. Once there, you can gather support from discontented nobles and—perhaps—seize the throne."

"No," said Philip.

"What else is there?" put in Perdiccas.

"You take the throne tonight," Philip said. "Ptolemaos murdered our father, and the throne is yours by right. We kill the king."

"Gods, man! You are insane," responded Perdiccas. "We have no allies we know of. The guards are loyal to Ptolemaos. We'd be cut down."

"Not so," said Philip. "Ptolemaos is not a popular man, so no one will feel any lingering loyalty when he is dead. I saw Archelaos ride from the palace this afternoon, and I am told he is heading for Thebes. So he will be no threat. With the king dead, the nobles will gather to choose a successor, but by then the guards will already have declared their loyalty to you."

"How can you be sure?"

"The nature of men," said Philip. "The desire to be led. And Attalus will speak to them. He is a captain of the guard, and they will listen to him. Is that not so, Attalus?"

"Perhaps," agreed the warrior cautiously. "But the risks are still very great."

Philip laughed. "Risks? I have lived with the prospect of assassination for years. What risks? We may die? All men die, rich and poor alike. But if I am to die, then let it be while I fight, not like some bullock in a pen waiting for the ax to fall."

Attalus listened as Philip outlined his plan, and his admiration for the young man grew. He found himself wishing that the boy were older; he would make a fine king, a man of power and insight. He glanced at Perdiccas. There was strength here also, but he was a lesser man than his brother. Still, if this lunatic venture succeeded, it was Perdiccas who would take the crown. Attalus waited until Philip had finished speaking, then turned to Perdiccas and knelt.

"I hope, sire, that when we have succeeded, you will not hold it against me that I served your father's murderer. I had no hand in it."

Perdiccas looked down at the man, then laid his hand on his shoulder. "I will forgive you that, Attalus. And I will see you rewarded for this night's work."

The three men left the room, Attalus leading the way through the palace to the corridor before the king's apartments. There the brothers waited while he strode forward to where the two black-cloaked guards were sitting outside the bedroom door.

Attalus gestured to the guards to follow him and walked on. The men rose, glanced at one another, then moved to the end of the corridor, where Attalus waited.

"Have you seen anything suspicious?" Attalus whispered.

"In what way, sir?" asked one of the men. Behind the guards the princes had moved out into the open. Attalus found his mouth dry. This is madness, he thought.

"Have you seen anyone in the corridor this evening?" he inquired as the brothers crept toward the bedroom door.

"Only you, sir. And the king himself. Is there some trouble?"

"Probably not. But be vigilant." Philip had opened the door; both princes were slipping inside.

"Of course, sir. We don't sleep on duty."

Attalus watched the door of the bedchamber close. "The world offers many surprises," he said. "Sometimes a man just happens to be in the wrong place at the wrong time."

"I don't understand," the man replied.

"No, I am afraid you don't," answered Attalus, his dagger flashing into the man's throat. The second guard stood rooted to the spot for a moment, then grabbed for his sword, but Attalus tore his dagger free and plunged the point through the man's eye.

From the king's bedchamber came a terrible scream. Attalus ran forward, throwing open the door.

Ptolemaos lay half out of the bed with two swords jutting from his chest and belly. The king fell to the floor and tried to drag himself toward Attalus, but Philip ran forward, wrenching loose his sword. Ptolemaos screamed again, then the blade hacked through his neck.

Philip rose, turned, and knelt before Perdiccas.

"You will never have to kneel to me," promised the new king of Macedonia, lifting Philip to his feet. "And I will never forget what you have done for me."

I N the eleven years since Parmenion's victory at Leuctra,
Derae had suffered many strange dreams—visions of darkness and evil, demon-haunted and terrifying. At first Tamis
would appear in her dreams, rescuing her, telling her of the
servants of the Dark God who sought to destroy them both. As
the years flowed on, Derae's powers grew and she found the
night attacks less daunting. Yet now she was lost within a
dark, troubled nightmare, shadows darting just out of her
range of vision as she spun and twisted, trying in vain to
glimpse them. But all she could see were gray castle walls,
water glistening on cold stone.

Darkness rose like smoke around her, and from within it she
heard the sound of rasping breath, the scratching of talons on
stone pavings. Piercing pain tore into her arms as a creature
of scale and slime leapt at her. White light blazed from her
fingers, and a terrible scream echoed along the stone corridors. Glancing down at her arms, she saw the marks of talons
in bloody tears on her flesh, but of the creature there was no

sign, only a fleeting memory of cold opal eyes and a wide-slitted mouth. Swiftly she healed herself and tried to soar, but the stone ceiling held her trapped, as did the walls and floor.

A black, stagnant pool of water ahead of her bubbled and rose, coalescing into the shape of a woman cloaked and hooded, pale of face and dark of eye. "So, you are the healer," said the woman, her voice deep and husky. "You are a pretty one. Come to me, pretty one!"

Derae laughed then, her fear evaporating. "What do you want of me?"

"I want to know who you serve. You trouble me."

"Why should you be troubled?" countered Derae. "I am, as you say, a healer. For more than twenty years I have dwelt in the temple. I do not even know you, lady."

"Can you walk the many futures?" the woman asked.

"Can you?" responded Derae.

"What I can do is none of your concern!" snapped the hooded newcomer.

"I see that you cannot," said Derae softly. "Why is it of interest to you?"

The woman smiled, but her features did not soften. "Can we not be friends? I, too, am a healer and a seer. I merely felt your power and wished to know more of you."

Derae shook her head. "We cannot be friends, you and I; we serve opposing powers. But then, you do not desire friendship, do you? Speak the truth—or do you fear it will burn your tongue?"

"Burn! You wish to see burning?" hissed the woman. Flames leapt from the walls, and Derae's robes caught fire, her skin blistering. She did not move or scream. A soft golden light enveloped her, healing her skin, wrapping itself around her in a protective cloak. Angry now, Derae raised her hand. Twin spears of barbed light flashed through the woman's chest, hurling her back and pinning her to the wall; she screamed in pain, then touched the spears, which disappeared in an instant.

The dark woman smiled. "Very fine," she said, "and I was

wrong about you. I have nothing to fear."

The castle shimmered and vanished, and Derae awoke back in the temple.

The battle in the ghostly castle disturbed her, and she sought out Tamis. The old woman was still asleep, spittle drooling to her chin. Derae touched her lightly, but she did not wake. The last two decades had not been kind to the old priestess: her powers were fading, along with her sight and hearing. Derae gripped her shoulder, shaking her more roughly.

"Eh? What?" muttered Tamis, rubbing at her eyes.

Derae brought her water and waited while the old woman adjusted from sleep to waking. "Why did you disturb me? I was dreaming of my first husband. What a man! Ha! Like a ram, he was."

Derae told her about the castle and the dark-cloaked woman. Tamis listened in silence, then shook her head. "I don't know who she was. We are not alone in this struggle, Derae. There are others like us, with talent and sight. Some serve the light, others the darkness. Why did it trouble you?"

"She was frightened of me, but when I defeated her, all her fear vanished. That makes no sense . . . does it?"

Tamis sighed and rose from the bed. Dawn light was seeping through the shuttered window. She dressed in a simple robe of white wool and walked out into the garden, Derae following her.

"You say you defeated her. How?" asked Tamis. Derae explained, and the old woman sighed. "You tried to kill her, and in doing so she defeated you, for that is not the way of the source. And those who do not serve the source serve only chaos."

"But that is not true," protested Derae. "I am a healer. I am not evil."

"No, you are not evil," agreed Tamis, her voice weary. "I have trained you badly. I have done so many things badly. My arrogance has been colossal. Cassandra tried to warn me, but

I would not listen. Yet I was wise once," she said suddenly, stooping to smell a budding rose. "I knew many secrets. But all wisdom is folly. We think we manipulate, but we are being manipulated. We think we have power, but we are as leaves in a storm. We do good works that lead to evil. All is confusion. All is vanity."

Derae took her hand. "Are you ill, Tamis? I've not heard you speak like this before."

"I am not ill. I am dying, Derae. And none of my work is finished. I wonder sometimes if we ever finish what we start. I am so tired of it all. I have done terrible things . . . terrible. I thought I was being clever." She laughed then, the sound a dry cackle that ended in a series of racking coughs. She cleared her throat and spit into the rosebushes. "Look at me! Beautiful Tamis! It is hard to believe that men once desired me."

"What did you dream?" Derae asked.

"Dream?"

"You said you dreamed of your first husband. Tell me of it."

"I saw how good it was to be loved, to be touched, to use and be used. I saw all that I have lost—all my mistakes, my vanities."

"Show me!" whispered Derae, laying her hands on the old woman's head. Tamis relaxed, and Derae swam into her subconscious, seeing the young Tamis writhing beneath a powerful, bearded young man. Derae did not watch the scene but floated high above it, twisting in the air, seeking . . . searching. Then she saw her, the dark-cloaked woman. She was laughing and pointing at the rutting couple. Derae moved closer. The woman was not alone; shadowy shapes hovered around her.

Derae surfaced into the cool of the dawn garden. "It was no dream, Tamis; it was the woman I spoke of. She came to you, filling your mind with despair."

"Nonsense. I would have seen her. I am still powerful!" protested Tamis. "Why do you seek to undermine me?"

"I do not," Derae told her. "I promise you. We are under attack, Tamis. But why now?"

"The dark birth is close," whispered Tamis. "So close. Maybe within the year, certainly within two. Was she truly in my head?"

"Yes. I am sorry."

"It does not matter. All powers fade." Tamis sighed. "I wish I could teach you more, but I cannot. And one day you will hate me." Tears fell from her eyes.

"You have taught me much, my friend . . . my dear friend. How could I ever hate you?"

"You saw the woman? Well, that is retribution of a poetic kind," said Tamis. "One day you will know why. But tell me, where is Parmenion?"

"He is in Susa. The great king has presented him with a prize stallion following his victory in Mesopotamia."

"He will be drawn into the battle for Macedonia," Tamis said. "That is the center now. All the powers are being drawn there; it is the place. Go there! Go there now! See it. Feel it!"

"I cannot go now. I am worried about you, Tamis."

"It is too late for your worries, my dear. The future is upon us. The Dark God is coming."

"But we can still stop him?"

Tamis shrugged and stared around the garden. "Look at the roses. There are hundreds of them. Every year there are thousands of blooms. If I were to ask you to trim and prune them all so that only one perfect bloom would emerge and all other bushes remained green, could you do it?"

"I think so, but it would take all my power."

"What if I asked you to prune all the roses in the world so that only one bush produced one perfect flower?"

"What are you saying, Tamis?"

"Go to Macedonia, my dear. I will sit and watch the roses grow."

Derae soared above the temple and fled west, passing over the mountains of Thrace and the plains of the great rivers Nestus, Strymon, and Axios. Floating in a clear blue sky, she relaxed her mind, closing her spirit eyes and riding the rhythms of power as they pulsed from the land below. She felt herself drawn south, over the sea and down toward a mountain range. Lower and lower she flew. Below her a group of horsemen were pursuing a lion. It ran into the rocks and then, out of sight of the pursuers, turned and prepared itself for the charge. One of the hunters, a handsome dark-bearded young man, had pulled ahead of the group. He galloped his horse into the rocks and leapt to the ground, a light hunting spear in his hand. The lion charged, but the hunter did not panic or run. Dropping to one knee, he gripped his spear firmly and waited for the beast to charge.

Derae sped like an arrow toward the lion.

Philip dragged his horse to a standstill as he saw the lion lope into the rocks. The joy of the hunt was on him, the intoxicating spirit of danger proving, as always, stronger than wine. He leapt lightly to the ground, his short stabbing spear held firmly in his right hand, the iron point honed to razor sharpness.

The years since the assassination of Ptolemaos had been good to Philip. No longer a slim young boy, the prince was now broad-shouldered and powerful with a trimmed black beard, glossy as the pelt of a panther, adorning his face. At twenty-three Philip of Macedon was in his prime.

When Perdiccas took the throne, Philip had known peace for the first time in years. He had moved south of the capital to the royal estates beyond the ancient capital of Aigai and there had indulged in all the pleasures enjoyed by Macedonian nobles: hunting, drinking, whoring. But of them all, it was the hunt that most fired his blood. Bears, wolves, deer, wild oxen, boars, and leopards—Macedonia was alive with game.

But the lion was growing scarce. Now a shaggy male had moved down from the mountains, attacking the sheep flocks, killing goats and cattle. For five days they had tracked it, losing the spoor only to find it again, moving always south. It seemed as if the beast were drawing them ever closer to Mount Olympus, the home of the gods.

Philip glanced south at the distant mountain. "Be with me, Father Zeus!" he whispered as he moved slowly into the rocks. He should have waited for his companions, but—as ever—Philip was anxious to make the kill, to be the first to strike.

The noon sun beat down on the prince's back as he inched his way forward. Lions did not like to be moving in the heat, he knew, preferring to find a shady spot to sleep. And this one had recently killed a large sheep, gorging himself on the fat-filled flesh. Philip hefted his spear. The point would have to enter behind the lion's shoulder, driving deep into his lungs and heart. Even then a single sweep of its paw could crush a man's ribs, the talons disemboweling the spearman.

Philip glanced back, seeing that Attalus and the others were still some distance away. The pale-eyed assassin would be furious if Philip made the kill without him. He chuckled. Attalus was already angry, for Perdiccas had taken the army west to challenge Bardylis, leaving him behind. Despite the assassin's aid eleven years earlier, Perdiccas had never trusted him or allowed him to rise to prominence; he was still a mere captain of the guard.

A low growl came from ahead, beyond the boulders. The sound was deep and rumbling. Fear touched Philip with fingers of fire, and he reveled in it as at the caress of a beautiful woman.

"Come to me," he whispered.

The lion charged from the rocks. It was huge, seeming to

Philip larger than a pony. There was no time to run to the side and deliver the killing thrust.

Philip dropped to one knee and grounded the haft of the spear, the point aimed at the lion's throat. It would not stop him, he realized. The haft would snap under the impact, then the fangs would tear at his face. Instantly he knew the day of his death was upon him, yet he stayed calm, determined that he would not die alone. This monster would walk beside him on the road to Hades.

Behind him he heard the sound of hoofbeats, but his friends were too late to save him.

"Come on!" he roared at the lion. "Come and die with me!"

Suddenly the beast twisted as if in pain, the charge faltering. Its huge head lifted, and a terrifying roar rent the air. . . . And the monster halted, inches ahead of the iron spear point.

Philip could smell the beast's rancid breath and found himself staring at the fangs, long and curved like Persian daggers. He looked up into the beast's tawny eyes.

Time ceased, the moment lingering.

Philip slowly stood and then reached out, touching the spear point to the lion's mane. The beast blinked but did not move. Philip sensed Nicanor behind him, drawing an arrow from his quiver.

"Let no one loose a shaft," said the prince, his voice soft and low.

The lion moved forward, its pelt rubbing against Philip's leg; then it turned and ambled away into the rocks.

Attalus ran to the prince. "I never saw anything like it," he whispered.

Philip shivered. "Nor I."

"Do we give chase?"

"I do not think so, my friend. And I have lost all appetite for the hunt." He glanced back to where the lion had been.

"Was it an omen of some kind? Was it really a lion?" Attalus asked.

"If it was a god, he had appalling breath," answered Philip, glancing nervously at the distant peaks of Mount Olympus.

The huntsmen took a leisurely route back to Philip's summer home twenty miles south of the city of Aigai. They were almost there when the rider came galloping from the north and rode alongside Philip. His horse was lathered and close to exhaustion.

"The king is dead," he said, "the army destroyed."

"Perdiccas dead? I do not believe it," cried Attalus. The rider ignored him and looked to Philip.

"The king advanced on the Illyrians, but our center gave way. Perdiccas tried to countercharge, but the enemy was expecting it. The cavalry was cut to pieces, the king's head placed on a lance. We lost over four thousand men."

Philip had never been close to his brother, but neither were they enemies. The younger man had admired the king for his prowess as a statesman and warrior. What now? he wondered. The king's son was only two years old, and the army—whatever was left of it—would never agree to a babe being crowned, not with the nation under threat. He rode away from the men and dismounted; sitting on a boulder, he stared out to sea. He had never wanted to be king, had never desired anything more from life than to be able to hunt, and drink, and make love. Perdiccas understood that, which was why he had never considered having Philip assassinated.

For his part Philip mostly avoided affairs of state. He had warned Perdiccas of the perils of attacking the Illyrians, but such battles were common and very rarely decisive; the losers would agree to pay large sums in tribute to the victors, and then life would go on. But for the king to fall on the battlefield, along with four thousand Macedonians! It was a tragedy of awesome proportions. The balance of power in northern Greece was delicate at the best of times, and with this catastrophe it would be thrown into turmoil.

Perdiccas had proved a good king, popular and strong. But he was obsessed with the desire to crush Bardylis, and nothing Philip had said would sway him.

"Send for Parmenion," Philip had urged.

"I need no half-blood Spartan," Perdiccas had replied.

"Would you like me to ride with you?"

For a moment he thought the answer would be yes. Perdiccas' handsome face softened, but then the hard look returned
to his eyes. "No, Brother. You stay in Aigai. Enjoy yourself."

As Philip had turned to leave, Perdiccas had reached out
and taken hold of the younger man's shoulder. "I never forgot
what you did for me," he said.

"I know that. You do not need to say it."

"There are some who have urged me to kill you, Philip.
There are some who believe . . . ah, what does it matter? I did
not kill Archelaos, and he has proved no threat."

"Do not fear for me, Brother," Philip told him. "I have no
wish to be king. But beware of Bardylis. If you lose, he will set
a tribute you may find hard to pay."

Perdiccas grinned. "I shall *not* lose."

Now Philip shook himself loose of the memory and called
the rider to him. "Where are the Illyrians now?"

"They have not advanced, sire. They stripped the dead, and
now they are camped four days' ride from Pella."

"Do not call me sire; I am not the king," snapped Philip,
waving the man away.

His thoughts raged like a storm in his mind. The balance of
power was everything! To the west the Illyrians, to the north
the Paionians, to the east the Thracians, and to the south
Thebes. While each nation had a strong army, there was little
danger of a full-scale invasion. But now, with Macedonia's
army destroyed, the land was open to any with the courage to
take it. Philip thought of his enemies. First Bardylis, the cunning king of Illyria, eighty years old, maybe more, but with a
mind as sharp as a timber wolf. After him Cotys, the king of
Thrace, just turned sixty, a greedy, ruthless monarch whose
avaricious eyes would now turn to the Macedonian mines no
more than a day's ride from his Thracian borders in the east.
Then the Paionians, tribesmen from the north who lived to
fight and plunder. After them the power-hungry Thebans, the
pompous Athenians. The gods knew how many others!

One fear at a time, he cautioned himself. What if, he wondered, he did not try for the crown? One name soared into his mind: Archelaos, his stepbrother. The hatred between them was stronger than iron and colder than a winter blizzard. Archelaos would fight for the throne, and his first action would be to see Philip dead.

Philip called to Attalus. "I am riding for Pella," he told the warrior. "It is likely that Archelaos has not yet heard the news. When he does, he will also come to the capital, but he will be traveling from Cercine. Take twenty men and see that he does not survive the journey."

Attalus smiled grimly. "A task I'll enjoy, for sure," he said.

THE CITY OF SUSA, PERSIA, AUTUMN, 359 B.C.

"IT is your own fault," said Mothac as Parmenion paced back and forth across the room. "Who else can you blame?"

The Spartan moved to the wide doors leading to the gardens, where he stood staring out over the terraces with their hanging blooms and trees garlanded with blossom. The scents were sweet and the view exquisite, but Parmenion turned away, his face flushed, his eyes angry.

"Blame?" he snarled. "Who else but that cursed Persian brat? He loses seventy men because he cannot be bothered to clear the fighting ground of boulders. Seventy! Then he had the brass balls to tell me it doesn't matter, they were only peasants."

"He is a royal prince, Parmenion. What did you expect when you revoked his commission? Praise? Another prize stallion?"

"Persians!" hissed Parmenion. "I am sick of them."

"No," said Mothac softly. "You are sick of Persia, my

friend. And you are too canny not to have understood the consequences of dismissing Darius."

"What are you saying? That I wanted my own commission revoked?"

"Exactly that."

"Nonsense! We have everything here that men could desire. Look around you, Mothac. Silks, fine couches, beautiful grounds. How many kings in Greece can boast such a palace? Slaves to obey our every desire and more coin than we could spend in two lifetimes. You think I willingly threw this away?"

"Yes."

"Let's get some air," muttered the Spartan, strolling out into the gardens and along the paved walkways. Mothac followed the general into the bright sunshine, silently cursing himself for forgetting his hat of straw. During the last ten years Mothac had grown steadily more bald, a calamity he blamed totally on the harsh Persian sun.

"How could he have been so stupid?" asked Parmenion. "He knew he could get no chariot support unless he cleared the ground. And he had a thousand men under his command. It would have taken no more than an hour, perhaps two. But no, our fine Persian prince leaves his men sitting in the sunshine and rides into the hills to bathe in a cool stream."

"We were finished here, anyway," pointed out the Theban. "The satrap wars are all but over. What else could the great king have asked of you? You have won his battles in Cappadocia, Phrygia, Egypt, Mesopotamia, and other places with names I cannot wrap around my tongue. We don't need any more wars. Let us just sit here and enjoy our dotage. The gods know we need no more coin."

Parmenion shook his head. "I am not ready for dotage, Mothac my friend. I want . . ." He shrugged. "I don't know what I want. But I cannot sit idle. What are the latest offers?"

"The satrap of Egypt requests your services to counter tribal attacks in the south."

"Too hot," said Parmenion.

"The Olynthians are hiring mercenaries. They would like

you to lead their forces into Macedonia."

"Macedonia again. Tempting. What else?"

"The king of the Illyrians, Bardylis, offers you employment, as does Cotys of Thrace. The Thracian offer is a good one: two talents of gold."

"What of the Macedonian king . . . Perdiccas?"

"We have heard nothing from him."

Parmenion sat silently for a while. "I am not anxious to return to Greece. Not yet."

Mothac nodded, remaining silent. He knew Parmenion's thoughts had turned again to Epaminondas. The Theban hero had crushed the Spartans, taking the Theban army to the outskirts of Sparta itself, where the Spartan king, Agisaleus, had barricaded the streets, refusing all challenges.

Glory days had followed for Thebes, but the Athenians, fearing Theban ambition, had allied themselves with Sparta, and bloody battle had followed bloody battle for seven years.

Then, while Parmenion was at the great court in Susa, came news of a battle near Mantinea. The Spartans and the Athenians together had come against Epaminondas. The Theban tried to repeat the tactics of Leuctra: the massed charge. But it was only partially successful, and a contingent of Athenian cavalry smashed a path to Epaminondas. The general died at the point of victory, and the man who killed him was said to be an Athenian captain named Gryllus, the son of Xenophon.

"He was a great man," whispered Mothac.

"What? Yes. How is it you always know my thoughts?"

"We are friends, Parmenion. I fear for Thebes now: Pelopidas dead in Thessaly, Epaminondas gone. Who is there to fight for Thebes?"

"I don't know, but I'll take no part in it. Xenophon was right. Greece will never be united, and the constant battles only weaken her further."

A slave girl ran from the house, bowing before Parmenion and then turning to Mothac. "There is a messenger, sir. He wishes to see the general."

"From whom does this messenger come?"

"He is a Greek, sir." The girl bowed her head and waited.

"See that he is given wine. I shall speak to him presently," Mothac told her.

Parmenion waited in the sunshine until Mothac returned.

"Well, what was it?"

"He was an Illyrian. Bardylis has withdrawn his offer to you. It seems that without you he crushed the Macedonian army and killed Perdiccas. It might be a good time for you to take the offer of Cotys. Thrace and Illyria will now fight over the spoils. Macedonia is finished."

"Who succeeded Perdiccas?"

"One of the princes . . . Philip, I think he said."

"I knew him in Thebes. I liked him."

"Oh, no," said Mothac. "Don't even think it."

"Think what?"

"I see that look in your eye, Parmenion. They have no army, and the wolves are gathering—it is folly to even think of it. Anyway, this Philip has made no offer."

Parmenion chuckled. "No army and strong enemies all around him. It is very appealing, Mothac."

"There is nothing appealing about death!" snapped the Theban.

Archelaos was murdered as he crossed the River Axios to the northwest of Pella, and with his death opposition to Philip from within Macedonia was ended. But it did not end his problems. The Illyrians had crushed the Macedonian army in the northwest, and now the Paionian tribes of the north had invaded, sacking two cities and thirty villages. Worse was to follow for the new king. In the east the Thracians were massing to invade, ready to install a distant cousin of Philip's, Pausanias, as a puppet ruler. And from the south came word that the Athenians were sponsoring yet another cousin, Argaios, and he was marching with an army to contest the throne.

"What surprises me," Philip confided to Nicanor, his closest friend, "is why anyone should wish to take over the kingdom now. There's precious little left that isn't already in enemy hands."

"You'll win, though, Philip. You will. There's not a man in Greece to outthink you."

Philip chuckled and threw his arm around his friend's shoulder. "I would accept that compliment more readily if there was any basis for it in fact. But I need a miracle. I need Parmenion."

"What can a Spartan do for us?"

"He can build me an army—and, by the bones of Heracles, I need one. Find him for me, Nicanor. Send out riders, use the seers. Anything. Find him."

Pushing the problems from his mind, he found himself remembering his days as a hostage in Thebes eleven years earlier, when he had watched the legendary Parmenion training the Sacred Band. There was something about the man, a calm that spoke of great strength, and in his pale eyes Philip had seen an understanding, sensing an affinity with the Spartan warrior.

Then had come Leuctra and the defeat of the awesome Spartans. Parmenion's victory. From that time Philip had begun to look for news of the Spartan's travels, listening eagerly to tales of his victories in Egypt and Persia. Satraps offered him fortunes in gold and jewels, vying for the favors of the greatest general of the age. Even the great king was said to be in awe of his skill.

Once an enemy army surrendered when they heard that Parmenion had been hired to lead a force against them. Even his name had power.

How I need you now, thought Philip.

Attalus approached the king as he stood by the window, his thoughts distant. "What of the babe, sire?" he whispered. "Do you wish it dispatched?"

It was a reasonable question, and Philip considered it. If allowed to grow, his nephew would one day perhaps seek to win his father's throne. And it was customary to eliminate all other claimants.

Philip sighed. "Where is Simiche?"

"As you commanded, the queen is a prisoner in her rooms. She still has three handmaidens, and the child is with her."

"I will do it," said Philip. He walked swiftly from the throne room and down the long corridor to the adjoining building in the east. Two guards saluted as he reached the queen's quarters; he nodded to them and entered Simiche's private chamber. The queen was a small woman, elfin-faced, her hair long and dark. She looked up as he entered and almost managed to keep the fear from her face. The toddler, Amyntas, smiled as he saw his uncle and tottered toward him. Simiche stood and gathered the child to her, stroking his dark curls.

Philip dismissed the handmaidens, who ran from the room. Simiche said nothing; she did not plead, she merely sat, cuddling her son. Philip was torn. His hand was on his knife hilt, but he stood in the center of the room confused and uncertain. Perdiccas could have ordered Philip's death, but he had not. Now Philip was standing before the woman Perdiccas had loved and the son he had adored.

He sighed. "The boy will be safe, Simiche," he said at last. "No harm will come to him. You will go to my summer home and raise him there. I will see you have a good allowance for his education."

"Do not deceive me, Philip," she replied. "If you plan to have us killed, do it now. Do not raise false hopes. Be a man and use that knife. I will not resist."

"You have my word, Simiche. There is no question of killing the boy."

She closed her eyes, her head dropping. Tears fell to her cheeks, the release of tension making her tremble as she hugged the boy to her, kissing his face. He struggled to be free of such intense emotion. Philip sat beside the queen, putting his arm around her. The boy reached out and giggled as he tugged the king's dark beard.

"May the gods bless you," Simiche whispered.

"They are not making good work of it at present," said Philip.

"They will," she promised him. "Perdiccas loved you, Philip, but he was in awe of you. He said you had greatness within you, and I believe that now. What will you do?"

He shrugged and smiled, ruffling the boy's hair. "I have no army and am being attacked from the west, the north, the east, and the south. I think I will shave off my beard and become a traveling actor, a reader of comedies."

She laughed then. "You will think of something. What is it that you need most?"

"Time," he answered without hesitation.

"Who is the greatest enemy?"

"The old wolf, Bardylis. His Illyrians have already crushed the army. If he marches on Pella, there is nothing I can do to stop him."

"It is said he has a daughter of surpassing ugliness," said Simiche softly. "Her name is Audata, and he has tried—unsuccessfully—to arrange marriages for her with lowly princes. I daresay he has given up thinking of a king for her."

"A bride of surpassing ugliness? Something I have always wanted," replied Philip, and their laughter filled the room.

The days passed with an ominous lack of movement from his enemies, and Philip worked long into the nights, preparing dispatches for Athens, to friends in Thessaly to the south and Amphipolis in the east. He sent Nicanor to Bardylis in Illyria, formally requesting the hand of his daughter Audata in marriage and promising to pay a tribute of five hundred talents a year from the day of the wedding. To the Thracian king, Cotys, he sent a long letter assuring him of friendship, but carrying the assurance was the cold-eyed Attalus.

Philip gave him two small metal vials, each marked with different letters. "This one," said Philip, "contains a deadly poison, but it is slow-acting. The other is an antidote. You must find a way to poison the king without suspicion falling on you. Cotys has three sons, and they hate each other. Once the old man is dead, they will never unite to threaten us."

Attalus smiled. "You are taking to this business rather well, my friend. I thought you had no desire to be king."

"A man takes what the gods thrust upon him," Philip answered. "But it is vital that Cotys die. Before the deed is done, seek out the pretender Pausanias and tell him you are disenchanted with me. Tell him you wish to serve him against me. I leave it to you how you kill him . . . but do it."

"I do not wish to sound like a Cretan mercenary, sire, but it would be pleasant to know that I will return to some honored position in your service."

Philip nodded and took the tall warrior by the arm, leading him to a couch by an indoor pool of marble. "You do not need to call me sire when there is no one else present. You are my friend, Attalus, and I trust you as I trust no other. You are the king's right hand, and as I prosper, so will you. Do you trust me?"

"Of course."

"Then do my bidding."

Attalus chuckled. "Already you sound like a king. Very well, Philip."

The door opened, and a servant entered and bowed. "My lord, the Athenian ambassador is seeking an audience."

Philip rose and took a deep breath. "Tell him I shall be with him presently." The king bade farewell to Attalus and then walked through to his bedchamber, where he changed his clothes, dressing himself in a long pale blue tunic and a Persian cloak of fine dark blue wool.

Then he sat, allowing his thoughts to drift over his problems, identifying each and preparing himself for the meeting. To remove Athens from the fray was an urgent priority, but it would prove costly. Once again the city was struggling to be the leader of all Greece. Since Parmenion had crushed the Spartans, the real power struggle had developed between Thebes and Athens, both forming alliances in bids to secure supremacy. Perdiccas had favored the Thebans, sending Macedonian troops to the independent city of Amphipolis in the east to aid them against Athenian aggression. Understandably this infuriated the Athenians, who had ruled Amphipolis.

It was an important settlement, controlling all trade routes down the great River Strymon, but its people wanted nothing to do with Athens and had been fighting for independence for more than fifty years.

But now the Athenians had dispatched an army to remove Philip from the throne, and he had no force to oppose them. If they succeeded, Amphipolis would fall anyway.

Placing a slender gold circlet on his brow, he walked out into the throne room to meet Aischines. The man was short and stout, his face the unhealthy crimson of the weak of heart.

Philip greeted him with a broad smile. "Welcome, Aischines, I trust you are in good health."

"I will not complain, sire," the man answered, his voice deep, his tones clipped and exact. "But I see that you are in the best of condition, like a young Heracles."

Philip laughed. "Would that I had only twelve labors to perform! However, I must not burden you with my problems. I have sent messages to Athens—a city I have always admired—and I hope our friendship will be lasting."

"Sadly, an attitude not shared by your late brother," said Aischines. "He seemed to prefer the Thebans and even—dare I mention it—sent troops against us in the battle to recover Amphipolis."

Philip nodded. "Sadly, my brother did not share my view of Athens. He did not see the city as the father of democracy, nor understand the true nature of her greatness. I think he was dazzled by the exploits of Epaminondas and Pelopidas and trusted our nation to prosper under the wisdom of Thebes. A great shame," said Philip, shaking his head. "But let us walk awhile and enjoy the cool of dusk as we talk."

The king led the way to the outer corridors and the royal gardens, pointing out different blooms that Simiche had planted from seeds sent from Persia. As they walked, Philip's mind was whirling. He needed the Athenians' acceptance, if not their direct support. An army financed by Athens was marching to steal his kingdom and place Argaios on the throne. As yet the Macedonian forces were unready for another major conflict, but could he be so rash as to surrender Amphipolis, a city so vital to the sea trade in the Thermaic Gulf?

Tread warily, Philip! he cautioned himself.

They halted by a high wall and sat beneath a tree heavily laden with purple blooms. Philip sighed. "I will be frank with you, Aischines," he said. "After all, your spies already know of my contacts with Thebes." Aischines nodded gravely, which amused the king since no such contacts had been made. "They wish to send me an army in order—as we are both aware—not to protect Macedonia but to stop Athens from regaining Amphipolis. I need no more lengthy wars fought on Macedonian soil, and I desire no new masters. Rather, I wish for friendship with the premier city of Greece."

"The Thebans," said Aischines carefully, "seek only the power of tyranny. They have no culture. Where is their philosophy? In the power of the sword? In the last hundred years they have known only two great men, and those you have already mentioned. When Pelopidas was slain in Thessaly and Epaminondas fell at Mantinea, they had no one to replace them. They are a failing power. Athens is once more in the ascendant."

"I agree," said Philip soothingly, "but what choices do I have? The Illyrians have invaded my upper kingdom. Paionians are pillaging to the north. The Thracians are massing on my borders, seeking to install Pausanias. I am threatened everywhere. If Thebes is the only answer, then Thebes it must be—five thousand *hoplites* would secure my throne."

"Only for Thebes, sire. Not for you."

Philip turned his gaze to meet Aischines' eyes. "I have known you only a few moments, Aischines, but I see that you are a man I can trust. You are a fine spokesman for your city and an honest, noble man. If you tell me that Athens wishes friendship, I will believe you, and I will spurn the offer of Thebes."

Aischines swallowed hard. Neither man had mentioned the Athenian force marching with Argaios. "There is still," he said, "the question of Amphipolis. As you are aware, she is an Athenian city, and we would much like to restore her to the league. You currently retain a garrison there, I understand."

"It will be withdrawn the moment we reach agreement," promised Philip. "Amphipolis is not considered by me to be Macedonian. In truth, the citizens requested our aid, and my brother—wrongly, as I believe—agreed to help them. Now, tell me, Aischines, what message should I send the Thebans?"

"I see that you are a man of culture and wisdom," said the ambassador. "I can assure you that Athens respects such men and desires only friendship with them. I shall send my report to the council immediately and will return to you directly."

Philip rose. "It has been a pleasant meeting, my dear Aischines. I hope you will join me tomorrow at the theater; there is a new comedy I have been waiting to see. The players are Athenians, and it would be an honor for them—and for me—if you would sit beside me."

Aischines bowed.

Philip accompanied him back to the palace and then returned to his rooms, his face darkening with fury. Nicanor was waiting for him.

"It did not go well with the Athenian?" asked his friend.

"Well enough," snapped Philip, "but if I give away much more of Macedonia, I shall be the ruler of three trees and a stagnant pool. Tell me something good, Nicanor. Cheer me!"

"We have gathered almost a thousand men from the remnants of the army. But morale is not good, Philip; we need a victory somewhere."

"Is the gold still getting through from Crousia?"

"Some, but I think the governor is holding back, waiting to see who is likely to win. He may already be communicating with Cotys or Pausanius."

"Then we can hire no mercenaries. So be it. A victory, is it? You have spoken to the officers, so tell me, which of them has the belly I need?"

Nicanor leaned back on the couch, staring at the ceiling. "Antipater is a good man. He kept his troops together well, and they fought a tight retreat. I think he is respected. The others? There is no one special, Philip."

"Send him to me. Tonight!"

"Who are we to fight?"

Philip laughed then and spread his hands. "The one thing we are not short of is enemies. But it will be the Paionians. What news of Parmenion?"

"He won a battle for the satrap of Cappadocia. He is in Susa, being honored by the great king. But we have got word to him. I must say, though, Philip, I cannot see why he should come. He must be rich by now. Why would he return to Greece? What can we offer him?"

Philip shrugged. There was no answer to that.

And the thought depressed him.

The faint light of predawn bathed the slopes of the low range of hills overlooking the River Axios as Nicanor gently shook Philip awake. The king groaned and sat up, pushing aside his blanket and stretching his back. Around him most of the thousand cavalrymen were still sleeping. Philip stood and rubbed warmth into his powerful arms, glancing up at the sentries on the ridge.

"Any movement?" he asked Nicanor.

"No, sire."

Philip lifted his bronze-reinforced leather breastplate and swung it into place, Nicanor adjusting the winged shoulder guards and tying them securely. A black-bearded warrior walked through the gloom and bowed before the king.

"The enemy have camped in a hollow about a mile from here, due north. I count they have almost twice our number: they were reinforced last night."

Philip wanted to curse. Instead he grinned. "You have done well, Antipater. And do not concern yourself with the numbers. Just remember that we are Macedonian and that the king rides with you."

"Yes, sire." The man looked away. Philip guessed at his thoughts. Only weeks before, another king had probably said something remarkably similar, and that enterprise had ended in massacre and disaster.

"I am not Perdiccas," said Philip softly. Antipater looked startled, but Philip thumped his shoulder and chuckled. "Now, we cannot consider two defeats in so short a time, can we?"

Antipater smiled nervously, unsure how to take this curious man. "Do you wish to talk to the men, sire?"

"No. Tell them I'll give a victory speech later and we'll all get drunk."

"A speech before might bring better results," Nicanor advised.

Philip swung on him. "Perdiccas was a good speaker, is that not right, Antipater?" The warrior nodded. "And did he not fill the men's hearts with fire on the night before the battle?"

"He did, sire."

"Then tell the men exactly what I said. Now let us move; I want to be above their camp at dawn. You, Antipater, will take half the men. I will command the others. We will hit them from east and west. I want no prisoners. Hit them hard—and hit them well."

An hour later Philip led his five hundred men up a steep hillside, where they walked their horses until they reached a ridge overlooking the enemy camp. There were scores of tents, and hundreds more men could be seen lying under blankets around dying fires. There were no sentries out, which in a strange way increased Philip's fury. He drew his saber and pointed to the right. The Macedonians mounted their horses and moved out to form a long line across the ridge. There they waited. The sun was still hidden behind the distant Kerkine mountains, but the sky was brightening. Shading his eyes, Philip saw Antipater and his force of five hundred come into view to the east, a cloud of dust billowing under the thundering hooves. Paionian warriors rolled from their blankets, grabbing for sword, lance, or bow. But then Antipater was upon them. For a while the Paionians seemed likely to hold, then their center broke and they fled for the hills, where the king waited. Philip lifted his sword.

"Let them hear you!" he bellowed, and the Macedonian war cry went up, a rolling wall of sound that echoed across the plain.

Philip kicked his black gelding into a run and galloped down the gentle slope. The Paionians were caught now between hammer and anvil as they fled before Antipater directly at Philip and his riders. Panic set in, and the tribesmen sprinted away in any direction that offered cover. The Macedonians bore down on them, cutting and killing. Philip dragged on his reins and saw a group of tribesmen, some sixty or seventy strong, trying to form a square behind their wickerwork shields. Blood lust upon him, he galloped his horse into their midst, hacking at men with his saber. A spear glanced from his breastplate, and a sword sliced his thigh, opening a shallow wound. Nicanor, seeing the king in peril, led twenty riders to his aid, and the square broke.

What followed was a massacre. The Paionians threw away their shields and swords and ran, only to be hunted down by groups of riders intent only on revenge and the death of their enemies.

By dusk, as Philip sat in the enemy leader's tent, his thigh bandaged, almost eleven hundred Paionians lay dead or wounded, for the loss of only sixty-two Macedonians, and one of those was killed when his horse stumbled and rolled on top of him. The camp was filled with plunder, gold and plate, silver coins, statues in precious metals. More than fifty Macedonian women had been held enslaved here, and so happy were they to be free that they gave to their rescuers with gusto the pleasures the Paionians had needed to obtain by force.

Philip ordered the treasures to be loaded onto carts and taken to Pella, then he fulfilled his promise and gathered the men about him in a great circle.

"Today," he said, his voice resonant and deep, reaching every ear without apparent effort, "you have enjoyed a victory. Your enemy lies dead in his hundreds, and the north will soon be free of his pillaging. That is today. That is the *beginning*. Do not misunderstand me—today was not a great victory. Yet it was historic. For it is the first of many, and I promise you this—there will come a day when the battle cry of Macedon will shake the foundations of the world! It will be heard across oceans; it will echo above mountains. There will not be a man alive who does not know of it and fear the sound. That is my promise to you, warriors of Macedon. That is the promise of Philip." He lapsed into silence and gazed at them. There was no cheering, and the lack of sound or movement from them left him momentarily confused. Then he looked at them again, seeing that many had no breastplates and only a few sported helms. "I will give you weapons," he said, "bright shining armor, sharp swords, greaves, helms, and lances. I will bring you gold and riches and grant you land for your sons to grow on. But for tonight I give you wine. Now . . . let us drink!"

There was polite applause led by Nicanor as the wine was brought out, and the men began to rise and move away to sit in groups around small camp fires. Philip sought out Antipater.

"Was it such a bad speech?" he asked the warrior.

"Not at all, sire. But most of these men are from Pelagonia and the valleys of the Pindos. The Illyrians now control their homelands; their wives and children are lost to them. If you could tell them about an expedition against Bardylis . . . ."

"But I cannot . . . and I will not lie to them, Antipater. Not ever. Tomorrow you will take your five hundred and scour the north. Hit any tribesmen you find. Drive them from Macedonia."

"We will lose more men to desertion," said Antipater softly. "They will seek to go home."

In the morning Philip was again among the first to rise. He bade Nicanor gather the men once more.

"Last night I made you promises," he told them. "Today I have something else to say. Many of you will be riding with

Antipater to push the Paionians from our lands. There will be those among you who will wish to return to your homes, seeking out wives and children. I understand that. What I ask of you all is this: choose from among yourselves a group of twenty men who will ride into the occupied lands, gathering news of lost families. Those men will receive full pay of twenty-five drachmas a month while they are gone, their wages held in Pella against their return. The rest of you will be home within three months; I promise that also. But there will come a time when I will call on you, and if you are men of honor, you will come to me. Is that fair?" Philip pointed to a burly, dark-bearded warrior in the front row. "You! Is that fair?"

"If it is true, yes," answered the man.

"I have no way but time to prove my words. But you are the first of Philip's warriors, and I will never let you down." His eyes raked the group, hovering on every face. "There will be decisions you do not understand in the early days, but know this, that I live for Macedonia, and everything I do will be to further her cause. I ask for your trust."

Spinning on his heel, he stalked to his horse. Behind him the burly warrior climbed to his feet. "The king!" he cried.

"The king! The king!" shouted the others, surging to their feet.

Philip bowed and waited until the roar had died down, then his own voice boomed out. "Macedon! Macedon!"

The warriors cheered and took up the cry as Nicanor moved alongside Philip. "A proud moment for you, sire," he said. "You have won their hearts."

Philip did not reply. Already he was thinking of the pretender, Argaios, and the Athenian army.

In the days that followed Philip worked tirelessly, gathering men from the south, hiring a group of two hundred Cretan archers at an exorbitant forty drachmas per man a month, continuing his discussions with Aischines, and waiting with ill-concealed tension for the news from Thrace and Illyria.

The treasury was running low, supplies of gold from Crousia in the east drying up, and there was now only enough coin to support a month of campaigning.

Then news came that the rebel Argaios had landed at the port of Methone, two days' march from Aigai. With him were three thousand Athenian *hoplites*, a group of eight hundred mercenaries, and more than a hundred rebel Macedonians.

Philip called Antipater to him. "What force can we muster against them?" he asked the officer.

"We still have five hundred men in the north under Meleager, harrying the Paionians. Another thousand are waiting in the east with Nicanor, against possible Thracian attack. We could recall either, but it would leave us open."

"How many here?"

"Not more than seven hundred, but half of these fought with you in your first battle. They would ride with you into the fire of Hades."

"It's not enough, Antipater, not against Athenian *hoplites*. Get Aischines here. Be polite, but get him here swiftly."

Philip bathed and dressed in full battle armor—breastplate, greaves, and bronze-reinforced kilt, his sword by his side—and waited in the throne room. Aischines arrived within the hour, looking startled when he saw the king arrayed for war.

"I had not expected treachery," said Philip, keeping his voice low and sorrowful. "I trusted you, and I trusted Athens. Now you land an army at one of my ports. I have messengers ready to ride to Thebes, and I suggest with regret, Aischines, that you prepare to leave Pella."

"There has been some mistake, sire. Please . . . trust me," said Aischines, his face reddening. "I have sent many messages to our leaders, and I am sure the force at Methone will not advance into Macedonia. There was some confusion when they set out. But they will not make war on an ally, and that you are, sire. An ally."

Philip stared long and hard at the man before he answered him. "Are you sure of this, Aischines, or are you merely hopeful?"

"I received dispatches today from Athens, and one is to be sent on to Mantias who commands the *hoplites*. They are to return home, I promise you."

Philip nodded. "Then send your dispatch today, sir, and with some speed. For the day after tomorrow I march on the traitor."

Antipater gathered the seven hundred horsemen, and despite what he had told Aischines, Philip led them that night on a lightning ride south, taking up a position at dawn on the slopes between Methone and Aigai, hidden from the road.

Two hours after dawn the enemy appeared in the distance. Philip shaded his eyes and scanned the advancing men. There were more than one hundred cavalry leading the force, and behind these almost a thousand *hoplites*. The foot soldiers were a motley crew, some sporting plumed helms and others wearing Thracian leather caps. The devices painted on their shields were many: the winged horse of Olynthus, the Theban club of Heracles, the crossed spears of Methone. But none bore the helm of Athena. Philip was exultant. The Athenians, as Aischines had promised, had not marched with Argaios.

Lying on his belly, Philip flicked his eyes left and right of the advancing enemy. They had no outriders and were moving in a straggling line stretched out for almost a quarter of a mile.

The king slid back from the peak, calling Antipater to him. "Send the Cretans to that outcrop of rocks. Let them loose their shafts as soon as the enemy is within range. You take four hundred men, keep behind the line of hills, and hit them from the north. I will wait to give you time, then come in from the south."

Antipater grinned. "Do not be so rash this time, my lord. Stay with your men and avoid charging single-handed into enemy ranks."

The first volley of arrows from the Cretans decimated the leading horsemen, their mounts rearing in terror as the rain of death fell from the skies. The smell of blood in their nostrils brought panic to the horses, making them almost impossible to control.

Then Antipater's four hundred came galloping from the north, their battle cries echoing in the rocks. The Macedonians smashed their way through the confused mass of the enemy cavalry, hacking men from their mounts, then thundered into the milling foot soldiers just as Philip's force hit them from the south.

The mercenary infantry, having lost more than half their number before they could form a defensive square, locked shields against a second attack, but Antipater wheeled his men and charged again at the cavalry, who broke and galloped from the battlefield.

Philip also pulled back his riders, and the Cretan archers loosed volley after volley over the shield wall of the mercenaries.

At the center of the shield square stood Argaios, his helm knocked from his head, his golden hair bright in the sunshine.

"Ho, Philip!" he shouted. "Will you face me, or do you have no stomach for the fight?"

It was a desperate last throw from a man already beaten, but Philip knew the eyes of his men were upon him.

"Come out!" he called, "And then we will see."

Argaios pushed his way clear of the shield wall and strode toward Philip. The king dismounted, drawing his sword and waiting. Argaios was a handsome man, tall and slender, his eyes the blue of a spring sky. He looked so like Nicanor that Philip could not help but flick his eyes to his friend, comparing them. In that moment Argaios attacked. Philip's shield only half deflected the blow, which glanced from his breastplate to slice a narrow cut on his cheek.

His own sword lashed out, hacking into his enemy's bronze-reinforced leather kilt. Argaios threw himself forward, their shields clanging together. But Philip, though shorter, was more stocky and powerful and held his ground. His sword lanced out, stabbing low, piercing Argaios' left leg above the knee. The pretender screamed in pain as Philip twisted the blade, severing muscles and tendons. Argaios tried to leap back, but his wounded leg gave out beneath him and he fell.

Throwing aside his shield, Philip advanced on the injured man.

Argaios' sword slashed out, but Philip danced away from the gleaming blade, then leapt forward, his foot pinning Argaios' sword arm to the dusty ground.

"I call upon the king's mercy," screamed Argaios.

"There is no mercy for traitors," hissed Philip, his blade plunging into Argaios' neck, through the windpipe and the vertebrae beyond.

By nightfall more than six hundred of the enemy lay dead, with a further one hundred mercenaries held captive. The forty Macedonian prisoners were stoned to death by the troops after a short trial presided over by Philip. Of the rest, sixty-two were mercenaries who were freed to return to Methone and thirty-eight were Athenian volunteers; these were freed without ransom, and Philip invited them to dine with him in his tent, explaining once more his policy of friendship with Athens.

By dawn Philip was still awake, hearing from Antipater of Macedonian losses. "Forty men dead, three crippled, seven recovering from wounds," Antipater told him.

"Find out the names and whereabouts of the dead men's families, then send one hundred drachmas to each. The crippled men will receive double that and a pension of ten drachmas a month."

Antipater was surprised. "The men will be heartened by this news," he said.

"Yes, but that is not why it is being done. They died for Macedon, and Macedon will not forget that."

Antipater nodded. "I will not forget it, either, sire, and neither will the warriors who ride for you."

After the officer had gone, Philip lay down on his pallet bed, covering himself with a single blanket. The Paionians were defeated, and one pretender had been dispatched. But still the major enemies had to be met.

Where are you, Parmenion?

THE THRACIAN BORDER,
AUTUMN, 359 B.C.

Parmenion tugged lightly on the reins as he saw the man sitting on the rock ahead. "Good day to you," said the Spartan, glancing at the surrounding boulders, seeking out any men who might be hidden there.

"I am alone," said the stranger, his voice agreeable, even friendly. Parmenion continued to study the nearby terrain. When he was satisfied the man was indeed alone, his gaze flicked down on the distant River Nestus and then up toward the far blue peaks of the Kerkine mountains and the borders of Macedonia. Returning his attention to the man on the rocks, he dismounted. The stranger was not tall but sturdily built, his hair gray, his beard curled in the Persian fashion, his eyes the color of storm clouds. He was wearing a long *chiton* of faded blue and a pair of leather sandals that showed little indication of wear. But there was no sign of a weapon of any kind, not even a small dagger.

"The view is pleasant," said Parmenion, "but the land is desolate. How did you come here?"

"I walk different paths," the man answered. "You will be in Pella in seven days. I could be there this afternoon."

"You are a *magus*?"

"Not as the Persians understand it, although some of the *magi* will one day walk the paths I use," answered the man smoothly. "Sit you down for a while and dine with me."

"Let's leave him here and ride on," said Mothac. "I don't like this place; it is too open. He's probably a robber."

"I have been many things in my time, Theban, but never yet a robber. I have, though, been waiting for you, Parmenion. I thought it wise that we sat and talked of the past, the future, and the echoes of the great song."

"You sound Greek," said Parmenion, moving to his left and continuing to scan the surrounding rocks.

"Not . . . exactly . . . Greek," said the man, "but it will suffice. You accomplished great deeds in Persia; I congratulate you. Your attack on Spetzabares was brilliant. Outnumbered, you forced him to surrender, losing only a hundred and eleven men in the process. Remarkable."

"You have me at a disadvantage, sir. I know nothing of you."

"I am a scholarly man, Parmenion. My life is devoted to study, to the pursuit of knowledge. My wish is to understand all creation. Happily I am not yet close to any real understanding."

"Happily?"

"Of course. No man should ever completely realize his dreams. What else would there then be to live for?"

"Look!" shouted Mothac, pointing to a dust cloud farther down the mountain slopes. "Riders!"

"They are coming to take you to Cotys," said the man. "Either that or to kill you. The Thracian king has no wish to see Parmenion helping the Macedonians."

"You know a great deal," said Parmenion softly. "I take it you also know a way to avoid these riders."

"Naturally," said the man, rising smoothly to his feet. "Follow me."

Parmenion watched him stride toward a sheer rock face that shimmered as he reached it. The Spartan blinked. The stranger was gone.

"He's a demon or a demigod," whispered Mothac. "Let's take a chance on the riders. At least they are human."

"Swords can cut a man faster than spells," said Parmenion. "I'll take my chance with the *magus*." Taking the reins of the stallion in his right hand, he led the beast toward the rock face. As he approached, the temperature dropped, the rocks seeming translucent. He walked on, passing through them, feeling weightless and disoriented.

Mothac emerged from the wall behind him, sweating heavily as he drew alongside his friend. "What now?" the Theban whispered.

They were in a huge subterranean cavern, enormous stalactites hanging from the domed roof. From around them came the steady, rhythmic dripping of water, and there were many dark pools shining on the cavern floor.

The stranger appeared some fifty paces ahead of them. "This way," he called. "You are only halfway home."

"Halfway to Hades more like," muttered Mothac, drawing his sword.

The two men led their horses across the cavern floor to a wide natural opening, leading onto a lush green meadow where a small house had been built, the roof red-tiled, the walls smooth and white.

Parmenion walked on into the sunshine and stopped. The countryside was hilly and verdant, but there were no mountains to be seen in any direction, and of the great River Nestus there was no sign.

Mounting their horses, the two men rode down to the house, where the stranger had set a wide table with cold meats, cheeses, and fruits. Pouring his guests goblets of wine, he sat in the shade of a flowering tree. "It is not poisoned," he said as his guests stared at the food.

"Are you not eating?" Parmenion asked.

"I am not hungry. But think on this: A man who can make mountains disappear is unlikely to need to poison his guests."

"A valid point," agreed Parmenion, reaching for an apple.

Mothac grabbed his hand. "I will eat first," said the Theban, taking the fruit and biting into it.

"Such devotion," observed the stranger. Slowly Mothac sampled all the meats and cheeses. Finally he belched.

"Best I ever tasted," he said. Parmenion ate sparingly, then moved to sit alongside the stranger.

"Why were you waiting for me?"

"You are one of the echoes of the great song, Parmenion. There have been many before you, and there will be many after. But I am here to offer my help. First, though, how is it you greet my magic with such indifference? Has anyone else ever moved a mountain for you?"

"I have seen the *magi* turn staffs into snakes and make men float in the air. And there is a magician in Susa who can make men think they are birds, so that they flap their arms and try to fly. Perhaps the mountains are still there but you stop us seeing them. I care not. Now, what is this great song you speak of?"

"It is a war between dream and nightmare. An eternal war. And you are part of it. Homer sang of it, transferring the battles to Troy. Other nations sing of it in different ways, placing it in different times, through Gilgamesh and Ekodas, Paristur and Sarondel. They are all echoes. Soon we will see the birth of another legend, and the Death of Nations will be at the center."

"I know nothing of this, and your conversation is plagued with riddles. I must thank you for your food and your hospitality, but let us speak frankly: who are you?"

The man chuckled and leaned back against the trunk of the flowering tree. "Straight for the heart, eh? Ever the general. Well, there's no harm in that, my Spartan friend. It has served you well over the years, has it not? Me? As I said, I am a scholar. I have never been a warrior, though I have known many. You remind me much of Leonidas the sword king. He was a man of great prowess and had a gift for making men great."

"The sword king died more than a century ago," said Parmenion. "Are you telling me you knew him?"

"I did not say I *knew* him, Parmenion. I said you *reminded me* of him. It was a shame he felt he had to die at Thermopylae; he could have made Sparta truly great. Still, he also was a strong echo of the great song, three hundred men against an army of two hundred thousand. Wondrously brave."

"When I was in Thebes," said Parmenion, "there was a man who tried to teach me to catch fish with my bare hands. Talking to you reminds me of those days. I hear your words, but they slip by me, the meanings obscure. How can you help me?"

"At this moment you do not need me, Spartan," said the man, his smile fading. Reaching out, he gripped Parmenion's arm. "But there will come a time. You will be given a task, and my name will come into your mind. It is then that you must seek me out. You will find me where first we met. Do not forget that, Parmenion—much will depend on it."

Parmenion stood. "I will remember, and once more I thank you for your hospitality. If we go back the way we came, will we see again the river and the mountains?"

"No. This time you will emerge in the hills above Pella."

The gray-haired man stood and offered his hand. Parmenion took it, feeling the strength in the grip. "You are not as old as you look," said the Spartan with a smile.

"There is great truth in that," the man answered. "Seek me out when you have need. And by the way, even as we speak, the Thracian king is dying, poisoned by one of Philip's friends. Such is the fate of greedy kings, is it not?"

"Sometimes," agreed Parmenion, vaulting to the stallion's back. "Do you have a name, scholar?"

"I have many. But you may call me Aristotle."

"I have heard of you, though never as a *magus*. It is said you are a philosopher."

"I am what I am. Ride on, Parmenion—the song awaits."

The trench was more than two hundred feet long, the fifty men digging with picks and shovels through layers of clay and rock, the sun beating down on their bare backs as they labored. Other soldiers worked to clear the debris, which they threw onto the backs of the trench.

Philip drove his pick into the ground before him, feeling his shoulders jar as the metal edge struck rock once more. Laying the tool aside, he dropped to his knees and dug into the clay, hooking his fingers around the stone and dragging it clear. It was larger than he had first thought, its weight as great as that of a small man. He was about to call for help when he saw several of the men looking at him and grinning. He smiled back, placed his arms alongside the rock, and heaved it to his chest. With a powerful surge he rose and rolled the offending stone to the bank. Then he climbed out and walked the line of the trench, stopping to speak to the workers, gauging their progress.

At each end the trench turned at right angles, the workers following the lines of ropes pegged to the ground. Philip walked back from the site and pictured the new barracks. It would be two stories high, with a long dining hall and seven dormitories housing more than five hundred men. The architect was a Persian who had been trained in Athens, and Philip had demanded that the building be completed by the next spring.

The workers were all soldiers from the Pelagonia and Lynkos districts to the northwest, land currently occupied by Bardylis and his Illyrians. The men worked cheerfully enough, especially when the king struggled alongside them, but he knew they remembered his promise that they could return to their homes within three months of the victory against the Paionians.

That had been five weeks ago, and still there was no treaty with Bardylis. Yet, looking on the positive side, Philip thought that was promising, for the Illyrians had not marched farther into Macedonian territory and Bardylis was considering Philip's offer to marry his daughter. As a gesture of good faith and "continuing brotherhood," Bardylis had requested that the Macedonian king hand over to Illyria all the lands between the Bora mountains and the Pindos range: six districts in all, including Pelagonia, rich in timber, with good grazing and fine pastures.

"Ugly brides do not come cheaply, it seems," Philip had told Nicanor.

Now the king was ridding himself of tension by sheer physical labor. The trench would be finished by tomorrow, then the footings could be completed and he could watch with pleasure the growth of the barracks.

No simple structure of wood and mud brick, the frontage would be carved stone, the roof clay-tiled, the rooms airy and full of light.

"But you are talking of a palace, sire," the architect had objected.

"And I want three wells and a fountain in the central courtyard. Also a special section for the commanding officer, with an *andron* to accommodate twenty—no, thirty men."

"As you wish, sire . . . but it will not be cheap."

"If I wanted cheap, I would have hired a Spartan," Philip replied, patting the man's thin shoulder.

The king wandered to a pile of rocks and sat down. A workman brought him a goblet of water from a cool stone jar; it tasted like nectar. He thanked the man, recognizing him as the burly bearded warrior who had led the cheering after the first battle.

"What is your name, friend?"

"Theoparlis, sire. Most call me Theo."

"It should be a fine building, Theo. Fit for the troops of the king."

"Indeed it will, sire. I am sorry I shall not enjoy the pleasure of living in it, but in two months I shall be returning to my wife in Pelagonia. Is that not true?"

"It is true," agreed Philip. "And before another year is out I will come to you there and offer you a place in this fine barracks and a house for your wife in Pella."

"I will look forward to your visit," said Theo, bowing and returning to his work. Philip watched him go and then swung his gaze to the east, where two riders were making their way from the city center. He drained his water and watched them. The lead rider wore a bronze breastplate and an iron helm, but Philip was more intent on the horse, a chestnut stallion of some sixteen hands. All Macedonian nobles were raised as horsemen, and Philip's love of the beasts was second to none. The stallion had a fine head, eyes set well apart—a good indication of sound character. Its neck was long but not overly so, the mane cropped like a helmet plume. Philip strolled toward the riders, angling so that he could see the stallion's back and flanks. Its shoulder blades were sloping and power-ful, which would give the beast long sweeping strides, making it fast and yet comfortable to ride. Straight shoulders, Philip knew, led to jarring steps and discomfort for the rider.

"You there!" came a voice, and Philip glanced up. The second rider, a short stout man riding a swaybacked gray gelding, was pointing at him. "We are looking for the king. Take us to him."

Philip studied the man. He was bald, but red and silver hair grew over his ears like a laurel crown. "Who wants him?" he asked.

"That is none of your concern, peasant," snapped the rider.

"Gently, gently, Mothac," said the other man, lifting his leg and jumping to the ground. He was tall and slim, though his arms were well muscled, showing the scars of many fights. Philip looked up into the man's eyes; they were pale blue, but the face was tanned to the color of leather, making them as gray as storm clouds. Philip's heart leapt as he recognized

Parmenion, but quelling the urge to run forward and embrace the Spartan, he kept his face free of emotion and wandered forward.

"You are a mercenary?" Philip asked.

"Yes," replied Parmenion. "And you are a builder?"

Philip nodded. "It is to be a barracks, I am told. Perhaps one day you will be quartered here."

"The footings are deep," observed the warrior, walking to the trench and watching the workmen.

"There are occasional earthquakes," Philip told him, "and it is essential for the foundations to be sound. It does not matter how pretty the building. Without good foundations it will fall."

"The same is true of armies," said the warrior softly. "Did you fight against the Paionians?"

"I did. It was a good victory."

"Did the king fight?"

"Like a lion. Like ten lions," said Philip, smiling broadly.

The man nodded and was silent for a moment, then he turned to the king and he, too, smiled. "I am glad to hear it. I would not wish to serve a coward."

"You seem sure the king will employ you."

The warrior shrugged. "Did you like my horse, sire?"

"Yes, he is a fine—how did you know me?"

"You are much changed from the boy I saw in Thebes, and I might not have recognized you. However, you are also the only man not working, and such, I would guess, is the king's prerogative. I am hot, and my throat is dusty, and it would be pleasant if we could find a place out of the sun and discuss why you asked me here."

"Indeed we shall," said Philip, smiling broadly. "But first let me say that you are a prayer answered. You have no idea how greatly you are needed."

"I think I have," answered Parmenion. "I remember a young boy telling me of a country surrounded by enemies: Illyrians, Paionians, Thracians. A soldier remembers such things."

"Well, it is worse now. I have no army to speak of and little but my wits to hold back our foes. Gods, man, but I'm pleased to see you!"

"I may not stay," warned Parmenion.

"Why?" Philip asked, a cold fear touching his heart.

"I do not yet know if you are a man I would wish to serve."

"You speak frankly, but I cannot question the wisdom behind the words. Come with me to the palace; there you can bathe and shave and refresh yourself. Then we can talk."

Parmenion nodded. "Did you really fight like ten lions?" he asked, his face expressionless.

"More like twenty," replied Philip, "but I am modest by nature."

Parmenion climbed out of the bath and strolled to the window, allowing the water to evaporate from his skin, cooling it. Running his fingers through his thinning hair, he turned to Mothac.

"What did you think of him?"

Mothac shook his head. "I don't like to see a king in a loincloth, digging dirt like a peasant."

"You've been among the Persians too long, my friend."

"Will we stay?"

Parmenion did not answer. The journey had been long across Asia Minor and into Thrace, crossing mountains and rivers. And despite the saving of a week's travel after the meeting with Aristotle, he was tired and felt the dull ache of the old spear wound under his right shoulder. He rubbed himself down with a towel, then lay on a couch while Mothac massaged oil into his back.

Macedonia. It was greener than he had imagined, more lush. But he experienced a slight disappointment, for he had hoped to feel that he had come home. Instead it was just another land, boasting tall mountains and fertile plains.

Dressing in a simple tunic and sandals, he wandered out to the courtyard to watch the setting sun. He felt old and bone-weary. Epaminondas was dead, slain at Mantinea just as

Tamis had foretold. Parmenion shivered.

Mothac brought him a pitcher of wine, and they sat in comfortable silence. As the sun set, Mothac lit a lantern and the two men ate a frugal meal of bread and cheese.

"You liked him, didn't you?" asked Mothac at last.

"Yes. He reminds me of Pelopidas."

"He'll probably end his life the same way," remarked Mothac.

"By heaven, you're in a sour mood," snapped Parmenion. "What's wrong with you?"

"With me? Nothing. But I want to know why we left Susa to come here. We had the life of princes; we were rich, Parmenion. What does this frontier land hold for us? The Macedonians will never amount to anything. And what do you have to gain here? You are known as the greatest general in the civilized world. But it is not enough, is it? You cannot resist the impossible challenge."

"You are probably right. But I asked you if you wanted to stay in Persia. I put no bridle on you, Mothac."

The Theban grunted. "You think friendship has no chains? Well, it has. Even to following you—and your pride—into this wilderness with its half-Greek barbarians."

Parmenion reached out and gripped his friend's arm. "You shame me, Mothac. And I am sorry if this enterprise does not meet with your approval. I don't understand all the reasons that drew me here. Partly it was the call of blood. My ancestors lived on this land, fought for it, died for it; I had to see it. But there is truth in what you say. I know what men call me, but are they correct? I have always led well-trained armies, mostly outnumbering the enemy. Here, as you observe, there is a challenge. The Illyrians are disciplined and well led, the Thracians ferocious and many, the Olynthians rich enough to hire the best mercenaries. What glory would there be in leading any of them? But Macedon?" He smiled. "I cannot resist it, my friend."

"I know," said Mothac wearily. "I have always known."

"That we would come to Macedonia?"

"No. It is not easy to put into words." He was silent for a while, his green eyes fixed to Parmenion's face. Finally he smiled, reaching forward to grip his friend's shoulder. "I think—deep inside—you are still the mix-blood boy in Sparta, striving to prove your worth. And if you succeed here—which is doubtful—you will hunt the impossible challenge else-where. And the foolish Mothac will be with you. And now I'll say good night." The Theban rose and walked away to his rooms.

For a while Parmenion sat alone, his thoughts somber, then he strolled out into the gardens beyond the courtyard and up the steps of the high wall, where he leaned on the parapet, looking south toward Thessaly.

Mothac was right, he knew. The boy Savra remained within the general Parmenion, sad and lonely, still seeking a home, a love, happiness. He had hoped to find it in Persia, in wealth and renown. But fame was no answer, and fortune merely served to remind him of all the joys he could not buy.

All was darkness beyond the city, but somewhere out there to the south Pelopidas had fallen, fighting alongside the Thes-salians against the tyrant of Pherae. The enemy advancing on all fronts, Pelopidas had charged into their center, cleaving his way toward the tyrant. It had changed the course of the battle, but the Theban had died in the charge. The victorious Thessalians had cut the manes and tails from their horses in honor of the dead general.

Parmenion shivered. He had thought Pelopidas invulnera-ble. "But no man is," he whispered. "May the gods bless your spirit, Pelopidas. May you know joy in the Hall of Heroes."

"Do you believe that he does?" asked Philip, moving up the steps and sitting opposite Parmenion.

The older man sighed. "It would be fitting. You should have seen him at Leuctra. Like a god of war he cleared the enemy, striking down the battle king."

Philip nodded. "While you charged the enemy center, send-ing their javeliners and archers running from the field. It was your victory, Parmenion, the forerunner of many more in

Cappadocia, Phrygia, Egypt, Mesopotamia. You have never lost. Why is that?"

"Perhaps I fight like twenty lions, sire."

"It was a serious question, *strategos*."

"Your barracks supplies the answer. The footings must be right, the foundations solid, the walls resting on firm ground. An army needs many things, but above all it needs confidence, belief that it will win the day. Training gives confidence; those are the footings. Good officers are the foundations."

"And the walls?" asked the king.

"Infantry, sire. No army can hope to conquer without good infantry."

"Could you build me an army within a year?"

"I could, but what would you do with it?"

Philip chuckled. "We are in a difficult position here, you and I. You are a mercenary, which means that at any time you could be standing alongside Cotys or Bardylis. I cannot tell you all my plans. And I would guess that unless I do, you will not serve me. How do we resolve this problem?"

"Tell me all you have done so far, sire, leaving nothing out. And that includes the murder of your stepbrother."

"Why not?" answered Philip. For almost an hour the king spoke of his efforts to stave off disaster, his wooing of Athens, his offer to Bardylis, and his assurances to Cotys in Thrace. At last he faded to silence and looked at Parmenion's face in the moonlight. The Spartan was expressionless, his eyes locked to Philip's.

"And that is all?" he asked finally.

Philip considered lying but on impulse shook his head. "No, that is not all. Cotys may already be dead." He watched Parmenion relax.

"Indeed he is, sire. But that still leaves the pretender Pausanius."

"Who also will soon be dead," said Philip, his voice barely above a whisper. "That is all I can tell you."

"How many men would you require within the year?"

"Two thousand horsemen and ten thousand infantry."

"Too many," said Parmenion. "They would be inadequately trained. Content yourself with six thousand foot soldiers. That should give you enough men to tackle Bardylis. How does your treasury stand?"

"Almost empty," admitted Philip.

"Then your first action must be to relieve the governor at Crousia and restore your fortunes. Then you must purchase armor and weapons. In Phrygia they make fine breastplates of baked leather, lined with thick cloth—not quite as effective as bronze but lighter. The Phrygian helm is also highly regarded."

"You are giving me good advice, *strategos*, but you do not say whether you will join with me."

"I'll stay for the year, sire. I'll train your army. After that . . . we'll see."

Philip stood and gazed out over the lantern-lit city. "Normally it is the king who is petitioned, but here you have reversed the position. What did I say that made you decide to stay?"

"It was nothing you said, sire. It was something you did."

"But you will not tell me?"

"Exactly, sire. Now, to the terms. Tomorrow I would like to meet those of your officers and friends who are presently in Pella. My position will be that of first general, answerable to no man but yourself. I will warrant no argument as to the methods I use in training the men, nobles or peasants. You will give me your full backing in everything connected with training. Do you agree?"

"I agree. But what will you be seeking to do first?" asked Philip.

"The formation of an elite force, the king's infantry companions, the royal guard—five hundred men, the best you have."

"Like the Sacred Band of Thebes?"

"Better," said Parmenion. "For they will be Macedonian!"

* * *

With the trench foundation complete, the soldier workers made way for the stonemasons, carpenters, and wall builders. Idle now, the men gathered in small groups to dice and gamble and talk of going home. Rumors spread through the ranks. The king was preparing to invade Illyria to win back their homelands, the Thebans were marching on Pella, the Thracians were massing an army.

Theo took little notice of the stories. He was more interested in events closer to the capital and listened intently to the gossip about the pale-eyed Spartan now seen with the king and his officers. Only yesterday those same officers had been seen running in the hills, sweat shining on their bodies, their legs trembling. It had been a source of much amusement for the men. Horsemen did not take well to running. The Spartan had run with them, long loping strides that carried him far ahead, drawing them behind him like tired hounds in pursuit of a stag.

But, despite the amusement it offered, it set Theo to thinking. Why should they run? What point was there?

Now a hundred volunteers had been sought to attend the Spartan at the new training field. Theo was the first to step forward.

One hour after dawn he rose from his blankets and joined the straggling line of men who wandered to the field where the Spartan sat waiting. The man was wearing a woolen tunic and carried no weapons. Yet around him were stacked wooden shields and a pile of short clubs.

When the men had gathered, he gestured for them to sit, then cast his eyes slowly over the group. "What is the prime objective in a battle?" he asked suddenly, lifting his hand, finger pointed. He stabbed it out in the direction of a man to the left of Theo.

"To win it," answered the man.

"Wrong." The finger moved again, and Theo could feel the tension around him as men willed it to pass them by. The

Spartan's hand dropped to his lap. "Does any man have an answer?"

Theo cleared his throat. "Not to lose it?" he said.

"Good," said the Spartan. "Think about that for a moment." His pale eyes studied them. "Victory in battle is a fickle spirit that floats in the air, never knowing where to settle. A cavalry charge smashes the enemy, forcing the opposing king to retreat. Has he lost? Not yet. If his flanks can close in around the cavalry, robbing them of mobility, he can yet draw victory to him. But if he does, has he won? No, not if the cavalry are tight-knit and continue to drive directly at him, killing his guards. Why did Bardylis destroy your army?" Once again the finger rose, pointing at a man at the rear of the group.

"The gods favored him," answered the man to a chorus of approval.

"Maybe they did," said the Spartan. "But in my experience, the gods always favor the clever and the strong. You lost because your king—a brave and dynamic man—threw everything into a single charge. When it failed, he failed. You failed."

"And the Spartans would have done better?" shouted a man behind Theo.

"Perhaps not," snapped Parmenion, "but *you* will. The king has asked me to find for him a special group of fighting men. They will be the king's companions, and they will fight on foot."

"We are horsemen," said the same man. Theo glanced around, recognizing Achillas.

"Indeed you are," agreed the Spartan, "and as such you will earn your twenty-five drachmas. But the men I select will be double-pay men. Each will have fifty drachmas a month. Those men interested should remain; the others are free to return to their duties."

Not a man moved: fifty drachmas was a fortune. They were all small farmers, needing money for the purchase of horses, or bulls, or goats, or cereal seed. It was not a sum to be dismissed lightly.

The Spartan stood. "Be warned that from every hundred I may choose only five, maybe ten men. The king desires the best. Now stand."

As they rose, Parmenion opened a box by his side and took out a small brooch the size of a man's thumbnail. It was made of iron. "On this brooch is the club of Heracles. When a man has five of these, he will have won his place in the king's company. With every badge goes a prize of ten drachmas. The first will be won by a man who can run. Ten circuits of the field. Prepare yourselves." The men began to remove their breastplates. "Stop," said Parmenion. "When you charge the enemy, you will not discard your armor. You will run as you are. Go!"

They set off at a murderous pace that faltered within a lap. Theo settled in at the center of the leading group, feeling his breastplate rubbing at the back of his neck. By five circuits the leaders had pulled half a lap clear of the following pack, and by seven they had started to overtake the back markers. Theo finished fifth and slumped to the ground as Achillas stepped up to receive his badge.

The Spartan waited until all the men had finished.

"Take up shields and swords," he ordered them. The swords were wooden but of the same weight and length as the short stabbing blades used by most *hoplites*. "Now we will see how you fight," he said. "Choose an opponent and form into two lines. You will fight only until a blow is struck that with a real sword would kill or disable. The loser will walk back to sit on the right, the victor to the left."

The contest took more than an hour, and by the end the men were cheering the finalists as they circled one another, blocking with shields, lunging, parrying. Theo had won his first two bouts but had been beaten on the third. Achillas had reached the last four but had lost to Damoras, who now fought Petar, a man from Theo's area in the north of Pelagonia.

Damoras was stronger, but Petar, the shorter man, had greater speed and his wooden blade cracked against Damoras' skull, causing his opponent to stagger. "Killing blow!" shouted Parmenion. Petar dropped shield and sword and punched the air with delight, taking his badge from Parmenion and holding it up for his friends to see.

"Now, gentlemen," said Parmenion, "for a little amusement. Pair off with the first man you fought." As the warriors shuffled into place, the Spartan lifted two badges from the box. "You will run five laps of the field, carrying your partner on your back. You may choose when to carry or be carried. But the first pair to return here will receive a badge each."

Theo found himself paired with a slender man from Lyncos. There was little chance of the warrior being able to carry him at speed, so Theo offered to do the carrying. The man leapt to his back.

"When you are ready!" yelled the Spartan. "Go!"

The fifty pairs set off. Theo, his powerful legs pumping hard, took an early lead, but before half a lap he felt himself losing strength. Gritting his teeth, he struggled on, being passed by several pairs. On the second lap he had to stop. The slender warrior tried manfully to keep up with the pack, but under Theo's formidable weight he stumbled and fell. Theo had regained his breath. The problem was trying to run while holding his partner's legs in place. Pushing the man in front of him, he ducked down, lifting the warrior to his shoulders. The man hooked his legs behind Theo's back and the huge Macedonian set off in pursuit of the pack. There was no question now of changing places, and Theo did not try to sprint. Conserving as much of his strength as possible for the final lap, he slowly reeled in the leaders. By the final circuit Theo was third. The second pair stumbled and fell, leaving him chasing Achillas and his partner.

Achillas was tiring as Theo came up behind. The man Achillas was carrying glanced back and shouted to his partner to put in an extra effort. But Achillas was finished; he dropped his partner and ran around to change places. It was all Theo needed. Putting in a last desperate push, he reached the finish two paces ahead of the second pair.

Parmenion stepped forward with the victors' badges, but the young warrior with Theo refused.

"I did not earn it," he said.

"What is your name, lad?" asked the Spartan.

"Gaelan."

"What shall I do with the badge, Gaelan?"

"Give them both to my partner. He did all the work."

"And what do you say?" Parmenion asked Theo.

Theo put his arm around Gaelan's shoulder. "We were a team." He took the badge from Parmenion and pressed it into Gaelan's hand. "We won as a team and will share the prize."

"Good," said the Spartan. "A fine way to end a morning's work. Go away and eat. Return in two hours, when the final badges will be won."

As Parmenion sat alone at the training field, drinking water and eating a simple meal of figs and fruit, the king rode up with two of his officers.

"How goes it, *strategos*?" Philip asked.

Parmenion rose and bowed. "There are some with promise," he said. "But we shall see." He strode forward, rubbing his hand down the chest of the king's horse. "A good animal— fine lungs and strong legs."

"A Thracian sire and a Macedonian dam," Philip told him, patting the stallion's neck. "But he's young yet; he'll learn. Will you sell me your stallion? He would make a magnificent breeder."

Parmenion laughed. "I'll not sell him, but you are free to put him in with your mares. I daresay he will enjoy the experience."

Philip nodded. "Tell me, are all Persian cavalrymen mounted on such beasts?"

"No, sire. He is special, from the great king's herd. Only the royal guard will have mounts of similar quality."

"And how many men make up the king's guard?"

"One thousand, sire."

Philip looked thoughtful, then he grinned. "Time for the hunt," he said. "I will leave you to your lunch." Touching heels to the stallion, he cantered away toward the distant forest, his officers trailing behind.

Parmenion finished his meal and thought back to the morning's work. The Macedonians were game enough, sturdy and tough, but still he sensed their suspicion. One year to train six thousand men, to build an infantry army from cavalrymen.

One day at a time, Savra, he cautioned himself. He glanced up to see the men returning; they formed a great semicircle around him and waited for his orders.

"I want you to pick three generals from among you," he told them.

"For what purpose?" asked Achillas.

Parmenion smiled. "What purpose does a general serve? You will lead your men into battle—here on this training field. Now, choose!"

Parmenion sat back and watched as the debates began, listening intently to the names proposed, studying the reaction of the men named. As he had guessed, Achillas was the first to be nominated, but the arguments raged on. Parmenion did nothing to interfere even when tempers began to flare.

Theo stood up. "Stop this!" he shouted. Silence fell. "We'll be here for days if this keeps up. Surely it is a simple task. The *strategos* has asked for three men. All those in favor of Achillas raise a hand." Two-thirds of the men did so. "Then Achillas is one," said Theo. "Now, many of you were shouting for Petar. How many in favor?" This time the vote was more evenly split, and Theo counted the hands before announcing Petar to be the second general. "Who will nominate a third?" asked the black-bearded warrior.

"I will," said Parmenion. "I nominate you, and there will be no voting on it. Let the three generals step forward." He stood with them before the seated men. "Each of you in turn will select a warrior to make up your army. One at a time, so that no one can say any general had a greater advantage. You will each choose twenty-five men. Achillas, you may begin."

Parmenion walked back to his seat and watched the process. In the early stages the chosen men stood, raised their hands, and walked out to stand behind their leader while the others cheered. But as the choosing continued, a hush settled over the waiting men. No one wanted to be left unchosen, and the tension grew. As the last man was selected, Parmenion turned to the generals. "Over there, by the trees, you will find shields and weapons. Go, arm yourselves." As they trooped away, Parmenion turned to the twenty-two men still seated.

"There is no worse feeling in the world than this," he told them. "When I was a young man in Sparta, many games would begin this way. Always I would be the one chosen last or chosen not at all. We can tell ourselves that it is unfair; we can tell ourselves the choosers were wrong." He scanned their faces. "But ultimately we must accept that we have been judged by our fellows. Some of you will have been left here because you are small, weaker than your friends. Others will be here because they are not popular with any of the three generals. It does not matter why. I am now your general for this . . . test. We will compete with the others, and we will see if they were wrong. Now follow me."

He led the disconsolate group to where the others waited. "Gentlemen, this will be your first battle as infantry units. The rules are simple. Each force has a general. The object for the enemy will be to kill or capture that general, which will be considered done if any warrior touches an enemy general. Is that understood? Good. Achillas, take your warriors to the southern end of the field, Theo to the west, and Petar to the east. When I give the signal, you can move forward against any other group. I will command the northern section. One last point: There are two badges to be won here. One will go to the general commanding the victorious army; the second will be awarded by that general to the man he believes was the most valiant of his men. Generals, take up your positions!"

The groups marched off, armed with shields and clubs.

Parmenion turned to the men waiting patiently behind him. "Look at the weapons," he said. There were clubs and shields, but beyond them ten-foot-long staffs left in a ragged pile.

Theo called his men together at the western edge of the field. "The most dangerous group will be led by Achillas," he told the warriors. "He is closer to Petar than to us. We will march across the field toward them but hold back as they clash; then we will hit the victor."

"What about the Spartan?" Gaelan asked.

"You've seen the men he has," Theo answered. "We'll keep a watch on him. I think he will also hang back."

Achillas' group was the first to move, and as Theo had suspected, they angled directly toward the men with Petar. With a great shout they surged forward, clashing with the enemy, clubs cracking against shield and skull. One of Petar's men broke through, racing at Achillas, who leapt back from a blow and then cracked his club against the warrior's chin, stunning him. Petar fell under a series of hits. But then Theo and his group charged in, taking Achillas from the rear. The warrior tried to seek refuge behind his men, but Theo leapt at him, bearing him to the ground.

"The Spartan!" yelled Gaelan. Theo rolled to his feet.

"Back!" he ordered his men. Pulling out of the melee, his group locked shields and watched the Spartan approach. His smaller group was also in tight formation.

"Do we charge them?" asked Gaelan.

"Wait!" replied Theo.

The defeated men sat down to watch the clash. Suddenly the Spartan's force surged forward, their long staffs lancing out to punch men from their feet. Theo's front line went down. "Move back!" Theo bellowed, and the men ran to the southern end of the field, turning once more to face the advancing formation. Swiftly Theo outlined a plan to Gaelan and the others. Then they waited, shields locked together. Once more the Spartan's army charged. The front rank again went down, and the enemy pushed on over them, closer to Theo, who had placed himself at the back of his force.

Inside the Spartan square Gaelan rose from beneath his shield and touched Parmenion on the shoulder with his club. "Killing blow!" shouted Gaelan.

A great cheer went up from the watching warriors. Parmenion took hold of Gaelan's arm and raised it in the victor's salute, then he led all the men back to the north of the field.

"This afternoon," he told them, "you saw almost all the major problems faced by infantry. Petar, you experienced what happens when a charge comes unexpectedly, the sheer force of it carrying the enemy through to the center. Achillas, you suffered the double envelopment, being hit on your flank as you engaged Petar. Theo, despite being the victor, you saw what happens when a foe is better armed, the spear giving greater length and penetration than the sword. Your ploy was a good one, and I do not belittle it; indeed, I will learn from it. But in a real battle, though you might have destroyed the enemy general, your troops would have been cut to pieces, and you would have died in the process."

He presented the badges, watching with pleasure as Theo handed the second to Gaelan.

"Tonight all badge holders will be given their prizes. Now, gentlemen, you may return to your duties—all except the generals."

As the men wandered away, Theo, Achillas, and Petar sat down with Parmenion. "Tomorrow," said the Spartan, "I will be riding south to Aigai to begin training the men there. I will be gone for a week. During that time you will bring the men here every day; you will make them run, you will fight mock battles, and you will issue badges. One of you will command; the other two will be underofficers. For this you will all be paid an extra drachma a day."

"Which of us is to command?" asked Achillas.

"Who would you choose?"

"Myself," Achillas said.

"And, if it was not to be you, who then?"

"Theo."

Parmenion turned to Petar. "For whom would you vote if not yourself?"

"Theo," answered the blond-bearded warrior.

"Before you ask me," said Theo, "let me say that I cannot make a choice. Achillas is an old friend and a warrior I respect. Petar is a good man, but I do not know him well. I sense that I will have the deciding vote on this issue, and I protest the unfairness of such a vote. You are the *strategos*. We are all strangers to you, and you have seen us—and judged us. So play no more games, Parmenion. You choose!"

"You have a fine mind," said Parmenion, "but do not complain of life's unfairness. It is never fair—at best it is impartial. I believe that all three of you have qualities of leadership, but at this moment I would not presume to judge which of you has the greatest potential. All of you are fine swordsmen, brave men. Each of you has won the respect of his fellows. I will ask you to decide now, among yourselves, who is to lead the training."

The men looked at one another, but it was Achillas who spoke first.

"It should be Theo," he said. Petar nodded in agreement.

"So be it," said Parmenion. "I thank you all. Now, Theo, let us walk together and discuss strategy."

"It is an insult!" stormed Attalus. "Twenty men! How can a king travel into hostile lands with only twenty men?" A murmur of agreement ran around the officers gathered in Philip's throne room.

"What do you say, Parmenion?" asked the king.

"Bardylis is the victor. He destroyed Macedon's army. He wants the world to see that you go to him as a supplicant and not as a king."

"And your advice?"

"Do as he says," Parmenion answered.

"What else would you expect from a Spartan?" hissed Attalus. Parmenion chuckled and shook his head as Philip gestured Attalus to silence.

"Give us the benefit of your reasoning," he urged Parmenion.

"It does not matter what the world sees now. In fact, it could be argued that it is better for Macedon to seem . . . vulnerable. What we need is time. Next year you will have an army the equal of Bardylis. A year after that and it will be the envy of Greece."

"But," said Nicanor, "there is the question of pride, of honor."

"This is the game of of kings, young man," Parmenion told him. "Today Philip must suffer for his brother's defeat. But soon it will be others who will feel the shame."

"What of you, Antipater?" asked Philip. "You have said little."

"There is little to say, sire. I agree with Attalus. The situation is not to my liking. Yet you must go or there will be no wedding. Without the wedding, an invasion is sure."

Philip sat back on his couch and looked at the four men. So different all of them, but each with unique skills. Cold-eyed Attalus, who could kill without remorse as long as it served to further his ambition. Nicanor, gloriously brave and doggedly loyal, a man who would ride into the whirlwind if Philip ordered it. Antipater, cool and efficient, a warrior respected by the army.

And Parmenion, who in a few short weeks had revitalized Macedonian morale, gathering a core of warriors and filling them with pride and camaraderie.

So different in looks, too: Attalus thin and hatchet-faced, his skin tight around his cheekbones, his teeth too prominent, giving him the appearance of a hastily covered skull; Nicanor almost feminine of feature, fine-boned and honest-eyed; Antipater, his black beard shining like a jaguar's pelt, his dark eyes keen, observing more than his expression showed; Parmenion, tall and slim, seeming younger than his forty-two years, his pale eyes so knowing.

On you all will I build Macedonia, thought Philip. "We will take only four riders," he said suddenly. "We here will ride to Illyria and collect my bride."

"That is worse than madness, sire," protested Attalus. "There are robbers, outlaws, people dispossessed of their homes."

"We will not ride alone all the way," Philip assured him. "Only the last few miles in Illyria. There we will be met."

"But why only four, sire?" Nicanor asked.

The king gave a cold smile. "Because I *choose* four. No man, not even Bardylis, tells Philip how many will accompany him."

After the meeting Philip walked with Parmenion out into the palace gardens. "How is the training coming, *strategos*?"

"Better than I had hoped. Until the new armor arrives from Phrygia, we are keeping the work simple—running, single combat, and a few elementary unit exercises. What is heartening, though, sire, is the quality of the men and their willingness to accept new ideas. I already have several underofficers of great potential."

Philip nodded, and the two men walked to a quiet area at the back of the gardens, sitting in the shade of a high wall. "I know it would be easier for you, Parmenion, if we could gather all the men in one place. But you know why I cannot. If word gets out that I am building an army, Bardylis will invade swiftly."

"Only if he believes he is the target," Parmenion pointed out. "When you see him, explain that you are planning to strike against the Paionians, that you are tired of their incursions into Macedonian territory."

"You don't know Bardylis; he's the wiliest wolf in all Greece. He must be around eighty now—even the goddess of death can't seem to summon up the courage to claim him."

"How strong is his hold on Illyria?"

"Strong enough," Philip answered. "There are three main tribes, but the Dardanoi of Bardylis are by far the strongest. And his army is well trained and disciplined. Better than that, they are used to victory. They won't crack."

"We'll see," said Parmenion.

Philip rose. "I am riding east to Crousia. The gold supplies have started again, but they are low. While I am gone, you will have charge of the army. All reports will come to you."

"How long do you plan to be away?"

"No more than two weeks. Then we head for Illyria—and my marriage."

Philip took two hundred warriors with him on the ride northeast toward the towering Cercine mountains north of Crousia. He had never seen the mines or met the governor there, Elyphion. But reports of the man were not promising: he had close links with Cotys, the late king of Thrace, and was a second cousin to the murdered pretender, Pausanius. But still Philip was prepared to forgive these connections if he could woo Elyphion to his cause.

They crossed the River Axios and rode across the great Emathian plain, passing through villages and towns, woods and forests. Game was plentiful here, and they saw the tracks of bear and lion, boar and deer. It was said that to the north there were panthers with black pelts, but none had been seen in a hundred years.

Just before dusk on the third day Philip led his troop up a high hill, cresting it as the sun was sinking behind the western peaks of Mount Bermion. The sky was heavy with broken gray clouds, and beyond them sunlight turned the heavens to purple and crimson. Philip hauled on his reins and stared out over the rolling grasslands, the forests and the mountains, shading his eyes against the setting sun.

"Why are we stopping, sire?" asked Nicanor, but Philip ignored him, his keen gaze swinging to the east, past the proud, rearing peaks of Mount Messapion and on to the mighty Cercine mountains, stone giants with beards of snow and cloaks of timber.

Around the king the men waited. Philip dismounted and walked to the hill's crest. The wind blew at his cloak, the night cold whispering against his bare arms, but the beauty of the land was upon him, and he felt nothing but the spell of the sunset.

Nicanor approached him, laying his hand on the king's shoulder. "Are you well, Philip?" he asked softly.

"Look upon it, my friend," said Philip. "Long after we are dust, the land will still be here, these mountains and forests, the plains and the hills."

"They are all yours. Everything you see belongs to you."

"No. That is folly. I am the steward, no more than that. But that is enough, Nicanor. This is a proud land. I can feel it seeping into my bones. I will not see it conquered—not in my lifetime."

Striding to his horse, he took hold of its mane and vaulted to its back. "Ride on!" he ordered.

Six days of easy traveling brought them to the foothills of the Messapion range, where they camped in a hollow surrounded by trees.

"Tell me more about the governor, Elyphion," Philip ordered Attalus. "I want to be prepared tomorrow."

Attalus spread out his cloak and lay alongside the fire. "He's fat, very fat. He dresses always in blue. He has three wives but spends most of his time with young boy slaves. He has been governor for eleven years. He has a palace that rivals any in Pella, even yours. He is a collector of statues and works of art, most of them Persian."

Philip grunted. "My gold supplies dry up, but he collects works of art and builds a palace! I think I am beginning to know the man. What of the mines themselves? How are they run?"

"How would I know, sire? I have never seen one."

"You will tomorrow," Philip assured him.

"What a fascinating prospect," muttered Attalus. Philip laughed and thumped him on the shoulder.

"Aren't you interested in where our gold comes from?"

"No," admitted Attalus, "only that it comes."

"What of you, Nicanor? Do you wish to see the mines?"

"If you command it, sire. But what is there to see? Men grubbing in the earth like moles. Darkness and stench. And as they go deeper, the constant danger of a roof fall. I want to be buried when I am dead, not before."

Philip shook his head. "Then I give you leave to seek the fleshpots of Crousia. Antipater will accompany me."

"A singular honor for him," Attalus sneered.

"It is always an honor to walk with the king," said Antipater, masking his anger, though his dark eyes remained fixed on Attalus.

"You do not like me, do you?" asked Attalus, sitting up and returning the soldier's stare.

"I neither like you nor dislike you, Attalus. In fact, I think of you rarely."

"Be careful how you speak to me!" Attalus snapped. "I make a bad enemy."

"Be silent, the pair of you!" stormed Philip. "You think we do not have enough trouble? When Macedonia is free, then—perhaps—I will allow you to declare your enmity. Perhaps. But know this, if either of you fights, I will have the winner executed. If you cannot be friends for my sake, then at least suffer one another. You understand me?"

"I wish for no enmity, sire," said Attalus.

"Nor I," added Antipater.

Philip settled down in his blankets, his head resting on his folded lionskin shabraque, and gazed at the bright stars—so distant, so far from all the troubles of the world. He closed his eyes and slipped into sleep.

He was walking on a grass-covered hillside under a silver moon when he saw the woman sitting beneath a spreading oak. He looked around, surprised that he was alone. When he approached her and bowed, she looked up, pushing back the dark hood of her cloak. Her face was pale and beautiful, her eyes dark and yet luminous.

"Welcome, great King," she whispered. He sat beside her.

"I am not great, woman. But I am a king."

"You will be great—that is the promise of Aida; the gods have decreed it. But there is something you need, Philip. There is a talisman you must acquire."

"Where do I find it?"

"It will find you. Look!" She pointed down the hill to where a small stream was sparkling in the moonlight. There sat a second woman. "Go to her—and know the joys of the universe."

Philip was about to ask a question when the dark woman vanished. He stood and walked to the stream. The woman there was little more than a girl, her figure slim, her breasts small and round. Her hair was red, like reflected firelight, her eyes green as jewels. When he knelt beside her, she reached out and stroked his beard, her hand dropping to his chest and stroking his belly. He realized he was naked, as she was, and passion flooded him. He pulled her down to the grass, kissing her face and neck, his hand caressing her inner thigh. He could feel his heart pounding.

"Love me!" she whispered. "Love me!"

He entered her, and so exquisite was his pleasure that his orgasm was instant. Incredibly, though, he stayed erect, his passion seeming inexhaustible. He felt her trembling beneath him, moaning and crying out. He rolled from her, but she would not let him go, stroking him with gentle fingers, caressing him with soft lips. Finally he groaned and rolled to his back, where he lay with his arms around her.

"Who are you?" he asked her. "I must know. I must have you."

"You will see me again, Philip. With you I will have a child, the son of a king."

"Where can I find you?"

"The time is not yet. I will meet you two years from now on the Island of Mysteries. There we will be wed; there your son will be conceived."

"Your name, tell me your name!"

"Tell me your name!" he shouted.

"What is it, sire?" asked Nicanor, moving to where the king lay. Philip opened his eyes and saw the stars, bright in the night sky.

"It was a dream," he whispered. "A gift from the gods."

Unable to return to sleep, Philip sat for the rest of the night reliving the scene of his vision. In two years, she had said, she would be on the Island of Mysteries.

Samothrace.

He had never been there—had never wished to. But now, he knew, only death would stop him from keeping that appointment.

Soon after dawn he woke the others, and they rode down into the valley of the mines. Crousia was not a large settlement; fewer than a thousand people dwelt here, and Elyphion's palace overshadowed the town with its white pillars and elegant statues, its high pointed roof bearing a beautiful relief showing the goddess Athena rising from the brow of her father, Zeus.

The two hundred riders reined in their horses before the building, and Philip dismounted. An elderly servant emerged from an outbuilding and stood slack-jawed, staring at the army before the palace.

"You!" shouted Philip. "Take my horse." The man stumbled forward.

"Are you . . . expected?" he asked, his eyes fearful.

"I would hope not," answered Philip, tossing him the reins and striding toward the huge double doors beyond the pillars. Attalus, Nicanor, and Antipater followed him into the building, and the four men stopped in the great hallway within. Persian carpets covered the floor, statues lined the walls, and an enormous mosaic decorated the ceiling, showing the Trojan prince, Paris, with the goddesses Aphrodite, Hera, and Athena.

Philip felt almost humbled by the awesome surroundings. He noticed that his muddy boots had marked the carpet and that his hands were grime-smeared.

"Elyphion!" he bellowed, the word echoing in the marble hallway. Servants ran from hidden doorways with panic in their eyes. One, a slender boy with golden hair, cannoned into Antipater and fell to his knees. The soldier helped him to his feet.

"Don't kill me!" the boy begged.

"No one is going to kill you," Antipater told him. "Fetch your master. Tell him the king is here."

"Yes, sir." The boy began to move toward the stairs, then turned. "I am sorry sir, but . . . which king?"

"The king of Macedonia," said Antipater.

An older man stepped forward and bowed to Philip. "Sire, perhaps you would like to wait in the *andron*. I shall fetch you refreshments."

"At last," said Philip, "a servant with his wits about him." The group followed the man into a long room to the right. Here there were silk-covered couches, and the walls were painted with hunting scenes: riders chasing a white stag, Heracles slaying the Nemean lion, archers loosing their shafts at a huge bear. "By the gods," said Philip, "it makes Pella look like a cattle shed. I would be envious if it weren't for the fact that it was built with my gold."

The servant brought them wine from Elyphion's vineyard—red, sweet, and fortified with spirits. Philip lounged down on a couch, lifting his filthy boots to the silk and smearing mud on the cloth.

His mood was dark, and his companions said nothing as they waited. At last Elyphion appeared. Attalus had said the man was fat, but this proved an understatement—great folds of flesh hanging beneath his chin, his enormous belly pushing at the blue Persian robes he wore. His dark hair was cut short and sat atop his head like a small, badly fitting cap. He tried to bow, but the belly defeated him.

"Welcome, sire," he said. "Had I only known of your visit, I would have prepared a sumptuous welcome." The voice was deep and attractive, as indeed, Philip noticed, were the man's large brown eyes.

"I came to see the mines," Philip said.

"But why, sire? There is little for a man of breeding to see. Great gaping holes in the earth and a few tunnels full of stench. I will gladly show you the smelting houses."

Philip's voice dropped low, and a dangerous glint showed in his eyes. "You will show me what I wish to see," he said slowly. "You will do this, Elyphion, because you are my servant. Now, take me to the mines."

The king rose.

"Yes, of course, sire, I will just dress; I will not be long."

"Attalus!" snapped Philip.

"Yes, sire?"

"If this fat fool disobeys one more instruction, take your knife and open his belly from groin to throat."

"Yes, sire," Attalus replied, grinning at the mortified Elyphion.

"Now, sir, the mines, I think," said the king.

"At once . . . sire," stammered Elyphion. The fat governor shouted for his carriage, and within minutes a wagon was brought to the front of the palace. Drawn by four black geldings, it resembled a giant chariot save that it had a wide cushioned seat. Elyphion settled himself in place, and a servant climbed in beside him, flicking the reins.

Despite their avowed disinterest in mining, Attalus and Nicanor rode behind Philip, unwilling to miss the king's visit.

They rode for almost an hour until they came to a small valley where the earth had been gouged as if by a huge pick. Far below them they could see the slaves digging in the earth and others shuffling from tunnels in the hillside.

Slowly the riders descended.

Nicanor's eyes raked the working groups. Both men and women labored here, their skeletal bodies covered in weeping sores, while around them stood guards armed with short, wicked whips. To the right a woman carrying a basket of rocks stumbled and fell, cracking her head against a boulder. She did not cry out but wearily pushed herself to her feet and stumbled on.

Ahead Philip rode to the nearest tunnel mouth and dismounted.

Elyphion climbed ponderously from the wagon. "As you ordered, sire. This is the mine."

"Take me inside."

"Inside?"

"Are you deaf?"

Elyphion walked slowly toward the darkness of the tunnel, halting to allow his eyes to become accustomed to the gloom. Lanterns hung from the walls, but the tunnel was full of choking dust. Elyphion's servant, the man who had led the king to the *andron*, poured water on a linen cloth and gave it to his master. Elyphion held it to his face and walked farther into the mine. The ground sloped ever down, and the air grew thick and stale. From far ahead they could hear the sound of metal tools hacking at rock.

A shower of dust clattered to Attalus' breastplate, and the warrior glanced nervously at the timbers shoring up the roof. One of them showed a split through which earth was filtering.

Still they walked on.

They came to the body of a young woman that had been pushed to the side of the tunnel. Dirt had covered her eyes and filled her open mouth. The tunnel roof was lower here, and they walked on with heads bowed. But it dropped lower still.

Elyphion stopped. "I don't know what you want to see, sire," he whimpered.

"Move on!" ordered Philip. Elyphion dropped to hands and knees and began to crawl forward. Philip turned to the others. "Wait here," he said, then followed the governor.

Nicanor turned to Attalus. "Do you think we could move back just a little, to where the roof is higher? Would Philip mind, do you think?"

Sweat was streaking the grime on Attalus' face. He felt cold and full of fear, but he stood his ground and looked at Antipater. "What do you think?" he asked.

"I . . . er . . . do not believe the king would object," Antipater answered. The three men inched their way back to the wider tunnel, stopping where they could just see the glint of sunlight in the distance. There they waited. Nicanor could not stop himself from staring at the dead woman.

"Why did they not bury her?" he asked.

"You saw the slaves," said Antipater. "They've barely the strength to stand."

"It's like a valley of the damned," whispered Antipater. Footsteps came from the tunnel entrance, and the three men moved back as a line of slaves bearing empty wicker baskets on their backs shuffled by them, heading into the gloomy depths of the mine.

"I am going back to the sunlight," said Nicanor. "I can't stand this."

"The king said to wait," Attalus reminded him. "I like it no more than you do. But let us be patient."

"I think I will go mad if I don't get out of here," Nicanor replied, his voice rising in pitch.

Antipater put his arm on the young man's shoulder. "Someone should go and tell the men that everything is all right. We have been down here a long time, and some of them may be concerned. Wait for us outside, Nicanor."

As Nicanor nodded and ran back toward the light, Attalus turned on Antipater. "Who are you to countermand the king's order?" he hissed.

"The man was close to cracking. If I had not allowed him to go, he would probably have run anyway."

"So? He would have run. What has that to do with you?"

Antipater nodded as understanding came to him. "I see. He might have fallen from favor. Gods, Attalus, do you have no friends? Is there no one you care for?"

"Only a weak man needs friends, Antipater. And I am not weak."

Antipater said nothing, and the two men waited in silence for what seemed an age. Finally the fat figure of Elyphion appeared, his blue robes streaked with grime. Behind him came the king, his face thunderous; he stalked from the tunnel out into the sunlight, dragging in great gulps of air, then he turned on Elyphion. The fat man stepped back a pace, seeing the fury in the king's eyes.

"What have I done, sire? Tell me? I am loyal, I swear it!"

Philip could hardly speak. "Someone get me a drink!" he thundered, and Nicanor ran forward bearing a water skin. Philip rinsed his mouth and spit out the water. "This is my gold mine," he said at last. "Mine. Macedonia's. Tell me something, fat fool, what do you need in order to get gold from the ground?"

"Tools, sire. Picks, digging tools . . . baskets."

"And who uses these tools?"

"As you see, slaves, criminals, thieves, murderers. Men are sentenced and sent here. Women also."

"You do not see it, do you?" roared Philip. Around them all work had ceased; the guards with their whips were no longer watching the laborers, who sank wearily to the ground, dropping their tools. All eyes were on the unfortunate Elyphion.

"I see only that I have done my best," whimpered Elyphion. "The gold is not as plentiful as once it was, but is that my fault? The veins go deeper, where we cannot follow."

Philip turned toward a guard. "You!" he bellowed. "Fetch everyone from the mine. Get them all into the daylight." The man bowed and ran toward the tunnel. "Elyphion," said the king softly, "I could forgive you your greed, your lust for wealth. I could even forgive your theft of my property. What I cannot forgive is your stupidity. Tools, yes. But what kind of an imbecile allows his tools to reach such a state? Starved to the borders of death, covered in sores, living without hope, how can these people work? Digging requires strength, powerful arms, a good back. For this a man needs food, good wholesome food, and wine for the spirit. Attalus!"

"Yes, sire."

"You will take over the running of this enterprise. I will leave you with one hundred soldiers. I want the slaves fed and rested for two weeks, and I will send others here. Find yourself a good foreman and break the work load so that each man works no longer than twelve hours." Philip looked into the warrior's eyes and suddenly smiled. Attalus had no liking for this role, and it showed. "Also," concluded the king, "you may keep one part in a hundred of all the gold mined."

"Thank you, sire," said Attalus, his eyes gleaming as he bowed low. "But what of Elyphion?"

"Who is the foremost judge in Macedonia?" responded Philip.

"The king, sire."

"Indeed he is. For his greed, I sentence Elyphion to five years working in this mine. See to it that he works well."

Elyphion threw himself to his knees. "I beg you, sire . . ."

"Get him out of my sight!" roared the king. Three soldiers dragged the weeping man away.

"What of his wives?" Nicanor asked.

"Buy them a house in Crousia and give them an allowance. The treasures are to be brought to Pella. Where is the man's servant?"

"Here, sire. My name is Paralus." Philip looked into the man's eyes. He was of medium height, his hair short and tightly curled, his nose hooked, his complexion dark.

"You are a Persian?"

"Phrygian, sire."

"How long have you served Elyphion?"

"Since he bought me eleven years ago, when I was twelve."

"How did you serve him?"

"At first I was his catamite—one of them. Then he had me trained to keep his accounts."

"Where does he hide his gold?"

"There is a storeroom beneath the palace."

"Attalus, have the contents sent to me—less one-hundredth. Now, Paralus, you have a new master. Will you serve him well?"

The servant glanced from Attalus to the king. "Sire, Elyphion promised me my freedom on my twenty-fifth year. He said he would then pay me for my work. Does his promise still hold true? Or do I remain a slave under this new master?"

"I give you a better promise. In three months you will be a free man. From this moment you will be paid according to the value Attalus sets on your work. Now I ask you again, will you serve us well?"

"I will, sire, and honestly."

"Let it be so," Philip told him.

ARDYLIS sat very still as the razor-sharp knife scraped away the hair beneath his braided topknot. The skin of his scalp was loose and wrinkled, but the servant's hands were steady as the blade caressed the skin.

"One nick and I will have your hands cut off," said Bardylis suddenly. The servant froze for a moment, then rubbed more oil into the king's face and head to soften the bristle. The knife slid over the skin above Bardylis' right ear, then the servant moved to stand in front of the king.

"Move your head back, sire," he said. Bardylis looked up at the man and offered his neck. The knife continued its work until at last the servant stepped back.

Bardylis stroked the skin of his face and head. "You did well, Boli," he told the man. "Now tell me, why did my threat not unnerve you?"

The man shrugged. "I don't know, lord."

"Then I shall tell you," said Bardylis, smiling. "It is because you decided that if you made a single nick, you would cut my throat and then run for your life."

Boli's eyes widened, and Bardylis saw that the truth had hit home. He gave a dry chuckle and pushed himself to his feet. "Do not let it concern you."

"If you knew that, lord, then why did you threaten me?"

"A little danger adds spice to life, and—by the balls of Zeus—when you reach eighty-three, you need a lot of spice. Send in Grigery."

Bardylis wandered to a bronze mirror and gazed at his reflection, hating the sagging skin of his face, the spindly limbs, and the thin, white hairs of his long mustache. There were times when he wished he had not been quite so skillful at recognizing traitors. Perhaps, he thought idly, I should have let Bichlys kill me. His son had been a fine warrior, tall and proud, but he had reached fifty years and still his father ruled the Dardanoi. The rebellion had been short-lived, his army had been crushed, and Bardylis had watched his son being slowly strangled to death.

He turned away from the mirror as the man who had killed his son entered. Grigery was tall, wide-shouldered, and slim-hipped. Though he boasted the shaved skull and braided top-knot of the Dardanoi, he had grown neither beard nor mustache, his clean-shaven face pale and handsome after the fashion of the southern Greeks.

Grigery bowed. "Good morning, sire. I trust you are well."

"Yes, I am, but the definition of well has a different meaning for the old. Is the Macedonian here?"

"He is, sire. But he brought with him only four men."

"Four? What, could he not find twenty Macedonians with the courage to enter Illyria?"

Grigery chuckled. "I would imagine not."

"Who are the four?"

"One is a common soldier named Theoparlis; another is the king's lover, Nicanor; the third is a soldier called Antipater—

he it was who led the charge against the Paiones. The last is a mercenary named Parmenion."

"I know that name," said Bardylis. "I offered him employment."

"He served the great king in Persia, I understand. He was also a friend to the Theban Epaminondas."

"More than that," said Bardylis. "Leuctra. The Spartan defeat. What other news is there?"

"Little of import, sire. Neoptelemus has agreed to increase his tribute. But then, you expected that."

"Of course. Now that his army is destroyed, he has little choice."

"He also offered one of his daughters in marriage, sire."

"The man's a fool. Much as I would wish it otherwise, my interest in women perished a decade ago. Still, let us turn to matters of greater importance; I want Philip well treated while he is here—but also he must be made to realize who is the master now."

"How should I engineer this, lord?"

"Be polite to the king but—out of his sight—goad his followers. It would be interesting to force one of them to challenge you. I would then of course have no option but to allow a duel to go ahead. You would then kill the man."

"Which one, sire?"

"Not Nicanor. I want the king mildly humbled, not aroused to fury. Fury leads to stupidity. Let it be the soldier, Theoparlis. And have Parmenion brought to my chambers tonight, but do not allow Philip to know of the invitation."

"You will employ him?"

"Why not? That would be a secondary blow to the Macedonian. Tell me, what do you make of Philip?"

"He seems anxious to please. However, it is difficult to judge the man. He has a great deal of charm and uses it well. He has cool eyes, and I would be wary of him in combat. But as to his nature . . . I have no idea."

"His brother was headstrong but a dynamic man," said Bardylis. "It interests me why Perdiccas let Philip live. Either he was considered no threat or Perdiccas was a fool. Similarly, why has Philip not slain the son of Perdiccas? They are an intriguing family."

"He was not slow to kill his own stepbrother," Grigery pointed out.

"I know." Bardylis sighed and returned to his throne. "Ah, if I was sure he would be a threat, he would not leave here alive. But a husband for Audata is not a prize I had thought to find. Invite him here for a private meeting. Bring him in an hour."

After Grigery had left, Bardylis summoned Audata to him. She was a tall, bony woman with a prominent nose, but though Bardylis knew many considered her ugly, he himself could see only the child he had loved since birth. She entered the room and hugged him.

"Have you seen him?" asked Bardylis, holding his daughter's hands.

"Yes. He is handsome, though I fear he is shorter than I."

"I want you to be happy," he told her. "And I still do not know if this is wise."

"I am twenty-seven years old, Father. Do not concern yourself over me."

"You speak as if twenty-seven were ancient. You still have time to bear healthy sons and watch them grow. I want that for you. I want you to know the joy I had while you were growing."

"Whatever pleases you," she said. They sat and talked until Grigery returned and announced Philip. Audata left swiftly but waited outside the throne room, watching the scene through the partly closed door.

Bardylis stood before the throne as Philip entered. The Macedonian walked forward and then knelt at Bardylis' feet, taking his hand and kissing it.

"A king should not kneel to another king," chided Bardylis.

"But a son should honor his new father," replied Philip, rising to his feet.

"A good point," agreed the Illyrian, waving Grigery away. "Come and sit with me; there is much we have to discuss."

Parmenion added the sylphium leaves to the boiling water, stirring it with his dagger blade. "What is it?" asked the Illyrian servant who had brought the water.

"Herbs from Macedonia. It makes a refreshing drink. My thanks to you."

Parmenion moved to a couch and sat down, waiting for the infusion to cool. Mothac had been furious when he had heard he was being left behind and had fussed around Parmenion like an old woman. "You will take the sylphium before going to bed each evening? You will not forget?"

"Of course I will not forget."

"You forgot in Egypt that time. Three days it was, when I was sick with a fever."

"I had other matters to worry about. We were being besieged at the time."

Mothac grunted, remaining unconvinced. "You have enough for five days, six at the very outside."

"I will be careful, Mother. I promise you."

"That's right! Mock! We are talking about your life, Parmenion. Just remember."

Parmenion swung his legs to the couch and relaxed, sipping the cooling drink. Like many of the southern Greeks, the Illyrians drank from shallow dishes. Only in Thebes had the Persian goblets found a natural second home. He finished the sylphium and settled back, his muscles weary from the long ride. The king had left his two hundred companions near Mount Babouna in the south, promising to return within five days. They had been met by Grigery and one hundred Illyrian cavalrymen. It was a tense ride to the palace of Bardylis, and Parmenion was weary hours before they sighted the long, single-storyed building. It was unadorned by statues, and there were no gardens, merely stables for the king's horses, but the rooms they had been given were comfortable, and each man had been assigned a servant.

Parmenion was just settling down to sleep when he heard the sound of knuckles rapping at his door. "Who is it?" he called.

"Grigery, sir. The king has requested your presence."

Parmenion sat up and rubbed the sleep from his eyes. He glanced to his cuirass and helm where they lay on the floor alongside his sword, then stood and walked to the door, pulling it open. Grigery bowed. Parmenion stepped from the room and followed the warrior along the wide corridor to the king's apartments. The man walked well, perfectly balanced, moving on the balls of his feet. He was an athlete, Parmenion knew—and more than that, a warrior to watch.

Grigery ushered him into an anteroom and announced him to Bardylis. To the Spartan's surprise, the king was alone. He did not rise from his couch when Parmenion entered but acknowledged the Spartan's bow with a wave of his hand.

"Welcome to my home, Parmenion. It is an honor to have such a famous general in Illyria."

"It hardly matches the honor for me, your Majesty. It is rare to be invited to a private audience with a king of such renown."

"You speak well, Spartan, but let us put aside such niceties," snapped the old man. "Come and sit beside me and tell me what you are doing in Macedonia."

Parmenion sat alongside the king. "A general moves where there is employment. I fear I almost outstayed my welcome in Asia. King Philip was kind enough to offer me a temporary commission."

"Temporary?"

"I am to train a few hundred warriors in order that he may guard his borders with Paionia. And also to supply him with a royal guard."

The king smiled, showing badly discolored teeth. "And what of Illyria? How does he feel about those borders?"

Parmenion thought swiftly. "He does not like the current situation, but then, would you? But I have told him there is little he can do. It would take considerable resources, an army of mercenaries, and even then he would face a less than even chance of success."

"You are extremely forthright," said the King, surprised.

"I am speaking no secrets, your Majesty. And I sense it would be . . . inappropriate to lie to you."

"Would you come to my employment?"

"Of course, sire. But I have given my word to Philip that I will stay one year and train his guard. After that? I will be seeking a new post. However, I do not think you need me. I am usually employed by men who have lost; very few victors have need of a mercenary general."

"That is true," Bardylis agreed. "Tell me, do you like Philip?"

"Very much. He is a kind man, in some ways a gentle man. Where I have traveled, such men are few."

"Is that why he did not kill the son of Perdiccas?"

"I imagine so, your Majesty. But it is difficult to know all that is in the king's mind."

"One last question, Parmenion: If Philip did raise an army, would you march against me?"

"Naturally, your Majesty. I would be a curious general if I did not."

The king chuckled. "I could have you killed, you know."

"All things are possible," admitted Parmenion, looking closely at the old king. "But I don't think you will."

"Why?"

"Because you're bored, sire, and small a threat as he is, Philip intrigues you."

"You are an observant man. I think I should watch you. But go now and enjoy your stay in Illyria."

For three days Philip was feted as Bardylis arranged banquets, athletic displays, dances, and the staging of a Corinthian comedy at a theater on the outskirts of the city. The Macedonian king seemed to be enjoying the pageants, though for Parmenion the days grew increasingly irksome. The warrior Theoparlis seemed tense and upset, and twice Parmenion had seen him in conversation with the sneering Grigery.

The Spartan approached Theo as the crowds left the theater.

"Is everything all right?" he asked.

"I am well," responded Theo, striding on ahead.

Parmenion put the problem from his mind as Philip came alongside, linking arms. "A good play, did you not think?" Philip asked.

"I am not a lover of comedies, sire."

Philip leaned in close. "To marry someone like Audata, a man must need to love comedy," he whispered.

Parmenion chuckled. "There is more to love than beauty, I am told."

"Yes, but looks must count for something. I sat with her for two hours yesterday, and throughout that time I sought one physical feature that I could compliment her on."

"What did you find?"

"I thought of telling her she had very nice elbows."

Parmenion laughed aloud, the tension easing from him. "What happened then?"

"We made love."

"What? In her father's palace? Before the wedding? And how did you manage it if you found nothing attractive in her?"

Philip looked suddenly serious. "I had a dream, Parmenion. I pictured the woman I saw in it, the woman I will meet next year on Samothrace." As they walked back to the palace, Philip told the Spartan of the mystical encounter.

"And you are sure it was an omen?"

"I would stake my life on it, and I would *give* my life to make it true. She was wonderful, the most beautiful woman I have ever seen. She is a gift from the gods, Parmenion, I know it. She promised to bear me a son, a child born of greatness."

As they approached the palace, Philip took Parmenion's arm and stopped. "This afternoon," said the king, "Bardylis wants me to see his army. It should be enlightening."

"Indeed it should," agreed Parmenion. "So what concerns you?"

"Theoparlis. He has grown sullen, and I think the man Grigery has been baiting him. He must not be drawn into a fight. Antipater has been asking questions about Grigery; it seems he is the king's champion and a demon with a sword."

"I shall prevent any duel between Macedonian and Illyrian," promised Parmenion.

"Good. Have you seen Bardylis again?"

"No. I think I convinced him there was no intention of a war with Illyria."

"Do not be too sure," warned Philip. "I think the man is a sorcerer, a reader of minds."

In the afternoon Philip and his companions watched the Illyrian cavalry charging across a wide field, their lances bright in the sunlight. Then the infantry marched forward in phalanx formation. Each man was armed with a spear and a short sword and carried a square shield of bronze-reinforced wood; they wore crested helms, breastplates, and greaves, though their thighs were bare. At an order from their general, the phalanx smoothly changed formation, moving out in a long line three men deep, spears leveled. Philip and his Macedonians were standing at the edge of the field when the king noticed the Illyrians on either side edging back.

"Stand firm, no matter what," whispered Philip.

With a thunderous roar the infantry charged. Philip watched the spearmen closing on him and for a moment wondered if this was the end of his life. It seemed that nothing could stop the charging mass and that within seconds an iron point would plunge into his unprotected breast. But he stood still with hands on hips, facing the charging men.

At the last possible second the phalanx halted. Philip gazed down at a spear point hovering a finger's breadth from his chest. Slowly he lifted his hand to it, rubbing his thumb on the metal. He looked into the spearman's eyes.

"There is rust on this," he said softly. "You should take better care." Then he turned away.

Not one of his company had moved a muscle during the charge, and this filled Philip with pride. Bardylis waved, and Philip joined the old king on a wide seat at the head of a table laden with food.

Parmenion was about to take his seat at the table when he noticed Grigery and Theo some twenty paces away. Once more the Illyrian was making some sneering comment, and even from this distance Parmenion could see Theo's face redden, his hand moving toward his sword hilt.

"Theo!" he roared, and the soldier froze. Parmenion walked over to the two men. "What is happening here?" he asked.

"This louse-ridden dog has challenged me," said Grigery.

"I forbid it," stated Parmenion.

"It is not for you to forbid anything in Illyria," retorted Grigery, his dark eyes gleaming.

Parmenion took a deep breath. "Did Theoparlis strike you?" he asked softly.

"No."

"I see. So, there was nothing like this," said Parmenion, lashing Grigery's face with a backhanded blow that spun the man from his feet. A great roar went up from the officers who were preparing to dine. Parmenion ignored the warrior, who was scrambling to his feet, and walked to Bardylis. He bowed low.

"Your Majesty, I must apologize for this unseemly scene. But your man Grigery has challenged me to battle with him, and I seek your permission to accept."

"It was not with you!" Grigery shouted.

"Then you do not wish to fight the man who struck you?" asked Parmenion.

"Yes . . . I mean . . ." His eyes turned to the king.

"All men have seen the beginning of this quarrel," said

Bardylis. "Now we must see the end. I give you permission to fight."

"Thank you, lord," said Parmenion. "Might I, as a guest, ask one favor? It seems only right, since we have interrupted a fine meal, to give you a spectacle not just of skill but of courage. Would you therefore have any objection if we fought in the manner of Mesopotamian nobles before their king?"

Bardylis stared hard at Parmenion. He had no idea of how Mesopotamian warriors fought but equally had no intention of disclosing this fact.

"As you will."

"Let a brazier be prepared," said Parmenion, "with hot coals to the depth of a man's forearm."

Bardylis ordered two servants to fetch the brazier. Parmenion walked some distance from the table, and Philip and the others joined him there.

"What in Hades is happening here?" Philip asked.

"I had no choice, sire. I promised you no Macedonian and Illyrian would fight. Whatever happens here will be seen to be between a Spartan and a warrior of Bardylis." He swung to Theo. "There is honey on the table. Fetch it—and some red wine. Find bandages and soak them in the wine."

"What is this manner of fighting?" asked Antipater.

"It is something new," Parmenion told him.

"You lied to Bardylis?" the king whispered.

"Yes. You need not worry, sire; he cannot read minds."

Four servants, using crossbars of thick wood, carried a burning brazier out into the field. Parmenion removed his breastplate and helm, tunic and greaves and, drawing his sword, walked out to stand before the brazier. Nonplussed, Grigery also stripped himself and moved to stand opposite him. The king and his officers formed a circle around the warriors and waited for the battle to begin.

"You need a fire to keep you warm, old man?" asked Grigery.

"Do as I do," Parmenion told him. The Spartan turned to the brazier and thrust his sword blade deep into it; leaving it there, he stood back with arms folded across his chest. Grigery plunged his blade alongside Parmenion's.

"Now what?" the Illyrian asked.

"Now we wait," the Spartan told him, locking his gaze to Grigery's eyes.

Slowly the minutes passed. The spectators' eyes flicked from the naked men to the blades, which had begun to glow a deep red.

The leather binding on the grip of Grigery's blade twisted and cracked, then smouldered, black smoke rising from it. Slowly it peeled away. Parmenion's sword had a metal grip, bound with fine gold wire over snakeskin. The skin burst into flame, the wire falling loose.

"When you are ready," said Parmenion, "take your sword and begin."

Grigery licked his lips and stared at the smoldering swords.

"You first," he hissed.

"Perhaps we should do it together. Are you ready?"

Grigery reached out, but the heat close to the hilt was unbearable, and his hand flinched back. He gazed around the crowd, seeing their fascination with the contest, and his eyes rested on the king, whose features were cold. Grigery knew what was expected of him, and he looked back at the red-hot sword.

"The longer you wait, the hotter it will become," said Parmenion mildly.

"You miserable whoreson!" screamed Grigery, his hand grabbing for his sword and wrenching it clear. The agony hit him as his flesh blistered and peeled away, sticking to the sword hilt. With a terrible cry he hurled the weapon from him. Parmenion reached out his left hand, drew his sword from the flames, and walked to Grigery.

The Spartan's face was without expression, but his breathing was quick and shallow, his teeth clenched and bared. Lifting the sword, he wiped the gleaming blade across Grigery's chest. The sizzling of burning hair and flesh carried to all the listeners, and Grigery leapt back, falling to the grass.

Parmenion turned to Philip and bowed, then he raised the red-hot blade and saluted Bardylis. Parmenion's arm flashed down, and the sword plunged into the earth by his feet. The Spartan walked through the crowd to where Theo waited with the honey, which he smeared on the blistered, weeping flesh. "The bandages," he croaked. Theo lifted them from the shallow wine dish, squeezed the excess liquid from them, and carefully wrapped the general's hand.

"How did you do that?" asked Theo.

"Can't talk . . . at . . . the moment," said Parmenion, closing his eyes as the cool bandages drew the heat from his palm. He felt sick and weak, and his legs were trembling. Gathering his strength, he looked at Theo. "Take the honey and the rest of the bandages to Grigery. Do it now!"

As Theo moved away, Parmenion heard footsteps approaching. He turned to see Bardylis and Philip, followed by a score of officers.

"You are an interesting man, Parmenion," said the old king, "and I should have known better than to allow a test of endurance against a Spartan. How is your hand?"

"It will heal, your Majesty."

"But you were not sure, were you? That is why you used your left."

"Exactly so."

"Are you strong enough to dine with us?"

"Indeed I am, sire. Thank you."

The pain was indescribable, but Parmenion willed himself to sit through the meal, even to eat, contenting himself with the knowledge that Grigery was nowhere to be seen.

LIFE was increasingly difficult for Derae as Tamis' mental condition deteriorated. The old woman now spent her days sitting in the temple gardens, often talking to herself, and at times it was impossible to communicate with her. Her sense of despair had grown, and the duties of the temple rested on Derae alone. Every day supplicants would arrive—long lines of sick or crippled folk, rich and poor, waiting for the hands of the healer.

The work exhausted Derae, especially now that the old helper Naza had died and there was no one to do the work around the garden or to gather the vegetables planted in the spring.

Only occasionally did Derae find the time—and, more rarely, the energy—to observe Parmenion.

Day by day she labored on.

Then she herself fell sick, a fever coming upon her swiftly, leaving her legs weak and her mind hazy. Despite her powers, she could not heal herself or tend to the sick who waited in vain outside the closed gates. Tamis was no help, for when Derae called out to her, the old woman seemed not to hear.

For eleven days Derae lay sick and exhausted, floating between strange dreams and confused awakenings. Once she awoke to see, with her spirit eyes, a man beside her bed. He had partly lifted her and was spooning a broth into her mouth. Then she slept again.

Finally she awoke and felt the sunlight coming through the open window. With no sense of the passing of time, she knew only that she was tired but no longer sick. Her bedroom door opened, and a man entered. Tall and gray-bearded, dressed in a tunic of faded red, he carried a dish of water to her bedside and helped her drink.

"You are feeling better, priestess?" he asked.

"Yes. Thank you. I know your voice, don't I? But I don't remember . . ."

"My name is Leucion. I came here a long time ago, and you advised me to go to Tyre. I took that advice. There I found love and a good wife, and we reared five sons and two daughters."

Derae lay back and spirit-gazed upon the man, remembering the look in his eyes as he had tried to rape her. "I remember. Why did you come back?"

"My wife died, priestess, and my eldest son now sits at the head of the table. But I never forgot you. I wanted . . . I wanted to see you again. To apologize. But when I came here you were ill, and there was no help. So I stayed."

"How long have I been in bed?"

"Eleven days," said Leucion. "At first I thought you would die, but I managed to get you to eat. I fed the old woman, too, but I do not think she even knows I am here."

"Eleven days? How is it that my bedclothes are so clean?"

"I changed them for you and washed the others. When you are well again, I shall leave."

Derae took the man's hand. "I thank you for your help, and I am glad you came back. I am glad also that your life has been happy. And if you are seeking forgiveness, I gave that a long time ago, Leucion."

"There are many people waiting for you. What shall I tell them?"

"Tell them I shall be with them tomorrow." Derae pushed back the covers and stood; her legs were unsteady, but she could feel her strength returning. Leucion brought her clothes and offered to help her dress. "It is all right, Leucion. I may be blind, but I can dress myself." She chose a simple white gown and walked to the gardens, where Tamis was sitting by the fountain.

"Please don't hate me!" whimpered the old woman.

Derae cuddled her, stroking her hair. "You look tired, Tamis. Why don't you rest?"

"It's all wrong. All of it. I haven't served the light at all. It's my fault, Derae." The younger woman took Tamis by the arm and led her to her own quarters. Tamis sank onto the bed and fell asleep instantly.

"Is she still taunting you?" whispered Derae, sitting beside the old priestess. "Let us see." She soared and looked around, but there was no one close and no sign or *feel* of the hooded woman. What, then, Derae wondered, was the source of Tamis' despair? With the priestess asleep, she decided to find out. Never before had she entered Tamis' mind unbidden, but it was useless now to try to elicit information. Her decision made, Derae's spirit flowed into Tamis, becoming one with the sleeping woman. She saw many years flow by; felt Tamis' hopes, dreams, despairs; saw a child of unique talent become a woman of power and influence; watched her grow; observed—and shared—her lovers and her bereavements. Finally she saw the first vision Tamis had seen of the birth of the Dark God and watched in horror as Tamis orchestrated the death of the Persian girl who was to bear the babe.

"We cannot use the weapons of the enemy," Tamis had said. And yet, fifty years ago, the seeress had entered the mind of the pregnant Persian, taking control of her limbs.

Then she had walked her to the top of the tower, forcing her to climb the parapet and leap to her death. Derae shook herself clear of the shared memory and, with growing unease, continued her journey. As the years moved on, her mood darkened. Tamis had begun to manipulate events. She it was who asked Xenophon to teach the boy strategy; she also used her powers to keep Parmenion separated from the other boys of his barracks, instilling in them a dislike for the young mix-blood.

But worst of all, Derae found the answer to a lifelong mystery.

Though she had loved Parmenion desperately, she had never understood why they had been so reckless in their love-making, so stupid and so open.

Now she saw. . . .

Now she knew. . . .

For, as with the hooded woman in Tamis' dream, so Tamis herself had floated above the lovers, using her power to blind them to peril, urging them on, driving them to their destruction.

Worse, it was Tamis who had spirit-led the raiders to her, Tamis who had caused her horse to bolt, leaving her with no escape. It was Tamis who had filled Nestus with the craving for vengeance, who had planted in him the desire to see Derae killed.

Tamis had engineered it all.

Parmenion had been manipulated, steered like a horse with invisible reins, led to Thebes, led to Persia, led to Macedonia.

But the last lie was the worst of all. Derae saw herself battling against her bonds in the sea after being thrown from the ship. The leather at her wrists had stretched in the water, and she had torn her hands free and swum for her life, the thunder of the breakers coming ever closer. She was strong and young, and she had battled the force of the deep almost to the beach when a huge wave picked her up and dashed her head against a rock. Seconds later Naza had waded out and dragged her into the shore.

"She is alive!" said the old man.

"Carry her to the temple," Tamis ordered. Alive! Not chained by the bonds of death at all. Lies, lies, lies! She could have left at any time and gone to Parmenion; she could have saved him from his life of emptiness and torment.

"Please don't hate me!"

Derae fled to her body and rose, staring down at the old woman as she slept. She wanted to strike her, to wake her and scream the truth at her.

A servant of the light? A woman who professed to believe in the power of love?

Derae staggered back from the force of her own hatred and ran from the room, colliding with Leucion in the corridor beyond. She almost fell, but his arms went around her.

"What is wrong, lady?"

"Everything," whispered Derae.

And the tears followed.

PHILIP watched the thousand-strong foot companions form into a fighting square and charge across the field. At a shouted order from Parmenion they halted, still in formation, and wheeled to the left. Another order saw the rear five ranks pull clear and stream out to widen the front line.

The discipline was good, and the king was well pleased. He saw the men gather up the *sarissas*—spears three times the length of a tall man—that Philip had personally designed. Each spear had an iron point and, at the base, a spike. The warrior in the front row of the phalanx held the *sarissa* shaft in the crook of his right arm, while a second man behind him took up the weight of the spear, ready to ram it forward into the enemy ranks. It was an unwieldy weapon, but Philip believed it would give the raw Macedonian infantry a tactical advantage in their first battles. The phalanx would advance against the enemy, who would come to meet them expecting the surging, shoving clash of armored men. But with the *sarissa* Philip felt he had an edge.

Parmenion was not so sure. "They are formidable, sire, at the front, but an enemy could sweep to the flanks, making them useless."

"True, *strategos*, but to do that an enemy would have to change the tactics of his entire army—tactics used for a century or more."

"Even so, we need a secondary tactic of our own," said Parmenion.

And he had supplied it.

No longer would Philip's cavalry adopt a frontal charge on the enemy; this would be left to the new infantry, the cavalry taking position on both flanks of the phalanx, forcing the enemy army in upon itself.

Day by day through the autumn and winter the army grew. Villagers and peasants flocked to Pella to undergo rigorous training in order to win the new Phrygian armor, the black breastplate and red-crested helm. By midwinter Parmenion had selected the men for the king's guard, each of whom had black cloaks of the finest wool and a bronze-edged shield bearing the star of Macedon at the center. These had been purchased with gold from the Crousia mines. Under Attalus, the mines had once more produced a plentiful supply of the precious metal, and Philip spent the proceeds even as they arrived in Pella: armor from Boeotia and Phrygia, horses from Thrace, marble from the south, cloaks from Thebes, builders from Athens and Corinth.

The barracks were finished now, and the guards lived there, eating the finest food, drinking only the best wine, but earning their privileges with extraordinary displays of endurance and stamina under the eagle eye of Parmenion.

Theoparlis and Achillas had remained with the king after his return from Illyria. Having seen their families in Pelagonia and supplied them with enough coin to last the winter, the two men now commanded phalanxes of infantry each two thousand strong.

Achillas had won glory in Paionia, where Philip had blooded his new troops the previous autumn. The Paionian king had been killed, his army put to flight. Philip rewarded Achillas with a golden-hilted sword.

For another hour Philip watched the soldiers in their training, then mounted his new black stallion and rode back to the palace at Pella.

Nicanor came to him there.

"The queen is now settled in the estate at Aigai," Nicanor told him. "Simiche said she was glad of the company."

"How is Audata?"

"She suffered sickness on the ride, but she is well. The physicians are with her; they are still concerned over the narrowness of her hips and her age. But the seers say the pregnancy will go well for her; according to Diomacus, she will have a daughter."

"She wanted to stay in Pella," said Philip, "but I told her it would be best to move south." He sighed. "She's not a bad woman, Nicci. But I do not want her here. This palace is for a special bride."

"The dream again?"

"It keeps coming to me, each time more powerful than the last. I can see her now more clearly than I see you."

"She is bewitching you, Philip," said Nicanor, his eyes betraying his concern.

"If she is, then it is an enchantment a man would die for—or kill for. She tells me we will have a son, a man of unique greatness. I believe her. And I must build a kingdom worthy of him. But I cannot do it while I am paying such a high tribute to Bardylis."

"What will you do?"

Philip smiled. "I have already done it. I have canceled the tribute."

"Does Parmenion know?"

"Is he the king here?" thundered Philip.

"No, sire; that is not what I meant. Bardylis will have no choice but to invade. Are we ready?"

"I think that we are," said Philip. "Macedonia's time has come, and I will not travel to Samothrace as another man's vassal. When I bring her home, it will be to a victorious nation. Either that or I shall be dead and have no concern for sons and glory." Taking Nicanor by the arm, he leaned in close. "What I am saying now must not be repeated to any man."

"I will say nothing," promised Nicanor. Philip nodded.

"Macedonia will be free," said the king.

Later, after Nicanor had left, Philip moved to the long window in the western wall and sat watching the sun falling behind the distant mountains.

He had not told Nicanor everything, nor would he.

The grand strategy had begun. First Bardylis, then Thessaly to the south, then Thrace to the east.

And then . . . ?

Ever since the first dream, Philip's ambition had grown day by day. He began to see events in a different way, on a larger scale. For centuries the great cities had sought to impose their will on their fellow Greeks, but all had failed. Mighty Sparta, invincible on land; Athens, queen of the seas; Thebes, lord of Boeotia. None had succeeded for long. They never would, Philip realized, for ultimately their dreams were small, bound to their own cities.

But if a nation should rise up strong, confident, and far-sighted, then the cities would topple and all Greece would be free to be united, to be led into battle by a single warrior king.

Then would the world tremble.

Philip shivered. What am I thinking? he wondered. Why has this ambition never shown itself before?

Because you are a king now, whispered a small voice in his mind. *Because you are a man of power and insight, wisdom and courage.*

By the time Parmenion arrived to give his report, the king had consumed several jugs of wine. He was in a merry mood, witty and convivial, but the Spartan sensed tension behind the good humor. The two men lounged on couches and drank until nearly midnight; it was then that Philip asked the question Parmenion had been waiting for.

"So tell me, *strategos*, are the men ready?"

"For what, sire?" Parmenion hedged.

"To fight for the freedom of Macedonia."

"Men are always ready to fight for freedom. But if you are asking me whether we can beat the Illyrians, I don't know. In another six months we will have two thousand more men trained; then my answer will be yes."

"We do not have six months," said Philip, refilling his wine cup.

"Why is that?" asked Parmenion mildly.

"I have canceled the tribute. We have less than six weeks before the Illyrian army crosses the mountains."

"May I share your reasoning?" inquired Parmenion.

"I spent the money on armor and weapons, so there is nothing left for Bardylis. Can we beat him?"

"It depends on what tactics he chooses and on the terrain. We need flat ground for the infantry and space for the cavalry to strike at his wings. But then, sire, it is down to the fighting soul of the army."

"How do you see the battle developing?"

Parmenion shrugged. "The Illyrians will begin confidently, expecting another easy victory. That will be an advantage for us. But when we push back, they will form the fighting square. After that it is down to strength, courage, and will. Something will crack, break—them or us. It will start with one man turning to run, the panic spreading, the lines shifting and pulling apart. Them or us."

"You are not filling me with confidence," muttered Philip, draining his wine.

"I am confident enough, sire. But we will be evenly matched. There is no question of a guaranteed victory."

"How is your hand?" asked Philip, switching the subject.

Parmenion lifted his left hand, opening his fingers for the king to see the scarred flesh of his palm. "It has healed well enough, sire, for me to hold a shield strap."

Philip nodded. "The men talk of that day. They are proud of you, Parmenion; they will fight for you; they will not break unless you do. They will look to you—you will be the fighting soul of Macedonia."

"No, sire, though I thank you for the compliment. They will look to the king."

Philip smiled, then laughed aloud. "Give me this one victory, Parmenion. *I* need it. Macedonia needs it."

"I shall do my best, sire. But long ago I learned the hazards of placing everything on a single race."

"You won, though," Philip pointed out.

"Yes," said Parmenion, rising. He bowed and walked from the palace, his thoughts in turmoil.

Why had the king taken such a terrible risk? Why not delay until the result was more sure? Philip had changed since the dream woman had come to him, becoming at times more moody and intense.

The following morning Parmenion called his main under-officers to him and walked with them on the training field outside Pella. There were twelve men in the group, but foremost of these were Achillas and Theoparlis, two of his first recruits.

"Today we begin a new series of training routines," he told them, "and the men will work as never before."

"Is there something we should know?" Theo asked.

"An army is like a sword," Parmenion told him. "Only in battle can you judge its worth. And now ask no further questions. Concentrate on the men under your command—find the weak ones and remove them. Better to be undermanned than to carry a coward into battle."

Slowly he looked around the group, meeting each man's eyes.

"Sharpen the sword," he told them softly.

THE LYNCESTIAN PLAIN,
SUMMER, 358 B.C.

THE two armies were drawn up in battle order on a dusty plain a day's ride into Upper Macedonia. The Illyrians, with ten thousand infantry and a thousand cavalry, outnumbered the Macedonians by almost two to one.

Philip dismounted and walked to the foot guards, who sent up a cheer as he hefted his shield and took his place at the center of their ranks. Parmenion remained mounted with Attalus and Nicanor beside him, four hundred cavalrymen waiting patiently behind. The Spartan looked beyond the three phalanxes to where Antipater commanded three hundred Macedonian horsemen on the right flank; the black-bearded warrior was issuing last-minute instructions to his men.

"By Hecate," whispered Attalus, gazing at the Illyrian lines, "there are enough of the whoresons."

"There will be fewer later," Parmenion assured him. The Spartan tied the chin straps of his white-crested helm and glanced once more at the enemy ranks less than a half mile distant.

Bardylis had drawn up his men in a fighting square with the cavalry to his right. The old wolf had gained the first advantage, Parmenion knew, for the square would be hard to break, and in the first stages of the battle, this could damage Macedonian morale beyond repair.

"Forward!" bellowed Philip, and the guards lifted their *sarissas* and marched toward the enemy, the phalanxes of Theo and Achillas close behind. Parmenion lifted his arm and touched heels to his stallion; the cavalry followed, angling out to the left of the marching men.

Dust billowed, but a strong wind dispersed it, leaving a clear field of vision. Parmenion watched the guards break into a run, his heart beating faster now as he studied their formation. It was still tight, compact. He willed it to remain so.

"Here they come!" shouted Attalus. Parmenion wrenched his eyes from the infantry to see the Illyrian cavalry charging across the plain.

"Remember the wedge!" yelled Parmenion, raising his spear and kicking the stallion into a gallop.

The Macedonians streamed after him.

Closer and closer came the horsemen, their lances leveled. Parmenion raised his buckler, chose his opponent, and then risked a glance to left and right. Attalus and Nicanor were beside and just behind him, the cavalry forming a giant spear point. Parmenion looked to the front, where bearing down on him was a yellow-cloaked rider on a chestnut gelding. Parmenion's eyes moved to the man's lance, which was resting across his mount's neck; as the point flashed up, he kneed his stallion to the left and his opponent's lance slashed the air by Parmenion's face. At the same time the Spartan stabbed his own weapon into the warrior's throat, hurling him to the ground. Blocking a thrust from another spear, he plunged his lance into the unprotected belly of an Illyrian rider. As the man fell, Parmenion's lance snapped. The Spartan drew his sword and hacked and cut his way deep into the enemy ranks.

The Macedonian wedge split the Illyrians, who tried in vain to gallop clear and re-form. But as they did so, Antipater came from the right, thundering into their flanks. Caught now in a pincer, the Illyrians battled for survival.

A sword clanged against Parmenion's helm, and a spear thudded against his breastplate, dropping to open a narrow gash in his thigh. His own sword rose and fell, spraying blood into the air.

Slowly the Illyrians were pushed back into a tight mass, where the majority could not fight, encumbered as they were by their fellows. Horses went down, trampling screaming warriors, and the cavalry battle became a rout, with the Illyrians forcing a path to the south and fleeing the field. Antipater set after them, but Parmenion, Attalus, and Nicanor recalled their own men and re-formed behind the battle lines.

Philip had no time to watch the clash of the horsemen. As the guards came within thirty paces of the Illyrian line, he ordered a halt. The phalanx slowed, then stopped, allowing Theo's regiment to link on the left, Achillas holding back to prevent a flank attack on the right.

They were close enough now to see the faces of the enemy and the wall of spears and shields that awaited them.

"Victory!" bellowed Philip.

The line moved forward, three hundred shields wide, ten deep. As they closed on the Illyrian square, the Macedonian front line dug in their heels and halted once more, the *sarissas* held loosely, points gleaming in the sunlight. The men in the second rank lifted the hafts of the long spears and, at a shouted order from Philip, ran forward, propelling the awesome weapons into the first Illyrian rank. The iron *sarissa* points cleared shields and breastplates, punching men from their feet. Then the spears were drawn back to plunge yet again into the second rank.

In that first clash it seemed to Philip that the Illyrians would break and run, such was the panic that threatened to engulf the enemy. But then an Illyrian warrior, speared through the belly, seized the *sarissa* that was killing him and held on to it. Other men saw this act of defiant courage and followed his lead, grabbing at the wooden hafts and rendering the weapons useless.

"Down spears!" shouted Philip, whereupon the men of the leading line dropped the *sarissas* and drew their short stabbing swords. "Forward!" the king yelled. Once again the Macedonians drove on, stepping over the bodies of the Illyrian slain. But now the battle changed and the advancing line was stopped by the wall of Illyrian shields; Macedonians began to fall before the stabbing spears of Bardylis' *hoplites*.

Achillas, who had held back, saw the charge falter.

"Level spears!" he called, and led his men in a second charge to aid Philip's right. Once more the Illyrians fell back, the deadly *sarissas* opening their ranks, but soon these, too, were seized and rendered useless and all three Macedonian phalanxes were locked in lethal combat.

Parmenion and the cavalry waited and watched with growing concern.

"Should we ride in?" Nicanor asked.

"Not yet," Parmenion told him.

"But they are holding us, and they have thousands more soldiers. The weight alone will force us back if they countercharge."

"Not yet," repeated Parmenion. The Spartan stared at the milling mass, wishing he could be in there at the heart, willing Theo to recall the maneuvers they had practiced so many times.

The Macedonian line in front of Philip was torn open by an Illyrian unit. The king ran forward, stabbing his sword into the groin of the leading warrior, who went down with a terrible cry. Philip leapt over him, ramming his shield into the face of a second warrior. Around him the guards tightened the line, but the king was now in the front rank, facing the spears and swords of the enemy.

To the king's left, Theo at last shouted the order Parmenion had been waiting for.

"Ranks seven! *Ranks seven!*"

The men to the left pulled back, while those to the right locked shields, powering forward, swinging the phalanx, and separating from the guards. As the gap between the regiments opened, the Illyrians surged forward like the sea rushing through a broken dike.

"Now!" screamed Parmenion, and the Macedonian cavalry kicked their horses into a gallop, aiming for the gap and the disordered Illyrians. Too late the enemy soldiers realized their peril and tried to re-form. But Macedonian warriors were now on both sides of them, the cavalry thundering toward them.

The Illyrians were tough men, seasoned in war. As best they could, they formed their shield wall and waited. But the cavalry smashed through them and on into the heart of the Illyrian square.

All was chaos and confusion now: the square broken, the Macedonians, tight and compact still, grinding their way toward Bardylis and his generals.

The old king stood firm, his own royal guard closing in around him. But the battle had now become a massacre, the Illyrian *hoplites* cut down in their hundreds by the advancing Macedonians.

Bardylis tried one last desperate move, ordering his guards to attack the line where Philip stood, but the regiments of Achillas and Theoparlis had closed in, stabbing at their flanks. Even so, four warriors hacked and cut their way through to Philip. The king killed the first with a stabbing thrust to the throat, his guards closing on the other three, scores of blades hacking them down.

Bardylis waited for death, drawing his own sword and hefting his heavy shield. But on a shouted order from Philip, the Macedonians drew back.

"Come forward, Father," called the Macedonian king. Bardylis sighed. Sheathing his sword, he eased through the last line of his guards and walked to stand before his son-in-law.

"I suppose you want me to kneel," said the old man.

"One king should never kneel to another," replied Philip,

returning his sword to its scabbard. "Was it not you who taught me that?"

"What do you require of me?"

"I want only my kingdom returned to me. All Illyrians and all of Illyrian blood will be moved to Illyria. The tribute will remain, save that it is you who will deliver it to me."

"You have traveled a long way in a short time, my son. And you fought well. What happens now to Audata? Will you throw her aside?"

Philip saw the anguish in Bardylis' eyes, and he moved to him, laying his hands on the old man's shoulders. "She is dear to me," Philip assured him, "and she is pregnant. She has her own estate now, near the sea. But I will send her to you for a visit when the babe is born."

Bardylis nodded, then turned to Parmenion, who had dismounted and approached. "I might have need of you now, Spartan," he said, forcing a smile.

Parmenion said nothing, but he bowed deeply.

The old man turned away and walked to the surviving guards.

At that moment a tremendous cheer rose from the Macedonian ranks, and Philip found himself hoisted to the shoulders of the guards and carried back from the field.

Parmenion stood and surveyed the battle site. Bodies were everywhere, men and horses; at that moment it seemed there were too many to count. Later he would learn of seven hundred Macedonian casualties, including Achillas and Petar. But six thousand enemy warriors had perished on this day, the power of Illyria shattered beyond rebuilding.

"Help me," came a voice from the ground by his feet, and Parmenion glanced down to see Grigery, his face a mask of blood. A sword had slashed across his brow, putting out both his eyes, and there was a deep wound in his groin. The life-blood was pouring from him.

Parmenion knelt by the dying man, cradling his head.

"Did we win?" asked Grigery.

"Yes, we won," said Parmenion.

"Who are you?" whispered the Illyrian, his voice fading.

"I am . . . Savra."

"Oh, gods, there is so much blood in my eyes. Wipe them clear. I can't see."

"Rest, my friend. Lie back. Do not struggle. There is nothing left for you to fight for."

Grigery lay quiet once more, and Parmenion thought he had died. But he spoke again. "I . . . thought we . . . would lose. You know what they call . . . the Spartan? The Death of Nations. Destroyed his own city. Everywhere he walks . . . death follows. Not any more, though, eh, Savra?"

Grigery's head sagged back, his last breath rattling in his throat.

Sadness hit the Spartan, and he rose and gazed at the sky.

Carrion birds were circling, waiting for the feast.

Derae sat at Tamis' bedside, waiting for the inevitable. The old woman had not eaten in over a week or spoken in days. When Derae took her hand, it was hot and dry, the skin loose over bone. Tamis' flesh had melted away, and her eyes had a haunted, lost look that filled Derae with sorrow.

She tried to use her powers on the dying woman but felt Tamis struggling against her.

It was close to midnight when the old priestess finally died. There was no movement or sound to indicate her passing. One moment her spirit flickered faintly, the next it was gone. Derae did not weep, though sadness filled her. Covering Tamis' face, she returned to her own room and climbed into bed.

Leucion had left by the bedside a jug of water and a bowl of fruit. But neither hungry nor thirsty, she drifted into a deep sleep.

The sound of music awoke her, and she opened her eyes to an unfamiliar scene. She was beside a great lake sparkling in a natural bowl at the center of a range of tall, snow-cloaked mountains. Beside her sat a woman of wondrous beauty, tall and elegantly formed, wearing a long *chiton* of shimmering gold.

"Tamis?" whispered Derae.

"As once I was," answered the priestess, reaching out and tentatively touching Derae's arm. "What can I say to you?" she asked. "How can I ask for forgiveness? I should never have lied, nor should I have meddled. Pride is not a gift of the source, and I fell victim to it. But we have little time, Derae, and I have much to tell you. Those ancient gateways I showed you, across continents and oceans—you must not use them. You must not pit yourself against the Dark God or his servants. They will corrupt you."

"I can fight them alone," said Derae. "It is what you trained me for."

"Please, Derae, listen to me! Go from the temple. Find Parmenion. Do anything you will—but do not follow my path."

Derae laughed then. "Where were your doubts, Tamis, when you led the raiders to me, when I was tied behind the leader's horse? Where were they when you floated above me, blocking my fears, urging me to rut with Parmenion and be damned for it?"

Tamis fell back from the Spartan's anger. "No, please! I have asked forgiveness of you. Please."

"Oh, Tamis, my friend," said Derae softly, her eyes cold. "I give you my forgiveness. But I saw how you prevented the last dark birth. How clever of you to enter the girl's mind and get her to leap from the tower. Perhaps that is the method I will choose this time. I will think on it."

"Stop this! I beg you, Derae. I was wrong. Do not continue my folly."

Derae closed her eyes. "I must stop the dark birth. You took away my life, Tamis—you lied, deceived, manipulated. If the Dark God succeeds, all is for nothing. I won't have that! I am a Spartan, and I will not surrender in this fight. Now," she *said, taking the woman's arm, "tell me all you know about the birth."*

"I cannot!"

"You owe me, Tamis! For all I have lost. Now tell me. Or I swear I will bring death to Philip of Macedon and all other servants of the Dark God."

Tears welled in Tamis' eyes. "You are my punishment," she whispered. "You are Tamis born again."

"Tell me what I need to know," Derae urged.

"Do you promise me you will not kill?"

"I promise you I will never stoop to murder."

Tamis sighed. "Then I will trust you, though my soul may be damned if you betray me. You have seen the events in Macedonia? Of course you have. The rise of Philip, the birth of a nation. That birth heralds the coming of the Dark God. His body of flesh will be conceived in Samothrace, during the night of the third mystery at high summer; it is all arranged. The mother will be Olympias, daughter of Neoptelemus, king of Epirus. The father will be Philip of Macedon. He has been primed, bewitched. You have but one real opportunity to succeed. In order for the Dark God to live, the conception must take place when the stars reach a certain alignment that will last for only an hour on that one night. If you are determined to go on with this quest, then you must journey to Samothrace and disrupt the ceremony."

"High summer is only ten days from now," said Derae. "How can I reach Samothrace in time?"

"The gateways I showed you lead to paths between worlds, between times. Listen to me, Derae, for this is the last time you will see me and you must learn your lessons well."

Derae opened her eyes to see dawn light creeping across the sky, the stars retreating before it. She rose and poured a goblet of water, sipping it slowly.

Samothrace, the Isle of Mysteries. She shivered. Tamis had once called it the Dark God's realm. The thought of the journey brought a sudden stab of fear, almost panic. Yet Parmenion will be there, she realized. For the first time in almost a quarter of a century they would be together. But what then? She was no longer the flame-haired adolescent of his memory, nor he the shy young warrior to be. More than time separated them now. Yet it would be good to be close to him once more.

She had watched with mixed feelings his successes for Philip: first, last year, the crushing of the Illyrians, but since then the march into Thessaly, securing the southern borders, the invasion of Paionia, and the besieging of the city of Amphipolis.

Now the wolves of the major cities viewed Macedonia with different eyes. Where once they saw only a lamb, ripe for ownership or slaughter, now they faced a lion—young and powerful, proud and arrogant.

Derae's pride at Parmenion's achievements was tinged with sadness, for the more powerful Macedonia became, the more deadly would be the effect when the evil one sat upon the throne.

Fear flooded her. She felt like a child facing a forest fire, a huge wall of flames that threatened to engulf the world. And what do I have to halt it? she wondered. Looking down, she saw the goblet of water in her hand. She smiled then and walked back to Tamis' room.

"I will keep my promise to you, Tamis. I will not murder. But if the servants of the Dark God come for me, then they will die. For I will not be thwarted in this."

The sheet still covered the body. When Derae pulled it back, all that lay there was a disconnected skeleton, the bones loose. As she lifted the sheet, the skull was dislodged from the pillow and fell to the floor, shattering into shards.

SAMOTHRACE, SUMMER,
357 B.C.

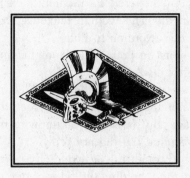

THE crossing had been calm, and the vessel glided smoothly into dock, the three banks of rowers backing oars to slow its progress. Seamen threw ropes to the men waiting at the quayside, and the great ship settled into place.

Philip strode down the gangplank, followed by Parmenion.

"I can barely contain my excitement," said the king as the two men stood on solid ground, staring at the tree-lined hills. "You think she is here already?"

"I don't know, sire," replied Parmenion, "but I am uneasy about your lack of guards. There could be assassins hired by any number of enemies."

Philip laughed and lightly punched Parmenion on the shoulder. "You worry too much. We are just travelers, wandering men, mercenaries. Few know of my plans."

"Antipater, Attalus, Nicanor, Theoparlis, Simiche . . . the gods know how many more," Parmenion muttered. "One wrong word is all it would take."

Philip chuckled. "It will not happen, my friend; this has

been ordained by the gods. And anyway, I have the Lion of Macedon to protect me." He laughed again at Parmenion's discomfort. "You know, you should really consider taking a wife or a lover. You are altogether too serious."

A tall woman in robes of black moved toward them, bowing deeply.

"Welcome to Samothrace, Lord Philip," she said.

"Wonderful," whispered Parmenion. "Perhaps a parade has been planned." The woman looked at him quizzically, then returned her attention to Philip.

"There is a feast in your honor tonight, and tomorrow a hunt in the high hills."

Philip took her hand, kissing the palm. "Thank you, lady. It is indeed an honor and a privilege to be greeted by one of such beauty and grace. But how did you know of my arrival?"

The woman smiled but did not reply.

She led them through the crowded city port to where two other women waited, holding the reins of two white stallions. The first pointed to a white palace a mile to the north. "Your rooms have been prepared, my lords. I hope the horses are to your liking."

"Thank you," answered Philip. The beasts were pretty to look at, but their chests were not deep, and this, he knew, indicated little room for lungs and heart and therefore a lack of stamina and strength.

The two men mounted the horses and rode slowly toward the palace, the walking women trailing behind.

In fields to left and right other horses were cropping grass. They were spindly-legged beasts, many of them roach-backed, the spine curving upward, thus making them uncomfortable to ride.

Philip found his disgust hard to conceal. "What is the point of breeding such useless animals?" he asked Parmenion.

The Spartan pointed back to the port. "Chariots and wagons, sire, but no horsemen. Obviously they do not concern themselves with riding."

The king grunted. Nothing offended a Macedonian more than poor horse breeding.

His good humor was restored at the palace when they were met by three beautiful women, dressed in robes of yellow and green. "Are there no men here?" he asked.

"Only you and your companion, sire," one of them replied. They were led to sumptuous apartments with silk-covered couches and gold-embroidered curtains.

"If there is anything you require, my lord, you have merely to ask," said a young raven-haired girl.

Philip smiled and took hold of her waist. "Exactly what is meant by anything?" he asked.

Her hand slid under his tunic, caressing the skin of his inner thigh. "It means exactly what you want it to mean," she told him.

Parmenion strode to the window, drawing back the hangings and staring out over the fields and meadows. He was tired and wished only for a bath. Hearing the girl giggling behind him, he cursed softly.

"What is wrong with you, *strategos*?" asked Philip, and Parmenion turned. The girls had gone.

"I am just ill at ease."

"You should take my advice. Enjoy these women; it is good for the soul."

"Maybe I will," Parmenion told him.

Philip filled two wine cups from a pitcher on a small table, passing one to Parmenion. "Sit with me awhile, my friend," said the king, leading Parmenion to a couch. "When I was in Thebes, they told me about your love for a priestess called Thetis."

"I do not wish to talk of it, sire."

"You have never spoken to me of her, nor of the other woman you loved. Why is that?"

Parmenion swallowed hard and looked away. "What point is there in talking of the past? What does it achieve?"

"Sometimes it lances the boil, Parmenion."

The general closed his eyes, fighting back the rush of memories. "I . . . have loved two women. Both, in different ways, died for me. The first was called Derae, and she was Spartan. Because of our . . . love . . . she was sacrificed, thrown into the sea off the coast of Asia. The second was Thetis; she was killed by assassins sent by Agisaleus. There have been no others. Never again will someone I love die for me. Now, if it please you, sire, I would prefer—"

"It does not please me," said Philip. "It is a fact of life that people die. My first wife, Phila, died only a year after our wedding. I adored her; on the night she died I wanted to cut my throat and follow her to Hades. But I didn't, and now I am about to meet a woman of dreams."

"I am pleased for you," said Parmenion coldly. "But we are different men, you and I."

"Not so different," Philip put in. "But you wear armor, both on your body and on your spirit. I am younger than you, my friend, but in this I am as a father to a frightened son. You need a wife; you need sons of your own. Do not concern yourself about love. Your father, whoever he was, gave you as his gift to the world. You are his immortality. In turn your sons will do that for you. Now, I will preach no more. I shall bathe, and then I shall send for that sweet-limbed young girl. You, I suspect, will walk around the palace grounds examining natural defenses and seeking out hidden assassins."

Parmenion laughed then, the sound rich and full of good humor. "You know me too well, young Father."

"I know you enough to like you, and that's a rare thing," said Philip.

The Spartan wandered out to the palace gardens and beyond to the hillsides overlooking the bay. He saw a flock of sheep and a young boy guarding them. The boy waved. Parmenion smiled at him and walked on, following a dry-stone wall that curved up to a high hilltop. He was drawn toward a grove of trees, their branches weighed down by pink and white blooms, where he sat in the shade and dozed.

He awoke to see a woman walking toward him, tall and

slender. He stood, his eyes narrowing to see her face. For a moment only, it seemed to him that her hair had changed color. At first it appeared to be the color of flame, flecked with silver, but as he looked again, it was dark. It must have been a trick of the light, he thought. He bowed to her as she approached. At first sight her robes were black as the night, but as she moved, the folds caught the light, shimmering into the rich blue of the ocean. Her face was veiled, a sign of the recently bereaved.

"Welcome, stranger," she said, her voice both curiously familiar and strangely exciting.

"Is this your land, lady?"

"No. All that you see belongs to the Lady Aida. I, too, am a stranger. Where are you from?"

"Macedonia," he told her.

"And before that?"

"Sparta and Thebes."

"You are a soldier, then?"

"Is it so obvious?" he asked, for he was dressed in only a pale blue *chiton* and sandals.

"Your shins are lighter in color than your thighs, and I would guess they are normally shielded by greaves. Similarly, your brow is not the deep brown of your face."

"You are very observant." He tried to focus on the face below the veil but gave up. The eyes as he saw them seemed to be opaque, like opals. "Will you sit with me awhile?" he asked her suddenly, surprising himself.

"It is pleasant here," she said softly. "I will bide with you for a little while. What brings you to Samothrace?"

"I have a friend—he is here to meet his bride. Where are you from?"

"I live across the sea in Asia, but I travel often. It is long since I was in Sparta. When was it you lived there?"

"Through my childhood."

"Is your wife a Spartan?"

"I have no wife."

"Do you not like women?"

"Of course," he answered swiftly. "I have no male lovers, either. I . . . had a wife. Her name was Thetis. She died."

"Was she your great love?" the woman inquired.

"No," he admitted, "but she was a good woman—loyal, loving, brave. But why must we speak of me? Are you in mourning? Or can you remove your veil?"

"I am in mourning. What is your name, soldier?"

"My friends call me Savra," he said, unwilling for her to hear the name being whispered in cities across the world.

"Be happy, Savra," she said, rising gracefully.

"Must you go? I . . . I am enjoying our conversation," he said lamely.

"Yes, I must go."

He stood and reached out his hand. For a moment she hung back, then touched his fingers. Parmenion felt his pulse racing and longed to reach up and draw aside the veil. Lifting her hand to his lips, he kissed it, then reluctantly released her.

She walked away without a word, and Parmenion slumped back to sit on the ground, amazed by his response to the stranger. Perhaps the conversation with Philip had touched a deep chord in him, he thought. She had disappeared now beyond the hillside. Swiftly he ran to catch a final glimpse of her.

She was walking toward the distant woods, and as the sunlight touched her, it seemed once more that her hair was red-gold.

The beginnings of a cramp in his left arm awoke Philip an hour after dawn. He glanced down at the blond acolyte whose head rested on his bicep and gently eased his arm loose. Someone stirred to his right. A second girl, dark-haired and pretty, opened her eyes and smiled up at him.

"Did you sleep well, my lord?" she asked, her fingers sliding slowly over his belly.

"Wonderfully," he told her, his hand seizing her wrist. "But now I would like the answers to some questions."

"Can the questions not wait?" she whispered, rolling to face him.

"They cannot," he told her sternly. "Who owns this palace?"

"The Lady Aida."

"I do not know the name."

"She is the high priestess of the mysteries," said the girl.

"Well, darling one, tell her I wish to see her."

"Yes, lord." The girl threw back the sheet and stood. Philip gazed at her long back and slim waist, his eyes drawn to her rounded hips and perfect buttocks.

"Now!" he said, more powerfully than he intended. "Go *now*!"

The blond girl awoke and yawned. "Out!" roared Philip. "And get someone to send in a pitcher of cool water." After they had gone, the king rose, squeezed his eyes shut against the hammering in his head, and dragged open the curtains on the wide window.

Sunlight lanced his brain, and he turned away from it, cursing. The wine had been strong, but it was the dark seeds that he remembered so vividly. The girls carried them in small silver boxes and had offered them to Philip after the first bout of lovemaking. They dried the tongue but fired the mind and body. Colors seemed impossibly bright, while touch, taste, and hearing were all enhanced. Philip's strength had surged, along with his appetites.

But now his head pounded, his body feeling weak. The latter sensation was not one he enjoyed.

Dressing in a clean *chiton* of dark green, he sat on a couch and waited for the water. The dark-haired girl brought it, and he drank greedily. She offered him the silver box, opening the hinged lid to display the dark, shriveled seeds.

"They will restore your strength," she promised.

He was sorely tempted but waved her away. "What of the high priestess?" he asked.

"She will be here at noon, lord. I will tell her of your request."

"How many other guests are there in the palace?"

"Only one at the moment, the Lady Olympias."

"Olympias? Where is she from?"

"Epirus, lord. She is the daughter of the king."

"I'll see her, then," said Philip.

The girl looked shocked and then frightened. "No, lord, that is forbidden. She is undergoing the rite of union. No man may see her before the appointed night, especially her betrothed. The gods would strike him blind!"

"Send Parmenion to me."

"He is not in the palace, lord. He was seen running in the hills just after dawn."

"Then tell him when he returns," snapped Philip. "Now leave me alone!"

After she had gone, the king felt momentary regret for treating her shabbily, but so great was his irritation that the feeling soon passed.

He paced the room for an hour, then ate a breakfast of pears and goat's cheese and wandered out to the meadows beyond the palace. His mood was not lightened by seeing the horses there, thin-legged and weak. He sat on a wide gate and scanned the hills, where sheep and goats were grazing, tended by a slim boy.

What is the matter with you, Philip? The women were wonderfully willing and endlessly creative. Normally, after a night of lovemaking, he awoke feeling like a young Heracles. Those cursed seeds, he thought. Never again! He saw Parmenion running down the hillside and shouted to him. The Spartan slowed his run.

"Good morning, sire. You are awake early."

"I have been up for hours," said Philip. Parmenion leaned against the fence, stretching the muscles of his calves. "You are still fast, Leon. I think you could beat them all even now."

"Would that it were true, sire. But I do not fool myself. What is wrong?"

"Is it so plain?"

"You look like thunder."

"It is the waiting, Parmenion. Two years I've longed for this day, and now I can bear it no longer. She is here. Her name is Olympias . . . and I am not allowed to see her. Gods, man! I am Philip! I take what I want!"

Parmenion nodded. "We have been here but a day, sire. Be patient. As you said, this was ordained by the gods, so let it take its own course. Why don't you run for a while? It will clear your head."

"I'll race you to that grove of trees," said Philip, suddenly sprinting away. The morning breeze felt good in his face, and the contest made him feel alive, his headache disappearing. He could hear Parmenion just behind him, and he powered on up the hillside. It mattered nothing to him that the Spartan had already run for more than an hour. The contest was everything. He hurdled a low boulder and raced for the trees a hundred paces ahead. His breathing was more ragged now, and he could feel the burning in his calves, but also he could hear the Spartan just behind him. He slowed in his run. Parmenion came alongside. Philip thrust out his arm, pushing Parmenion off balance. The Spartan half stumbled and lost ground, giving Philip just the edge to reach the first tree and slap his palm against it.

"Unfair tactics!" Parmenion shouted.

"Victory," answered Philip weakly, sinking to the ground and raising his arm, his face red, his breathing fast and shallow. Within minutes he had recovered, and the two men sat in the shade gazing out over the fields and mountains, but again and again Philip's eyes were drawn to the white marble palace.

"I'll have a home like that," he said. "Even the gods will be glad to live there. I'll have it all one day, Parmenion."

"Is that all you want, sire?"

"No. What does any man want? Excitement. Power. I think of Bardylis often—old, withered, as good as dead. I look at myself and I see a strong young body. But I am not fooled,

Parmenion. Bardylis is only a reflection of the Philip to be. I want to live life to the full. I want not a single regret to haunt my dotage."

"You are asking a great deal, Philip," said Parmenion softly. "All men have regrets, even kings."

Philip looked at Parmenion and smiled. "For two years I have asked you to call me Philip when we are alone, yet you wait till now. Why is that?"

The Spartan shrugged. "These are strange days. Yesterday you spoke to me like a father. Then I met a woman, and I felt excitement such as I have not known in a decade. Today I feel . . . different—like a man again."

"Did you bed her?"

Parmenion chuckled. "Sometimes, Philip, your predictability dazzles me. No, I did not bed her. But in truth, I wanted to. And that sensation has been a stranger to me for too long. By the way, how many women did you have in your rooms last night? By the sounds it must have been a troupe of dancers."

"A mere twenty or thirty," answered Philip. "So what was this woman's name?"

"I don't know."

"Where does she live?"

"I don't know that, either."

"I see. You don't think it might be a little difficult to further this relationship? What did she look like?"

"She wore a veil."

"So the general Parmenion has fallen for a woman whose face he has not seen and whose name he does not know. I am at a loss to understand the nature of your arousal. Did she have nice feet?"

Parmenion's laughter rippled out. He lay back on the grass and stared at the sky. "I did not see her feet," he said. Then the laughter came again; it was infectious, and Philip began to chuckle, his dark mood evaporating.

After a while both men returned to the palace, where the king ate a second breakfast. The dark-haired girl came to him just after noon. "The Lady Aida will see you now, lord," she said. Philip followed her down a long corridor to a high-ceilinged room where statues of young women lined the walls. A woman was waiting by the southern window, and she turned as Philip entered. She was dressed in a dark, hooded robe, her face pale as ivory. Philip swallowed hard as he recognized her from his first dream.

"At last we meet," she said.

"Where is my bride?" whispered Philip.

"She will be waiting for you," said the hooded woman. "Tomorrow, on the night of the third mystery, she will be brought to your rooms. But there is something you must do, King of Macedon."

"Name it."

"You will not go to her until the third hour after midnight; you will not see her before then. At that appointed hour she will conceive your son—not a moment before, not a minute after. You will lie together in the third hour. If this is not done, there will be no marriage."

Philip laughed. "You believe I will have a problem in that area?"

"I hope not, Philip," she answered coldly. "Much depends on it. This son will be greater than any warrior before him, but only if he is conceived in the third hour."

"As I said, I see no reason to fear failure."

"Then I will give you two. If you fail, all your dreams of greatness will come to nothing; the gods will desert you. And secondly, you already have a son: Arrhidaeus. He is simple-minded, his limbs weak; your wife Phila died in giving birth to him. Apart from this one chance, Philip, all you will sire are daughters. What I offer you now is a chance—your only chance—to sire a perfect heir."

"How did you know of Arrhidaeus?" whispered Philip.

"I know all your secrets. I know the secrets of the world. Be prepared, King of Macedon. Olympias will await you."

Aida watched the Macedonian turn and stalk from the room. As the door closed behind him, she returned to her high-

backed chair and sat, her thoughts uneasy, her emotions confused.

Philip was a powerful man, his personal magnetism compel-
ling, yet something was wrong, and Aida's tension grew. So
much depended on this union, so many plans laid over so
many years.

Aida had been a child when her mother first told her of the
dream of the dark birth and of the many failures that had
followed. Only once in each fifty-year cycle did the harmony
of the universe falter, giving rise to a unique moment of plane-
tary confusion.

When the last alignment took place in Mesopotamia, Aida
was fourteen. Her mother had bewitched the great king and
prepared an acolyte of exceptional beauty. The wedding night
had proceeded as planned, but the girl—her mind dazed by
the drugs—had wandered from the balcony, falling to her
death on the marble stone of the courtyard. Aida's mother had
been desolate, and for two months she refused to speak; then,
just when it seemed she would recover, she slashed her throat
with a bronze knife.

Now the moment was here once more. There would be no
balcony for Olympias, no danger to the princess. Philip was a
ram who would need no assistance to fulfill his . . . necessary . . . task.

So what could go wrong? Aida did not know. But she felt the
icy touch of fear.

She closed her eyes and soared, her spirit rising high above
the palace, moving over the green hills, seeking, ever seeking,
without knowing what she sought.

The assassins sent from the city of Olynthus were dead,
their boat destroyed in a sudden storm. Only one had reached
the Samothracian shore, and his head had been crushed by a
heavy rock wielded by two of Aida's acolytes. There was no
danger from assassins. Aida would know.

But she could not dismiss her fears. She trusted her talents
and her intuition. Although she could not walk the paths of the
past and future, still Aida was powerful, reading the hearts

and minds of men, anticipating events. The rulers of the city of Olynthus feared Philip. It was not difficult to second-guess their intentions, especially now that the king's former favorite, Nicanor, entertained an Olynthian lover at his home in Pella.

The storm had been costly—two of Aida's acolytes sacrificed, their hearts torn from their bodies. But it was worth more than even those to ensure that the lord of fire could be born in the flesh. Aida would sacrifice a nation for such a holy miracle.

Returning to her body, she opened her eyes.

Where is the peril?

Think, Aida! Use your mind! She had searched the island, the seventeen villages and four ports. Nothing. She thought of Tamis, almost wishing her alive so that she could focus her hatred once more.

Would that I could have killed you a dozen, dozen times! The old priestess had been a constant sore for decades. Curiously, her death had done little to ease Aida's hatred. All that power wasted on the whore, she thought, remembering with exquisite distaste Tamis' lovers.

The other priestess had worried her at first, but she also was flawed.

Where, then, the danger?

Closing her eyes once more, she flew across the seas, hovering over the temple. A tall man was tending the garden, and there were no supplicants waiting in the meadows. Swiftly Aida armored herself with protective spells, then entered the temple. It was empty.

Where are you, my dove? she thought.

Returning to Samothrace, she searched the island once more—carefully, thoroughly, each hill and wood.

At last, weary and almost spent, she returned to the palace and walked to the kennels below the outer wall. The black hounds began to bay as she entered. Pulling open the wooden gate, she moved in among them, crouching down as they surged around her. Summoning the image of Derae, she cast the picture into the mind of each hound, imprinting it, holding

it until the baying stopped. Then, lifting her arm, she pointed
to the open gate.

"Go!" she shouted. "Taste of her blood, break her bones!
Go!"

Derae sat in a hollow below the branches of a flowering tree,
her mind alert. She sensed the search and located Aida's spirit
as she soared from the palace. Calming the fluttering of panic
that beset her, she leaned back against a tree trunk, her arms
crossed, her hands on her shoulders. She merged her mind
with the tree, feeling her way into the bark, through the
oozing sap that killed most insects, on into the capillaries
where water was drawn to the leaves and flowers.

She was Derae no longer. She was the tree, her roots deep
and questing, seeking moisture and goodness from the dark
earth, her branches growing, stretching, flowing with slow
life. She felt sunlight on her leaves and concentrated on the
seed-bearing blossoms that would ensure her existence
through eternity. It was peaceful within the tree . . . so peaceful.

At last she withdrew her spirit and searched for Aida. The
witch woman had returned to the palace. Derae rose and
walked slowly down to the meadows, close by the wood,
where tonight the acolytes would celebrate the third mystery.
There was a stream here, and she drank deeply.

In the distance she heard the baying of hounds, ready for
the hunt.

Adjusting her veil, she waited, sitting on a boulder, not
looking in the direction from which she knew he would come.
His footfalls were soft, unconsciously stealthy.

"We meet again, lady," he said, and she turned.

"How are you, Savra?"

"I am well—even better now that I have seen you again."

Her spirit eyes scanned his face. The boyish features had
long since been replaced by the angular, almost harsh lines of
the man. Yet still he was the Parmenion of memory. Her
Parmenion!

"How prettily you speak—for a soldier."

"Not usually, lady. You bring out the best in me. What is your name?"

She was suddenly torn, filled with the desire to remove her veil, to show him her face, to tell him how she had missed him through all those lonely years. She turned away. "No names," she said at last.

"Is something wrong?" he asked, moving closer.

"Nothing," she replied, forcing gaiety into her voice. "It is a beautiful day."

A sleek black hound padded from the woods, coming closer to them. Suddenly its lips drew back to show long fangs, a low growl rumbling in its throat. Parmenion stepped in front of Derae, his hand on the dagger at his side.

"Be off with you!" he roared, and the hound backed away several paces—then charged at Derae. Parmenion's dagger flashed into the air. The hound leapt at the woman, but the Spartan threw himself at it, his arm curling around the dog's neck, the dagger blade plunging into its side. As he rose to his feet, two more hounds came running from the woods.

Parmenion turned to see Derae walking toward the palace, the hounds closing in on her.

"No!" screamed Parmenion in the sudden realization that he could not reach her in time. Yet even as the beasts prepared to leap, they slumped to the ground. She did not turn to see this apparent miracle but walked on through the palace gate.

Parmenion moved to the hounds. They were sleeping peacefully. Bewildered, he sheathed his dagger and ran into the courtyard.

There was no sign of the woman.

"Look at this," said Philip, pointing to the long white cloak and the silver full-faced helm that lay on one of the couches. "Can you believe I am supposed to wear that *during* the consummation?"

Parmenion hefted the helm. It was beautifully crafted of

shining silver edged with gold, the ear guards embossed with
what appeared to be demons bearing jagged knives. At the
nape of the neck were protective plates of silver, no wider
than a man's thumb. There was no crested plume, but to the
sides two black ram's horns curved from the temples to the
neck.

"It is stunning," said the Spartan, "and very old. The workmanship is rare."

"Rare?" stormed Philip. "Rare it may be. It is also rare to
ask a man to mount a woman wearing such a . . . such a . . .
bridal hat!"

Parmenion smiled. "You said yourself that this marriage has
been ordained. Surely you expected a little ritual. Even Bardylis made the wedding ceremony last a full day, with dances,
speeches, and athletic contests between his guards."

"Yes, he did," said Philip, "but there I was at the center.
Here I feel like a bystander, an incidental player." He stalked
to the window and stared out over the night-dark woods and
the distant fires. Parmenion joined him. "Listen to them," said
the king as the night breeze carried sounds of laughter and
music from the woods. "You know what they are doing?"

"No, sire."

"Neither do I . . . and that irritates me, Parmenion. They
are probably dancing naked around those fires, and I am
sitting here waiting to be led into my bride like a prize ram.
Am I so ugly that I need a helmet to disguise myself?"

"I think," offered Parmenion, "that you are nervous. I
would also advise you to hold back on the wine; you have
drained almost a full pitcher."

"Wine has no effect on my abilities," snapped Philip. "Why
don't we sneak out there and watch them. What do you
think?"

"I think that would not be wise."

"Gods, man, you are so staid!" Philip slumped down on a
couch and poured the last of his wine. "Get me some more
drink, would you; there's a good fellow."

Parmenion wandered out into the deserted corridor, following the stairs down to the kitchens. It was close to midnight, and even he was beginning to feel a sense of rising excitement over the forthcoming wedding.

The mysteries fascinated Parmenion, as indeed did the culture of this volcanic isle. Xenophon himself had been initiated here but had told Parmenion little of the ceremonies save that they involved arcane knowledge of the "greater gods." One of these, Parmenion recalled, was Kadmilos, the ram-horned immortal, the spirit of chaos.

The Spartan walked into the empty kitchens, located a pitcher of wine, and returned to the king's rooms. Philip was once more drinking happily.

"You found some more," said Parmenion, seeing the golden pitcher beside the king.

"A woman brought it. You cannot fault the hospitality here, Parmenion, and it is the finest wine I've ever tasted. Have some."

"I saw no woman, sire. From where did she come?"

Philip shrugged. "The palace is like a maze. Who knows? Come. Drink."

Parmenion poured a goblet of the king's wine and tasted it. It was strong, heavy, and almost sweet. Just then they heard the chanting, and he put down his wine and wandered to the window. A torch-lit procession was moving from the woods. "Your bride is coming, sire," said the Spartan. Philip leaned out, his hands gripping the stone sill.

At the front of the procession, dressed like an ancient Minoan princess, was a flame-haired girl of great beauty, her hair tied with golden ribbons, her breasts bared and rouged, her hips clad in swirling silk.

"By all the gods of Olympus!" whispered Philip. "Is that not a sight on which to feast the soul?"

Parmenion swallowed hard. The girl was the image of Derae: the wide-set eyes, the full, sensual mouth. The Spartan stepped back from the window, tearing his eyes from the scene. The procession moved on into the palace, the chanting becoming muffled and distant. Philip poured yet another goblet of wine, draining it at a single swallow.

"It is almost time, sire," said Parmenion. "You should prepare."

"Yes," replied Philip, his voice slurring. "Pre . . . prepare." He struggled from his *chiton*, staggered toward the white cloak, and fell onto a couch. "Damn!" he muttered. "Legs betrayed me." Parmenion ran to him.

"What is it, sire?"

"Don't . . . don't know. Help . . . me up." Parmenion pulled the king upright on the couch. "I'll be all right. Get me some water."

The Spartan heard sounds of footfalls in the corridor outside and listened as the door of the bedchamber opened. Moving to the hangings between the rooms, he drew them tight, then took water to the king. Philip's eyes were swollen and bleary. "They are here, sire," whispered Parmenion. "You must stir yourself." Philip took the water, which spilled to his naked chest. He tried to drink, but his head sagged back, the goblet falling from his hand.

Parmenion cursed softly. It was beyond belief. He had watched Philip on many drinking bouts; the man's capacity for wine or ale was legendary. Never had Parmenion seen him like this. And after only two pitchers of wine? It was inconceivable.

The smell of sweet incense drifted through the hangings, and he heard the acolytes withdraw from the chamber. Silently he crept across the room, opening a small gap in the drapes. The room beyond was lit by yellow-flamed lanterns, and the naked form of Olympias lay on the broad bed. She was writhing and moaning softly.

Parmenion cursed again and returned to the king.

The hour was upon them.

And Philip lay in a drunken stupor.

Derae slipped from the palace after the torch-lit procession had passed by. Swiftly she made for the hills and the old stone circle half-hidden by the trees of the apple orchard. Her spirits were high, and she fought to stem the heady sensation of victory.

"I did it, Tamis," she whispered. "I stopped him. There will be no Dark God!"

Running down a hillside, she saw the darkness of the trees looming. Her spirit eyes caught a flicker of movement in the shadows, and she dropped to her knees, waiting, scouring the trees.

There! By the undergrowth to the right.

Derae's spirit swept into the sky, hovering over the trees. A young woman in black robes was waiting, knife in hand. Derae flew to the left, but another woman crouched there, similarly armed.

Returning to her body, Derae retraced her steps up to the hilltop, then made an angling run to the left. She was only a few minutes from the stone circle. Once she was there, no assassin could follow.

She could hear her pursuers crashing through the undergrowth, shouting to other, unseen companions.

Suddenly she sensed Aida!

Darkness fell on her like a cloak thrown over her head. She was blind! Panic swept through her as, falling to her hands and knees, she crawled forward. Leaves brushed her face. Her fingers ran over the bush. It was thick and high. Crawling into its center, she pulled the branches around her, scooping dead leaves and dirt over her robe.

Then her spirit rose again.

Her blindness remained, but now her concentration deepened. Fire blazed from her eyes, and the spell of darkness gave way.

A scaled hand lanced for her face, talons sinking deep into her spirit flesh. The pain was agonizing, but her own hand came up to grip the reptilian wrist. Flames burned along the length of the arm, sweeping down over the demon and enveloping him in fire.

In an instant Derae was armored in breastplate and greaves of white silver, a Spartan helm on her head and in her hand a sword of blinding starlight.

"Where are you, Aida?" she called. "Face me if you dare!"

"I dare, child," came the whispering sound of Aida's voice, and Derae spun to see the dark-cloaked woman hovering nearby. Aida smiled. "Foolish girl to come here in the flesh. Even now the sharp knives are closing in on your hiding place. Fly to it, Derae!"

"I have beaten you," Derae shouted. "It does not matter if I die."

"And how have you beaten me, child? I am still here."

"There will be no dark birth," answered Derae, glancing down to where the acolytes were searching the undergrowth, moving ever closer to her hidden body. She did not want to die and fought to contain her fear.

Aida's laughter cut through her like a cold knife. "You think a child—even a talented child—can thwart the powers of Kadmilos?" She raised her arms. Black snakes fountained from her fingertips, hissing through the night air to cover Derae in a writhing mass, their fangs glittering in the moonlight.

Ignoring the pain, Derae closed her eyes. The snakes changed color, shifting from black to red, their shapes twisting into tiny circles, until they fell from her as rose petals, drifting down to the ground.

"You cannot harm me," said Derae softly. "Whereas—"

A dazzling sphere of light blazed up around Aida, trapping her at its center. Derae fled for her body just as an acolyte discovered it.

The knife blade swept down, but Derae's hand grabbed the wrist. Rolling to her knees, the priestess lashed her fist into the woman's face, hurling her back. Then she was up and sprinting for the stone circle.

Behind her the pursuers screamed their hatred. Derae ran on. A hurled knife flashed by her head as she leapt over a fallen stone column. Turning in the center of the circle, she raised her arms. The world shimmered. As the gateway closed around her, she heard Aida's voice whisper in her mind.

"There will be another time, my dove!"

Olympias lay on the silk-covered bed, her body floating on a sea of pleasure, her skin tingling, her mind exploding with colors. She licked her lips, running her fingers over her breasts and belly, aware of an almost painful desire.

"Philip!" she called. The room was spinning, the drugs in her system approaching the height of their powers. She had danced at the fire, felt the touch and caress of a score of acolytes, their lips soft and sweet with wine. The secrets of the third mystery had come to her with the music of the night, the breeze from the distant holy peak of Korifi Fengari. She would give birth to a god-king, a man of awesome talents. His name would echo throughout history, his deeds remaining unequaled as long as the stars hung in the sky. "Philip!"

Even in her drugged state she could feel the passing of time, sense that the mystical hour was almost spent. She rolled to her side.

The curtains parted.

There he stood, naked but for his cloak and the ram-horned helm of Kadmilos. He strode toward her, and she opened her arms. For a moment he stood and gazed at her body, then harshly he entered her. She screamed, her hands pulling at his back, the metal mask of the helm cold against her face.

Her fingers moved up to touch the metal, stroking the black horns.

His head lifted, and she found herself gazing into the eyes within the helm. Then the drugs overwhelmed her, and she slid into darkness, her last thought a strange one.

In the lantern light Philip's green eyes seemed—impossibly—to have changed to blue.

THE TEMPLE, SUMMER, 357 B.C.

Derae awoke just before noon. Throwing back the sheet, she moved to the window, her heart light. She had seen Parmenion, and she had destroyed the plans of Aida. Today she would leave the temple and journey to Macedonia, there to await Parmenion's return.

She knew now that he still loved her, and they would at least have many years to enjoy together. She felt young again, full of life and laughter.

It had been so easy to drug Philip's wine. All the years of fear had been so unnecessary.

The sun was warm on her face, but at her back she felt the blast of cold air and turned swiftly. A shadow was growing on the wall by the door, swelling like a winged demon. Derae prepared herself for the attack, but it did not come, the shadows swirling into a cloak around the spirit form of Aida.

"What do you want here?" Derae asked.

"I wanted to thank you," said Aida. "Without your help and that of your miserable predecessor, my dreams could not have been fulfilled." The hooded woman laughed, the sound chilling. "You can walk the paths of the past and the future. Walk them now—and weep, my dove!"

In an instant she was gone.

Derae sat back on the bed and closed her eyes, flying once more to the palace on Samothrace, feeling her way back through the hours. She saw herself bringing the wine to Philip, pouring him a drink, watching him drain it. She saw her flight and her battle with Aida.

Then, with a sense of dread, she returned to the palace, watching Parmenion's attempts to rouse the king. She cried out when she saw the Spartan stand up and remove his clothes, donning the helm and cloak of the chaos spirit.

"Oh, sweet heaven!" she whispered as he embraced the naked girl.

Derae fled the scene, opening her eyes back at the temple. *"Without your help . . . my dreams could not have been fulfilled."*

She saw it all now, the arrogance and the stupidity.

Tamis had seen the vision of the dark birth and then the face of Parmenion. Believing him to be a human sword she could wield against the forces of darkness, Tamis had entered his life, molding his future, forcing him along a path of bitterness and hatred. She had created in him the perfect warrior, the perfect killer of men. . . .

The perfect human father for the Dark God.

Anger flared in Derae. The years of dedication, of healing, the years of hopes and dreams. All for nothing!

Now there would be no life with Parmenion, no journey to love in Macedonia.

She gazed out of the window, over the rolling hills and meadows and the cloud-shrouded mountains, seeing again the visions of bloodshed and horror that had haunted her for decades. Armies marching across bloody battlefields, widows and orphans, ruined cities, fallen empires. Sometimes the Dark God had been Greek, at other times Persian—a chief from Parthia, a young prince from the tribes to the far north.

Once he had even been black, leading his troops from the lush jungles far to the south of Egypt. These myriad futures no longer existed in the same form. Derae allowed the oceans of time to lift and carry her into distant tomorrows, and there she saw a young man with golden hair, his face beautiful, his armor bright with the glow of gold.

In every future the armies of Macedon were marching, their long spears stained with blood.

She studied the golden figure through hundreds of possible—even probable—futures. All were the same: the Dark God triumphant, becoming immortal, a creature of blood and fire, the human flesh burning away, the full evil of the horned one sitting on the thrones of the world. Despite her despair Derae searched on, finding at last a glimmer of hope like the fading spark of a winter fire.

The child had been conceived at the last stroke of the unholy hour, giving him at least a spark of humanity. The Dark God would be powerful within him, but at that moment Derae decided to spend her life fanning that spark, seeking to feed the human spirit within the devil who was to be.

"At the last you were right, Tamis," she said sadly. "We cannot fight them with their own weapons. There can never be victory there." And like the old priestess before her, Derae prayed for guidance.

And she saw, as Tamis had seen, one man standing beside the Dark God, a strong man—a good man.

Parmenion—the Lion of Macedon.

PHAEDRA closed her eyes, seeking to locate the source of the danger. Around her the sounds were all reassuring: the steady, slow, almost rhythmic hoofbeats of the royal guard, the rolling of the brass-rimmed wagon wheels over the shifting shale and scree, conversation and laughter from the soldiers on either side of the heavily curtained carriage.

But somewhere deep within her Phaedra could hear the screams of the dying, while scenes of blood and violence flashed across her mind. Yet she could not pin them down. She opened her pale blue eyes and gazed across the carriage cabin to where Olympias lay on pillows of down-filled silk. The princess was asleep. Phaedra longed to reach over to her. Anger flared briefly, but the seeress swiftly quelled it. Olympias was beautiful, but that beauty was now marred by her marriage to the barbarian from Pella, ruined by the babe swelling her belly to twice its size. She tore her gaze from the sleeping face.

"I don't love you anymore," she whispered, hoping that by

speaking the lie she could make it true. It was a vain hope.

We are sisters again, no more than that, thought Phaedra. Their love was now as dead as the blooms of summer. The seeress sighed, remembering their first meeting three years before. Two fourteen-year-old girls in the king's palace; Phaedra shy and yet blessed—cursed?—with the gift of seeing, and Olympias, gregarious and joy-filled, her body already sleek, her skin glowing with health, her face beautiful beyond imagining.

Phaedra felt comfortable with the princess, for she had never been able to *see* her life or read the secrets hidden in the dark corridors of her mind. Olympias made her feel ordinary, and that was a gift beyond price.

No one understood the loneliness of seeing. Every touch brought visions. A kind, handsome man stoops to kiss your hand, but you see the lecher, the dominator, the possessor. A woman smiles, pats your arm, and you feel her hatred at your youth. All the cobwebs of the human soul laid bare to your all-seeing eyes. Phaedra shivered.

With Olympias it was so different. No visions, no unpleasantness. Just love, first as sisters, then . . .

The carriage lurched as the huge wheels rolled over a stone. Phaedra pulled back a curtain and stared out of the window. To the left was the glittering Lake Prespa, beyond it the rearing Pindos mountains separating Macedonia and Illyria.

Olympias yawned and stretched. Running her fingers through her flame-red hair, she sat up and smiled at Phaedra. "Where are we?"

"Soon we will reach the plain," answered Phaedra. "There we will be met by the king's escort."

"I am hot and thirsty," Olympias complained, "and this awful wagon is making me feel sick."

Phaedra stood, opening the flap on the roof of the cabin and calling out to the driver. He hauled on the reins, and Olympias stepped down into the sunlight. Immediately the Epirite captain of the guard dismounted, bringing a water skin and filling a silver cup. Olympias smiled. "Thank you, Herkon, you are most kind."

Phaedra watched the young man blush. She did not need to touch him to know his thoughts. As she stepped down alongside Olympias, the vision struck her again, this time with awesome power. She saw horsemen thundering down the slopes, the wagon overturned, Herkon dead, his throat slashed open. . . .

She screamed and fainted.

She awoke to see a man bending over her, dabbing at her face with a water-soaked cloth. "They are coming," she whispered.

"Who is coming? What are you talking about?" Herkon asked.

The air was suddenly filled with the thunder of hoofbeats. For a moment only Phaedra thought the vision had returned, but then Herkon lunged to his feet, his cavalry saber hissing from its scabbard.

From the slopes of the mountains came hundreds of riders, bright cloaks streaming behind them like rainbow banners.

"Illyrians!" shouted Herkon, running for his horse. The fifty soldiers of Epirus drew their weapons—then the attackers were upon them. Olympias ran to where Phaedra lay, dragging the girl back under the wagon. Dust rose in choking clouds. Olympias covered her mouth with a linen kerchief, and the two women huddled together, listening to the clash of weapons and the screams of the dying. A horse reared close to the wagon, the rider falling headfirst to the ground, his face striking the wheel.

It was Herkon, his throat open, his dead eyes gazing at Olympias, who turned away her head.

The battle seemed to rage for hours, but at last the dust began to settle. Shapes could be seen, men moving among the wounded Epirites and killing them with sharp daggers. Olympias drew a slender knife from the hidden sheath high on her thigh and waited. Phaedra closed her eyes, unable to bear the terror any longer.

"Look what we have here!" called a warrior, squatting down to look under the wagon. Dropping to his knees, he crawled toward the women, his hand reaching out. Olympias plunged the knife into his eye, and he dropped without a sound, his head pinning the dagger firmly in the socket. Olympias struggled in vain to free it. But then a group of warriors took hold of the wagon, overturning it. Olympias rose, her green eyes angry, her chin held high.

"You will die for this," she promised them.

"No one will die," said a tall handsome warrior with blond hair and a braided forked beard. "But Philip of Macedon will pay a fine price to get you back. If you are kind to me, Princess, it may be that your short stay with us will be pleasant."

Olympias' eyes swept the group, her contempt apparent. Then she glanced beyond them to the eastern hills. A line of riders appeared, and at their center rode a warrior on a huge gray horse. The man wore armor of gleaming bronze and a helm with a white horsehair plume.

"I think you will find," she said slowly, "that Philip of Macedon has already set the price—and it is you who will pay."

"Arcetas! Look!" shouted a man, pointing to the stationary riders. Arcetas swore. He scanned the Macedonian line, counting no more than seventy cavalrymen.

"To horse!" he bellowed. "They are too few to stop us. Cut them down!"

The Illyrians mounted and galloped toward the waiting Macedonians.

"Watch, Phaedra," whispered Olympias, dropping down beside the terrified seeress. "Watch how my husband fights!" Phaedra opened her eyes to see the sunlight gleam from the bronze breastplate of the Macedonian on the giant gray. He drew his sword, holding it high.

And the Macedonians hurtled down to meet the charge, the gray rider forming the point of a wedge that cleaved the

Illyrian ranks, splitting them, destroying their momentum. Olympias saw the fork-bearded Arcetas straining to reach the gray rider. Dust swirled, but still she could just make out the fight that followed as their swords clashed. There was no question in Olympias' mind as to the outcome, no fear for the safety of the gray rider. She merely waited for the inevitable and leapt with joy as the gleaming sword swept through Arcetas' neck, his head lolling, blood fountaining into the air.

"That is the price, you whoreson!" she shouted.

The Illyrians broke and fled, the Macedonians re-forming their lines and galloping after them. But the rider on the gray, followed by three officers, approached the women.

"Philip!" called Olympias, running to meet him.

"No, my lady," he answered, removing his helm. "It is I, Parmenion."

They found a camping site in a grove of trees close to the River Haliacmon. Parmenion went to the wounded men, who had been placed away from the main group lest their cries during surgery upset the women. The Macedonian had lost seventeen men in the battle, with seven hurt. The crushed Illyrians had suffered more than eighty dead. Parmenion knelt by a young soldier who had lost three fingers of his right hand. The boy's face was gray with shock and pain and shone with sweat.

"I am useless now," he whispered. "What shall I do?"

"The gods gave you two hands, Peris; you must learn to use the left. It is not so bad. You are not a foot soldier, so you will not need to worry about forming the line. You are a cavalryman—aye, and a good one. You have too much courage to let such a small wound overcome you."

"I am no good with my left, General."

"We will work on it, you and I."

Parmenion moved on to the next man, but he had bled to death. The general covered the dead man's face with a cloak and moved on.

The surgeon, Bernios, rose to greet him as he finished his rounds. "We did well," said Bernios, wiping the sweat from his bald head with a bloodstained towel.

"Had we been an hour earlier, there would have been no battle," replied Parmenion. "That would have been better, my friend."

"Indeed it would, General. But—" The man shrugged and spread his hands. "—it could have been considerably worse. We might have been an hour later, and then the king's new bride would have been stolen from him. I believe Philip would have been mildly aggrieved."

Parmenion smiled. Slapping the surgeon on the shoulder, he returned to the main camp. The women's quarters had been set back into the trees, where they could enjoy privacy, while the fifty-one surviving soldiers sat around four camp fires. Parmenion called to Nicanor, signaling the young man to follow him.

"Are there scouts out?" asked the general.

"Yes, sir. Six men patrolling the hills. Three others are stationed north, west, and east of the woods."

"Good. You fought well today. The king will be proud of you."

"The king long since ceased to care about me," answered Nicanor with a shy smile. "But I truly do not mind, Parmenion. Do not concern yourself for me. I was his favorite for a time. Now there are others. I am getting old, you see. I am twenty-seven now." Nicanor shrugged. "But Olympias is very beautiful, don't you think?"

"Yes," answered Parmenion too abruptly. Nicanor looked up sharply, but Parmenion turned away. "See to their needs," he said over his shoulder as he walked to his blankets.

The younger man took up a wineskin, which he carried back to the queen's camp fire. Olympias was sitting on some cushions brought from the carriage; the girl he took to be her maid was tending the blaze.

"I have some wine for you, ladies," said Nicanor, bowing deeply.

Olympias flashed him a dazzling smile. "And you are, sir?" she asked.

"Nicanor. I am Parmenion's first captain."

"Join us, Nicanor," ordered the queen. He filled their wine cups, added water, then folded his cloak to make a seat. "Why is Parmenion not here?" Olympias asked.

"He is . . . er . . . weary, my lady. He did not sleep much last night. He was concerned to be here on time. He feared . . . well, he feared the Illyrians might raid, and he was right. He usually is; it is most galling."

"And yet you like him?"

"Oh, yes, my lady. He is a fine general, the best in the world. He has built Philip's army into a force to strike fear into the hearts of all our enemies."

"But he is not Macedonian," Olympias pointed out.

"Half-Macedonian," replied Nicanor. "He was raised in Sparta."

"Perhaps, then, we should forgive his bad manners in not attending us. Spartans are not renowned for their courtesies."

"I do not believe he meant to be discourteous," Nicanor said. "Far from it. He ordered me to see to your needs. I believe he felt you would sooner rest and recover from your ordeal than endure his company."

Olympias smiled and, reaching out, touched Nicanor's arm. "You are a good friend to your general and a powerful advocate. I shall forgive him instantly. And now, Nicanor, I would like to rest."

The young man rose and bowed once more before gathering up his cloak and walking back through the trees.

"You are shameless," said Phaedra. "You quite dazzled the poor man."

Olympias let the smile fade from her face. "This is a foreign land," she said softly. "I will need friends here. Why did Parmenion not come?"

"Perhaps it was as the officer said, that he was weary."

"No. He would not meet my eyes when he rode up. Still, what does it matter? We are safe. The future is bright."

"Do you love Philip?" asked Phaedra suddenly.

"Love? He is my husband, the father of the child I carry.

What has love to do with it? And anyway, I have met him only once—on the night of the wedding in Samothrace seven months ago."

"What was it like on the Isle of Mysteries when he made love to you?"

Olympias leaned back, smiling at the memory. "The first time was magical, strange . . . but in the morning it was as it always is. The man ruts and grunts, sighs and sleeps." She yawned. "Fetch me my blankets, Phaedra. And some more cushions. I will sleep now."

"You should sleep in the carriage. You will be warmer."

"I want to see the stars," answered Olympias. "I want to watch the Huntress."

Olympias lay down, her mind lazily drifting back to Samothrace and the night of the mysteries. The women, scores of them, had danced in the grove, drinking, laughing, chewing the sacred herbs that brought visions, bright colorful dreams. The torch-lit procession then filed to the palace, and Olympias remembered them carrying her to Philip's bed.

She had waited, her mind spinning, the colors supernaturally bright . . . red hangings, yellow silks, golden cups.

And he had come to her—his face, as ritual demanded, hidden by the helm of chaos. She had felt the metal against her cheek, felt his body cover her like a fire-warmed cloak.

Wrapped in her blankets, the new Queen of Macedonia slept beneath the stars.

Parmenion lay awake staring at the same stars, recalling the same night. His sense of shame was strong, painful almost. There were many deeds in his life that had left him with sorrow, others that had caused scars to both body and spirit. But shame was new to the Spartan.

The night had been like this one, stars like gems on sable, the air clean and fresh. Philip was drunk as he waited for his bride; he had collapsed on a couch just as the women brought his new wife to his bedchamber.

Parmenion had glanced through a gap in the curtains to see Olympias, naked, her body glistening, waiting . . . waiting.

He tried to tell himself that it was vital that the wedding be consummated on this night, reminded himself that Philip had told him exactly that.

"If I do not perform within the sacred hour, the wedding will be canceled. Can you believe that, Parmenion?"

But that was not why the Spartan had donned the ancient helm. He had looked upon the naked woman—and he had wanted her, as he had desired no one since his love had been stolen from him a quarter of a century before. He had made love to her, and when she slept, he went to Philip, dressing the unconscious king in the helm and cloak and carrying him to her bed.

You betrayed the king you swore to serve. How will you redeem yourself?

The night was chilly, and Parmenion rose. Wrapping his black woolen cloak tightly around his shoulders, he strolled out to where the sentries kept watch.

"I'm awake, sir," said the first man. In the darkness Parmenion did not recognize him.

"I did not doubt it," the general told him. "You are a soldier of Macedon." He wandered from the woods and down to the banks of the Haliacmon. The water was dark as the Styx but glimmering in the starlight. He sat on a boulder and thought of Derae.

Five days of love—fierce, passionate love. Then they had taken her from him, carrying her to the shores of Asia, where they hurled her into the sea to drown, her hands tied behind her. A sacrifice to the gods, for the protection of Sparta.

And how Sparta had needed protection! Parmenion remembered the battle at Leuctra, where his strategic genius had seen the fall of the Spartan army, the crushing of Sparta's dreams.

"You are Parmenion, the Death of Nations," the old seeress had told him. How right she was. Last year he had led the

Macedonians against the Illyrian king, Bardylis, devastating his army. The old king had died within seven months of the defeat, his country in ruins.

Looking up at the stars, Parmenion pictured Derae's face, her flame-gold hair, her green eyes. "What am I without you?" he whispered.

"Talking to yourself, General?" said a voice from close by. A young soldier moved from the shadows of the riverbank.

"It happens when a man gets old," Parmenion told him. The moon emerged from behind the clouds, and the Spartan recognized Cleiton, a young soldier from eastern Macedonia who had joined the army the previous autumn.

"It is a quiet night, sir," said Cleiton. "Were you praying?"

"After a fashion. I was thinking about a girl I used to know."

"Was she beautiful?" asked the young man, laying his spear against a rock and sitting opposite the general.

"She was very beautiful . . . but she died. Are you married?"

"Yes, sir. I have a wife and two sons in Crousia. They are moving to Pella as soon as I can afford to rent a house."

"That may be some time."

"Oh, I don't think so, sir. There'll be another war soon. With fighting wages, I should see Lacia again within six months."

"You want a war, then?" Parmenion asked.

"Of course, sir. It is our time. The Illyrians are destroyed, the Paionians also. Soon it will be to the east in Thrace or south against Pherai. Or maybe Olynthus. Philip is a warrior king. He will see the army is looked after."

"I expect that he will," agreed Parmenion, rising. "And I hope you get your house."

"Thank you, sir. Good night."

"Good night, Cleiton." The general returned to his blankets, but his sleep was haunted by dreams. Derae was running on a green hillside, her eyes wide with fear. He tried to go to her, to explain that all was well, but as he approached, she screamed and sped away. He could not catch her and stopped by a stream, where he gazed down at his reflection. Pale eyes in the bronze mask of chaos stared back at him. Pulling the helm from his head, he called out to her.

"Stop! It is I, Parmenion."

But she did not hear him and vanished from sight.

He awoke with a start and sat up. His back was aching, and a slow, painful pounding hammered within his skull. "You fool," he told himself, "you forgot your sylphium." There was water heating on a fire. Dipping a cup into the pot, he almost scalded his fingers. Then, adding his dried herbs to the liquid, he stirred it with his dagger, waited for it to cool, and then drained the infusion. Almost at once the pain departed.

Bernios approached. "You look dreadful, my friend," said the surgeon. "Do you ever sleep?"

"When I need it."

"Well, you need it now. You are not a young man anymore. Your body needs rest."

"I am forty-three years old," Parmenion snapped. "That is hardly ancient. And I can still run twenty miles should I so choose."

"I did not say you were decrepit, I merely pointed out that you are no longer young. You are very sharp this morning—that also is a sign of age."

"My back aches, and do not tell me it is because I am old. There is an iron spear point lodged under my shoulder blade. But what of you? Why do you not sleep?"

"Another man died in the night. I sat with him," said Bernios. "No one should die alone. He was stabbed through the belly; there is no worse pain than that. But he didn't complain, save at the end."

"Who was he?"

"I did not ask—and don't lecture me about it. I know the importance you place on such details, but I cannot remember all the faces."

"What did you give him?"

"The gift of poppies," answered Bernios. "A lethal dose."

"That is against the law. I wish you would not tell me these things."

"Then don't damn well ask!" responded the surgeon. He was instantly contrite. "I am sorry, Parmenion; I also am weary. But you are beginning to worry me. You have been tense now for days. Is something troubling you?"

"It is nothing of importance."

"Nonsense. You are too intelligent to concern yourself over trifles. Do you want to talk of it?"

"No."

"You are ashamed of it?"

"Yes," admitted the Spartan.

"Then keep it to yourself. It is often said that confession is a healing process. Do not believe that, Parmenion; it is the mother of all pain. How many know of your . . . shame?"

"None save myself."

"Then it did not happen."

"It would be pleasant if it were that simple," said Parmenion.

"Why complicate it? You expect too much of yourself, my friend. I have some bad news for you: you are not perfect. Now get some rest."

"Walk with me," Olympias commanded Parmenion as they made camp on the second night in a hollow on the Emathian plain. The Spartan followed the queen as they strolled toward the small campfire set by Phaedra. The queen saw that he was ill at ease and took his arm, enjoying the sudden tension in his muscles. So, she thought, he is not impervious to my beauty. "Why have you avoided me, General?" she asked sweetly.

"It is not a matter of avoiding you, your Highness. But my duty is to see you safely to your husband in Pella. That priority engages my mind, and I fear I am not good company."

She sat down on her cushions, a gold-embroidered woolen shawl around her shoulders.

"Tell me about Philip," she said. "There is so much I do not know. Is he kind to his servants? Does he beat his wives?"

Parmenion settled himself beside the fire. "Where would I start, lady? He is a king, and he behaves like one. No, he does not beat his wives—or his servants—but neither is he soft or weak. There is only one other wife, Audata, the daughter of King Bardylis. But she dwells now in Pelagonia—by choice."

"She has a child by Philip, I understand," she said, her hand unconsciously moving to her own swollen belly.

"She has a daughter, a beautiful child."

"Strange from so ugly a mother," snapped Olympias before she could stop herself.

"There are many kinds of beauty, my lady, and not all of them fade as swiftly as the flesh," he told her, his voice cool.

"Forgive me," she said swiftly. "It is hard not to be jealous. And I wish us to be friends. Will we be friends?" she asked suddenly, her green eyes holding to his own.

"All the days of our lives," he told her simply.

After he had gone, Phaedra moved close alongside the queen. "You should not flirt, Olympias, not among these Macedonians."

"I was not flirting, though he is a handsome man, save for that hawk nose. Philip is a warrior king, and he will take many wives. I need to ensure that my son remains the true heir to the throne, and it is never too early to win allies. Parmenion destroyed the power of the Spartans, raising Thebes to greatness. Last year he crushed the Illyrians. Before that he fought for the great king. He has never been defeated in battle. A good friend to have, do you not think?"

"You have learned much," Phaedra whispered.

"Oh, there is more that I know. The king has three advisers he trusts above all others. First is Parmenion, preeminent in strategy; then comes Attalus, cold and deadly, the king's assassin. Lastly there is Antipater, the second general, a tough, worthy warrior."

"What of the women?"

"Philip thinks little of women, save for Simiche, his brother's widow. He trusts her, confides in her. I will win her friendship also."

"Your plans seem well laid," commented Phaedra.

"They were set in Samothrace by the Lady Aida. She knows all things, past and future. I was chosen, and I will not disappoint her."

"Did you love her?" asked Phaedra.

"Are you jealous, sister of my heart?"

"Yes, jealous of all who touch you or even look upon you."

"You should take a man. I will arrange it for you if you desire it."

"I can think of nothing worse," said the seeress, snuggling close to her friend.

At that moment there came the sound of music from the camp fire of the soldiers, soft and mournful. A voice was raised in song—not a battle hymn but a love song of surprising gentleness, accompanied by the high, sweet tones of a shepherd's pipes. Olympias stood and walked through the trees to where the soldiers sat in a great circle around the piper and the singer. She shivered as she gazed upon the scene: men of war, in breastplates and greaves, their swords beside them, were listening to a tale of two lovers. The singer was Nicanor. He saw the two women approach and faded to silence, the soldiers standing as the new queen walked among them.

"No, please," said Olympias, "do not stop, Nicanor. It is beautiful." He smiled and bowed; the piper began to play, and Nicanor's voice once more rang out. Olympias settled down in the circle with Phaedra close beside her. The seeress shivered, and Olympias opened her shawl, the girl once more snuggling in close with her head on the queen's shoulder. Nicanor sang for more than an hour. The soldiers did not cheer or whistle as each song ended, yet there was tremendous warmth in the air and Olympias felt like a child again, safe and comfortable with these tough riders. Phaedra was asleep, her head a weight on Olympias' shoulder.

Parmenion appeared and crouched down beside her. "I will

carry her back for you," he said, his voice soft so as not to wake the sleeping seeress.

"Thank you," answered Olympias. When Parmenion knelt and lifted Phaedra to his arms, she murmured but did not seem to wake. The soldiers banked up the fires and drifted to their blankets as the general led the way back to the carriage. Nicanor opened the door, and Parmenion laid the seeress on the cushions within, covering her with two woolen cloaks.

"Your singing was beautiful, Nicanor," said Olympias. "I shall treasure the memory."

He blushed. "The men like to hear the songs; it reminds them of home and family. I cannot tell you how much your pleasure means to me." Bowing, he backed away. Parmenion followed, but Olympias called him back.

"Will you sit with me a little while, General?" she asked.

"As you wish," he answered. Her fire had died low, and he added fuel, building the blaze. The first cold winds of winter were sweeping across the plain, and already there was snow in the mountains. "What is it you fear?" he whispered.

"Why should I fear anything?" she responded, sitting close to him.

"You are young, lady. I am not. You hide it well, but it is there."

"I fear for my son," she said, her voice so low that he could barely hear her. "He will be a great king—if he lives. He *must* live!"

"I am a soldier, Olympias. I can make no promises as to his safety. But for what it is worth, I will protect him as best I can."

"Why?"

It was such a simple question, yet it ripped at Parmenion's mind with a whip of fire. He could not answer it directly and turned to the blaze, idly stoking it with a branch. "I serve Philip. He is Philip's son," he said at last.

"Then I am content. They say in Epirus that Macedonia will soon move against the cities of the Chalcidice. They say that Philip seeks to rule Greece."

"I do not discuss the king's plans, lady, nor am I always party to his thoughts. As far as I am aware, Philip seeks to secure Macedonia. For too long the country has been ruled by others, its security resting on the whims of politicians in Athens, Thebes, or Sparta."

"Yet Philip took Amphipolis, an independent city."

"No one is independent. It was an Athenian enclave, giving them a foothold in Macedonia," he told her, uncomfortable with her direct line of questioning.

"But then what of the Chalcidean League and Olynthus? Are they not a threat? Olynthus has close ties with Athens, as have the cities of Pydna and Methone."

"I see you are a thinker and wiser than your years. Yet you are not wise enough to hold your tongue on matters best not discussed in the open. Do not trust me overmuch, Olympias. I am the king's man."

"That is why I do trust you," she answered him. "I am Philip's woman. My son's life rests on his survival. If a king dies, is it not the Macedonian way for the new king to kill his predecessor's heirs?"

"It has been, lady, though you will be aware that Philip did not kill his brother's son. But what I am saying to you is that you should trust no one. Not me . . . not Nicanor . . . not anyone. Direct your questions to Philip."

"Very well, Parmenion. I am chastened. Will you forgive me?" Her smile was an enchantment, but Parmenion fought to remain untouched by its magic.

"Now *that* is a weapon you should use," he said.

"Ah, how wise you are. Will I have no secrets from you, Parmenion?"

"As many as you wish, lady. You are very beautiful and yet intelligent. I think you will continue to captivate the king. But make no mistake, he is also a man of wit and discernment."

"Is that a warning, General?"

"It is the advice of a friend."

"Do you have many friends?"

"Two. One is Mothac, the other Bernios. Friendship is not

a gift I give lightly," he said, holding her gaze.

Reaching out, she touched his arm. "Then I am honored. But is not Philip a friend?"

"Kings have no friends, lady. They have loyal servants and bitter enemies. Sometimes the two can be interchangeable; it is the mark of the man how well he recognizes this."

"You are a fine teacher," said Olympias. "But one last question, if I may."

"As long as it does not touch upon strategy," he answered, smiling. For a moment she was silent. The smile had changed his face, making him almost boyish.

"No, not strategy—at least, not directly. I was wondering about you, Parmenion. What ambitions are there for a man with your reputation?"

"What indeed?" he said, rising. Bowing to her, he turned and strolled back to the soldiers' camp fire, checking on the sentries before allowing himself the luxury of sleep.

Back in the carriage Phaedra lay awake, her heart pounding. When Parmenion lifted her, she had been jerked from sleep by the power of his spirit. It was too strong to read, and she had felt swept away by a sea of images of enormous intensity. But through them all was one overriding vision. It was this which made her heart beat so, which left her mouth dry and her hands trembling.

All her life Phaedra had known of the one way to lose the curse of *seeing*. Her mother had told her of it.

"When you give yourself to a man, the powers will wither and die like a winter rose."

The thought had been so disgusting that Phaedra would sooner keep the curse than surrender it in that way. In truth, the thought was still disgusting—but the rewards! She summoned the vision from memory, watching again the glories of the future.

How could she not take the risk?

Sitting up, she wrapped a shawl around her shoulders and stared at the stars shining bright beyond the carriage window.

She could hear Parmenion and Olympias talking by the fire. His voice was soft, almost gentle, yet his words were confident and born of an inner strength.

"I could grow to love him," Phaedra assured herself. "I could will it so." But she did not believe it. "It does not matter, anyway," she whispered. "I do not *need* to love him."

She waited until Parmenion had gone and pretended sleep when Olympias climbed into the carriage. Slowly the hours passed. Steeling herself, Phaedra slipped from the carriage and moved stealthily through the camp, seeking out where Parmenion lay; he had made his bed away from the soldiers in a sheltered hollow. As she gazed down on his sleeping form, her courage almost fled from her, but, steeling herself, she slipped from her dress and lay down beside him, carefully lifting the single blanket over her slender body. For some time she lay still, unable to summon the courage to wake him. But again the vision came to her, more powerfully than before. Gently her fingers touched the skin of his chest. He was still impossible to *read*, random scenes pouring over her like a wave and engulfing her senses.

Her hand slid lower, stroking his belly. He groaned in his sleep but did not wake. Her fingers touched his penis and—for a moment only—she recoiled. Gathering her courage, she touched him again, fingers circling him, feeling him swelling under her touch. He awoke then and turned toward her. His right arm moved over her, his hand touching her shoulder, sliding down over her breast.

"I have you!" she thought. "You are mine! And our son will be the god-king. He will rule the world!"

And she saw again the vision of a battle king leading his troops across the world.

Parmenion's firstborn.

My son!

THE TEMPLE, ASIA MINOR, WINTER, 356 B.C.

Derae lay on her bed and loosed the chains of her soul, floating free of the temple and soaring into the blue winter sky. In the distance clouds were bunching for a storm, but here by the sea the day was fine. Gulls arced and dived around her invisible form, and she gloried in their freedom.

Swiftly she sped across the sea, crossing the trident-shaped land mass of the Chalcidice and on to Pella, seeking, as always, the lover fate had denied her. She found him in the throne room . . . and wished she had chosen another day for the journey. For beside him stood Olympias.

Sadness struck Derae like a blow.

The mother of the Dark God!

The mother of Parmenion's child.

Hatred touched her, and her vision swam. "Help me, Lord of All Harmony," she prayed.

She watched Olympias walk forward into Philip's embrace, saw the momentary spasm of jealousy on Parmenion's face.

"What did we do to you, my love?" she thought, remembering her years with Tamis as they had battled to prevent the conception of the Dark God. According to the old seeress, Parmenion was the sword of the source, the one man capable of preventing Kadmilos from being born in the flesh. How vain they were . . . and how stupid. Tamis had secretly manipulated events in Parmenion's life, creating in him a warrior like no other in the civilized world: a fighter, a killer, a strategist beyond compare. All this so that he would be ready to destroy the Dark God's plans. Instead, the opposite had been achieved.

Derae's anger grew. For a moment she wanted nothing more than to use her power to obliterate the baby in the belly of the new queen. Frightened by the impulse, she fled back to the temple.

And here her anger turned to sadness, for she floated above her own body, staring down at the careworn face and the silver-streaked hair. Once she had been a beauty like Olympias. Once Parmenion had loved her. Not anymore. No, she thought. If he could see you now, he would turn away, his eyes drawn to the youthful skin and the earthly joys of girls like Olympias.

Returning to her body, she slept for two hours.

Leucion awoke her. "I have prepared a bath for you," he told her. "And I bought three new gowns for you at the market."

"I need no gowns. And I have no coin."

The clothes you have are threadbare, Derae. You are beginning to look like a beggar. Anyway, I have my own money."

For a moment only she considered rebuking him but dismissed the thought. Leucion was a warrior who had chosen to travel to the temple to serve her. He asked for nothing in return.

"Why do you stay?" she asked him, her spirit eyes scanning his hawklike face, so stern and strong.

"Because I love you," he answered. "You know that. I have said it often enough."

"It is my vanity that makes me continue to ask," she admitted, "but I feel guilty, for there will never be any more than we have. We are brother and sister, now and always."

"It is more than I deserve."

She traced a line on his cheek, her finger running the length of his jaw. "You deserve far more. You must not let your mind drift back to our first meeting—that was not you. There are forces in the world that use us, abuse us, discard us. You were possessed, Leucion."

"I know," said the silver-haired warrior. "I, too, have studied the mysteries. But the dark one can only enhance what is already there. I almost raped you, Derae, and I would have killed you. I did not know there was such darkness in my soul."

"Hush! There is darkness in every soul, and light also. For you the light was—ultimately—stronger. Be proud. You have saved my life and remain my only friend."

Leucion sighed, then smiled. "It is enough for me," he lied.

The warrior prepared a fire and left Derae sitting before it, her thoughts distant, her spirit eyes watching the dancing flames.

"I need help," she whispered. "Where are you, Tamis?"

The fire surged to life, the flames dancing high, twirling in on themselves to form a woman's face. Derae lifted her hands, soft light spilling from her fingers and surrounding her with a shield of brightness.

"You do not need protection against me," said the face in the fire. "And you can no longer call upon Tamis. I am Cassandra."

The face became more solid, framed by hair of flickering flames. Warily Derae let the spell of protection fall.

"You are the Trojan priestess?"

"Once upon a distant day," answered Cassandra, "I warned Tamis of her folly. But she did not listen. When Parmenion sired the Dark God, Tamis was filled with despair. Her soul is far from us now, broken like crystal, fragmented like the moon on water."

"Can you help her?"

"No. Though all others forgive her, she cannot forgive herself. Perhaps in time she will return to the light. For myself I doubt it. But what of you, young Spartan? How can I help you?"

"Tell me how to fight the evil that is coming."

"My gift in life—if a gift it can be called—was to speak the truth and never to be believed. That was hard, Derae. But I obeyed the source in all things. Tamis was corrupted by pride. She believed *she* alone was the instrument to bring down Kadmilos. Pride is not a gift of the source. In teaching you the ways of the mysteries, Tamis instilled in you a sense of that same pride. My advice is to do nothing. Continue to heal, to work with those in pain, to love much."

"I cannot do that," Derae admitted. "I was as much to blame as Tamis. I must at least try to make it right."

"I know," said Cassandra sadly. "Then use your mind. You have seen Aida and her wickedness. Do you not think she also has seen you? If she is prepared to destroy a Persian child, will she not—even more powerfully—seek to destroy you?"

"She and I have met twice," said Derae. "She has not the power to overcome me."

"There speaks pride," answered the face in the fire. "But Aida has many servants and can call upon spirits, demons, if you will. They have the power. Believe that, Derae!"

The fear returned, and Derae felt the cold breeze from the curtained window behind her. "What can I do?" she whispered.

"All that a human can do. Fight and pray, pray and fight. Yet if you fight, Aida wins, for to fight successfully, you must kill, and in killing there is the joy of the dark, touching, corrupting, changing."

"Then I should let her kill me?"

"That is not what I am saying. The battle between light and dark is not without complexity. Follow your instincts, Derae. But I advised you to use your mind. Think of what Aida must do in order for her dream to be fulfilled. There is one great enemy she must kill."

"Parmenion?"

"There speaks the voice of love," said Cassandra. "Not Parmenion. Who is the great enemy, Derae?"

"I don't know. How many men and women are in the world? How can I see them all, follow all their futures?"

"Think of a fortress with high walls. Impregnable. Where would the enemy most wish to be?"

"Inside," answered Derae.

"Yes," Cassandra agreed. "Now use your mind."

"The child!" whispered Derae.

"The golden child," Cassandra confirmed. "Two souls in one body, the dark and the light. As long as the spirit of the child lives, Kadmilos can never truly conquer. There is a bird, Derae, that builds no nest. It lays its egg in the nest of another, alongside other eggs. When it hatches, it is larger than the other chicks, and one by one it pushes them from the nest to fall to their deaths on the ground below. It does this until it is the only survivor."

"And Kadmilos will push out the child's soul? Where will it go? How can I protect it?"

"You cannot, my dear; you have no link to it. When the birth is close, the child's spirit will be thrown into the underworld, the caverns of Hades, the void. There it will burn like a bright flame—for a little while."

"What then?"

"Its brightness will summon the creatures of the dark, and they will destroy it."

"There must be a way!" protested Derae, pushing herself to her feet. "I cannot believe it can end like this!" Walking to the window, she felt the breeze on her face and struggled for calm.

"You say I have no link," she said at last, turning back to the face in the fire. "Who does?"

"Who else, my dear, but his father?"

"And how can Parmenion travel to the underworld?"

"By dying, Derae," said Cassandra simply.

For weeks the words of Cassandra returned to haunt and torment Derae, but no matter how hard she tried, she could not summon the fire woman again.

"Perhaps she was a demon," offered Leucion after Derae had finally confided in him.

"Would that she were," said Derae, "for then I would be able to dismiss her words. No, Leucion, she was no demon. I would have sensed any evil. What am I to do?"

The warrior shrugged. "All the world's problems are not yours, Derae. Let others take up the battle. I know very little of the ways of the gods. They do not—thankfully—take too much interest in me, and for my part I avoid them utterly. But surely it is they who must concern themselves with the coming of this . . . chaos spirit."

"You do not know the whole story, nor will I tell it," answered Derae, "but Tamis and I are in large part responsible for the coming evil. Cassandra gave me advice similar to yours. But do you not see why I cannot take it? I live to heal.

I serve the power of harmony. How could I live the rest of my life in the knowledge that I had brought such horror into the world?"

Leucion shook his head. "Some mistakes cannot be rectified. But even so, lady, why should you blame yourself? You did not set out to do the work of darkness."

"No, I did not," she agreed. "But I was raised in Sparta, Leucion, and no Spartan would consider leaving the fight until it was won or he lay dead upon his shield. The babe must have a chance at life. Cassandra says that if the soul is still alive when the child is born, then Kadmilos will be forced to share the body. That would give us a chance to work on the child, to hold the chaos spirit at bay."

"But for this the man you love must die," pointed out Leucion. Derae closed her eyes, saying nothing. "I do not envy you," said the warrior, "but it seems there is a contradiction here. Cassandra tells you there must be no killing or else you serve the darkness. Yet in order to win—albeit temporarily—you must kill Parmenion. There is no sense in it."

Turning away from him, Derae moved to the window, staring out over the hills and the distant sea beyond. Leucion left her there and wandered out into the gardens. The roses were growing wild now, the blooms crisscrossing each other in a profusion of colors, the pathways becoming choked. Leucion strolled up to the ramparts of the eastern wall, sitting on the parapet and gazing over the fields. Suddenly he blinked.

A man had appeared in the center of the meadow and was walking toward the gate. Casting his eyes beyond the newcomer, Leucion scanned the ground for any dips or hollows. Surely he would have seen him when first he looked east. The stranger's tunic was bright yellow, almost gold, his hair short and gray, his beard curled in the Persian fashion. He could not have just stepped from the air, Leucion assured himself. Unless . . . the warrior's mouth was suddenly dry.

Unless he was a god—or a demon.

Cursing himself for leaving his dagger in his room, Leucion ran to the parapet steps and down to the eastern gate, which lay open to the fields. Stepping out, he waited for the new-comer.

"May the blessings of Olympus be upon your home," said the stranger cheerfully.

"You cannot enter," said Leucion. "Be on your way." Sweat dripped to his eyes, and he blinked it away. The man did not seem to be armed, but this was small comfort to the warrior. If this stranger was a demon, he would need no sword to dispatch a human opponent.

"I come seeking the healer," the man said. "Is she here?"

"There is no one here but me. Now go—or work your sorcery and be damned to you!"

"Ah," said the man, smiling, "I see you observed my ar-rival. I am no threat to you or the lady who dwells here. You could say I am a friend. An ally."

Leucion's face darkened. "*Friend*, you are hard of hearing. If you do not turn away, I will be forced to fight you."

The stranger backed off a step. "How can I convince you? Wait! I have it." Lifting his hand to his breast, he closed his eyes. Leucion felt a weight in his right hand and, glancing down, saw that he now held a gleaming short sword. "There," said the man. "Is that more comfortable?"

"Who are you?"

"My name is Aristotle. And think on this, friend. Had I wished to harm you, I could have made the sword appear not in your hand but in your heart. Yes? And another point to consider: The last time someone came here intent on bringing harm to the healer, she needed no help, did she, Leucion? When you and your friends sought to rape and kill her. You remember?"

Leucion dropped the sword and staggered back. "I . . . I have tried to atone for that day."

"And you have done well," the man said, walking through the gateway. "Now show me to her, there's a good fellow. Ah, I see there is no need."

Leucion swung to see Derae standing on the pathway.

Wearing a new gown of glimmering green, her hair shining gold and silver in the sunlight, she looked to Leucion indescribably beautiful.

"What do you want here?" she asked the stranger.

"I wish to talk of times of peril, my dear."

"You are not of the source," she said, her voice cold.

"Neither am I of chaos. I am my own man."

"That is not possible," she told him.

"All things are possible, but let us say that I dwell upon the borders of both lands, serving neither. Yet we have a common purpose, Derae. I have no wish to see Kadmilos take on the mantle of flesh."

"Why come to me?"

Aristotle chuckled. "Enough of games, healer! An old friend asked me to visit you, to help where I could. Her name is . . . was? . . . Cassandra. Now may we go inside? I am hot and thirsty, and my journey has been long."

Derae was silent for a moment. As she closed her eyes, her spirit leapt free, merging instantaneously with the soul of the stranger. Yet fast as she was, the man was faster still, closing vast areas of memory, locking them away from her, allowing her only to glimpse bright fragments of his life. She withdrew from him and turned to Leucion.

"Aristotle is to be our guest for a little while, my friend. I would be grateful if you would treat him with courtesy."

Leucion bowed. "As you wish, lady. I will prepare a room for him."

After Leucion had gone, Derae moved to stand by the sword Aristotle had created. "A small though clever example of power," he said.

"Not small," she told him, "and let us see it for what it is." Kneeling, she held her hand over the blade, which shimmered and changed, becoming a long black snake, its head hooded. "Had he tried to stab you with this, the snake would have reared back and killed him."

"But he did not," said Aristotle lamely.

"Understand this and understand it well. Had he died, I would have sent your soul screaming into Hades."

"The point is well taken," he assured her.

"See that it is."

PELLA, MACEDONIA

"I will build him an empire," said Philip as they lay on the broad bed, his hand resting gently on Olympias' distended belly. "He will have everything he needs."

"You were magnificent on that first night," she said.

"I remember nothing of it, more's the pity. But I remember the morning after. You have been a fire in my blood for two years—ever since the dream. Only the gods will know how I have missed you these last seven months. Why did you have to spend so long in Epirus?"

"I suffered problems with the pregnancy. To have traveled might have meant losing your son."

"Then you were wise to wait. Everything I have built has been for you—and for him."

"He will be your heir?" she asked, whispering the question.

"My only heir, I promise you."

"What of your sons from future wives?"

"They will not take his place."

"Then I am content, Philip. Truly content. Will you attack the Olynthians?"

Philip chuckled and sat up. "Parmenion told me you were a student of strategy. I did not believe him. Why do you concern yourself with such matters?"

Her green eyes hardened. "My father was a king, from a line of kings. You think I should learn to weave and grow flowers? No, Philip, that is no life for Olympias. Now tell me about the Olynthians."

"No," he said, rolling from the bed.

"Why? Do you think me stupid? I want to help you. I want to be a part of your plans."

"You *are* a part of my plans," he said, swinging to face her. "You are the mother of my son. Can you not be content with that? I have many advisers, but few are those with whom I share my private thoughts. Can you understand that? No one can betray my plans if no one knows the full extent of them."

"You think I would betray you?" she snapped.

"I never met a woman yet who knew when to hold her tongue!" he roared. "And you are proving no exception." Philip threw a cloak around his shoulders and strode from the room.

It was close to midnight, and the corridor beyond was deserted, only two of the seven lanterns still flickering. The king marched to the end of the corridor, wrenching open the doors. The two guards beyond snapped to attention. Ignoring them, Philip stepped out into the moonlit gardens. The guards glanced at one another, then followed him.

"Leave me be!" he thundered.

"We cannot, sire. The Lord Attalus—"

"Who is the king here?" he bellowed, glaring at them. They shifted uneasily, and his anger passed. He knew their problem. If the king walked away into the night to be murdered, their own lives would be forfeit; they were in an impossible situation. "I am sorry, lads. A burst of temper, no more than that." He sighed. "Women! They bring out the worst and the best in any man." The men grinned. "All right, follow me to the home of Parmenion."

The half-naked king and the two black-cloaked guards crossed the gardens to the western wing of the palace. Lantern light could be seen from Parmenion's quarters, and the king did not bother to knock on the narrow side door. Opening it, he stepped inside.

Parmenion was sitting with his servant and friend, the Theban Mothac. Both men were poring over maps. The Spartan glanced up, showing no surprise at the king's entrance.

"And what are we studying?" asked Philip, striding across the room to stare down at the maps.

"The upper reaches of the River Axios, north of the Bora mountains," said Parmenion. "The maps came today. I commissioned them last year."

"You are anticipating problems in that area?" Philip inquired.

"There is a new Illyrian leader named Grabus who is trying to organize a league with the Paionians. They could prove troublesome."

Philip sat on a couch and swung to Mothac. "Pour me some wine, Theban," he commanded.

"Why?" responded Mothac, eyes blazing. "Have you lost the use of your arms?"

"What?" shouted Philip, his face reddening, his earlier anger returning with redoubled force.

"I am no Macedonian—and not your servant," Mothac told him. Philip lurched to his feet.

"Enough!" stormed Parmenion, leaping between the two men. "What nonsense is this? Mothac, leave us!" The Theban made as if to speak, then spun on his heel and stalked from the room. "I am sorry, sire," the Spartan told the king. "He is not himself. I cannot believe he would act in that manner."

"I'll see him dead," snarled Philip.

"Calm yourself, sire. Here, let *me* pour your wine. Sit for a while."

"Do not seek to soothe me, Parmenion," muttered Philip, but he sank back to the couch, accepting the silver cup. "I've had my fill of people today."

"A problem between you and the queen?" asked Parmenion, seeking to change the subject.

"She is inside my mind. When I look at the sky, her face is there. I cannot eat, I cannot sleep. She has bewitched me. Now she wants to hear all my plans. I'll not have it!"

Parmenion kept his expression even. "She is very young, Philip. But she is the daughter of a king; she has been well trained and has a fine mind."

"It is not her mind that interests me. I am surrounded by men with fine minds. A woman should have a fine body and a sweet temperament. Do you know that she raised her voice to me? Argued with me! Can you believe that?"

"In Sparta women are encouraged to speak their minds. In all matters—save war—they are considered the equal of men."

You think I should *explain myself*? Never! This is not Sparta. This is a man's kingdom, ruled by men, for men."

"The kingdom," said Parmenion softly, "is yours. It will be ruled as you say."

"And never forget that!"

"Why would I forget?"

"Will you discipline your servant?"

"No, sire, for he is not a servant. But I apologize on his behalf. Mothac is a lonely man, a man of sorrows and sudden tempers. He has never taken well to being treated with scorn."

"You take his part? Against *me*?"

"I will take no man's part against you, Philip. But listen to me; you came in here full of anger. And, in anger, you treated him like a slave. He reacted. True, he reacted in a manner unworthy of him, but still it was a *reaction*. Mothac is loyal, trustworthy, and the finest of friends."

"You do not need to speak for me," said Mothac from the doorway. He walked across to Philip and knelt. "I ask your

pardon . . . sir. It was ill-mannered of me. And I am sorry to
have brought such shame to the house of my friend."

Philip looked down at the kneeling man, his anger still
great. But he forced a laugh. "Maybe it was as well." Standing, he raised Mothac to his feet. "Sometimes, my friend, a
crown can make a man too arrogant, too swift to react in the
name of pride. Tonight is a lesson learned well. Now . . . let
me pour *you* a cup of wine. And then I shall bid you good
night."

Philip filled a cup, passing it to the astonished Theban.
Then he bowed and left the house. Parmenion watched him
walk away in the moonlight, flanked by his guards.

"He is a great man," said Mothac, "but I do not like him."

Parmenion pushed shut the door and looked into his friend's
eyes. "Most kings would have had you killed, Mothac. At best
they would have seen you whipped or banished."

"Oh, he is clever, all right," the Theban responded. "He
values you and your talents. And he has the strength to overcome his baser desires. But what is he, Parmenion? What does
he want? Macedonia is strong—no one can doubt that. Yet
still the army grows, the recruiting officers moving from village to village." Mothac sipped his wine, then drained it in a
single gulp. Sinking back to the couch, he pointed at the maps
spread on the wide table. "You asked me to coordinate information from lands surrounding Macedonia. We now have a
constant stream of news from merchants, soldiers, travelers,
wandering actors, builders, and poets. Do you know what is
happening in Upper Macedonia?"

"Of course," answered Parmenion. "Philip is building a line
of fortress towns against any future Illyrian invasion."

"True. But he is also forcibly expelling any of Illyrian blood
from lands they have held for centuries. Vast tracts of timber-
land, valleys, and pastures—all stolen from their owners.
Some of the men expelled are former soldiers in the
Macedonian army."

Parmenion shrugged. "For centuries the Illyrians have

been blood enemies of Macedon. Philip is trying to end the threat once and for all."

"Oh, yes!" snorted Mothac. "I can see that; I am not a complete dullard. But who acquires these lands? It is the king or Attalus. Last month three Pelagonian timber merchants were stripped of their wealth, their lands, their houses. They appealed to the king, but before the appeal could be heard, they were mysteriously slain, along with their families."

"That's enough, Mothac!"

"Indeed it is," replied the Theban. "So, I ask again, what does he want?"

"I cannot answer you; I do not believe Philip himself could answer you. But think on it, my friend. An army needs to be fed. The soldiers require payment. Philip's treasuries are not overly full; therefore, he must give his soldiers victories and plunder. But there is sense to it. A nation is strong only while it is growing. After that the decay begins. Why does this disturb you? You saw Sparta and Athens struggling for supremacy; you watched as Thebes battled to rule Greece. What difference now?"

"None whatever," Mothac agreed, "save that I am older and, I hope, wiser. This is a land of great riches. If farmed with care, Macedonia could feed all of Greece. But now the farmers are being lured to Pella for fighting wages, and war-horses are being bred before cattle and sheep. All I see ahead is war and death. Not because the realm is in danger—merely to satisfy the glory quest of a barbarian king. You do not need to tell me what he desires. He will attempt to conquer Greece. I will see Thebes once more besieged. He will make slaves of us all."

The Theban put down his wine cup and pushed himself wearily to his feet.

"He is not as dark as you believe," countered Parmenion.

Mothac smiled. "Try not to see him as a reflection of yourself, Parmenion. You are a good man, but you are his sword blade. Good night, my friend. Tomorrow we shall speak of more pleasant things."

* * *

Leaden clouds hung like a pall of smoke over Pella, distant thunder rumbling angrily in the sky as Olympias carefully made her way to the seat beneath the corner oak in the southern garden. She moved slowly, right hand supporting her belly, often stopping to stretch her back.

Her days with Philip were unsettling, alternating between the comfort of touching and sharing and the agonies of stormy rows when his face would redden and his green eyes would blaze with anger.

Were I still slim, I would win him over, she told herself. And I will be slender again. It was irksome that her graceful walk had become more of a waddle and that she could no longer embrace her husband, moving in close, arousing him. For in the ability to arouse lay power. Without it Olympias felt lost, insecure.

There were cushions on the long seat beneath the oak, and she stretched herself out, feeling the relief from the deep ache at the base of her spine. Every morning for months, it seemed, she had vomited, every night her stomach heaving, leaving her mouth tasting of bile.

But these last few days had been the worst. Her dreams were troubled, and she could hear her baby crying as if from a great distance. And with the dawn, she would awake believing him dead in her belly.

She had tried to seek comfort in the company of Phaedra, but her friend was often missing from the palace—spending hours, days it seemed, in the company of Parmenion. It perplexed Olympias, knowing how strongly her companion loathed the touch of man.

The rain began, gentle at first, then stronger, splashing to the stone pathway and bending the blooms of the garden. Here beneath the towering oak Olympias felt safe; the branches above her were thick and shielding, almost impenetrable.

Parmenion ran along the stone pathway toward his home, saw her, and changed direction. Ducking under the outermost branches, he approached her and bowed.

"Not a safe place, my lady. Lightning may be drawn here. Let me cover you with my cloak and see you to your quarters."

"Not yet, General. Sit awhile," she said, smiling up at him. Shaking his head, he chuckled and sat down, stretching out his long legs and brushing raindrops from his shoulders and arms.

"Curious creatures are women," he remarked. "You have beautiful rooms, warm and dry, yet you sit here in the cold and the wet."

"There is a kind of peace here, do you not find?" she countered. "All around us the storm, yet here we are safe and dry."

The thunder came again, closer now, lightning forking the sky.

"The appearance of safety," Parmenion replied, "is not quite the same as being safe. You look sad," he said suddenly, instinctively reaching out and taking her hand. She smiled then, holding back the tears with an effort of will.

"I am not really sad," she lied. "It is just . . . I am a stranger in a foreign land. I have no friends, my body has become lumpy and ugly, and I cannot find the right words to please Philip. But I will when our son is born."

He nodded. "The babe concerns you. Philip tells me you have dreams of its death. But I spoke to Bernios yesterday; he says you are strong and the child grows as it should. He is a good man and a fine surgeon. He would not lie to me."

The thunder was now overhead, the wind screaming through the oak and shaking it violently. Parmenion helped the queen to her feet, covering her head and shoulders with his cloak, and together they returned to the palace.

Leading her to her rooms, Parmenion turned to leave, but Olympias cried out and started to fall. The Spartan leapt to her side, catching her by the arms and half carrying her to a couch.

Her hand seized the breast of his tunic. "He's gone!" she screamed. "My son! He's gone!"

"Calm yourself, lady," urged Parmenion, stroking her hair.

"Oh, sweet mother Hera," she moaned. "He's dead!"

The Spartan moved swiftly into the outer rooms, sending in the queen's three handmaidens to comfort her, then ordered a messenger to fetch Bernios.

Within the hour the surgeon arrived, giving the queen a sleeping draught before reporting back to Philip. The king sat in his throne room with Parmenion standing beside him.

"There is no cause for concern," the bald surgeon assured Philip. "The child is strong, his heartbeat discernible. I do not know why the queen should think him dead. But she is young and given, perhaps, to foolish fears."

"She has never struck me as being easily frightened," offered Parmenion. "When the raiders attacked her, she killed one of them and faced down the rest."

"I agree with the surgeon," said Philip. "She is like a spirited horse—fast, powerful, but highly strung. How soon will she give birth?"

"No more than five days, sire, perhaps sooner," the surgeon told him.

"She will be better then," said the king, "once the child is suckling at her breast." Dismissing the surgeon, Philip turned to Parmenion. The Spartan was holding hard to the high back of the king's chair, his face ghostly pale and blood streaming from his nose and ears.

"Parmenion!" shouted Philip, rising and reaching out to his general. The Spartan tried to answer, but all that came from his mouth was a broken groan. Pitching forward into the king's arms, Parmenion felt a rolling sea of pain engulf his head.

Then he was falling . . .

. . . and the pit beckoned.

Derae's spirit hovered above Parmenion's bed, feeling the unseen presence of Aristotle beside her.

"Now is the moment of greatest peril," his voice whispered in her soul.

Derae did not answer. Beside the bed sat Mothac and

Bernios, both men silent, unmoving. Parmenion was barely breathing. The seeress flowed her spirit into the dying man, avoiding his memories and holding to the central spark of his life, feeling the panic within the core as the growth reached out its dark tendrils in his brain. It had been an easy matter to block the power of the sylphium, but even Derae was amazed at the speed with which the cancer had spread. Most growths, she knew, were obscene and ugly imitations of life, yet still they created their own blood supply, feeding from it, ensuring their own existence for as long as the host body would tolerate them. Not so this cancer: it multiplied with bewildering speed, spreading far beyond its own core. It was unable to feed itself, and its longest tendrils merely rotted, corrupting the fatty tissues of the brain. Then another tendril would spring up, following the same pattern.

Parmenion was moments from death, gangrene and decay entering his bloodstream and carrying corruption to all parts of his body. Fresh cancers were flowering everywhere.

Derae hunted them down, destroying them where she found them.

"I cannot do it alone!" she realized with sudden panic.

"You are not alone," said Aristotle, his voice calm. "I will hold the growth in the brain."

Calming herself, Derae moved to the heart. If Parmenion was to live through this ordeal, his heart needed to be strong. All his life he had been a runner, and, as Derae expected, the muscles were strong. Even so, the arteries and major veins were showing signs of wear, dull yellow fat clinging to the walls and constricting the blood flow. The heartbeat was weak and fluttering, the blood thin. Derae began her work here, strengthening the valves, stripping away the pale yellow wastes clogging the veins and restricting the flow of blood, breaking them down to be carried away to the bowels. His lungs were good, and she did not tarry there but swam on into the gallbladder, where wastes had been extracted from the blood only to congeal into stones, sharp and jagged. These she smashed into powder.

On she moved, destroying the cancer cells lodging in his kidneys, stomach, and bowels, finally returning to the central core, where Aristotle waited.

The growth in the head was unmoving now but covering still a vast amount of the brain, squatting within it like a huge spider.

"We have him now at the point of death," said Aristotle. "You must hold him here while I seek him out in the void. Can you do it?"

"I do not know," she admitted. "I can feel his body trembling on the edge of the abyss. One error, or the onset of fatigue. I don't know, Aristotle."

"Both our lives will be in your hands, woman. For he will be my link to the world of the living. If he dies in the void, then I will be trapped there. Be strong, Derae. Be Spartan!"

And then she was alone.

Parmenion's heartbeat remained weak and unsteady, and she could feel the cancer pushing back against her power, the tendrils quivering, seeking to grow.

There was no sensation of waking, no drowsiness. One moment there was nothing, the next Parmenion was walking across a colorless landscape under a lifeless gray sky. He stopped, his mind hazy and confused.

As far as his eyes could see there was no life, no growth. There were long-dead trees, skeletal and bare, and jagged boulders, rearing hills and dark distant mountains. All was shadow.

Fear touched him, his hand moving to the sword at his side. Sword?

Slowly he drew it from its scabbard, gazing down once more on the proudest memory of youth, the shining blade and lionhead pommel in gold. The sword of Leonidas!

But from where had it come? How did he acquire it? And where in Hades was he?

The word echoed in his mind. *Hades!*

He swallowed hard, remembering the blinding pain, the sudden darkness.

"No," he whispered. "No, I can't be dead!"

"Happily that is true," said a voice, and Parmenion spun on his heel, the sword blade extending. Aristotle leapt back. "Please be careful, my friend. A man has only one soul."

"What is this place?" Parmenion asked the *magus*.

"The land beyond the River Styx, the first cavern of Hades," answered Aristotle.

"Then I must be dead. But I have no coin for the ferryman. How, then, shall I cross?"

Aristotle took him by the arm, leading him to a group of boulders where they sat beneath the soulless sky. "Listen to me, Spartan, for there is little time. You are not dead—a friend is holding you to life even now—but there is something you must do here." Swiftly Aristotle told Parmenion of the child's lost soul and the perils of the void.

The Spartan listened in silence, his pale eyes gazing over the twisted landscape that stretched for an eternity in every direction. In the far distance shapes could be seen, darker shadows flitting across the gray land.

"How could any man find one soul in such a place?" he asked at last.

"It will shine like a light, Parmenion. And it must be close, for you are linked to it."

"What do you mean?" responded the Spartan, fear in his eyes.

"You understand full well what I am saying. You are the boy's father."

"How many know of this?"

"Myself and one other: the healer who holds your life back in the world of the flesh. Your secret is safe."

"No secret is ever safe," whispered Parmenion, "but this is not the time for debate. How do we find this light?"

"I do not know," Aristotle admitted. "Nor do I know how to protect it when we do. Perhaps we cannot."

Parmenion stood and stared hard in all directions. "Where is the Styx?"

"To the east," answered Aristotle.

"And how do I tell which is east? There are no stars save one, no landmarks that I could recognize."

"Why would you seek the river of the dead?"

"We must start somewhere, Aristotle. We cannot just wander this desolate plain."

Aristotle stood. "To the best of my recollection it is beyond two jagged peaks, higher than the surrounding mountains. Let's see . . ." Suddenly the *magus* swung on Parmenion. "Wait! What was that about stars?"

"There is but the one, flickering there," answered the Spartan, pointing to a tiny glistening dot of light high in the dark sky.

"There are no stars in the void. That's it! That is the soul flame."

"How do we reach a star?"

"It is not a star! Look closely. It is a tall mountain; the light rests there. Come. Quickly, now. For it will draw evil upon itself, and we must reach it first."

The two men began to run, their feet kicking up gray dust that hovered behind them before settling once more into place, undisturbed by any breeze.

"Look!" shouted Aristotle as they sped across the plain. Far to the left shadows were merging, huge, misshapen creatures lumbering toward the light. "It draws them with the power of pain. They must blot it out, destroy it."

There was little sense of time passing as the two ran on, but the mountains loomed above them dark and threatening as they reached the lower slopes. Here there was a forest of dead trees, bleached white like old bones. Parmenion cut to the left, seeking a path.

"Not that way!" screamed Aristotle.

Parmenion tried to turn, but a long branch curled around his throat, twigs like talons piercing his spirit flesh. His sword smashed through the bough, and he hurled himself to the ground, where white roots pushed up through the dead earth, skeletal fingers that tugged at his arms.

Aristotle leapt forward with arms extended, and a searing burst of light shone from his hands, bathing Parmenion. The roots turned instantly to powder, and the Spartan lurched to his feet.

"That was unfortunate," said Aristotle, "and such a display of power will bring our enemies the more swiftly."

Sword in hand, Parmenion followed the *magus* up the slope toward the light. As they approached a scattered group of boulders, dark shadows detached themselves from the rocks, skittering into the sky. Parmenion saw that they were birds without feathers or skin, black skeletons swooping and diving above them.

A low moan came from within the boulders. Parmenion halted in his run, turning to seek the source of the cry.

"There is no time," Aristotle shouted.

Ignoring him, Parmenion edged to the right.

At the center of the boulders lay a young woman, chains of fire holding her arms pinned to the rocks. Several skeletal birds were pecking at her flesh, peeling it back in bloody strips that healed instantly. Parmenion ran at the birds, shouting and waving his arms; they rose from the body, wings clicking. His sword smashed one to shards; the rest flew clear. Kneeling down, he gently touched the woman's face, lifting her head.

"I know you, do I not?" he said as her eyes focused on him.

"Yes," she answered weakly, her voice dreamlike. "I showed you my youth when you were in Thebes. Are you a dream, Parmenion?"

"No, lady." Extending his sword, he touched the blade to the chains of fire, which fell away. Sheathing the weapon, he helped Tamis to her feet.

Aristotle ran to his side. "I tell you there is no time for this. The demons are gathering."

"The child is born?" Tamis asked.

"Not yet," answered Parmenion. "Come with us." Taking her arm, he led her up the slope. Far behind them the shadows were gathering, merging, like a dark river flowing toward the mountain.

Higher they climbed, and here a cold wind whispered through the rocks. The light was closer now, a flame of pure white as tall as a man, burning upon a black boulder. Around it the skeletal birds were circling, their high-pitched cries echoing across the mountain.

A darker shadow formed by the fire . . . growing, spreading.

"Aida!" whispered Tamis, running forward.

The dark woman raised her arms. Darkness oozed from her fingers to flow over the fire, which guttered, shrinking down until it was merely the size of a lantern flame.

"No!" screamed Tamis. Aida spun, dark spears flashing from her hands. A golden shield appeared on Tamis' left arm, the spears glancing from it. Aristotle tore open his tunic, his hand circling a tiny golden stone hanging from a chain of silver. The flame on the boulder rose into the air, struggling free of the dark slime that was seeking to smother it.

"Take it, Parmenion," shouted the *magus*. The Spartan ran toward the flame, which floated onto his outstretched hand, settling upon his palm. There was no sensation of heat, yet an inner warmth touched Parmenion's heart and the flame grew, curling in on itself, becoming a globe of soft white light.

Tamis and Aida flew at each other. Lightning blazed from Tamis' eyes, searing through the robes of the dark woman. Aida fell back—and vanished. Tamis turned to Parmenion, her hands trembling above the globe.

"It is the unborn child," she said, "the child of your flesh. I understand now. Kadmilos must kill it or forever share the body." Her fingers touched the globe, the light spreading over her hands. "Oh, Parmenion! He is so beautiful."

"What can we do?" the Spartan asked, turning to glance

down the mountain, where the demons were gathering, some walking, others slithering across the stones, their cries drifting on the cold wind.

Aristotle moved alongside him. "I believe Mount Thanatos is close by. If I am correct, there is a gateway to the Elysian Fields, the Hall of Heroes. But they might not let us enter."

"Why should they not?" Parmenion asked.

"We are not dead," answered Aristotle, forcing a smile. "At least not yet."

"Look!" said Tamis, pointing down the mountain, where dark-armored warriors on skeletal horses were riding toward them.

"The gateway, then," agreed Parmenion. The sphere burning brightly in his hand, he started to run up the slope, the two sorcerers close behind.

"STILL she interferes," hissed Aida, opening the eyes of her body and rising from the ebony throne.

"What happened, mistress?" whispered her acolyte, Poris. The woman in the black robes stared down at the kneeling girl.

"There are three who struggle against us, keeping the child alive. Tamis—curse her—and the man Parmenion. There is another also, a man I do not know. Wait beside me!" Once more the dark woman closed her eyes, her body slumping back against the ebony throne. The slender acolyte took Aida's hand, touching her lips to it.

For some time she sat stroking Aida's fingers, then the dark woman sighed. "The man is a *magus*. His body lies waiting for him at the healer's temple. The woman Derae lies there also, her soul in Pella holding Parmenion's body among the living. Well, they have stretched themselves thin, my dear. Very thin. And it is time they died."

"You will send the nighthunters, mistress?"

"Three should be sufficient. There is only an old man guarding their bodies. Walk with me, my pretty one."

Poris followed her mistress out into the cold stone corridors of the palace and down to the torch-lit tunnels below. Aida opened a leaf-shaped door and entered a small room; it was empty of furniture, save for a raised stone slab at the center. Aida traced her fingers on the carved lettering there. "Do you know what this says?" she asked Poris.

"No, my lady."

"It is Accadian, carved before the dawn of our history. It is an incantation. Tell me," she asked, laying her hand on the girl's shoulder, "do you love me?"

"More than life," the girl assured her.

"Good," answered Aida, pulling her into a tight embrace, "and I love you, child. You are more than a daughter to me. But Kadmilos must be served, and his well-being is all that concerns me." The slender dagger plunged into Poris' back, through the ribs and into the heart. The girl stiffened, then sagged into Aida's arms.

The woman in black eased the corpse onto the slab and began to speak the words of power. Smoke rose from the letters engraved on the stone, covering the dead girl. A foul smell filled the room, the stench of decay. Aida waved her hand, and the smoke drew back into the rock. All that now lay upon the slab was a tracing of white-gray ashes.

Shadows danced on the dark walls, grotesque shapes that once had been men.

Moving to each of them, she touched her hand to their misshapen brows. "The temple is unprotected," she told them. "Find the body of the woman Derae and devour her flesh—and all with her."

The shadows faded.

Aida walked to the slab, dipping her fingers into the ashes.

"I shall miss you, Poris," she murmured.

Cresting the mountain, the hunted trio ran down the scree-covered slopes. Tamis fell and slid toward a precipice, but

Aristotle hurled himself in her path, seizing her white robes and hauling her to safety.

On they sped, the cries of their pursuers coming ever closer. From above them came the sound of leather wings, and Parmenion glanced up to see huge shapes hovering around them, their skins scaled, their forms barely human. But they did not attack, and the Spartan ignored them as he ran on.

"To the left!" shouted Aristotle, pointing to a pass between rearing black peaks.

Behind them the ghostly riders were closing fast. Parmenion risked a glance back over his shoulder, then returned his gaze to the pass ahead.

They were not going to succeed. With a muttered curse he halted and spun, sword in hand, to meet the enemy. There were more than twenty riders, faces hidden by the winged helms they wore. In their hands swords of red flame glittered like torches.

Tamis came alongside Parmenion. "Go on; I will hold them," she cried.

"I cannot leave you to face them alone."

"*Go!*" she shouted. "The soul flame is everything."

For a moment only he hesitated, then turned and ran on. The riders swept toward the seeress, and her hands came up, white fire blazing across the void to hurl four demons from their mounts. The rest charged on, sweeping out to pass Tamis by. Once more the lightning flared, scything through the first rank, the long-dead horses collapsing with bones cracking and splitting.

Two riders bore down on the seeress. The first she slew with a spear of light, but the sword of the second pierced her breast, jutting from her back and setting light to her robes. Tamis staggered, but she did not fall. Blasting the rider from his mount, she half turned and saw that Parmenion and Aristotle had reached the pass.

Ignoring the dying woman, the riders galloped on after the running men. Tamis sank to the dust, her mind swimming. She saw again her first passing, remembering the pain and the bitterness. Her soul had fled to the farthest corners of the void, lost and alone. It was there that the servants of Kadmilos had found her, binding her with chains of fire, sending the death crows to rip at her spirit flesh. In her despair, she had been unable to find the strength to fight them.

Taking hold of the sword of fire, she drew it from her body, casting it aside.

So many mistakes, Tamis, she chided herself. But here, at the end, perhaps you have atoned. Far ahead of her she watched the soul flame reach the Elysian gates. The riders of Hades had halted some distance away, unable to cross the open pass before the gateway without further orders.

The quest is with you now, Parmenion, my son, she thought. And I did—despite my mistakes—train you well.

At last content, she surrendered to the second, final death.

The gates were carved from shining black rock, as tall as three men, as wide as ten. Beyond them were green fields, flowering trees, tall snow-capped mountains, and a sky the blue of dreams. Parmenion ached to walk there, to put behind him the gray, soulless horror of the void.

But two guards stood in the gateway.

"You cannot pass," said the first.

Parmenion approached the man. The guard's armor was archaic, the breastplate gilded, the bronze shield huge and oval, the helm full-faced and red-plumed. Only the blue of the man's eyes could be seen.

Parmenion lifted the flame. "This is the soul of a child in peril. The lord of chaos seeks to walk the world of flesh, stealing his life, his body."

"The world of flesh is nothing to us," said the second guard.

"Is there no one beyond the gate to whom we can appeal?" put in Aristotle.

"Here there is no bending of the law," the first man answered. "The word is absolute. Only the souls of dead heroes may pass this way, and those we will recognize by a star of light that shines on their brows."

Parmenion heard movement behind him and turned. The horsemen had begun to edge forward, and beyond them a vast army of demons had filled the mouth of the pass.

"At least take the soul flame," Aristotle urged the guards.

"We cannot. He is of the living . . . as are you."

Moving to a nearby boulder, Parmenion opened his palm, willing the flame to flow from his hand. The white light streamed to the rock, leaving the Spartan with a powerful sense of loss. Drawing his sword, he ignored the guards and moved to stand at the center of the pass.

"Wait!" shouted the first sentry. "Where did you come by that blade?"

"It was once mine in life," Parmenion answered.

"I asked how you came by it."

"I won it in the general's games. Once it was wielded by my city's greatest hero, the sword king, Leonidas. He died more than a century ago, defending the pass of Thermopylae against the Persian invaders."

"A century? Was it so long? You are Spartan, then?"

"I am."

"Then you'll not stand alone," said the man, walking from the gateway and taking a position on Parmenion's left.

"Go back," said Parmenion, his eyes on the horde before them. "It is senseless enough for one man to die in this way, and a second sword will make no difference."

The sentry laughed. "There are more than two, brother," he said. "Boleus will soon fetch the others." Even as he spoke, the sound of marching feet could be heard from behind them, and three hundred armored warriors moved out to form three fighting lines across the pass.

"Why do you do this for me?" Parmenion asked.

"Because you carry my blade," answered the sword king of legend, "and because you are a Spartan. Now stand back with your friend and the soul flame. The demons shall not pass while we live."

Behind them the gateway disappeared, leaving only a cliff wall, black and impenetrable.

*   *   *

"You have powerful friends, it seems," remarked Aristotle, taking Parmenion's arm and guiding him back to where the globe rested on the rocks.

The Spartan was still dazed. "He is . . ."

"I know who he is—Leonidas, the sword king. The men with him are the heroes who died at Thermopylae, and they are risking eternity for you, Parmenion. It is a humbling thought. But then, the Spartans were always a strange people."

"I cannot allow it," whispered Parmenion. "They died once for their city and for Greece. They don't know who I am. I humbled their city, destroying its greatness! I must save them!"

"They know all they need to know," hissed Aristotle, seizing the Spartan's arm. "The babe is everything!"

Parmenion tore himself loose from Aristotle's grip, then saw the globe flickering. The soul of a child. *His child!* Glancing to his left, he saw the Spartan fighting lines—shields locked, spears pointed—and beyond them the vast army of demons.

The sword king laid down his shield and sword, striding back to where Parmenion stood. "They are waiting for something," he said, "but it gives us time to talk. What is your name, Brother?"

"Savra," Aristotle said swiftly.

The Spartan shook his head. "That was my name as a child," he said softly. "Now I am Parmenion."

The sword king was silent for a moment, then he lifted his hands to his helm and removed it. His face was regular, though not handsome, his hair long and golden, his eyes the blue of a summer sky. "I have heard of you; you have sent many Spartan brothers to the Elysian Fields."

"Yes. I wish there had been time to tell you the truth. But you were beside me so fast. Can you open the gateway and withdraw?"

"No. Nor would I if I could. It would have changed nothing, Parmenion. It still changes nothing. We stand together."

"I don't understand," Parmenion whispered.

"That is because you are from a different age, Brother. At Thermopylae we led a united Greek force against the invader. We stood firm then, and died. We did not die gladly, but we did die willingly, brother beside brother. You are a Spartan, and that is enough for us. Our blood is in your veins."

"You accept me?" asked Parmenion, all the tortures of his childhood roaring to the surface: the rejections, the beatings, and the endless humiliations.

Placing his hands on Parmenion's shoulders, the sword king smiled. "Come stand beside me, Brother, and the demons shall see how Spartans do battle."

In that moment all Parmenion's bitterness dissolved, as if a fresh spring breeze had whispered through the cobwebbed recesses of his mind.

Acceptance! By the greatest Spartan who had ever lived!

Drawing his sword, he followed his king into the battle line.

THE TEMPLE

I⊤ seemed to Leucion that the night was more beautiful than any he could remember. The sky was clear, sable-dark, the distant stars glittering like spear points, the moon a huge coin of shining silver. He had once received a coin like that, minted in Susa, when he had served as a mercenary in Egypt. Since most of the warriors were Athenians, the Persians had stamped the coin with the owl of Athena. His wonderment at its beauty had lasted only one night, when he had given it to a Numidean whore.

Now, staring at the moon from the ramparts of the temple, he wished he had kept it. Sighing, he turned from the wall and wandered down the steps to the moonlit garden. There were no colors to the roses now; all were shades of gray under the moon, but the fragrance remained.

Walking through the healing hall, he mounted the stairs to Derae's room and sat between the two beds. On one lay the sorcerer Aristotle, arms folded across his chest, his right hand curled around the stone on his necklet. On the other was

Derae, still dressed in the gown of green that Leucion had purchased in the market. Reaching out, he stroked her cheek.

She did not move, and he recalled with fondness his return to the temple, when he had found Derae in the grip of a fever. He had bathed her, tended her, fed her. He had been happy then; she was his, like a child.

Her face was pale, and she was scarcely breathing. For two days she had been thus, but Leucion was not concerned. Five, she had said. Then she would return and all would be as it once was: the healing of the sick, then the slow walks in the gardens, quiet conversations on moonlit nights.

The sorcerer moaned softly, his right arm sliding clear of the neck chain. Leucion leaned forward to peer at the golden stone. It was streaked with black lines and seemed to glow faintly. Returning his gaze to Derae, he was struck again by her beauty. It touched him like a spell, painful and yet welcome. Stretching his back, he rose, his scabbard rattling against the chair and breaking the silence. He was uncomfortable with the sword now, the years at the temple having dulled his warrior's spirit. But the sorcerer had said it was necessary that the bodies be guarded at all times.

From what? Leucion had inquired.

Aristotle had shrugged. "From the unpredictable," he had replied.

Leucion turned toward the door and froze.

It was no longer there. The wall, too, had disappeared, to be replaced by a long narrow corridor of pale, glistening stone. The silver-haired warrior drew his short sword and dagger, eyes straining to pierce the gloom. Two shadows detached themselves from the corridor walls, and Leucion stepped back as their huge misshapen forms moved slowly toward him. Their heads and shoulders were scaled, their arms and torsos the gray of decaying corpses; their taloned feet scraped on the stone, and as they came closer, Leucion saw with sick dread that their mouths were rimmed with pointed fangs.

As he backed away once more, his legs touched the bed on which Derae lay.

The first demon hurled itself at the warrior. Leucion sprang
to meet the charge, ramming his short sword into the beast's
belly and ripping it up toward the heart. Talons tore at his
shoulder, slicing through flesh and muscle and snapping his
collar bone. As the demon fell, the second creature lunged for
the wounded warrior, talons closing on his right side, shattering the hip beneath. Leucion plunged his dagger into the
beast's neck, just below the ear. Gray slime pumped from the
wound, drenching the warrior's hand and burning the skin. In
its death throes the demon hurled Leucion from him, and the
warrior fell to the floor, dropping both dagger and sword.

Blood was pouring from the wound in his shoulder, and the
agony of his broken hip was almost unbearable. Yet still Leucion struggled to rise.

Gathering up his short sword, he pushed himself to his feet,
taking the weight of his body on his left leg. The two demons
were gone, but the corridor remained.

"I did it," he whispered. "I saved her."

Five talons the length of swords hammered through his
back, bursting from his chest before closing in on themselves
and dragging him back.

Blood bubbled from his ruptured lungs, and his head fell
forward.

The demon hauled the body across the bed, where Leucion's limp arm fell upon the golden stone on Aristotle's chest.
The stone blazed into light. New strength poured into the
dying warrior. Reversing his sword, he plunged it back into
the belly of the demon behind him.

The talons slashed into his body once more, ripping clear his
head.

Dropping the body, the demon staggered, then its slitted
opal eyes focused on the still form of Derae. Saliva dripping
from its fangs, it advanced.

The demon horde filled the mouth of the pass, standing motionless, their eyes on the three hundred crimson-cloaked warriors who barred their path to the light.

"Why are they waiting, do you think?" Parmenion asked the sword king.

"They are waiting for him," whispered the king, pointing his sword at a dark, rolling storm cloud in the distance.

"I see no one."

The king was silent, and the cloud came closer, moving across the land, blotting out the slate-gray sky. As it neared, Parmenion saw that it was no cloud, merely a darkness deeper than any he could have imagined. The beasts cowered from it, running to hide behind boulders or in nearby caves.

The darkness slowed as it reached the pass, and then a breeze blew across the waiting soldiers, carrying with it the touch of terror. All the fears known to man were borne on that dread breeze, all the primal horrors of the dark. The line wavered. Parmenion felt his hands begin to tremble, his sword dropping to the ground.

"Spartans, stand firm!" the king shouted, his voice thin, reedy, and full of fear. Yet still it was the voice of the Spartan king, and the warriors' shields clashed together in a wall of bronze.

Parmenion knelt, gathering his sword. His mouth was dry, and he knew with grim and terrifying certainty that nothing could withstand the power of the dark.

"All is lost," said Aristotle, pushing through the line and tugging at Parmenion's arm. "Nothing can stand against him in his own kingdom. Come away, man! I can return you to the flesh!"

Parmenion shook him loose. "Go, then!" he commanded.

"You fool!" hissed Aristotle, his hand cupping the stone at his breast. Instantly he was gone.

The darkness rolled on toward them while from within the cloud came the sound of a slow drumbeat, impossibly loud, like controlled thunder.

"What is that noise?" asked Parmenion, his voice shaking.

"The heartbeat of chaos," answered the sword king.

And still the Spartans stood firm.

The demonic army gathered itself and edged forward, filling the pass, while the dark hovered behind them.

The warmth of life touched Parmenion's back, and he swung to see the globe of light swelling upon the boulder, growing, bathing the rocks, rising, glowing like sunlight over the pass.

The horde faltered, shielding their eyes from the brightness, and Parmenion felt the weight of fear lifting from his heart. The heartbeat of chaos sounded again, louder, and the dark oozed forward.

Light and dark, terror and hope, came together at the center of the pass, merging, twisting, rising higher into the sky, swirling into a great streaked sphere, lightning lancing from its center.

The army of Hades stood still, all eyes turned to the colossal battle being waged in the sky. At first the darkness appeared to swamp the light, but the soul blazed back, rending and tearing, shining clear in golden shafts that lit the pass with sudden flashes.

Higher and higher the battle swirled until at last only the faintest sparks could be seen. Then there was nothing save the unremitting gray of the Hades sky.

The sword king sheathed his blade and turned to Parmenion.

"Who is the child?" he asked, his voice hushed, his tone reverential.

"The son of the Macedonian king," answered Parmenion.

"Would that he were Spartan. Would that I could know him."

"What is happening?" asked Parmenion as the demonic army began to disperse, the creatures of the void moving sullenly back from the pass, seeking their eternal homes of shadows and gloom.

"The child is born," said the sword king.

"And the Dark God was defeated?"

"I fear not. They are locked together, and will remain so, in a constant struggle. But the child will be mighty. He may yet conquer."

"Then I failed," whispered Parmenion.

"There is no failure. He will be a child of light and dark. He will need friends to guide him, to help him, to strengthen him. And he will have you, Parmenion."

The gates to the Elysian Fields shimmered open, the sunlight glorious. The Spartan king took Parmenion's hand. "Your life beckons you, Brother. Go back to it."

"I . . . I have no way to thank you. You have given me more than I believed was possible."

The king smiled. "You would do no less for a kinsman, Parmenion. Go. Protect the child. He is born to be great."

Aristotle opened his eyes just as the demon reached for Derae.

"No!" he screamed. A shaft of light smote the creature's chest, pitching him back against the far wall, his skin blistering, flames licking from the wound. Within moments fire covered the beast, black smoke filling the room.

The *magus* rose from the bed, a sword of golden light appearing in his hand. Moving swiftly forward, he touched the blade to the blazing beast, which disappeared instantly.

The corridor vanished, the walls of the room reappearing; Aristotle gazed down on Leucion's dismembered corpse.

"You fought valiantly," whispered the *magus*, "for there would have been more than one." The sword flowed into Aristotle's hand, becoming a ball of fire, which he laid on Leucion's chest. The body was healed of all wounds, and the head was drawn back into place. "It is better for Derae to see you thus," Aristotle told the corpse, reaching out to close the dead eyes. Fishing into the pouch at his side, he produced a silver obol, which he placed in Leucion's mouth. "For the ferryman," he said softly. "May your journey end in light."

Returning to the bed, Aristotle took Derae's hand, calling her home.

Mothac was beside the bed when the miracle occurred. The color flowed back into Parmenion's face, the flesh filling out, but more than this—his hair thickened and darkened, the lines around his eyes, nose, and chin fading back and disappearing.

He looked younger, a man in his twenties. Mothac could not believe what he was seeing. One moment his master and his friend was dying; the next he looked stronger than he had been for two decades.

Lifting Parmenion's wrist, he felt for the pulse. It was beating strongly, rhythmically.

At that moment a tremendous cheer went up from the soldiers ringing the palace. Louder and louder it came.

Parmenion stirred and awoke. "By all the gods, I don't believe it!" Mothac shouted.

Parmenion sat up, embracing his friend, feeling Mothac's tears wet against his face. "I am back. And I am well. What is the reason for the cheering?"

"The king's son is born," said Mothac.

Parmenion threw back the sheet covering his body and walked to the window. Thousands of soldiers had surrounded the palace, chanting the name of the heir to the throne.

"Alexander! Alexander! Alexander!"

Bibliography

ANDRONICOS, M., *Sarissa* (Bulletin de Correspondence Hellenique 94).

ANDERSON, J. K., *Xenophon* (Duckworth 1974).

ARISTOTLE, *Ethics* (Penguin Classics, trans. J. A. K. Thomson, introd. Jonathan Barnes, rev. ed. 1976).

ADRIAN, *Campaigns of Alexander* (Penguin Classics, trans. Audrey de Selincourt, rev. J. R. Hamilton 1971).

AUSTIN, M. M. & VIDAL-NAQUET, P., *Economic and Social History of Ancient Greece* (Batsford 1977).

BENGTSON, H., *The Greeks and the Persians* (Weidenfeld 1968).

CASSIN-SCOTT, *The Greek and Persian Wars* (Osprey 1977).

CAWKWELL, GEORGE, *Philip of Macedon* (Faberer 1978).

COOK, J. M., *The Persian Empire* (Dent 1983).

DIODORUS SICULUS, *Books 15–17* (Loeb).

ELLIS, J. R., *Philip I and Macedonian Imperialism* (Thames and Hudson 1976).

FITZHARDINGE, L. F., *The Spartans* (Thames and Hudson 1980).

FLACELIERE, R., *Daily Life in Greece* (Macmillan 1966).

FORREST, W. G., *A History of Sparta* (Duckworth 1980).

HAMMOND, N. G. L. & GRIFFITHS, G. T., *History of Macedonia Vol. II* (OUP).

HATZOPOULOS, M. B. & LOUKOPOULOS, L. D., *Philip of Macedon* (Heinemann 1981).

LANE FOX, ROBIN, *Alexander the Great* (Omega 1973).

————, *THE SEARCH FOR ALEXANDER* (ALLEN LANE 1980).

KEEGAN, JOHN, *The Mask of Command* (Cape 1987).

KERENYI, C., *The Gods of the Greeks* (Thames and Hud
1951).

LAZENBY, J., *The Spartan Army* (Aris and Philips).

MAY, C., *The Horse Care Manual* (Stanley Paul 1987).

PAUSANIAS, *Guide to Greece Vol. I* (Penguin Classics, trans. with introd. by Peter Levi 1971).

———, *Guide to Greece Vol. II* (Penguin Classics, Trans. with introd. by Peter Levi 1971).

PLUTARCH, *Lives* (Routledge, trans. J. and W. Langhorne).

RENAULT, MARY, *The Nature of Alexander* (Penguin 1975).

RUTTER, N. K., *Greek Coinage* (Shire Archaeology 1983).

SEKUNDA, NICK, *The Army of Alexander the Great* (Osprey 1984).

STARR, CHESTER G., *The Ancient Greeks* (OUP 1971).

SYMONS, DAVID J., *Costume of Ancient Greece* (Batsford 1987).

WYCHERLEY, R. E., *How the Greeks Built Cities* (Macmillan 1962).

XENOPHON, *A History of My Times* (Penguin Classics).

———, *The Persian Expeditions* (Penguin Classics).